DEMONSPAWN

GLENN BULLION

For Katie, thank you. I love you.

CHAPTER 1

"Alex, you're not really human."

The words still haunt me in my sleep. Whenever I start to think I've got a hold on everything, on the wild direction my life has taken, I end up doing something creepy. Creepy enough to actually make me stop in my tracks and go "What the hell?"

I look back now over the first twenty-three years of my life and kick myself constantly for not taking some kind of action earlier. I mean, I knew I was different. I just didn't know *how* different. But I guess I can't get too mad at myself. Who the hell was I going to talk to? What could I have done?

It all started when I was in kindergarten. I shudder when I think back to my grade school years. Five years old. Undersized. Quiet to the point of not being noticed by anyone, except for the kids whose attention you didn't want.

I don't remember my father. He left when I was four, apparently not very happy that my mother got pregnant a second time. My little sister Alicia was six months old when he left. My mother had no time for us at all. Funny thing is I don't blame her a bit. My first year of school she became a single parent with two kids, trying to put herself through law school, and put food on the table all at the same time. The earliest memories I have is of coming home, doing homework while my mother did hers, and taking turns giving Alicia a bottle. I could change a diaper before I could write cursive.

I wouldn't trade any of it.

It was recess time near the end of the school year. Everyone from kindergarten up to fifth grade ran around like maniacs on the playground. Me, I sat in a far corner in the shade and scribbled in a coloring book. I didn't have any friends. My early-life quietness mixed with a dash of low self-confidence meant people didn't exactly flock to get to know me. It was a hot day, but I was always a big fan of the heat. I was minding my own business when I heard some raised voices coming toward me.

"Would you just leave me alone?"

That was followed by some laughter and a familiar voice that I hated.

"Aw, you scared? You afraid of the fire?"

I looked up to see a black girl that I'd seen before. A step behind her was Tommy Barnes, a fourth-grader whose main hobby was torturing kids smaller than he was, which included me. A few steps behind him were Tommy's gang, his little group of followers whose main hobbies were laughing at whatever Tommy did.

The black girl I finally recognized as Cindy Marshall. She sat on the other side of class from me. Nice girl, everyone seemed to like her enough. But for whatever reason Tommy decided that this was her day. Cindy backed away while Tommy shoved a lighter he'd found in her face. Eventually he had her pinned against the wall not too far from me. I tried my best to ignore them. I'm ashamed to admit that I was glad Tommy was leaving me alone for a change.

"Oh come on, it's just a little fire." Tommy thrust his hand out again.

"Stop it!" Cindy said. Tears fell down her face.

I focused back down to my coloring. I was in the middle of a portrait of my little sister that I had every intention of hanging on the fridge. The scary part is that I actually managed to ignore the scene just a few yards away from me, at least until I heard Cindy scream.

I didn't catch what happened, but it didn't take a genius to put it together. I looked up to see Cindy crouched against the wall, cradling her hand. Tommy and his goons actually had a look of shock on their faces. It looked like Tommy had hurt Cindy, probably got the lighter too close. Cindy raised her hand up to defend herself and got it burned.

Tommy's remorse didn't last long. I saw his face go from concerned to a stupid smile when he realized his buddies were watching him.

"Oh come on, you little girl. I didn't hurt you."

He moved in with the lighter again.

I'm not sure why I stood up. Guilt from doing nothing before? A sudden surge of bravery? Stupidity? Tommy would pull my pants down in front of everyone in school, push me down, whack me with a dodge ball as hard as he could. And I was going to confront him.

"Tommy." My voice cracked a little. "Leave her alone."

He looked both amused and annoyed.

"Well, look at this. Little Alex Teague. How's your dad? Oh I forgot. You don't have one."

You gotta love how cruel kids can be.

"You're not scared of fire, are you?"

He shoved the lighter in my face far closer than he did with Cindy. I was right next to her as I put a hand in front of my face. I actually felt something massaging my arm, and it made me laugh.

"That tickles!" I called out, and lashed out with my other hand. I knocked the lighter away. It fell into the grass not too far away.

Tommy and his buddies were surprised. I didn't know why. I didn't know until later in life that he held the lighter right to my arm, and my reaction was to laugh.

"Oh you think that's funny?" he said. "Let's see how funny you think it is when I rub your face in the wall."

He grabbed me by the shirt and forced me against the brick wall. It didn't take much for him to lift me into the air. I saw a pair of girl-hands reach in and grab Tommy's arms.

"Leave him alone!" Cindy said.

My princess in shining armor.

"What is going on over here?" Miss Treadwell, the recess monitor, said. What a bang-up job she was doing. I can't be too mad at her. She had a hundred kids or so to watch, and she'd just got done breaking up a fight on the other side of the playground.

Tommy quickly dropped me to the ground. Cindy helped me up. Miss Treadwell didn't know the whole story, but she knew enough to grab Tommy by his arm. She gave all of us, Tommy's buddies and Cindy and me, a stern look.

"Everyone come with me."

I groaned, knowing quite well the rest of the day was going to be bad.

I wasn't wrong. I sat in an empty office for three hours. Every now and then the secretary would pop her head in to let me know my mother was still on the way. I was scared, and I don't really know why. I knew I didn't do anything wrong. But all these crazy ideas went through my head. Like my mom busting into the room and yelling at me, or Tommy waiting outside to smack me around a little more.

Somewhere near the end of hour three Miss Jenkins, the school nurse, joined me inside the room. All the young boys who were old enough to have crushes had one on her. A twenty-something nurse, very hot, with a nice smile. I guess she was good at being a nurse too.

"Well, what happened to you today, Alex?" she asked.

I shrugged. I didn't want to talk about it. I just wanted Mom to come get me so I could run home and hide.

"Let's have a look at you." She pulled up a seat and sat across from me.

"Is Cindy okay?"

She gave me a curious look. I guess she was surprised that I was worried about her. She gave me a quick once-over, moving my head around, checking for bruises.

"Yeah, she's fine. Her parents are on the way. She's a little shaken up.

3

That Tommy, I hope his parents bust his ass."

My jaw dropped. She noticed.

"What?"

"You said...a bad word."

She smiled and turned a light shade of red.

"Sorry. I just don't like seeing that. Picking on kids smaller than they are."

"You mean me."

She didn't say anything, but that's exactly what she meant.

Never again, I told myself. *This will never happen again.*

"Oh my God." Miss Jenkins grabbed my right arm and studied my forearm under the wrist. "Doesn't this hurt?"

"Does what hurt?"

"I'll go get the burn kit. I'll be right back."

She left the office. She was gone maybe a minute or so before I realized what she'd said.

Burn kit?

I twisted and turned my arm to see what she was talking about. I didn't see anything at all, just a fleshy arm. I guessed maybe she saw something I didn't. What did a burned arm look like, anyway?

The door to the office opened. I thought it was Miss Jenkins, but it was Mom. I was relieved and terrified at the same time. She still wore her dress from where she worked as a receptionist at the law firm. In her arm she carried my little sister Alicia in the car seat. She set it down and rushed out to hug me. Finally, after three hours of waiting my stress went away.

"Are you okay?" she asked. "I'm so sorry I couldn't get here earlier. I left when school called, but then the babysitter said she couldn't stay, so I had to get your sister."

It was funny. Mom was just as stressed out as I was. I thought she'd be mad at me.

"It's okay, Mom."

"The principal told me what happened. Are you okay?"

Now I was embarrassed. Tommy really didn't do anything to me besides tickle my arm. Not exactly life threatening.

"Yeah Mom. I'm fine."

She sat in the chair Miss Jenkins was just at and held her head in her hands. The day was catching up to her. I'm glad I was too young to really know what she went through, or else I'd feel bad all the time. Answering the phone for a hundred pissed off lawyers' clients, trying to study during her breaks, then receiving a call that your pathetic son was the victim of a bully at school. Mom was a strong woman.

"You ready to go home?" she said with a small smile.

I smiled back and nodded.

Miss Jenkins came back in the room. She carried a burn kit under her arm.

"Oh. Mrs. Teague?"

"Miss, actually."

"Ah. I'll just put some ointment on Alex's arm and wrap it up. Then he's okay to leave."

"Arm?" Mom looked at me. "What's wrong with your arm?"

"Nothing."

She grabbed both of them gently and looked them over. Then she stepped out of the way so Miss Jenkins could see.

Her mouth opened. It was a moment before she spoke. "There was a burn. Across half his forearm."

"Are you sure?"

Mom's tone kept Miss Jenkin's quiet. She smiled and turned red once again.

"I, uh, must have been seeing things. You're okay to leave, Alex."

I didn't need to be told twice. I grabbed Mom's hand and was ready to go. I peeked in on my sister as Mom picked up her car-seat with her free hand. Alicia was sound asleep. I'm glad she slept through Mom having to rescue me at school. Mom was always telling me how I would have to take care of my sister when I got older. I didn't want Alicia's first memories to be Mom having to save me.

As we walked out the door we saw Cindy and her parents standing down the hall. I'd seen each of them after school. They took turns picking up Cindy. They were talking with Miss Treadwell, the lady who was responsible for all the kids during recess. I could tell Cindy's father was fired up. He was about the size of a football player. He talked loudly and waved his hands in the air. Cindy's mother, a much smaller woman, stood slightly behind him and in front of Cindy, almost like she was protecting her.

I could feel Mom slowing down as we neared them in the hallway. I groaned quietly. I just wanted to go home, not stand around while my Mom talked.

Cindy's parents turned their attention from Miss Treadwell to Mom and me. Miss Treadwell took the chance to quietly escape. Smart woman.

He gave my Mom a quick smile, and then looked down at me.

"Are you Alex?"

His voice boomed through the hallway. I wanted to stand behind Mom and hide, like Cindy was doing with her mother.

"Yes," I said. I sounded like a little mouse.

He reached his sledgehammer-like arm out and extended his hand. I shook it gingerly. My hand vanished in his fist.

"Thank you very much. Cindy told us all about what happened, how you stood up to that...boy, for her."

I felt my face growing hot. I looked at him, then at Cindy, who was giving me a small smile from behind her mother.

"You're welcome," I said to both of them.

Cindy's father laughed and focused on Mom.

"Hi. I'm Larry. This is my wife, Chandra."

"Pleased to meet you," Chandra said. She shook Mom's hand and gave me a smile.

They started talking. About the incident, the teachers, the first year of our school lives, a little of everything. I could only listen for about a minute before my attention started to wander. My eyes fell on Cindy, who looked to be as bored as I was.

"Hi," she said quietly.

I gave my sister a final look and walked over to Cindy.

"Are you okay?" I asked.

"Yeah. Thank you for helping me. Tommy was being a jerk."

"You get used to it."

"We should play together from now on. If we do, Tommy and his stupid friends will leave us alone."

I hesitated for a moment. Friends with a girl? I'd be made fun of every single day. No one would want to hang out with me.

So life wouldn't be any different. I'd actually have one friend to play with. She would just happen to be a girl.

"Good idea," I said.

"Okay. Tomorrow after lunch, meet me at the jungle gym. We'll be friends."

I smiled and nodded.

And that was the start of something great.

CHAPTER 2

Cindy and I grew up together, along with my sister Alicia. We were inseparable. Grade school was definitely a rough time for me, for all of us. Kids teased us about our little group. They ripped into Cindy and me for being best friends with the opposite sex, and Alicia for actually being friends with her brother. We also had to put up with some racial crap too. Apparently even now some people think whites shouldn't hang out with blacks. Definitely scary. But that didn't stop us. Mom was as busy as ever when we were in school, and that just let us spend more time with each other.

The funny part was how everything changed in high school. Suddenly Cindy made me a very popular guy, and the same thing happened when Alicia was a freshman and me a senior. What happened was both girls grew up.

Alicia was nothing like me. Short and small, long blond hair, always hanging out in the sun to get a tan. All the guys in school told me how hot she was, which bothered the hell out of me. She was my damn sister. Let's not hear about how hot she is.

Cindy, on the other hand.

Wow. I first realized it in middle school when we were playing basketball in her backyard. It's funny that I remember that. But I remember thinking to myself as she went up for a rebound how attractive she was. A very strange thought to have about someone you've known since kindergarten. Bright smile, lean body, funny and sweet, with a brain to top it all off.

She was my best friend, plain and simple. I knew everything about her. She was hard not to like. There were plenty of times she could have ditched me for the more popular crowd, one that would have made growing up a little easier for her. But she never did.

The next event in my life that made me lose quite a bit of sleep happened in my senior year. We were about two months in, just around the corner from Homecoming. I was already in coast mode, not really caring about classes too much. Senior year can have that effect. Cindy, on the other hand, studied her ass off. When she wasn't running track at school she was studying for college. Alicia was a freshman, and spent her first month of high school with her eyes wide, taking everything in. She was nervous at first, but smiles and stares from all the guys relaxed her pretty quickly.

That morning started out like most others during my school years, me waking up about ten minutes late. I stumbled out of bed like a zombie and nearly fell into the shower. As I woke up I could hear Alicia already downstairs in the living room watching TV. She actually liked going to school, unlike me. After drying off I gave myself a look over in the mirror.

I'd like to think I'm not ugly, but we're all our own worst critic. Nothing about my features really stood out. Plain face, brown hair, blue eyes. I did work out every day, and it definitely showed. When I was in eighth grade I thought working out and getting a good body would have the girls beating down my door. I was wrong. But selfish reasons aside, I actually like keeping in shape.

After a shower I spent about twenty seconds looking through my dresser to pick out the daily wardrobe. A pair of black shorts and a plain green tee shirt. Good enough.

Alicia wrinkled her face as I walked down the stairs.

"You're going to school in that?"

I looked over her clothes. Tight jeans and a tee-shirt showing off about an inch of her stomach, a school no-no.

"School is for learning. I'm trying to get educated, not win a fashion contest."

"Please. You haven't learned anything in years."

I smiled. We definitely got in our share of fights, but she made me laugh just as much.

"Yes I have. I learned yesterday that Mister Johnston gets mad if you fall asleep in his class."

"I'll try to remember that. You ready to go?"

"What? Go? What time is it?"

She rolled her eyes. "It's time to go. Try waking up a little earlier."

"Christ. Hold on."

I trotted into the kitchen to get a Pop-tart. Alicia kept talking to me.

"Mom left a message last night. She said she'd be stuck in Ohio a few more days."

I nodded. That was nothing new. All Mom's hard work paid off. She was now a successful lawyer. Of course that involved a lot of time away from home.

I stuffed the Pop-tart in my mouth and snatched the keys to my truck off the table. A hand-me-down gift from Mom when she got a more business-like Mercedes to show off to clients. Still, I loved my truck, and thanked Mom a lot when I saw her.

"Oh, Mom said I could drive," Alicia said as we left the house and walked down the sidewalk.

"Like hell she did. You're lucky I don't make you ride the bus."

"Yeah, right. The only reason girls even think you're alive is because you're my brother."

The sad part is I'm sure she was half right.

I picked Cindy up every day ever since I got my license. She only lived a few blocks away from us. I pulled in front of her house and gave my morning two quick honks. I saw her father Mister Marshall poke his head out the front door. I knew I'd grown up since kindergarten, but he still looked like he could crush a watermelon in his hand. He gave a friendly wave and called into the house.

A moment later Cindy hugged her father and trotted down the sidewalk. She looked great, as always. Jean shorts, showing off her runner's legs, and a white blouse with puffy shoulders. Throughout high school, whenever she happened to be single, guys would bug me all the time about what she liked, what was she in to, could I get her number, blah blah. It annoyed the hell out of me, but I can't say I blamed them.

"Hey guys," she said as she opened the rear door. "Come on, Jeeves, let's get a move on."

Alicia laughed.

"Ha ha," I said. It was still too early. I didn't have a comeback ready yet.

Cindy leaned forward between us from the back seat.

"So, Leese," Cindy said. Everyone called Alicia *Leese*. I was the only one who didn't. "You figure out who you're going to Homecoming with yet?"

I groaned. I love Alicia and Cindy, but they did have their share of girl conversations.

"I don't know. Brian's asked me. So has Todd. But I really want to go with Josh. But he won't even look at me."

"I'll talk to him for you."

"Nah, don't worry about it. I can get his attention." I rolled my eyes. "What are you and Daryl doing?"

Daryl was Cindy's boyfriend. They'd been going out since the end of junior year. I didn't have any problem with him, but I could tell he didn't like me. Was he jealous of Cindy's friendship with me? I have no idea.

"I thought we'd all go together."

"Not me," I said. "No date here."

"Well, have you asked somebody?"

"Nah."

I wasn't that big into school events. I skipped out on junior prom the year before.

"Come on, Alex. It won't be any fun without you."

"Don't worry, Cindy. We'll get him a girl."

"Uh, guys, I don't need a girl."

They didn't say anything, but I could sense the two of them looking at each other, making plans with their eyes. I knew I was in for it. I'd have to figure out how to fight them off.

I parked in the senior lot like I did everyday. We took a few final jabs at each other, and then went our separate ways. We didn't share any classes together. The only time we saw each other during the school day was lunch.

Lunch couldn't come fast enough. I had a bad day. I was late for three classes, and each teacher let me know about it. I forgot I had a test in physics I hadn't studied for. Three people asked me if Cindy was going to Homecoming with anyone, and by the third time I told them she had a boyfriend I was ready to attack people.

As I walked to the cafeteria I saw Cindy and Daryl kissing near their locker. He didn't have lunch when we did, but always stopped for a little public affection before heading off to his next class. He made Cindy happy, and for that I was glad. Her last boyfriend broke up with her in the middle of our junior year. She was crazy about him, a senior named Jay. The bottom line was he found another senior he liked better, and dumped Cindy over the phone. It took a lot of baseball games and pizza to get her mind off of him.

I bought a lunch and headed over to our normal table. We sat with a few of Cindy's track friends. I sat across from Alicia and gave her a friendly nod.

She took a bite of pizza and nodded in return. There's nothing like sibling communication.

"I'm still on the hunt for a Homecoming date for you."

I winced. "Alicia, don't."

"Why not?"

"Because. I really don't want to go anyway. And I don't want to think I'm so pathetic that I need my little sister to find a date for me."

"Well, you are, aren't you?"

"Ha ha."

"Seriously, Alex. When's the last time you had a girlfriend? Eleventh grade?"

Tenth, actually, but I felt no need to correct her.

"Yeah. So?"

"Come on. Look. This is the last year I'll have a chance to do anything like this with you and Cindy. Then I'll be all alone here."

I was saved from more torture by Cindy approaching. I saw a good chance to change the subject.

"Cindy. Hey." She sat next to me. "You still coming over tonight to watch the ballgame?"

One of our favorite pastimes. Baseball.

"Yeah. I've gotta go out with Daryl to buy some clothes. But I'll be over after that."

Alicia waved her hand around, remembering something.

"Oh, before you two get lazy tonight, I need you to drive me over Tammy's house. She wants me to hang out with her in her haunted house."

Tammy just moved into town that year. Alicia and her were pretty good friends. She'd been over our house a few times. But this was the first I'd heard about any haunted house.

"Huh?"

Alicia smiled. "Oh yeah. She tells me she can't sleep or anything. Noises during the night, all of that. Just like in the movies."

Cindy laughed at the idea. "Whatever."

And I agreed. I didn't give it another thought.

"Have fun with that."

The rest of the day was normal. Cindy never rode home with us. She stayed after for track, so it was Alicia and I by ourselves. She filled me in on all the potential dates she'd interviewed for Homecoming, along with plans of renting a limousine. That sounded a little too much for Homecoming, but I didn't argue with her. Alicia was hard to argue with once she set her mind on something.

As the sun started to set I went into the basement for my daily workout. The basement was full of different pieces of workout equipment and weights I'd gathered over the years. I leaned against the wall and did some curls while Alicia ran around upstairs getting ready to go over Tammy's house. She actually took a shower and changed clothes to do that. I asked her what the big deal was.

"If we happen to bump into any guys I have to look good."

All I could do was laugh.

I was nearly done my workout when a familiar pair of dark, toned legs walked down the stairs. Cindy put a hand over her eyes.

"Holy Christ! Blinding white skin! Man, Alex, put your shirt on. I haven't eaten dinner yet."

I laughed. I always worked out just in a pair of shorts. I talked while I squeezed out a few more reps.

"I will in a second. Can you believe that women everywhere aren't falling over me?"

"Oh yeah. So hard to believe."

I stared straight ahead, trying to concentrate. But I swear, out of the corner of my eye, I saw Cindy checking me out. I admit, best friend or not, I stole looks at her myself. But never did I think she did the same.

When I turned to look at her she quickly turned her head. Was she really stealing looks or was I imagining things?

"So you and Daryl do your thing?"

"Yeah. We talked about Homecoming. He's gonna rent a limo tonight for six people. He'll get a total and we'll split it however we need to."

I put the curl bar down and gave Cindy a look.

"Cindy, I don't think I'll be going."

"Yeah you are."

I sighed. "Cindy."

She mocked my tone. "Alex."

"It's too late now to be asking around for dates."

"It's never too late. I know Leese has a list about a mile long right now. Or just go stag. But you have to come."

"Oh, do I?"

"If you don't, I won't go. Then Leese probably won't go. Then Daryl will blame you and he won't be happy."

"You're serious?"

She nodded. She certainly looked it.

I took a deep breath. Alicia and Cindy both had their ways of getting what they wanted out of me.

"Alright. But tell Leese to call off the search. If I can't find anyone to go with I'll just go alone."

"Good. I knew you'd see it my way." She flashed that bright smile of hers.

I heard the basement door open at the top of the steps.

"Hey!" Alicia called. "You taking me to Tammy's or what?"

"Yeah. Hold on a minute. The house ain't going nowhere."

I grabbed my shirt and slipped it on.

"Do I look alright?"

The corner of Cindy's mouth curled up slightly, almost into a smile. I was dying to know what was going on inside that head of hers.

"Yeah, you look good."

We went upstairs to see Alicia already by the front door. Patience definitely wasn't one of her better qualities. Tammy's house was about ten minutes away on the other side of town. Alicia was bouncy when Cindy told her I was going to Homecoming. She started reading off her list. Literally, a *list*, that she started on during school. Suddenly I didn't have the heart to tell her I didn't want her help.

We pulled up in front of Tammy's house. She was sitting on the front steps, which I thought was weird. It was a little too hot to just hang out on the front porch. Cindy and I got out of the truck along with Alicia to say a quick hello. Tammy stood up and walked toward us.

I was startled as she drew closer.

Tammy was always a cute girl, which is why her appearance caught me off guard. She looked almost sick. Her skin was pale white along with dark circles under her eyes. She tried to smile a little, but it didn't quite happen. She looked exhausted, like she could pass out at any time.

"Hey Tammy, how you doing?" Cindy asked.

"I'm...okay, thanks."

Alicia gave me a look and glanced at the time on her cell phone.

"Come get me at ten?"

"Why don't you guys just hang out here?" Tammy asked. There was something in her voice. It bordered on desperation.

"Eh, I don't know," I said. I looked at Cindy. "We were gonna get a pizza and watch some baseball."

"We can do that here. Come on. It'll be fun. It'll be nice to have a cute guy around."

Cindy laughed. "Alex? Cute? Maybe in an ugly bulldog way."

Everyone laughed back. I did too, but I wasn't flattered by Tammy's comment. She wasn't trying to flirt. I could see she just really wanted our company. I wasn't sure why. I shrugged.

"Sound okay to you, Cindy?"

"Yeah. Maybe I'll call Daryl when he's done working on his car and get a *real* cute guy over here."

"Funny."

I was the last one to step into the house. I immediately folded my arms. It was like walking into a freezer.

"Jesus, Tammy. You trying to make ice cubes in the living room?"

The girls looked at each other for a moment, then back at me.

"I'm fine."

"Yeah, Alex. Stop being such a bitch."

It's hard to describe what happened next. The girls were chatting, but I wasn't listening. Cindy and Alicia sat on the couch while Tammy went into the kitchen to get drinks for everyone. I didn't move an inch from the front door.

Something was wrong.

I didn't know what the *something* was. I studied everything I could see. The house looked normal enough. The living room was right in front of me with a TV, couch, and chair. The dining room was to the left, complete with a table and chairs. Through an open archway I could see Tammy in the kitchen. Pictures of Tammy and her parents were on the walls. There was nothing out of the ordinary.

I felt something lightly touch the back of my head. It felt like fingers.

I whirled around. There was only the front door.

Even though I was freezing I could feel the sweat on my forehead.

"Alex? You deaf over there?"

I turned to see Cindy giving me a concerned look.

"Huh? What?"

"You okay?"

No, I wasn't. But I did manage a nod.

I was terrified, and I didn't know why. It was just like stepping into a creepy basement, only this was Tammy's living room. I looked in every direction before I sat down next to Cindy. The only thing I couldn't see very well was the stairs leading upstairs in the far corner.

Tammy handed me a glass of soda and I smiled graciously. I wiped the sweat from my forehead before taking a drink. She put the ballgame on to satisfy me and Cindy while she and Alicia talked.

"So where's the folks at tonight?"

"They're out having dinner. Thanks for coming over."

"Oh yeah, anytime. Party at your place."

Everyone laughed but me.

"Come on man, that was at the knees," Cindy said, shaking her head at the ballgame. "Alex, was that a strike?"

"Huh? Oh yeah."

I wasn't paying attention, and Cindy knew it. I felt her eyes on me, trying to figure out what was wrong. I said nothing. We teased each other a lot, but we cared for one another more than words could say, and we knew when something was wrong with the other. But she wouldn't ask me now, in front of everyone, and I was thankful for that, because I didn't know myself.

I knew I just wanted to leave.

*****

An hour passed. The sun had set outside. I could see the glow of the streetlight just outside the dining room window. Alicia and Tammy still talked about everything they could think of. Tammy looked much better than she did when we got to her house.

I wish I could say the same for me.

The nightfall made the house creepier. The living room and kitchen lights were on, but that didn't help any. I stole a glance into the kitchen. There was something there. I didn't know what it was, but something was in the kitchen watching us. I could feel a set of eyes on us. I could actually tell who it was looking at too. It looked at Cindy for a few seconds. Then to Alicia. Then it stared at Tammy a little longer. It seemed more interested in her. Its eyes fell on everyone as they spoke, but it kept going back to Tammy.

Cindy touched my shoulder. I jumped. I wouldn't have cared if Alicia or Tammy noticed, but they didn't.

If I looked like I felt, then I understand the concern in Cindy's eyes. I felt nauseous, like I could throw up at any second. I was still freezing. The goosebumps on my arms were evidence to that. The back of my shirt was damp with sweat.

"Alex, you look terrible," she said. There was no sarcasm, no humor in her voice. She was worried about me. "What's wrong?"

I opened my mouth to say something.

"Get out."

The voice was quiet, almost a whisper, but still crystal clear. It chilled me to the bone. I couldn't tell if it was a man or woman. It came from a few feet away to my left, near the kitchen. I spun my head and pressed back a little against Cindy.

There was nothing there.

I could no longer feel the presence of whatever it was in the kitchen, but that didn't calm me down. Alicia and Tammy were still talking behind me, but I didn't hear a word they said. I could only hear the thumping of my heart and feel the touch of Cindy's hand on my shoulder.

Tammy noticed me staring. She muted the TV. Alicia stopped talking, curious about what was going on. The house was dead quiet nearly half a minute. Finally, Alicia spoke.

"Uh, guys? Did I miss something?"

I turned and searched each of their faces. They were confused, not frightened.

"You guys didn't hear that, did you?"

Alicia shrugged for the rest of them. Cindy shook her head. But I saw Tammy's expression begin to change.

Another whisper behind me. This time closer.

"I will kill you."

I jumped off the couch and spun around. I knew I wouldn't see anything, but looked anyway. Cindy jumped up too. Alicia looked annoyed.

"What the hell is wrong with you?" she asked.

A loud thump brought everyone to their feet. It was right above us. It sounded like something fell upstairs.

Then there was a softer thump.

Then another.

Footsteps. There were five or so before they stopped.

"I thought you said your parents were at dinner?" Alicia said. I could hear a little shakiness in her voice.

"They are."

A creaking noise from the kitchen. We looked in and had a clear view of one of the cabinets opening by itself, revealing a collection of pots and pans. Even after it opened we just stared, not quite sure what else was going to happen.

"It's the ghost," Tammy said.

Alicia gave her a look. "The *what*?"

"I told you, we have a ghost here."

"I thought you were just kidding."

Tammy looked irritated. "Oh yeah. Ha ha."

The kitchen cabinet closed with a loud bang. Then another slowly opened.

I'm not sure if the girls realized it, but they drew closer to me. Ironic, as I was probably more scared than any of them.

"It just makes noise," Tammy explained. She tried to be calm, but her voice told us otherwise. "Scary as shit. But that's all it does. It'll stop in another minute. It doesn't do anything when other people are over."

"I guess it likes us," Cindy said, trying to lighten the mood. I could hear the fear in her voice too.

They couldn't hear the voice. Apparently I could.

I will kill you.

The ghost definitely didn't like us.

"What do you say we go outside? Get some air?" Alicia suggested.

"I'm for that."

I nodded. We started to circle around the couch, me pulling up the rear. We made it halfway to the door.

It was no longer a whisper. It was a roar that echoed in my ears.

"Fucking bitch!"

I heard a smack, and saw Tammy stumble and cry out in pain. She fell to one knee and brought a hand up to her face. I got to her first and knelt down in front of her.

Her expression said it all. A look of terror and surprise. The ghost had never hit her before. A red mark was already forming under her eye.

"Tammy, are you-?" Cindy never got to finish.

Alicia started screaming. I looked up to see every chair, every end-table, everything on the first floor bouncing up and down at a speed that just wasn't possible. The noise was deafening. I could see the kitchen cabinets flying open and closed.

Then the laugh came.

I could tell the girls heard it too. The laugh seemed to come from all around and last forever. There was no joy in it. It was an evil, frightful sound that made every hair on me stand up.

Alicia was the first one to the door. She swung it open and tried to shout something to us, but we couldn't hear her over the noise and laughter. I pulled Tammy to her feet, who was crying freely, and walked her the few remaining feet to the door. Cindy took over for me and was a foot behind Alicia. I hoped that shutting the door would stop the madness.

Before I shut the door behind me I heard a female voice barely rise above the laughter.

"Please help!"

I saw Alicia running to my truck. Cindy was right behind her, still walking Tammy by the shoulders. I was about halfway down the sidewalk when I slowed down. I watched Cindy put Tammy in the back seat. Alicia was already inside, and starting to cry.

Cindy shut the door for Tammy and turned to face me.

"Come on, Alex. Let's get the hell out of here."

Even as I fished in my pocket for the keys, I couldn't believe I was doing it. I tossed them to Cindy.

"Go back to my house. I'll be there in a while."

I turned around. From the moment I stepped into Tammy's house I was more terrified than any of the girls. Now, I was strangely calm, and ready to go back inside.

I took a step forward, then a hand grabbed my shoulder and spun me around. Cindy grabbed both my arms.

"Are you crazy? Alex? What the hell is wrong with you?"

There was anger in her voice, along with fear.

"You didn't hear it, did you? The voice? Asking for help?"

"The only thing I heard was shit bouncing around. And that laugh. Jesus," she shuddered at the memory, only a minute old.

"There's someone in there who needs help."

Cindy took a deep breath and looked over my shoulder at the now-quiet house.

"Okay, I'll go with you."

She straightened her blouse and lowered her head slightly to look at the ground, apparently preparing herself mentally for going back in.

"No. Just take Alicia and Tammy back to my house."

"I'm not letting you go back in there alone. So get that crap out of your head right now."

Cindy, my tough friend who had saved me from the big bad bully when we were in kindergarten. She definitely had a strong side. Despite everything that was happening, I felt myself smiling just a little. It dawned on me as I stood on the sidewalk that I'd never have another friend like her.

My smile only annoyed her more. She already thought I was nuts.

"What the hell is so funny?"

"Nothing. Look, Cindy. Tammy and Alicia can't drive, remember? Trust me, everything will be okay."

She looked worried. "Alex-"

I smiled. Back then I usually gave in to Cindy. But not this time. Suddenly I was confident, even enough to make jokes.

"Look," I cut her off. "Next haunted house I promise we'll tackle together."

She sighed and backed off. But she wasn't completely giving up.

"I'm dropping them off at your place, then I'm coming back."

I nodded.

I turned around and stared at the house. I heard Cindy pull away quickly behind me.

CHAPTER 3

I took a deep breath and walked back to the door. I knew deep down if it weren't for the female voice I heard on the way out, I'd be driving the truck instead of Cindy.

I stared at the door for at least twenty seconds before reaching out. I couldn't hear any of the terrifying noises. The only sound I could hear was the door creaking open.

I took a single step inside. The first place I looked was the kitchen. Every cabinet was shut. The dining room table was where we'd left it, but the photo of Tammy and her family was face down. A few pictures from the walls had fallen as well. The TV was still muted, but it wasn't centered on the stand anymore. It sat at a slight angle from everything bouncing up and down.

I grew cold again, but I didn't feel anything watching me.

"Uh, hello?"

I didn't expect a response. I jumped when I got two at once, overlapping each other. One was the genderless voice that threatened us. The other was the female voice.

"I'll kill you forever."

"Help me."

I shut the door behind me. For reasons I can't explain, I was terrified, yet somehow I was thinking clearly. I tried to think about what could possibly be happening. Ghosts fighting each other?

"I, uh, I'd like to talk to the lady, please."

She didn't respond. There was only that evil laugh. Softly, at first, then louder.

A blood curdling scream cut off the laugh. It was a woman's scream coming from upstairs. A man cut her off, shouting at the top of his lungs.

"I told you, bitch! You belong to me! You fucking understand me? You don't leave this house unless I tell you to!"

"I'm sorry, Richard! I'm so sorry!"

I ran up the stairs, taking two at a time. As the top of the stairs drew closer I realized I was an idiot for even being there. A quick picture of Tammy on the floor flashed through my mind. Whatever was in her house attacked her, and here I was trying to find it.

"Hello?" I called out.

Another scream. It came from the end of the closed bedroom at the end of the hall.

I passed a bathroom and Tammy's room on the way down the hall. I recklessly threw the door open. I didn't expect to see anything. I thought in the back of my mind I'd see an empty master bedroom, that way I could question my sanity for a while. But I was wrong.

In the corner next to the bed was a woman. She cowered with her legs curled up to her chest and her arms trying to shield her face. Standing over her was a large man with his back to me. He held a long belt in his right hand.

"Please, Richard! This isn't you!"

"Oh it's me, you bitch."

He swung as hard as he could. The woman managed to get her arm up, but the belt still struck her face. She cried out in pain. I was so stunned I couldn't move. I just stood there with my mouth open. It wasn't until the man brought his arm back for another swing that I managed to reach out and grab the belt. He felt the resistance on his arm and spun around.

The man's face was twisted in an expression I'd never seen before. Rage mixed with hatred. His lips almost curled into a snarl. He focused his gaze on me.

"What the fuck are you doing in my house?! This is my house!"

I backed up a step and bumped into the door frame. He took a step toward me with his arm in the air.

Then he vanished.

It wasn't a poof-vanish thing. It actually took a second or two. He just slowly faded away. I didn't realize I covered up with my arms to protect myself.

The woman looked up at me from the corner.

"How did you do that?"

It took me a moment to answer. "Uh, do what?"

She shook her head and quickly climbed to her feet. She was still terrified. She looked around, as if the guy could come back at any second.

"You have to get out of here," she said. She grabbed me by the shoulders. I was surprised that I could actually feel her hands. "The demon has him now. And it's getting stronger. I've tried telling them, but they can't hear me. I shouldn't have asked for your help."

"Whoa, wait. Who? Demon? What's going on?"

Sadness crept over her face. "Richard. My husband. Please believe me when I say he was good. But not now. You have to go. Please-"

She didn't get to finish. She vanished like Richard did. Suddenly I only saw the master bedroom. There was nothing out of the ordinary about it. Pictures of Tammy and her parents were on a large dresser. A clothes hamper was near the closet. Some nice white curtains decorated the windows. The only thing unusual was that I just got done talking to a ghost.

Then there was that creepy voice.

"You can't have her. She's mine."

A loud scream came from downstairs.

I turned and ran. It only took me a few seconds to move across the hallway and down the stairs. I grabbed a hold of the railing and stopped dead in my tracks when my eyes fell on the living room.

There was blood everywhere. On the carpet, the walls, the couch, everywhere. Near the dining room table was Richard and his wife. She was already dead. He straddled her on the floor. He stabbed I don't know how many times. He'd raise the long knife he held, thrust it into his wife, laugh, and then start over again. Where her chest used to be was nothing but a large gaping hole. The force of each thrust would make her head move just a little.

I looked at the front door, ten feet away. I didn't have a clue to what was going on, and I didn't want to know anymore. I just wanted to get away.

Richard stopped laughing and stabbing and turned to face me. I realized I was holding my breath. I tried to let it out without making a sound.

"I told her. I told her she was mine," he said. He was talking to me. "But she wouldn't fuckin' listen. I didn't want for this to happen. But she brought it on herself. I had to put a pillow over her head while she was sleeping. Then I cut her up just to make sure. You can never really be too sure."

He stood up and dropped the knife to the floor. Then he turned around and stared right at me.

"Wait a minute. You. You're...on her side, aren't you?"

He took a step forward. The blood-soaked carpet made a squishy noise. I took a step backward up the stairs. His eyes filled up with hate.

"I'll put you in Hell with her!"

I ran back up the stairs. I remembered seeing a window in the master bedroom. That was my goal. Get out of the house, and keep on running till I couldn't run anymore.

I didn't get the chance. As I passed by Tammy's bedroom a hand reached out and grabbed me by the arm. I was pulled inside and tumbled to the floor. I looked up to see Richard's wife closing the door and locking it. No blood, no stab wounds. She looked fine except for the panic on her face.

"He'll be up any second. Maybe you can help me!"

"H-How?"

"If you can see us, then you can help. You can act in our world."

I didn't understand a word she was saying. She reached down and grabbed my hands. For some reason I expected her to reach right through me, but that didn't happen. Her hands were warm to the touch.

As she helped me up there was a pounding at the door.

"Oh Susannnn," Richard said. "Open the door, sweetie."

"No!"

Another voice. The one with no sex that I kept hearing. Susan heard it too.

"Open the fucking door!"

"That's the demon," Susan said. "Richard wasn't always this way. The demon did it."

"That's right. And now you're both mine."

Susan looked at me again. "I don't want to die anymore."

Richard kicked the door open. I jumped in front of Susan, like I could protect her.

"Leave us alone!" I said. My voice came out almost a whimper.

Richard stepped forward and thrust out with a knife. I didn't even know he had another one. I felt a pressure in my stomach and couldn't breathe. I looked in Richard's eyes to see an eerie red glow. He still had that sick smile on his face.

He pulled the knife out and I fell to my knees.

"Hi, Susan. Now, where were we?"

"I'm sorry, Richard. I'm so sorry!" Susan said, sounding exactly like she did earlier in the master bedroom.

The first thing I felt was surprise. There was no pain. My breath slowly came back to me. I looked down, expecting to see me kneeling in a pool of my own blood. But there was nothing. Not even a hole in my shirt.

Richard couldn't hurt me.

Susan was cornered next to the bed. Richard's back was to me. I reached up and grabbed his shoulder.

He screamed in pain. It wasn't just his voice, but that other voice too, mixed in with his, both screaming. I backed up a step, not expecting that at all. He dropped to one knee and turned to face me.

He wasn't smiling anymore. He was afraid. Afraid of me.

"What are you?" he asked in the same mixed voice.

Now I was afraid. I was afraid of the question he was asking. A ghost was asking me what I was? Not *who*, but *what*? I'd never been so confused and afraid in my life.

I reached out and grabbed his shoulder again. His face took on a look of agony. He dropped the knife to the floor. My hand felt tingly, like it had fallen asleep. I didn't let go. Richard curled into a fetal position.

My hand went *through* him. It felt like pushing into a bucket of water. Then a second later he was gone.

I stayed like that for a minute, my hand on the floor holding myself up. Movement in the corner made me flinch. It was Susan. I'd almost forgotten about her.

She searched the room. A look of relief touched her face.

"He's gone, isn't he?" she asked. "The demon is gone?"

As she said it I noticed I wasn't cold anymore. All the strange feelings I felt when first coming into the house were gone.

"How did you do it? What did you do?"

I didn't say anything. Maybe I was going into shock.

"I've been trapped here for so long. I've died so many times. Now I can finally move on."

She helped me to my feet. She looked different. Almost brighter.

"Thank you. I don't know how you did it, but thank you."

I finally found my voice.

"That makes two of us."

"I tried to get their attention. The parents who live here now and their daughter. But I just couldn't get through to them. The demon was too strong. But you saw and heard. How is that?"

I was getting frustrated with her asking the same question.

"I don't know, okay? I don't know anything."

She backed up a step. "I'm sorry." She gave me a second before talking again. "I'm a ghost." She actually smiled. "I'm sure you figured that part out by now. Richard and I lived here in this house. Everything was fine until he started changing. A demon slowly took him over. He ended up killing me and himself. I was trapped here, until now. Now the demon is gone."

She closed her eyes and raised her head up, still smiling, as if looking toward Heaven.

"Did I...kill it or something?"

"You tell me. I have no idea." A tear rolled down Susan's face. "I wonder if Richard is waiting for me. The *old* Richard. On the other side? What do you think?"

"I don't have a clue."

She reached forward and gave me a hug. I jumped a little before returning it. Only one thought went through my head.

I'm hugging a dead woman.

"You're confused," she said. "So am I. But you've got some kind of gift there. You take care of it. I'll keep an eye on you for a while."

Then she was gone.

I saw in my head pictures of Susan, getting murdered over and over again in some kind of *ghost limbo*. A demon and a ghost fighting constantly with Tammy and her parents living around them. And they were never aware of it.

I barely remember leaving the house. I do remember glancing around and seeing nothing was out of order. The pictures we knocked off the wall, the blood-soaked carpet, it was like nothing ever happened.

When I walked out the front door I saw my truck pulling up by the sidewalk. Alicia got out before Cindy even parked. Tammy was right behind her, then Cindy. All of them looked concerned. I had to try hard to remember where they even went. Then it hit me, I told them to go to my house.

Despite bringing up the rear Cindy sped past the others and got to me first. She gave me a quick hug then held me at arm's length. Alicia and Tammy stood at her side.

"Jesus, Alex, are you okay? They wouldn't stay away. They wanted to come."

"He looks sick."

"He's shaking. What happened? Are you alright?"

I didn't say anything. I just stared at Cindy, then Alicia. I had so many questions, but I couldn't even form the words in my head. But somewhere deep down, I knew I did what I set out to. I helped the ghost in that house.

Tammy broke away a few steps and eyed her house up and down. Maybe she was expecting to see blood drip down the wall or curtains moving. I don't know. But she didn't get any closer.

"Alex, I'm so sorry," she said. "Nothing like that has ever happened. Usually it just makes noises at night. And when people come over it doesn't do anything. I kept telling everyone at school. They wouldn't believe me. I live in a fucking haunted house."

I looked at her.

"Not anymore."

CHAPTER 4

The next few days were a blur. I didn't even go to school. I stayed in bed most of the time, eating and watching some TV. Alicia and Cindy took turns staying home with me. I heard them out in the hallway a few times. Alicia wanted to call Mom, but Cindy talked her out of it. They were both worried about me.

On the third day Alicia stuck her head into my bedroom. She was dressed and ready for school, dressed to impress like she always was.

"Hey bro," she said. "You awake?"

"Yeah."

"Cindy's picking me up and taking me to school. Then she's coming over."

I didn't respond. I just waved a hand. She sighed with sadness. I heard her go down the stairs, then the front door open and close. I was alone.

Over the last few days I spent a lot of time in my room alone. I half-expected Susan to just pop up. She'd explain what was going on with me, talk about the afterlife, how I was able to help her, blah blah. But that didn't happen. I was left alone with my questions that I still couldn't wrap my head around.

How long was Susan in that house?

Did she know how much time had passed since she'd died?

Could she actually see Tammy and her parents all the time? Walk right through them, like in the movies?

The demon. Was it like a person? Did it have arms and legs and a body, or just a voice that controlled Richard?

What did I do to Richard? I only touched him, but it seemed to do the trick.

Was that really Richard in there, being controlled? Or did the demon make itself look like Richard?

How could I hear and see them so clearly?

Am I psychic?

What the hell is going on with me?

I was so depressed after Alicia left. So many questions with no answers, and as I laid there more questions kept coming up. I knew I'd never have the answers to all of them. Maybe not even *any* of them.

I heard the door open and close downstairs, followed by some footsteps coming up the stairs. I saw a shadow fall against the wall. I knew who it was, but turned in bed to greet her anyway.

Cindy leaned in the doorway with her arms crossed. When our eyes met she smiled and shook her head at the sight of me. I imagine I looked pretty bad. No one ever looks good in the morning, and when they're depressed, it shows even more.

"Girls are just lining up outside to jump in bed with you," she said.

I tried to manage a smile, but couldn't quite pull it off. Cindy saw my mood and got serious.

"I'll be downstairs. If you need anything just holler."

I nodded.

After she left I sat up in bed. For the first time in a few days my thoughts drifted to something besides my situation. I wondered about Cindy. This would be the second day she took off school to stay with me. How did her boyfriend Daryl feel about that? Hopefully he wasn't making a big deal out of it. Cindy and I were just friends. But I remember a girlfriend I had in ninth grade. Donna was her name. She got crazy-jealous over Cindy. She said we spent too much time together.

I pulled myself out of bed and stretched. A few minutes later I was in the shower, my first in quite a while. The questions were still in the back of my mind, but the truth in its simplest form started to settle in as I lost myself in the hot water.

Ghosts are real.

Demons are real.

Somehow, I can interact with both.

In the end, this didn't change anything. I still had to go to school. I still needed to get dressed and work out later in the day. I still had to get ready for Homecoming. I still had to make dinner for Alicia and me.

After my shower I threw on a simple pair of shorts and a tee-shirt. I smelled breakfast cooking as I walked down the stairs. Cindy must have been watching a movie as a DVD still played in the living room. I could see her in the kitchen hovering over the stove.

"Hope you're making enough for two."

She turned around to give me a smile. "I heard you upstairs. You haven't been eating a lot. I'm not that good a cook, but you'll get over it."

I laughed. I couldn't remember the last time I laughed.

"I don't even cook for Daryl, so keep this a secret."

I pointed at her. "Speaking of Daryl. Homecoming next Friday, right?"

"You're still going?"

"Yeah. Why wouldn't I?"

"Well, you know. We thought you might not go."

"Nah. You guys wouldn't have any fun without me."

"You're probably right." She paused for a moment. There was a bit of uncomfortable silence. "Listen, I'll never bring it up. But if you want to talk about what happened, you know I'm here for you, right?"

I smiled. My best friend since kindergarten. We knew things about each other that we didn't even share with our boyfriends and girlfriends, when we had them. We teased each other a lot. Our friendship was full of humor and practical jokes. But we knew when to be serious, and we took care of each other.

"Thanks, Cindy. I appreciate it."

"Now shut up and help me finish breakfast."

*****

Things quickly got back to normal. It's funny how life does that. After a full day of school and hanging out with my sister and Cindy, my mind went from dwelling on haunted houses to getting ready for Homecoming. I did get a quick update from Tammy that her house was now "normal", but besides that, I didn't think about it too much.

I did think about Homecoming. Much more than I really wanted to. I blame that on Cindy and Alicia. They kept putting it in my head on how I needed to look my best. Since I was going alone, they made it their personal goal to make sure I left Homecoming with someone. The funny part is the more they kept putting the focus of Homecoming on me, the more I stopped caring. I was only going to spend time with my two best friends. And I hate to admit it, but their argument of "This will be the only time we get to do this" worked. Cindy and I were seniors, this was it for us. Alicia would spend the next three high school years without us. I didn't want to be the one to keep our little group apart on our only Homecoming night.

The big day came up quick. Three hours before the dance, Alicia was in her room doing whatever it is ladies do to get ready for something important. Me, I was downstairs working out in a pair of shorts. That shows how much I was stressing over the dance compared to Alicia. I couldn't help but laugh as every now and then I'd hear a scream followed by "My fucking hair!" from upstairs.

It didn't take me long to get ready at all. After I was dressed and happy enough with what I saw in the mirror I went downstairs. It took Alicia another twenty minutes to get ready.

"Are you excited?" she asked.

"Eh, it should be fun."

"Oh, come on, Alex. You aren't pumped up at all at seeing every hot girl in school dress up to impress guys?"

"Aren't they dressing up to impress their dates?"

She smiled fiendishly. "Well, yeah. But let's put it this way. I'm going with Tom from my algebra class. But he's not my boyfriend."

I just rolled my eyes.

There was a honk outside. Alicia took a deep breath.

"How do I look?"

She looked great, as usual. My sister and I were nothing alike physically. I always thought she had the looks in the family. I gave her a thumbs-up.

"Remember to grab the camera. Mom said she wants enough pictures to fill a book."

I grabbed the digital camera from the dining room table and followed Alicia outside. Cindy stood there in front of a white limousine. I still felt renting a limousine was overboard, but there was no arguing with them.

I tried to keep my mouth from opening as I approached Cindy. I spend so much time with her that I forget how hot she is sometimes. She wore a white dress that stopped at the knees. Her hair was done up nice. She had the top of a red rose in her hair. She looked amazing.

She gave Alicia a quick hug and they fawned over each other for a minute. I just laughed. Finally, Cindy looked me up and down. I had on a pair of dress pants and a white collared shirt, nothing too fancy.

"Wow. You're not ugly."

"Ha ha. You're hilarious."

"Where's Daryl?" Alicia asked.

"He's in here, enjoying the limo."

Cindy said it as straight as could be, but that was the first clue that something was wrong. I missed it completely. He should have been with his girlfriend.

I waved the camera around. "Let's go pick up Alicia's guy. Then we got pictures to take."

"He's not my *guy*," she snapped. "He's just my *date*."

We piled into the limo. Daryl looked sharp. He was busy talking on a cell phone. He nodded a simple greeting to all of us, then went back to his conversation.

Alicia's date Tom didn't live too far away. Daryl didn't say a word to any of us during the drive over. He was more interested in calling his boys.

Tom seemed like a nice enough guy. He gave Alicia an awkward hug when she greeted him in front of his house. I caught him checking her out a few times, but he didn't act like a sleaze.

We got Tom's mother to take pictures of all of us in front of the limo. I felt a little out of place since I was the only one without a date. But things got even more awkward.

After about ten pictures Cindy had a request.

"Miss Madison, would you mind taking a few pictures of Alex, Leese, and me?"

If Alicia felt like I did, she did a great job of hiding it. I stole a quick glance at Daryl. He already focused his attention back to his cell phone. If I were him, I'd be a little upset. Cindy didn't ask for any pictures taken with her boyfriend, but with her best friend and his sister.

Miss Madison, Tom's mother, smiled and nodded. "Sure, hon."

We posed for a few pictures. Cindy put her arm around my shoulders once. Just a playful gesture, but still made me nervous enough to glance at Daryl. He didn't seem to care, or hid it well.

One of the fears I had about Homecoming was how our group would do. Cindy, Alicia, and I got along great. But what would it be like when two other guys, especially boyfriends and dates, were brought into the picture? Even when we were all seeing people at the same time, we didn't double-date or anything like that. Would Cindy and Alicia ignore me? Would Tom and Daryl not like the best friend and older brother being there?

It wasn't too bad. I did feel a little like an extra wheel, but everyone talked to me, even Daryl. He seemed distracted, but alright for the most part. I didn't notice until later that he and Cindy were barely talking to each other.

The limousine was nice. Plenty of room for us to stretch out. I kept an eye on Tom, simply because he was funny, although he didn't mean to be. I could see he wanted to scoot closer to Alicia, but didn't quite know how to do it.

The dance itself started out pretty well for me. I was actually surprised to see other people rented limos as well. Weird. We went into the school gym together. Whoever was responsible for putting the dance together did a great job. The gym looked great. Nice lighting, plenty to drink, a band playing near the back. Kids and teachers danced, badly, I might add, on the floor.

"Wow!" Alicia said when we stepped inside. She elbowed me. "And you wanted to skip out on this?"

"That's cause he's stupid," Cindy said.

"You guys thirsty?" Tom asked. He walked over to the punch table.

I actually had fun. I mingled and talked to some people I knew in my classes. Every now and then Alicia and Tom would go out and dance. Daryl and Cindy didn't dance, which I thought was weird because I'd seen them dance before. Hell, Cindy loved to dance. I would try to work out in the basement only to have her screw with my radio and start dancing. Very distracting, for obvious reasons.

Throughout the night we ended up splitting up a few times. We'd see people we knew and would break away to talk. After talking to a girl named Lisa who pulled me aside to say hello, I ended up alone on the side of the dance floor. I looked around, trying to find the group. I spotted Tom and Alicia on the floor sharing a slow dance. I smiled, it was their first of the night. I wondered if Tom finally got up the nerve to ask her to dance or if she did. Alicia did seem to like him.

I couldn't see Cindy and Daryl anywhere. So I sat down on one of the chairs lined up along the wall. It actually felt good. My legs were killing me. I was starting to want to get to the next phase of the night. Cindy and Alicia mentioned something earlier about getting dinner after the dance.

I was having fun, but I don't dance. I also didn't have a date, so slow dancing was out of the question. I leaned back and watched the couples. I loved watching some of the pairings out there that I never would have dreamed of. Lou, a brainy guy from my psychics class, apparently came with Crystal, one of the senior cheerleaders. I'd love to know how he pulled that off. Such an odd pair, but she was actually laughing and dancing close to him. It made me smile and gave hope that a semi-quiet weightlifting baseball fan might find his match.

I felt a tap on my shoulder. I turned to see Cindy standing there with her hands on her hips.

"What are you doing?" she asked. "The dance is out there. Come on, Alex, there's gotta be one girl here who drank too much spiked punch and is looking for a guy to dance with."

I laughed. "My legs are hurting. Give me a break."

She sat next to me. "You work out twenty-five hours a day and can't handle a school dance?"

"Man, you're on a roll tonight."

She smiled. "Thank you. I try. Seriously though, you having fun?"

"Yeah. What's not to like?"

She pointed at Alicia. "Looks like someone else is having fun too."

"Yeah. She spent all week talking about this thing, but never really talked about Tom. But it looks like she might like him."

No sooner did the words leave my mouth when Alicia hugged Tom's neck and kissed him.

"Aww," Cindy said. "We're gonna have serious girl talk later."

"Hey, where the hell is your man? You giving me a hard time about slow dancing. I haven't seen you two dance at all yet."

She shrugged. "Don't know where he is. He said he had to take care of something. Then ran off on that stupid cell phone of his."

It wasn't so much what she said, but how she said it. I knew something was up.

"Everything okay with you two?"

She hesitated and wouldn't look at me. "I don't think so."

"You want to talk about it?"

"No."

That was all I needed to hear. We sat in silence for a minute or so.

"Alex, I'm being serious here. Are you gonna dance with someone tonight or not?"

That came out of nowhere. I gave her a confused look.

"I don't think I'll lose much sleep if I don't, Cindy."

"Well, remember when your Mom called yesterday and I answered the phone?"

I nodded. No big deal there. Mom usually called a few times a week when she was away. And Cindy was over the house a lot. She talked to Mom just as much as I did.

"She told me that if you weren't coming with a date, that I had to make sure you danced with someone and get some pictures."

"What? Will *she* lose sleep or something?"

She shrugged defensively. "Hey, don't look at me. I'm just repeating what she said."

I shook my head. I'd have to give Mom a hard time when she got back.

"So, look. I talked it over with Daryl. He's cool with us dancing one song."

I wrinkled my face. "What? Are you kidding me?"

"Don't look so disgusted. I was the first person you danced with anyway. Remember?"

I did remember. We were seven years old, in her backyard. Cindy wanted to practice so she could ask Danny Thompson to the dance.

"Yeah. I still have nightmares about it sometimes."

"Oh, you're so damn funny. Come on, this song's half over. I want to at least say we danced a little so your Mom won't kill me."

I reluctantly let her grab my hand and pull me forward. I knew if I didn't give in she'd bug me about it forever. She led me over near Alicia. I felt awkward as hell. I'm not much of a slow dancer anyway. Plus Cindy was my best friend who had a boyfriend.

"Come on," she said as she put a hand on my shoulder. "White boys can at least slow dance, can't they?"

"I'm sure a lot of them can."

"Jesus, Alex. You've done this before."

She grabbed my hands and put them on her hips. Then she wrapped her hands around my neck. I made sure to stand as far away as I possibly could.

"You take my breath away."

"Huh? What?"

"That's the song that played in my backyard. When we first danced."

I smiled. "Oh yeah. I remember. Your father sneaked up behind you while I tried not to laugh. Then he scared you and you cried like a little girl."

"I *was* a little girl, you asshole."

Alicia and Tom made their way closer to us. I didn't even see them till she spoke.

"Be careful, Cindy," she said. "I don't think Alex has touched a girl in a while. He might try to hump your leg or something."

"I'm sorry, did we break up your tonsil-hockey game?" I said.

Alicia's face turned red. Tom tried not to laugh. His shyness seemed to be gone.

Then Alicia did something weird. I saw her eyes go to Cindy, then back to me, then she smiled. I wasn't sure I wanted to know what was going on in that blond head of hers.

I saw something out of the corner of my eye that caught my attention. Someone was waving near the doors that led back into the school away from the gym. When they saw I was looking at them, they waved more frantically, then started motioning for me.

I squinted to see who it was. I felt my heart beat faster. I could start to see some features I recognized. Long brown hair, wearing long blue-jeans and a blue blouse. She was wearing the exact same clothes from when I'd first met her.

It was Susan.

I just froze. For a second I doubted what I was seeing. But when she realized that I saw her, I could see Susan's motions getting more frustrated. Finally, she pointed right at me, then gestured for me to follow her. She disappeared through the doors and took a right out of eyesight down the hall.

Cindy was talking to me.

"Hello? Alex? I'm right here. Damn, no wonder you can't get a girlfriend."

I grabbed her hand and looked at Alicia. She was in the middle of a kissing session with Tom. I decided to leave her alone.

"Whoa. What's up?" Cindy said.

I didn't say anything. I led her across the floor toward where I saw Susan. We stepped through the open doors into the hallway.

"What's going on?"

"I need to make sure I'm not crazy."

"You've always been crazy."

I looked in the direction I saw Susan walking. I caught a glimpse of a foot disappearing around the corner at the end of the hall.

"Come on."

I let go of her hand and jogged. Cindy tried to keep up, but her shoes weren't exactly made for running. Her heels echoed in the empty school hallway. A feeling of dread crept over me. I was chasing a ghost in an empty school. Cindy's shoes being the only sound made everything more creepy.

I made it to the end of the hall first. I turned to see the door leading upstairs to the second floor just coming to a close, about ten feet away.

"Alex? Where the hell are we going?"

I slowly opened the door leading upstairs while Cindy stood a few feet behind me. I was cautious, like something could jump out at me at any second. The stairwell was dimly lit. There was a window at the top that let in a lot of light during the day, but not now.

"Alex? Any day now."

I looked at my best friend. She had her arms impatiently crossed in front of her.

"Do you trust me?"

She didn't hesitate. "Alex, we've known each other since we were five. What do you think? Tell me what the hell is going on."

I thought about the absurdity of what I saw. A woman, a *ghost*, waving at me across the school gym floor where two hundred couples danced.

"I'm not sure I trust myself right now."

I walked up the stairs. I heard Cindy take a deep breath behind me and follow me. My own footsteps sounded ominous in the hallway. Cindy's heels sounded just the same. I felt her grab my hand from behind.

We made it to the door guarding the upstairs. It creaked as I pushed it open slowly. The lights were off on the second floor. I guess no one felt the need to turn them on, considering the dance was in the gym.

"Christ. Who knew school could be so scary," Cindy whispered behind me.

There was some light coming from our left. I turned and felt my breath get caught in my chest.

Susan stood there, about halfway down the hall. She was looking into the only lit classroom on the floor.

Cindy poked her head out under mine. We both were looking in the same direction, but we weren't seeing the same thing.

"Wow. Miss Munroe teaching Spanish late tonight?"

"You don't see her, do you?"

"See who?"

I didn't respond, as there was no need to. The only thing Cindy saw was light from a classroom spilling out into the hallway. I saw that, plus a woman who was dead, murdered by her husband who had been possessed by a demon.

Susan turned her head toward me. She smiled, but I could see there was no happiness in it. She gestured with her head toward the classroom.

Then she was gone.

"Let's go see what's up," Cindy said, and took a step in front of me.

"Whoa, whoa." I grabbed her shoulders to stop her. Then I took the lead.

"Wow, Alex. You're my hero."

We walked toward the classroom, moving as quietly as we could. As we drew closer we could hear some sounds. It took me a moment to recognize it as moaning. I heard some rubbing, then what sounded like a belt coming off.

Cindy smiled. "Looks like someone couldn't wait till the dance was over. Let's see who it is."

Somehow, deep down, I knew who at least one of them was. I tried to reach out and stop Cindy, but I was too late. As her face went into the light I watched her amused smile turn to shock and horror.

She stood up and stormed into the room.

"What the fuck is this?!"

I was a step behind her. I already had an idea of what I'd see. Daryl was sitting in Miss Munroe's chair. His shirt was unbuttoned and his belt on the floor. Straddling his lap was Tiffany Sears, a senior whose reputation with the guys was well known. Her dress was pulled up to her hips, revealing white panties, and one strap was off. I can only imagine what the scene would be like if we came five minutes later.

"Cindy!" Daryl said. His eyes said it all. He quickly forced Tiffany off his lap. She straightened her dress. "Look, I can explain-"

"Can't anyone get any privacy anymore?" Tiffany said.

I didn't even have the chance to be stunned before Cindy gave Tiffany a look that could kill.

"You're in a fucking school classroom, bitch!"

"Don't you call me a bitch!"

Tiffany slapped Cindy with an open palm. Daryl started to get out of his sex-chair. I managed to take a step forward before Cindy struck back, although it wasn't with an open palm. She punched Tiffany square under the eye. Tiffany reeled back a few steps and fell on her ass.

I was surprised to see Daryl raise his fist. He had a dangerous look in his eye, and he was looking at Cindy.

He never had a chance to swing, although I believe that's exactly what he was gonna do. I was in front of Cindy faster than I would have thought possible. I had a hand around Daryl's throat and the other locked around his wrist. Daryl was a few inches taller than me and could easily have broken my grip. But he didn't. Seeing him raise his fist to my best friend made my mind go blank. His knees actually buckled before he stumbled back into the chair.

"I don't need this," Tiffany said. She climbed to her feet and stormed out of the room.

"Come back here!" Cindy was only a few steps behind her.

I stood there staring at Daryl. I was furious for only a few seconds longer. Then I noticed the look Daryl was giving me as he rubbed his neck.

He was terrified.

His face had a look like he'd just seen a monster. And he was staring right at me. What did I do exactly? Just force him to sit down? Or did he see something about me that the girls missed?

He finally recovered enough to get out of the chair. He circled around me

34

to the door, but never took his eyes off me. I was just scared from the look he gave me. I couldn't move myself.

"Wait, Cindy!" he said. "We have to talk!"

Daryl ran out of the classroom. I was ready to follow when I felt a hand grab my shoulder. I spun to see Susan.

"Don't, Alex," she said. "Cindy will be alright."

I was speechless for a moment. Susan was amused by my reaction. She smiled, then shrugged sheepishly.

"Stop staring at me like that," she said. "It's making me feel weird."

It was another ten seconds before I could talk.

"What in the *hell* is going on?"

"We've been watching you, just like I said I would. You saved me. And I couldn't really leave without paying you back somehow."

I gestured around the classroom. "This is payback?"

"Well, we saw your friend was heading for trouble. We figured you'd want to know."

Actually I *was* grateful. The last thing I ever want to see is Cindy with a broken heart. It was a good thing to get what kind of guy Daryl was out in the open before their relationship went crazy-far.

I nodded. "Thank you. Very much."

She smiled. "After what you did for us. Least we could do."

"We. Who is *we*?"

As soon as I asked the question there was a familiar voice from the corner of the room behind me.

"Hi, Alex."

I turned to see Richard leaning against the wall near the classroom door. That sight in itself freaked me out. He was a ghost, right? How could he lean against a wall? He was dressed in the same clothes as the last time I saw him, which was when he was trying to stab his wife.

"Alex, this is my husband, Richard."

I was afraid for a second. But then Richard smiled, and I could tell right away he wasn't what I dealt with in Tammy's house.

"Nice to meet you," I said.

Richard extended his hand. I shook it. Then he looked at Susan.

"Honey, it's almost time for us to go."

"Are we out of time already?"

"Afraid so."

She sighed, then leaned forward to hug me. It caught me off guard.

"You're gonna do a lot of great things, Alex. You take care."

I didn't know what to say. "Uh, you too?"

Susan laughed. "Cindy is out on the football field. You go take care of her."

"How do you know-?"

Before I could finish, she was gone. She did the two second fade-out routine once again. I turned around, knowing what I'd see. Sure enough, Richard was gone too.

I stood there for a moment, alone in the classroom in silence. My mind was still processing what just happened. Like last time, I wasn't sure I could handle it just yet. So I forced myself to think about the only thing that mattered at that moment.

Cindy.

I left the classroom and walked back down the dark stairs. I didn't go through the school gym. I took a side door and walked across the campus to the football field. I could see a dressed-up couple on the bleachers on the opposite side of the field, sharing some time together, and a familiar female with her back to me on the nearest side all by herself.

I didn't want to look at her too long and make her feel self-conscious, but I could tell Cindy was crying. She wiped at her eyes with her hand as I sat next to her. I knew Cindy better than anyone, and I knew more than anything she probably wanted to be left alone. But I wanted to make sure she was okay first.

I sat next to her without talking for a minute. She wouldn't look at me. I made sure to keep my distance.

"Daryl and I broke up."

I wanted to make a joke just to hear her laugh. But that would have to come later. Now was serious time.

"Probably a good move."

"What kind of an idiot am I?"

I looked at her. "What?"

"He told me he's *in love* with her." She rolled her eyes. "That he was tired of waiting for me. That he had *needs*. He *needs* to get his ass kicked. I'm a smart person, aren't I?"

The one thing about Cindy I haven't really touched on yet. She's *very* intelligent. When she wasn't running track or hanging out with me, she was studying. Hell, sometimes she'd study over my house. She wanted to be an accountant, and work in her father's accounting firm.

"You're the smartest person I know, Cindy."

"Then how the hell didn't I see this coming? I thought we...would be together for a while."

"Bottom line, Cindy, Daryl is an asshole and you can do a lot better. Hey, at least Tiffany will have a nice black eye tomorrow."

"Yeah. This is definitely a Homecoming I'll never forget."

Cindy laughed for a moment, but that laughter turned to crying. I felt my heart breaking along with hers. I scooted closer and wrapped an arm around her. She leaned her head onto my shoulder and cried for I don't know how long. I'd seen her cry before. But this was definitely a bad one.

"You want some alone time?"

Her answer surprised me. "No. Hang out with me for a while."

After a few minutes she calmed down. I took that as my cue to get my arm off her and scoot away. She leaned back and looked up at the moon. It was a beautiful night.

"I guess I'll live, right?"

She tried to smile. I just nodded.

"You'll be fine."

"That's cause I got friends like you."

My turn to smile.

"How the hell did you know what was going on up there anyway?"

I frowned and looked away. I thought back to ten minutes ago up in the classroom. Still so surreal. Standing in the middle of a school classroom and talking to two ghosts.

For a brief moment, I thought about lying to Cindy. I never lied to her before, but the truth sounded so strange, even to me. I wasn't even sure I could say the words.

"A, uh, *ghost*, told me. Can you believe that?"

She was quiet. I looked at her to read her face. She was studying me, trying to figure out if I was joking.

"At Tammy's house, I helped a ghost. I don't have a clue how, but there was a ghost trapped in Tammy's house. And she showed up at the damn dance tonight to tell me what was going on, as a favor."

I regretted opening my mouth. Cindy stared at me for a few seconds, and those few seconds ate at me. Would she laugh? Would she walk away? Would she simply not believe me?

"Is that why you freaked out for a few days?"

I nodded. "Ghosts are real, Cindy. So are demons. And I can see them both. It kind of freaked me out."

She put a hand on my shoulder. Her face didn't show any humor or disbelief, only concern.

"You could have told me," she said. "I believe you. You know that, right?"

I smiled and nodded, but that was an understatement. I was so relieved. Even when she didn't try or was upset herself, Cindy found a way to lift me up.

"Are *you* gonna be okay?"

She managed to smile. "Hey, Daryl's mistake. Not mine. Besides, my best friend sees ghosts. How cool is that?"

"Let's find Alicia and Tom and go do something."

"Sounds good."

CHAPTER 5

It was definitely a night I'd never forget. Alicia and Tom did become a couple for a few months. It was a while before Cindy was completely over Daryl. I'm not sure if she missed him directly, or the fact that she was cheated on.

We eventually let Alicia in on my wonderful little secret. Her only response was "Cool". I never did tell Mom. I'm not really sure why. I didn't see her much, and I guess I just didn't want our few conversations to be about ghosts.

Actually the next few years of my life were what you would call "normal". I didn't wake up in the middle of the night to see ghosts all over my room. I wasn't like that little kid in that movie who saw dead people, seeing ghosts everywhere he looked. In fact, I started to believe my experience with Susan and Richard was a once-in-a-lifetime kind of thing. Maybe I couldn't see ghosts or demons or whatever. Maybe I'd never see another ghost again.

If only.

It was a week away from my twenty-third birthday when my life changed forever. I had an okay job that paid the bills working at a warehouse shipping dock. Not the best job in the world, but better than nothing. Cindy was graduating college with a degree in accounting. I was so proud of her. She was full of motivation and intelligence, two qualities I lack. Alicia was a senior now in our old high school. It's amazing what happens between the ages of fourteen and eighteen. Alicia grew up fast. She definitely didn't need me to watch out for her anymore, even though I still did.

It was a Saturday. I went through my morning routine of waking up and stumbling into the shower. While I was in the bathroom I heard the front door to my apartment open and close.

"Is that you, baby?"

39

A soft, familiar voice responded. "Yeah."

Julie, my girlfriend. We'd been dating for almost a year. I have absolutely nothing bad to say about the woman. We met one night while I was out running around town with Alicia, Cindy, and a group of our friends. We traded numbers and hit it off pretty well.

After a shower I walked into the living room. She had her roller-blades in the corner. Every Saturday morning she roller-bladed on the nearby bike trail and came over my place.

She looked great. She was showing off her tan legs with a pair of white shorts and a tank top that hugged every curve.

"Hey," I said. I looked her up and down. "You can grab a shower if you want. I'll dig us up some breakfast."

"Okay."

"We still heading over your parents tonight for dinner?"

"I guess so."

Three short answers in a row, and no eye contact. Something was wrong.

"Julie? You alright?"

She finally looked at me. Sadness filled her eyes.

"We have to talk."

I don't think a good conversation has ever happened that started out with those words. I wasn't wrong this time either. Basically, in her words, "We're not working out."

I don't remember everything she said. She gave me a bunch of reasons about why she was breaking up with me. She apparently felt it coming on for the past few months. Weird, because we just had sex in the middle of the week. How did that work? Was she thinking "I wonder if we should break up" while we were naked in bed?

I said some things back. I can't remember, but nothing nasty. Then she cried a little, and left. She said she'd be back in a week or so to get her things.

I sat on the couch and didn't move. Shock, I guess. It took a year to build up our relationship. To get to know each other and become a part of each other's life. It took about twenty minutes to end all of that.

We were supposed to have dinner with her parents. Now I didn't know what I'd do. I didn't know what I'd do the next day either. Or the day after that.

I was desperate to do anything to keep my mind busy. I started cleaning my apartment. It was overdue anyway. I had a simple one bedroom apartment on the top floor of a three story building. The kitchen was bare, but it worked just fine. There was a dining room, but as a male bachelor, had no need for a dining room table. I kept my weights there instead. In the bedroom I had a full-sized bed with a small dresser. The living room, of course, had the entertainment center with a computer in the corner.

Normally Alicia or Cindy would stop by on Saturday to see how I was doing, grab lunch, whatever. They didn't that day, and I was actually glad. I knew Alicia spent the night over one of her friend's house, and was probably still hanging out with her. Cindy was spending the day helping her parents with some yard work. I thought that was funny considering she lived right next to me.

Cindy snatched up the empty apartment next to me about a year after I moved out. I don't know how the hell she did it, having to work a job, and go to school full time. I know her parents helped her out with money sometimes, but I know I couldn't handle it. I loved having her next to me. Our friendship hadn't died any at all since high school. We still saw each other almost every day. Living next to each other definitely helped with that.

She called around six o'clock. I'd just got done watching a DVD. She was surprised when I answered the phone.

"Hello?"

"Hey. I thought you were having dinner with Julie's folks?"

I closed my eyes tight. I hadn't been upset since that morning, but hearing her name made the heart jump.

"Nah," I said simply. "Why the hell you call then?"

"To leave a message on your machine, dumbass. You guys want to come out tonight? Dave and Tina are heading out to Lumbermill's in the city. It's eighteen and over, so Alicia's coming too. You guys in?"

I thought about it for a moment. I didn't really want to drive to the city to go to a club. Staring at attractive women certainly isn't a bad way to pass the time, but I'm not really a club guy. I don't drink or dance. So basically I give up fifteen bucks to go stand and hang out with my friends.

But if I didn't go, I'd dwell on Julie all night long.

"Yeah, sure."

"Cool. We're gonna head out around nine."

"Gotcha."

She hung up.

It didn't take long to get ready and look halfway decent. Just a pair of jeans and a short-sleeved shirt to try to show off the arms. I was watching TV when I heard someone knocking at Cindy's door just outside my apartment. Then there was a familiar voice.

"Yo Cindy! You in there?"

It was Dave, one of Cindy's friends that she'd met in college. No doubt his girlfriend Tina was with him. About ten minutes later I heard someone else knocking at her door. Looked like the night was getting started.

I locked the front door behind me and walked into Cindy's apartment. We never knocked on each other's doors. We just had a rule that went unspoken. If the door was locked, it meant naked people were usually inside.

Dave and Tina were sitting on the couch. Jenny, another of Cindy's friends, was in the kitchen getting a drink. She was the only other black friend that Cindy had. Cindy was nowhere to be seen, probably in the bedroom still getting dressed.

"Hey Alex!" Dave said. "What's up, man?"

Dave and Tina were alright. Always happy and smiling.

"Hey, how's it going? You two getting drunk tonight?"

"I'm gonna try my best, if Tina lets me."

She elbowed him in the side and laughed.

Jenny waved from the kitchen.

"Alex. Long time no see."

"Hey, Jenny. How's it going?"

"Are we all here?"

"Everyone except Alicia."

Almost like she sensed her name, Alicia gave a quick knock on the door, then stepped inside.

"Hey, everybody."

Cindy's voice came from the bedroom.

"Leese? Is that you?"

"Yeah."

"Come in here and tell me if I look good."

I laughed. Definitely funny cause Cindy always looked good.

We did some small talk for a few minutes until Cindy and Alicia came out of the bedroom. Cindy wore blue jeans and a half-shirt. She'd have no trouble getting the attention of the guys at the club. I always noticed a pattern in the way she dressed. If she showed off her upper body, she wore jeans. If she showed off those legs of hers, then she covered up top. It was always a half and half thing with her.

"Everybody ready?" Cindy asked, then looked right at me. "Hey Alex, where's your woman? Did she finally get smart and dump your ass?"

Despite Cindy throwing a dart and hitting a bulls-eye, I didn't flinch or anything. I just threw on a poker face.

"Eh, she couldn't make it tonight."

Dave pointed at me from the couch. "Listen, if you two ever do break up, let me know. I'd drop Tina for her in a second."

"Like hell you would, asshole," Tina said. "You've never had such good sex."

"Whoa. Too much info," Jenny called from the kitchen.

I could have won an acting award. No one suspected anything.

Except, of course, for Cindy and Alicia. I caught the two of them trading looks, then Cindy stared right at me while Dave and Tina were elbowing each other. I could see the sadness in her eyes. I gave a small smile and shrugged.

"Okay, we ready to go? Who's driving? The Teague family again?"

Alicia and I drove the few times we headed out. Alicia wasn't old enough to drink, and I simply didn't drink.

"That sounds fine to me."

"Cool. Me and Tina will go with Leese so we can make out in the back seat and gross her out like last time."

Everyone started filing out of the apartment. Then Cindy spoke up.

"Oh, Jen, we'll be out in a second. I need Alex's help with something."

"Sure," Jenny looked at me. "Your truck unlocked?"

"Yeah."

She left. It was just Cindy and me. She put her hands on my shoulders.

"Alex, I'm *so* sorry," she said. "What happened?"

I shrugged. "It wasn't working out."

"What?"

"That's what she said. She said she just didn't feel it was working out."

"That fuckin' bitch."

Her tone made me laugh. "I'll be okay."

"I didn't mean what I said." She gave me a hug. "She's an *idiot* for breaking up with you. She'll never find someone else like you."

"Thanks, Cindy. Do me a favor. Just keep this quiet for tonight. I don't want everybody freaking out and wanting to talk about Julie all night."

She nodded. "No problem. What a stupid bitch. Listen, nine thousand women will be all over you at the club. So don't worry about it."

"Yeah, right."

We left the apartment. Jenny was waiting in the back seat of my truck. Alicia was driving away with Dave and Tina, but slowed down when she saw me. We locked eyes, and I smiled and nodded, letting her know I was okay. She nodded back, letting me know she understood. Sibling communication.

The night started out normal enough. The drive through the city wasn't fun, but that was expected. Groups of people walked around everywhere. Every street was jammed with traffic. But we eventually made it to the club and parked close to each other. Then the six of us walked up together. We all got a nice little drinking armband except Alicia.

It's like an assault on the senses when you first step into any club. You go from a quiet, wide open outside to a loud, claustrophobic inside. It was so loud I could barely hear anyone talk. It was so crowded I could barely move. The lines at the bar were so long that it would take minutes to get a drink of any kind. Wow, what fun.

We split up after a while. Dave and Tina went to the dance floor and started grinding on each other. Alicia went to the bathroom while Jenny, Cindy, and I all waited for a drink.

It was so loud that whenever you wanted to talk to someone you had to get right next to their ear. And Jenny would put a hand on me whenever I leaned close to talk. Weird.

"What you want?" I asked her, pointing at the bar.

"Just a beer is fine. Thanks."

I looked at Cindy. "Water."

I gave her a look. That's what I had in mind.

I handed everyone their drinks and we found a corner to stand in. Cindy leaned close to me.

"Any woman's phone number in here you want, let me know. We'll get it."

I shook my head. Cindy always looked out for me. Probably a little too much.

"Jesus," Jenny said. "Look at those two."

I followed her finger. Dave and Tina were making out like crazy on the dance floor. I thought any moment he'd throw her to the ground and make their own porn film.

"Leese will be dropping them off at a hotel tonight."

Someone behind Dave and Tina caught my attention. There was a red-headed woman standing next to the platform where the DJ was and others were dancing. She wasn't dancing or drinking. She leaned against the railing and stared right at me.

I took a sip of my water. I expected when I looked back over at her that she'd be looking somewhere else. I was wrong. She still stared right at me. And it wasn't an "I think you're sexy" stare. There was a curiosity in her body language.

I looked at Cindy. "Hey. Do you see that redhead over there? Don't stare. But do you see her?"

Cindy casually searched to where I was gesturing. "I don't see any redhead."

I looked back to the DJ. Sure enough, she was gone. I searched around the dance floor. In just a matter of seconds, I couldn't find her. You gotta love clubs.

"Can't blame her, though," Cindy said with a smile. "I'd stare at you too."

I opened my mouth to throw a joke out when Alicia joined us.

"Hey guys," she said. "One of the pool tables is open upstairs. Let's get some games in."

I liked that idea. I'm not great at pool, but like playing it. We made our way up the stairs to the second level of the club. Near the back were the pool tables. Alicia and Jenny played first. I cheered my little sister on as always, while Jenny gave me dirty looks. Cindy sat next to me and rested an arm on my shoulder.

They were about halfway done their first game when I heard a voice off to my left.

"Hi guys."

We all turned to look at her. The redhead I'd seen staring at me not too long ago. Now that she was only ten feet away I could get a good look at her.

Very gorgeous. Red hair that stopped past the shoulders. Deep green eyes. A skirt that went just above the knees. Rather pale skin. A bright smile. Absolutely amazing body. She looked about our age, maybe a little older.

"You guys mind if I play with you?"

Alicia looked at all of us. When none of us objected, she shrugged.

"Sure. You can have winner of our game if you want."

"I want to play him, if that's alright." She pointed at me.

I saw Alicia give me a look. She smiled and nodded, like she was proud of me that I could attract such a beautiful woman.

The redhead sat next to me while we waited for Jenny and Alicia to finish. I didn't say a word to her. Cindy nudged me, trying to get me to talk to her.

I somehow knew she wasn't interested in me. She was here for another reason. I just didn't know what it was.

Alicia finally beat Jenny. She pretended to put Jenny in a headlock while tossing the pool cue to me.

"Well, you ready?" the redhead said to me.

I nodded. Cindy and I locked eyes for a moment before I started racking. Her eyes said it all. She was wondering what was wrong with me, why I wasn't chatting up this beautiful woman.

"Aren't you the stud with all these women," she said. She never took her eyes off me at the other end of the pool table.

She was playing a game of some kind. Was she actually flirting or interested in me? Something deep down told me no.

"I'm Alex. That's my sister Alicia. My friends, Jenny and Cindy."

"I'm Victoria. Nice to meet all of you."

"Hi," Cindy said, flashing her smile. "Alex is a little shy, so you have to forgive him."

"I think I can manage that. He is cute."

I broke the rack, sinking a ball. I missed my next shot. She took hers, sinking the one ball. It almost felt like a duel of some kind.

"So do you live around here?" she asked.

"All my life."

"I'm a traveler myself. I'm in town for a few days. Looking to make some friends."

"Ah."

"You guys come out here a lot?"

"Every now and then."

"You don't look like a drinker to me."

"One day we'll get him drunk," Jenny said from next to Cindy. Now suddenly she felt the need to help out too.

"Nah. I like a guy who's in control."

I ended up beating her. She faked disappointment and handed her cue to Alicia. She touched my shoulder. I wanted to pull away, but didn't. I didn't want to make my hesitance of Victoria obvious.

"It was nice meeting you. I hope we meet again sometime."

I watched her walk away and disappear into the crowd of people. I heard Jenny behind me.

"I'll give you credit, Alex. Any other guy would have been all over her. Julie is a lucky woman."

Yeah, right.

I felt a hand on my shoulder. I knew it was Cindy.

"You *are* something."

I looked at her. "What do you mean?"

"Any other guy would jump on the rebound express. And a hot redhead, no question about it."

I smiled. "You were trying to get me to talk to her at first."

She shook her head. "Bad idea. She was too pushy."

"Yeah. Not my type."

"What *is* your type, Alex?"

The question caught me off guard. I looked at my friend.

"Don't really know. But I know it's not that."

She smiled. "I'm so glad we're friends." She was serious. No humor in her voice.

Again, the sudden bonding surprised me. I gave her a quick, playful hug. She did the same.

"What would I do without you?"

"You wouldn't make it a week. Now get me some more water, bitch."

I laughed.

I complain about clubs a lot, but I usually end up having fun. I always have the company to thank for that. I always have fun with Alicia and Cindy, of course. Dave and Tina just made me laugh. They were a funny couple. Jenny was quiet, but I liked her too.

There was one more surprise in store for me.

It was getting close to the end of the night. Dave and Tina ran off to who-knows-where. Jenny actually met a guy, and was at the bar talking to him. Alicia had to go to the bathroom. It was just me and Cindy, leaning against the wall with our waters.

"So, you having fun?" she asked me.

"Yeah. I just get tired of you whipping my ass at pool."

"You let me win."

"Bullshit. I wouldn't let my own mother win."

She laughed. "I'm glad you had fun."

I knew what she was referring to.

"I'll probably hide in bed all day tomorrow," I said. "But thanks for looking out for me."

"That's what friends are for. Tomorrow I'll pull you out of bed and get us a pizza. We'll become one with the couch and watch some movies."

I laughed. "Sounds good."

"Now, what do I have to do to get you out there and dance with me?"

"Probably a lot of beer. But I don't drink. So that's that."

"Come on, Alex. It'll be fun. I'll hang all over you like Tina does to Dave."

"We'll probably get arrested then. Come on, you know white people can't dance."

Her turn to laugh. "Well, I'm gonna dance. And if you don't come I'll look stupid dancing all alone."

She walked out to the dance floor. I shook my head while holding up the wall. But I couldn't take my eyes off her. Cindy grew up from a spunky five-year-old girl to a sexy woman, all right in front of me. She had that beauty that went across all races. Once people found out we were friends, color didn't matter. I had whites, blacks, Asians, Hispanics, all asking if Cindy was single. Everyone wanted to talk to her. Can't say I blame them.

Maybe somebody spiked the water, I don't know. But I decided I was gonna dance badly with her. She was trying her best to have fun with me. What better way than to laugh together at how bad a dancer I am.

I took two steps away from the wall when suddenly a pair of arms slipped around me. I looked into the eyes of Victoria, the hot redhead. I noticed for the first time that she was about an inch shorter than me.

"Put your arms around me. Right now. Make it look like we're dancing."

Her voice had changed from earlier. The flirty tone was gone. She wore a smile, but she was all business. I thought I heard a slight accent that I didn't hear before.

She squeezed me. I actually felt the air rush out of my lungs. For a few seconds I couldn't draw a breath. Then she eased her grip.

"I could kill you right here, right now, and no one will really notice. Now put your arms around me."

"No. Fuck you. You won't hurt me, cause you want something from me. Now let me go."

I don't where that came from. I'd never been threatened before in my life, unless you count schoolyard bullies that Cindy saved me from. But there I was, mouthing off to someone who obviously wasn't what she seemed.

She actually smiled.

"Fair enough."

She let me go. But she did grab a hold of my hand. The entire time she never let the smile fade from her face.

"Who are you?"

I was confused. "I told you. My name's Alex. I don't know what you're problem is, but I think you got me confused for someone else."

"Okay. Enough games. Listen to me. I don't know who or what you are.

But this place is under my protection. Get to whatever business you have and leave."

I felt a hand on my shoulder.

"Hi guys," Cindy said. "I was looking for you, Alex."

Victoria's personality shifted once again.

"Hi, Cindy," she said. "Listen, I'll get right to it. You and Alex aren't dating, right?"

"Nope. Not at all. He's all yours."

"Just what I wanted to hear."

Victoria winked at me. Then she walked away.

I watched the curvy stranger. Her words still bounced in my mind.

Who are you? What are you?

"Man, that is one aggressive bitch."

I didn't smile. "You ain't lying."

"Hey. Did I mess up there? It looked like you needed saving. But if you're interested..."

"Oh no, Cindy. You definitely saved me."

"Good. I'm picking your next girlfriend. No one's ever breaking up with you again."

I looked at Cindy and smiled. "It's a deal."

CHAPTER 6

The rest of the night went smoothly. It ended up being almost three in the morning before everyone got home. Cindy wanted to stop by my place and watch TV, but I was tired. I just wanted to get to bed. I wanted to go to sleep and dwell on the fun stuff. I wanted to forget about girlfriends that broke up for reasons unknown and hot redheads that were freakishly strong and got people mixed up.

I don't know what time I woke up the next morning, but the sun was up high. The first thing I did when I woke up was reach over for Julie. She always stayed over my apartment on the weekends. My heart sank when I realized she wasn't there, and the memory of the day before flooded back.

That's right. I'm single again.

I sat up in bed for a minute, taking it all in. I'd have to get used to sleeping alone on the weekends one more time.

I was confused though when I heard the TV. I poked my head out the bedroom and looked toward the living room. I saw Cindy sitting on the couch, waving the remote control around. She saw me out of the corner of her eye.

"Hey, zombie. Glad you could wake up."

Cindy stopping by unannounced was nothing new. It only stopped when I was dating someone. When she was single I did the same thing to her.

"Damn, did you sleep here last night?"

"Nah. I had three male models waiting for me when I got home. Why the hell would I sleep here?"

"Funny."

"Don't come out of there naked, please."

"If only you could be so lucky."

I took a quick shower. After I threw some clothes on Cindy was in the kitchen pouring two glasses of soda. She handed me one.

"Okay. Donuts are right behind you. I've got eighty movies in the living room."

"What time is it?"

"One o'clock."

I nearly spit out some soda. "In the afternoon?"

"No. In the morning. Don't let that damn sunlight fool you. It lies."

"How the hell do you get up so early?"

"Because Alicia called me. To check up on *you*, she calls *me* and wakes me up. You've got a hell of a sister."

The attention was starting to get embarrassing.

"I broke up with a girlfriend, that's all. I didn't have surgery or anything."

"Okay, we'll ignore you from now on. Now watch a movie with me. But I swear if you try to hold my hand I'll beat your ass."

"I'll try to behave."

We sat on opposite ends of the couch and started a movie. Cindy curled her legs up under her like she always did, a gesture I always thought sexy. She was an action movie person, like myself. She put in *The Matrix*. It was relaxing, just hanging out with my best friend. But my mind started drifting in between action scenes and Keanu Reeve's superior acting. I started thinking about Julie. I went back and forth between self-pity and anger. It wasn't only Julie either. I was just unhappy. I was a suddenly single shipping dock worker. Not really much to brag about there. Nothing compared to Cindy, who was a college graduate with a good job doing something she loved.

Julie was icing on the cake with how I felt about myself at that time.

"What the hell happened?"

Cindy looked at me. "Huh?"

"We had sex on Wednesday night. Then Saturday morning she tells me it's not working out? How do you go from naked time on one day, then three days later, oh it's not working out? After a damn year?"

She wrinkled her face. "Christ, Alex. You could have kept some of that to yourself."

"Sorry. But you get what I'm saying."

Cindy didn't say anything. She just looked at me, sympathy in her eyes. Maybe she didn't know what to say.

"Remember Marie, two years ago? She at least had a reason for breaking up. She was screwing someone behind my back. That's a reason, right?" I paused. "Did I goof up somehow and not know it?"

Cindy uncurled her legs and leaned toward me slightly. "Do you want to know what's wrong with you?"

"Hold on," I said, and put my soda on the coffee table. A definite plus about our relationship was that we knew each other so long that honesty was never a problem. We could be honest with each other, even if it was painful, and we'd still be friends. "Okay, what's wrong with me?"

"Absolutely nothing."

I was surprised, to say the least.

She continued.

"Alex, you've got faults, like we all do. You're a little more down on yourself than you should be. Sometimes you can be a little too quiet. Not as bad as when we were little, but it's there sometimes. But don't change. Ever. Forget those stupid bitches. You're awesome just like you are. That's why you're my best friend."

I let her words sink in. Right then I knew I would get over Julie. I could get through anything, because of friends like Cindy.

"Thanks, Cindy."

We turned our attention back to the movie.

"I never thought my best friend would be a goofy white dude."

I threw a couch-pillow at her.

*****

Monday came around, and the weekly grind started once again. Nothing exciting ever happened during the week. I woke up, went to work, then came home. I didn't see Cindy too much during the week because of her working late with her father. Alicia did stop by twice. We had dinner together. She filled me in on the normal topics. Guys she was interested in, classes she had trouble with.

I felt bad for her. At least when I was growing up at the house, she had me for company, since Mom wasn't home much. Now with me gone, it was just her. Although I had a suspicion she had more people over the house than she let on.

It felt like forever for Friday to come around. It would be my first official weekend without Julie. Surprisingly, I was okay with it. Single life had its perks too. On Friday, when I got home, I kicked my shoes off and threw a quick dinner in the microwave. I could do whatever I wanted. I never had to see her parents again, and I'm sure they were grateful they never had to see me either.

At around seven the front door to my apartment opened up. Cindy poked her head in, still wearing her cute dress from working at her father's firm.

"Hey Alex? You're not naked in here, are you?"

"Nah."

"Oh, damn," she joked. "Everyone's coming over my place tonight. You coming over?"

I knew *everyone* consisted of our usual friends. At least minus Alicia, as Friday was her night she usually hung out with her school friends.

"Yeah. What time?"

"About an hour. I gotta take a shower."

"Good. You smell."

"You're so damn funny."

She closed the door.

I did a quick workout before deciding I'd be first at Cindy's place for a change. I got dressed and walked the three feet separating our front doors. I was greeted by music playing in the living room. I could hear her shower at the end of the hall.

"Hey Cindy!" I called. "I'm in here."

I stole a soda from her fridge. I walked around her apartment, studying her decorating skills. She had pictures everywhere. Most were of her, Alicia, and myself. She also had pictures of her parents and her grandma. I hadn't seen her grandma in a few months. I smiled as I looked at the picture taken just last year of Cindy, Grandma, and me. We were posing in front of a roller coaster at the Kings Dominion amusement park. Cindy was giving me bunny ears as I flexed an arm in front of her. Grandma was playfully pulling on Cindy's arm, as if wanting to go back on the roller coaster. That was a fun time.

"Alex!"

I jumped. The voice was five feet away. I looked up to see Cindy, completely naked. Her body had a sexy sheen from the shower water. My mind barely had a second to process what I was seeing before I closed my eyes and threw an arm over my face.

"Jesus, Cindy!"

"What the fuck, Alex," she said. I heard her storming down the hallway. "Why didn't you say you were here?"

"I did! I screamed at the top of my lungs! I said, 'Cindy, I'm in your apartment. Please do not come out of the bathroom without any clothes on.'"

"Bullshit."

"Seriously, Cindy. I yelled out when I first came in."

She was talking from her bedroom now.

"Well, I didn't hear you."

"I did, I swear. I've seen enough naked women in my lifetime. No need to add you to the list."

She was quiet for a moment. I was trying to figure out if she really was mad at me. Hell, I'd done worse by accident over the years, like the time I ran over her foot with her car.

She stepped out of her bedroom, dressed this time. Shorts and a tee-shirt. She walked by without even looking at me.

Yikes.

Before I could defend myself there was a knock at the door.

"Come in."

It was Dave. Tina was a step behind.

"Hey guys," he said. He saw the scowl on Cindy's face. "Uh, we interrupting something?"

"No," she said, then motioned for them to come in.

Dave looked at me. "Dude, why the hell didn't you say Julie broke up with you last weekend? Man, I feel like an ass now."

I waved him off. "Don't worry about it. I'm good now."

Tina pointed at me. "Her mistake, Alex."

"Thanks, Tina."

Jenny showed up not too long after they did. Dave and Jenny fought over what to watch on TV. Everyone just talked about their work week, what was happening in their lives. Cindy barely looked at me. I decided to steer clear of her for a while.

We had our share of fights over the years, like all friends do. Some were dumb, and some not so dumb. She didn't agree with me dating Marie, a bartender I met while we were out one night. Turned out she was right about that one. I gave her a hard time when she lent her last boyfriend Roy three hundred bucks to "fix his car". Turns out I was wrong. He paid her back. But I still insist he was on drugs.

Now apparently we were fighting because I saw her naked for half a second.

Everyone was vegging out. They raided her fridge a little and were fighting about what movie to watch when Dave had an idea that would change my life.

"Hey, you guys want to get out of here? I know this great place we could hang out at."

"Where?" Jenny asked.

"It's a cabin in the woods. Awesome place. Right by a lake. I left a grill there from when I was there last time. We could cook some food. No one ever goes there."

Jenny shrugged. "I'm up for it."

Everyone looked at Cindy. "Sure."

My turn. I saw this as a chance to go home, get away from Cindy's evil stare. But when I looked at her the evil look was gone. She looked better, although she still wasn't smiling.

"I'll tag along."

"Sweet," Dave jumped up. "We brought Tina's truck. We'll take that. Give Alex a night off from driving. I'll buy food and gas."

"Sounds like a plan."

It was a little cramped in the back of Tina's truck, but it wasn't too bad. Tina sat in front with Dave, of course. I tried to avoid sitting next to Cindy, but Jenny didn't want to sit next to the window. So, stuck I was. Nothing like being forced to rub shoulders with someone you know is mad at you.

Dave stopped at the grocery store. He and Tina ran inside while Jenny got out to make a call on her cell phone. I got out just to stretch my legs, and to get away from Cindy. To my surprise, she got out with me.

We avoided eye contact for a moment, then looked at each other. She gave me a half-hearted smile, a sign she had cooled off a little.

"Are we cool, Cindy?" I finally asked.

"Yeah, we're cool."

Some more silence. There was still some discomfort there.

"I don't know what you're thinking, but I swear that was an accident. Come on, you know me. I don't do crap like that on purpose."

"You don't have a clue why I'm mad, do you?"

I was quiet. Well, I *thought* I knew, anyway.

"Uh, maybe because I saw you with no clothes on?"

"No. You saw me with no clothes on, and you looked away like I was the ugliest thing you ever saw. You actually covered your eyes, like I was blinding you or something."

I can only imagine the look on my face. Probably a mix of plain dumb confusion and surprise.

"Huh?"

"Do you think I'm pretty, Alex?"

I was a little annoyed, simply because I had no idea of what was going on.

"Is this a joke? What are you talking about?"

"It's a simple question, with a yes or no answer. Do you think I'm attractive?"

The simple question with a yes or no answer made me uncomfortable enough to stall for time. I caught Jenny sneaking a peek at us, but she quickly looked away and kept on with her phone call.

"Cindy, what the hell does it matter what I think? There's a thousand guys out there who think you're attractive."

"I'm not asking a thousand guys. I'm asking you. And you just gave me an answer, I guess."

"No, I didn't. Don't put words in my mouth."

She threw her hands in the air. "Why does this have to be so damn hard? It's a simple question."

It *was* a simple question. But it was wrong somehow to tell your best friend that she was the most beautiful woman you'd ever seen. I stole looks at her all the time, but that was always followed by guilt. You aren't *supposed* to be attracted to your best friend.

"You're gorgeous. Come on Cindy, what's this about? You even know you're gorgeous. You don't need me to tell you."

She took a deep breath and smiled. "Then why did you cover your eyes back at the apartment?"

I barely held in my frustration. Women are weird.

"Did you want me to stand there and stare like a pervert? I'm not gonna stare at a naked woman with my mouth hanging open."

I saw Dave and Tina walking across the parking lot with a bag of groceries. It was time to get moving.

Cindy surprised me with a tight hug. Then she climbed back in the truck. I shook my head. I still didn't know what the hell just happened, but whatever it was, I was glad it was behind us.

"Christ. Next time I'll stand there like a deer in headlights. That'll make everyone happy."

It didn't take us too long to get to where Dave had in mind. He took a turn off the highway down a dirt road through some trees. It was a little creepy considering the only light came from the moon. But after about five minutes of driving he slowed down.

It was a hell of a scene. It was just like he described. The moonlight threw wicked shadows across the worn-down cabin. Right behind the cabin was a pier leading to a huge lake. The moonlight shimmered off the surface of the water. The sounds of nature were all around us. It was freaky. Ten minutes ago we were on the highway. Now that all seemed so far away.

"Wow," Jenny said.

"Yeah, I know," Dave said. "Awesome. Alex, give me a hand?"

I helped him unload groceries. He turned the radio on. The women walked around a little, just exploring. Apparently the cabin was completely empty except for an old wood stove. I would have brought some wood if I knew that was the case. Nothing beats the smell of an old wood stove.

Dave fired up a lantern he kept in the truck and started cooking some burgers on the grill he left there. It felt like a mini camp-out. Dave certainly found a gem when it came to fun and relaxing spots to hang out. It was exactly what he promised.

Dave and I sat in the back of the truck while the women danced to the music. They laughed and carried on, bragging about who the better dancer was. Dave took a bite of a burger and leaned closer to me.

"We gotta get more light on them."

I smiled. Dave's subtle way of suggesting Tina, Jenny, and Cindy dancing was entertainment all by itself. I couldn't argue with him there.

I always thought it was funny how women could dance together, and no one blinked an eye. But look out if two guys were caught dancing together.

Dave leaned over again. "Is it just me, or is Tina hot?"

I actually think Cindy's got her beat. Of course I'm not gonna tell Dave that.

"Watch me start some trouble. Hey, Jenny!"

She didn't stop dancing. She cast Dave a look. "What?"

"Stop staring at me. I caught you staring."

"Uh, no," she said with a smile.

"Don't try to hide it. You want some of the Dave."

His own girlfriend was the first to laugh.

"Please. You think *everyone* wants a piece of the Dave."

"Well, they do, don't they?"

Tina stopped dancing. "Ha. A *tiny* piece was enough for me. I think I'm ready to move on. Jenny, you can have him if you want."

Jenny stopped dancing too and pretended to study Dave. "Eh, no thanks. He probably couldn't handle me. Besides, I don't date white guys. I only hang out with you guys cause I'm bored."

"Hey now," Cindy said. She grabbed a soda and leaned against the truck next to me. "What's wrong with white guys?"

"Nothing. It's just they're so...white."

I laughed at that. Jenny didn't joke much, which made her jokes more funny.

Cindy pointed at Dave. "Survey time. Would you date a black woman?"

"I'd like to. But Tina won't let me."

Cindy looked at Tina, but dismissed her with a wave. "We already know you'll date anyone, as shown by exhibit A." She pointed at Dave.

"Damn, that's harsh," he said.

"Alex, would you date a black woman?"

"I'll date anyone that looks at me twice without turning away."

Tina laughed at that one. Dave just nodded approval.

"Nah, I'm serious. Would you go out with a black woman?"

The answer was yes. This is the twenty-first century. If a woman was attractive, funny, and intelligent, it didn't matter what the color of her skin was. But I thought I'd play with Cindy some more.

"Depends on who it is. Hell, what does she look like? Beyonce? Gabrielle Union?"

Cindy shrugged. "I don't know. Like me. Would you date a black woman who looked like me?"

I heard Dave cough a little next to me. It was guy code, but I couldn't understand it. I hung out with Cindy and Alicia too much.

"Well, yeah, I would."

"What about you?" Jenny asked. "Would you date a white guy?"

"I have before. Race doesn't matter to me."

"Ah ha. You say that, but you're single now, aren't you? White guys are the devil."

We shared a laugh.

Jenny started staring at something behind me. I turned my head to see what she saw. I could only see trees and shadows.

"Jenny? What's up?"

"What is that back there?"

Dave turned around too. "That's just an old house. All tore up. No one lives there."

Cindy shook her head. "What are you talking about? I don't see anything."

"It's there. Look just above the tree line. You can see part of the roof."

He was right. I'm sure it was easier to see during the day. But I could see what looked to be a roof through the tops of the trees.

"Holy shit," Jenny said. "Is that the McEllen house?"

Tina frowned. "The *what?*"

"I heard there was supposed to be an old house in the woods somewhere that was haunted."

Cindy looked at me. I didn't say a word, but I had a sinking feeling I knew where this was all leading.

Dave shook his head. "Nah. I went there with some buddies last time I was here during the day. There's nothing in there. Creepy though, I'll say that. But nothing jumped out at me."

"How was it creepy?"

"Just was. There were books and shit all over the ground. There were still plates on the dining room table. It was freaky."

"What happened there?" Tina asked.

I tried not to groan.

"Supposedly the McEllens lived there and some people tried to rob their house. They were a rich family. All of them were killed. That was like twenty years ago."

Jenny's face lit up. "Let's check it out?"

Dave shrugged. "Sure. I've got a flashlight or two behind the seats. But there's nothing up there."

"Tina? You in?"

She pointed at Dave. "You'd better hold my hand."

"I'll do more than hold your *hand.*"

"Cindy?"

She didn't hesitate. "No. I'll pass."

"You're no fun. Alex?"

I shook my head. "Not a good idea, guys. If that house is haunted, you don't want to go anywhere near it."

"You watch too many movies. Haunted houses aren't real," Jenny said.

"I was in a haunted house once. Scariest thing that ever happened to me."

I didn't elaborate. I saw Cindy get ready to say something, probably back me up. But I shot her a look that told her otherwise. I didn't want everyone to think she was crazy along with me.

"Oh, come on. Like Dave said, there's nothing up there. I just want to see it. We're not gonna go inside and call up the dead or anything."

They started to leave. I stared at Cindy and shook my head.

I didn't want to go at all. Five-year-old memories rushed back to me. Tammy's freezing house. Watching Richard raise a knife repeatedly over his head and thrust it into his wife. That creepy, genderless voice that cost me many nights sleep. The look on Tammy's face after she was struck by an invisible hand.

But these were my friends. Dave was probably right. There was nothing there. But if somehow, some way, my friends got hurt, I would never forgive myself.

"Wait up."

Cindy looked at me. "Alex."

I could read her face. She was only concerned for me.

"But I'm not feeling too good," I added. "Is it alright if we make it quick?"

Jenny was excited. "Yeah, we won't stay long. It'll be fun though. Like a haunted house ride at the theme park."

Cindy took a breath. "I'm right behind you."

"Cindy-"

"You said the next haunted house we'd hit together."

I grinned. I'm surprised she remembered that.

Dave knew the way, so he led us. Everyone chatted quietly as we hiked through the woods, like we'd disturb someone if we weren't quiet. Cindy casually fell back next to me in the back of the group.

"What are we doing?" she asked. "This is just stupid."

"I know. But it's probably nothing. And someone needs to keep an eye on everyone."

"Don't you step six inches away from me."

"You wuss."

"I mean you. I'm watching out for *you*."

I was touched. "Thanks."

CHAPTER 7

It took us about five minutes to reach the house. Nature had started to claim it a long time ago. Trees and bushes nearly surrounded the place. Some even grew into the windows, where there was no glass. The front door hung on by a single hinge. It looked like it came right out of a horror movie. Dave was right. It definitely had a creepy vibe to it. But any old house is creepy to me.

"Wow! Isn't it awesome?" Jenny said.

"So a family died in here?" Tina asked.

"Supposedly," Dave answered.

Cindy and I kept quiet.

"We going inside?"

"Yes! Man I should have brought my camera."

We slowly walked up the grown-over path and to the front door. The smell was the first thing I noticed. It smelled like a musty old basement, just the scent of age.

There was a couch turned over on its side in the living room. I couldn't help but wonder if that happened during the family's last night alive, assuming all of that was true. The carpet was soaked with rain water from a leaky roof. We made squishy noises as we filed into the living room.

I'm sure they noticed more than I did. Like the paintings that were ruined and still hanging on the walls. Were they just random paintings, or pictures of the house's old owners? A stairwell that was missing a few steps led to a second floor. I could make out the dining room and see the table Dave talked about.

I grew very cold. I had trouble concentrating.

Jenny waved one of Dave's flashlights around.

"Wow. This shit fascinates me. This is like walking through history right here."

Tina didn't look impressed. "Yeah. Smelly, dirty history."

"Come on, Tina. Isn't the mystery cool? I mean, what happened here? Who lived here? What were they like?" She picked up a piece of paper from the ground. It nearly fell apart in her hand. "This is a bill from the eighties!"

"Christ. They could have at least paid their bills," Dave said.

Jenny shot him a look. "Let's look around."

The next stop was the dining room. I could feel goosebumps all over me. Cindy was nearly stuck on me. She walked right with me, but just far enough not to touch and bother each other.

I froze when we went into the dining room. My eyes fell on the corner of the room. Dave, Tina, and Jenny spread out and looked around. The lantern and flashlights threw shadows everywhere.

"You were right, Dave. Damn, I bet this mush on the table is old food. That's just crazy. I wonder what happened here."

"It's definitely got the eerie thing going," Dave said. "I was actually disappointed the first time I came here. I was hoping a chair would move or something. But there's no ghosts here or anything."

"Yes there is."

Everyone looked at me. I kept my eyes locked on the corner. There was something there, just like in Tammy's kitchen, standing there watching us.

Cindy grabbed my arm.

"What are you talking about?" Tina asked.

"There's something there."

Dave moved near the corner and held up his lantern. "You mean right here?"

"Yeah."

"Come on, man. That's not funny," Jenny said. The smile disappeared from her face.

I frowned. I wish I knew *how* I knew. But I can't explain it. All I could see was a dark corner. But I could feel a set of eyes watching us.

Strangely though, I wasn't afraid like I was five years ago.

"I don't think it's evil or anything. Just...curious."

"Alex. Come on. Stop that shit. Don't be a dick."

It was quiet for a moment. Dave, Tina, and Jenny all traded looks. Jenny shook her head, obviously a little mad at me.

"Come on guys, let's go check out the upstairs. Alex can play down here with his ghost."

Cindy opened her mouth to defend me while our friends walked back to the living room. I grabbed her hand and shook my head. The further away the three of them were, the better. I wish Cindy wasn't with me either, but she was too stubborn. I looked at her as we heard their footsteps going upstairs.

"They'll never believe me anyway."

"Well, I do."

Suddenly a man stepped out of the corner. He was nicely dressed with a shirt and tie. Starting to go bald a little.

"You can see me?"

I flinched. I stood in front of Cindy.

"You *can* see me, can't you?"

It took me another moment to find my voice. "I-I couldn't see you till just now. But I knew you were there."

Cindy gripped my arm a little tighter. "Alex? What's going on?"

I didn't answer. The new arrival had my complete attention.

"Wow," he said with a smile. "I've had a lot of visitors over the years. Thrill-seekers, homeless people looking for a place to stay, but none have ever been able to see me."

I didn't respond. I was too stunned.

He started to walk *through* the dining room table. I backed up another step. He emerged and stood in front of me.

"Wow, who's this young lady with you? She's cute."

He reached out to touch Cindy. I put a hand on his chest and shoved him back. Cindy jumped next to me and got behind me slightly.

"Don't touch her."

The man didn't look angry, but surprised.

"You *pushed* me?"

"Well, don't go reaching for my friend."

He ignored me. "You...can reach into where I am? I wonder if that means-"

He reached out and grabbed my arm. His hands were warm and coarse. He pulled me forward until I braced myself with a foot on the floor.

"Hey!"

I heard Cindy suck in a breath behind me.

"Alex!"

"Yeah, Cindy. I'm okay."

"Where are you?"

I turned around. "Huh? Right here."

I reached out to grab her shoulder. My fingers sank into her clothes, like they were made of water. I pulled them back quickly. She turned and kept calling my name. Her face was full of panic.

I imagine mine was the same.

I looked at my hands.

"Guys! Alex is gone!"

There was a herd of footsteps upstairs followed by the gang running through the living room and staring at Cindy from the doorway.

"Cindy? What's going on?"

"Alex. He just disappeared."

"Uh, guys? I'm right *here*."

"Come on, Cindy. Not you too. No games, okay?"

"This isn't a fucking game! He was right here," she said, gesturing with her hands. "I was holding onto him. Then he just vanished!"

The three of them looked at each other. The girls looked nervous, but Dave only shrugged.

"Well, let's look for him. We'll split up."

"Split up? Are you kidding me? In this creepy ass place?"

Jenny stared at Tina. Cindy looked scared, but determined.

"We need to find Alex. Jenny and I will go upstairs. You two start down here."

Jenny didn't move. Cindy had to grab her hand and pull her away. I heard them walk upstairs. Dave and Tina went back to the living room, then went through the front door to look outside.

I walked to the dining room table and tried to touch it. My hand went right through it. I actually pushed my arm through up to the elbow. It felt like when my arm went through Richard, all those years ago, like sticking my arm in a bucket of water. It was effortless to move my arm around, but I could still feel the table around me.

I pulled my arm out and stared at the man. He stared back at me, looking stunned himself.

"Amazing," he said. "Who are you?"

"How about who the hell are *you*?" I said.

"Oh, I'm sorry. Manners. I'm George McEllen."

McEllen.

"You used to live here."

"Yeah, till those bastards came and took everything. My family, my life. All gone in five minutes."

I felt sad for him. The look in his eye said it all. He looked at the table.

"We were eating right here. They came in through the back door. Shot my daughter Pam first. Then Sharon, my wife. Then me. All for the famous McEllen fortune they heard about."

"I'm so sorry."

George smiled solemnly and nodded.

"Why are you still here?" I asked.

"I wasn't. I felt someone in our home. I wanted to see who it was."

"You...can *feel* things from the other side?"

He looked confused. "Other side?"

"You know. When you die."

He smiled. "It's a little hard to explain. But you'll find out one day. Everyone does."

I didn't say anything. He continued.

"I think the question is what's up with you? I've seen a lot of people come through here. Even psychics come through, looking for the fortune. And they can sense things, I won't lie. But talk to me and touch me? That's a new one. You *are* alive, right?"

It was a joke. I had trouble laughing.

"Well, I'm gonna leave now. It was nice meeting you. Certainly an experience. And that's saying a lot, since I've been dead who knows how long."

"Wait." I pushed my hand through the table one more time. "How do I stop doing this?"

He shrugged. "You got me there, son. I'm sure you'll figure it out. Oh, one more thing before I leave. There's a cabin not too far from here. Check out under the stove. I want you and your friends to have what's there. Call it a reward for such an interesting night."

I was so confused and scared. But I wanted to talk to George a while longer.

"Wait!"

It was too late. He walked back into the corner like it was a doorway. He vanished into thin air.

I heard Dave and Tina arguing in the living room.

"I'm telling you, Tina. This isn't a damn joke. Hell, this was all Jenny's idea!"

"This just seems like something you'd do. You and Alex, to get a laugh."

"Oh, get a grip. I was upstairs with you. You see how freaked out Cindy is? You think that's a joke?"

I walked into the living room. I didn't expect them to see me. But when my foot squished on the carpet Dave looked up.

"Alex! Holy shit, man!"

Tina poked her head near the stairwell. "Cindy! Jen! He's down here!"

I was *real* again. I didn't move. My jaw just hung open. I heard footsteps upstairs. Cindy and Jenny trotted down. Cindy nearly ran. She ran forward and hugged me. Even though I knew they could see me, I half-expected Cindy to walk right through me. I was thankful that she didn't. I wrapped my arms around her, not wanting to let go. No demons, no reliving a murder. But I'll never forget the first time I pushed my arm through a solid object.

"Hey," Jenny said. "That wasn't cool."

Tina nodded. "Yeah. We were really worried."

I searched everyone's faces. They really thought I played some kind of joke on them.

I wouldn't try to convince them otherwise. But I wouldn't lie, either.

"Can we leave?" I asked.

"Yeah. Let's get the hell out of here."

We filed out of the house. Cindy kept a hand on my shoulder for a while before letting it fall. I gave the house one final look as it got smaller.

Goodbye, George McEllen.

I remembered his last words.

Check out under the stove.

No one said much to me as we packed up our little party. I guess they were actually mad at me for *pranking* them. Dave set the grill in the back of the truck. Tina walked around and threw empty cans into a bag. I stole a look at the cabin.

"Hey guys. Come with me for a sec."

I led the way to the bare cabin. I wondered if this belonged to George and his family as well when they were alive. I felt like we were trespassing. I knew once we left I'd never come back.

But George wanted us to have something.

"Dave, help me move this stove."

He looked at everyone, then shrugged. He handed the lantern over to Tina.

The floor of the cabin was wooden planks. But as we dragged the heavy stove we could see two sets of hinges close to the wall.

"A trap door?" Jenny said. Her explorer enthusiasm was returning. "That's cool!"

"How did you know that was there?"

I didn't answer Tina. There weren't handles of any kind, but we could see the door itself. It was about two feet by two feet. Dave had to stab his pocket knife into the door to be able to lift it.

There was a hole dug in the dirt, about a foot deep. Sitting there, hidden away for over twenty years, was a brown burlap sack.

"Holy shit!" Dave said.

I lifted it out. Everyone was quiet as we carried it back to the truck. I emptied it on the lowered tailgate.

Money. Stacks of wrapped money, all neatly marked. I couldn't tell how much was there just by looking, but I'm sure it was more than I had in my bank account at the time.

None of us spoke. We just stood there and stared at it. Cindy was the first one to find her voice.

"Damn," was all she could say.

"Can...we keep that?" Tina asked.

Dave grabbed a stack and looked it at. It was marked ten thousand. Ten thousand dollars in one little stack of money. I'd seen that in the movies, but never for real. He started dividing the stacks.

"Guys, I don't really think we should keep this," Cindy said. She actually took a step back, like she was looking at something horrible. "I mean, this isn't ours."

"Actually, we *can* keep it," I said.

"What do you mean?"

I didn't want to say it, because I knew the looks I'd get. But there was nothing else I could say.

"George said he wanted us to have this. George McEllen."

I wasn't wrong.

Tina frowned. "George McEllen? The guy who was killed here?"

"Oh come on, Alex. You want us to believe you can talk to ghosts?" Jenny said. Her tone said it all. She was irritated and annoyed.

I shrugged and looked at each of them. "Look, I really don't care what you all believe. But we can take this money and not feel guilty."

They all looked at each other. Cindy kept her eyes on me. I could tell by looking at her that unlike the others, she didn't doubt me. She believed me.

She took a step back toward the truck and looked at Dave. "How much is there?"

"One hundred five thousand, but that last stack looks a little light."

"What's that six ways?" I asked.

Cindy didn't blink. "Seventeen thousand five hundred."

Gotta love accounting majors.

"Wait a minute. Why *six* ways? There's five of us here."

"For Alicia. She's part of the group."

I looked around, waiting for someone to argue. We were all friends, but money does strange things to people. I was waiting for a fight. I was surprised when I didn't get one.

Dave shrugged. "Shit. Seventeen thousand dollars is about seventeen thousand more than I have right now."

"Alright, it's all good. Let's get out of here."

We did just that. As we drove back everyone talked about what they were gonna do with their new-found treasure. I was thankful for that, as I thought everyone would ask me ghost questions. I guess money is more important than ghosts. Cindy didn't say much. I knew she probably still had mixed feelings about keeping such a large amount of money. Normally I'd feel the same way. Hell, when I was in fifth grade I found a hundred dollars on the playground, and gave it to a teacher so she could found out who it belonged to.

But this was different. George said we could have it.

How many times does that happen?

I was lost in my own thoughts as we drove back to Cindy's apartment. One hundred thousand dollars. Is that what cost George and his family their lives? Is that what a family's lives were worth? If I had five more minutes with George McEllen I would have asked him if they found his killers.

We divided up the money in Cindy's apartment. For some reason I kept thinking of all the crazy movies I'd seen. All of a sudden, during the money counting scene, everyone would turn on one another. Someone would fight over five dollars, and bad things happened. That didn't happen. We just split up the money, no drama involved. I kept Alicia's share. Cindy gave everyone plastic bags to carry it in. Then Dave, Tina, and Jenny left. Cindy and I were alone in her apartment.

We didn't talk for a minute. She collapsed on the couch. I took a soda from her fridge, even though I wasn't really thirsty. I just needed to do something normal, anything at all. Drinking a soda was a good place to start.

I sat on the other end of the couch. Cindy took a deep breath.

"What happened?"

"I met the guy who lived there. He was a ghost. He somehow *sensed* we were there."

"You disappeared right in front of me," she said. "You were right here, a foot away, and you disappeared."

I smirked and nodded. "Believe me, I'm freaked out too. Even George was. I put my hand *through* that dining room table, Cindy. Then he told me to look in the cabin and take what we found." I paused for a second. I was strangely calm up to that point. But talking to more ghosts, and putting my hands through tables, was starting to get to me. "What the hell is happening to me?"

She scooted closer. "Hey, listen. Nothing changes, okay? Whatever is going on, it doesn't change who you are. You still have me. You still have Alicia."

"Come in the bathroom with me for a minute."

She smiled. "You'd better keep your sex fantasies to yourself."

I laughed. I needed that. I needed Cindy to be herself and make jokes.

"I just want to see if I can make it happen again."

"Again, keep that sex stuff to yourself."

We walked down the hall to her bathroom. I leaned on her sink while she stood behind me.

"Okay. What are we doing?"

"If I disappear, let me know. Okay?"

She shrugged. "Sure."

I stood there trying to make it happen. I know George grabbed me, then that's when I vanished. But I thought I could make it happen myself. If I just concentrated hard enough on becoming invisible.

"Uh, I can still see you."

"Okay, thanks."

"You're still ugly, too."

"Thanks again."

I stood there staring at myself for another two minutes. I wasn't sure what was supposed to happen, even if it worked. Would I still see my own reflection? I was resting my hands on her sink. Would they sink right through the porcelain?

"Do you want me to turn on the fan?"

I turned around to look at her. "What?"

"Well, you know. When people hang out in the toilet, it's usually doing something else. And the fan's usually on. I figure having the fan on might help you concentrate."

I laughed hard. "You are the craziest woman I've ever known."

She laughed too. "My best friend since birth is standing in my bathroom trying to turn invisible. And *I'm* the crazy one."

"This isn't gonna happen tonight. I'm just too freaked out. I'm gonna go to bed."

"You wanna stay here?"

Nothing unusual or sexual about that. We stayed with each other all the time. Usually it was just a matter of falling asleep on the couch while we were watching TV.

"Nah. Thanks, though."

"Sure. Just come on over if you need me. I'll be up a little while."

I nodded. She reached forward and gave me a quick surprise hug.

"I know I give you a hard time a lot. But I thought I lost you tonight. Don't know what I'd do without you."

I gave her a squeeze and let go. "Don't worry, Cindy. I'm not going anywhere."

She smiled and nodded.

I remember my next actions clearly. I picked up my plastic bag with thirty-four thousand dollars in it. I gave Cindy a wave. I walked from her apartment to mine. The first thing I did was slide the plastic bag under my bed. Then I remembered I didn't lock the door behind me. I usually didn't, Cindy always came over unexpectedly, and I didn't want her fumbling with her key. But that night, I felt weird enough to want to lock the door. A lot of money in a plastic bag will do that.

I reached for the deadbolt knob.

My hand passed right through it.

I pulled my hand back like I touched a razor knife. I stared at the door a moment longer. Then I placed my hand on it. The sensation was still like running my hand through water.

"Amazing," I said out loud.

I knew what I wanted to do. I took a deep breath.

I walked through the door.

There was a quick flash of darkness as my head passed through. I was standing outside my front door. I was breathing hard and didn't even know it. Hell, was I actually breathing? Did people who could walk through walls breathe?

I turned toward Cindy's apartment. I had to see her, share this with her.

I walked through her front door too. A part of me was still afraid of the unknown, of what the hell was happening to me. But the excitement of the experience was finally starting to win me over.

I couldn't see inside Cindy's kitchen from the front door, but I could see a shadow moving in there.

"Cindy! Can you hear me? This is incredible."

She stepped out of the kitchen carrying a cup of pudding. She still had on her jeans, but had took off her shirt moments ago. She only had on a black bra, which she filled out very well.

"Whoa."

She walked right toward me, then turned and sat on the couch. She put the TV on and did that sexy leg curl thing she did.

"You can't hear me, can you?"

She didn't budge.

I ran my hand through the back of the couch a few times. I was already getting used to the feeling.

Cindy grabbed her phone and hit a speed-dial number.

"Hey, Leese. It's me. What's going on?"

I could only hear her end of the conversation.

"Yeah, I know it's late. But don't act like you were sleeping. Some crazy crap is going on. I'll let Alex fill you in on most of it. But I will say you're seventeen thousand dollars richer. Alex really looks after you. Yeah, you heard me. *Seventeen thousand dollars.*"

I smiled. I admit, I was half tempted to walk through the couch and just watch Cindy talk in her bra. How many chances would I get to do that in a lifetime? But it felt weird, basically spying on my best friend. I turned to the door.

"Nah. It didn't come up."

I stopped. So much for feeling weird.

"Leese, believe me, that's the last thing I was thinking about tonight. And look, it's never gonna happen. And I'm cool with that. So forget it. Okay?"

What the hell are they talking about?

"Alright, look. I'm tired. I'm gonna go to bed. Stop over tomorrow if you get some time."

Cindy hung up. She looked frustrated. I was curious. What was that about?

She stretched out on the couch. I couldn't take my eyes off her. Then guilt finally settled in once again and I looked away. I stepped through the two doors back into my apartment.

I looked at the front door and pushed a few fingers into it.

"Okay. Turn off now," I said.

It didn't work.

I started to panic. What if I couldn't turn it off? What if I was stuck this way forever?

Then I calmed down when I touched the door a sixth time and my hand felt solid wood.

I took a deep breath.

It was definitely a crazy night.

CHAPTER 8

In that one night, I found over one hundred thousand dollars, and also learned that I could walk through walls and turn invisible, as well as still talk to ghosts. You think that would turn a life upside-down, but the day to day stuff didn't change. The money just sat there in my savings account. Cindy didn't bring that night up. Neither did Alicia. She knew about it, and asked a few questions. But after that, it was pretty much business as usual.

But I did answer, and ask, a lot of questions about myself.

A month passed. Everyday after work I spent a few hours trying different things. I even borrowed Cindy's video camera so I could study what was happening. I found out a lot. But for every question I answered, it seemed another popped up.

In that month, I learned to control what I could do. I could go invisible and walk through walls just as easily as flexing a finger. But I could only do both at the same time, not one or the other. If I was walking through things, that meant no one could see me. I didn't know why. I also couldn't see my own reflection when I vanished. But yet if I looked at my hands, I could see them. Gravity also seemed to have some weird effect. If I walked to the third floor of my apartment building, I could will myself to float down through the floor to the second. But I couldn't float *up*.

I didn't do anything else besides those experiments. I didn't go spying into the women's locker room or rob any banks. In fact, I never vanished outside my own apartment. I tried to keep everything as normal as I could. Cindy was stressed out more than usual. Work was rough for her. But besides that everything was the same. Alicia must have thanked me a thousand times for her gift of seventeen grand. I'd stayed in the past few weekends with Cindy and Alicia. Julie was becoming a memory.

I'd just put a pot of spaghetti on the stove when the front door opened.

Cindy skulked her way inside. She threw a newspaper on the coffee table, kicked her heels off, and laid down on the couch. She wore a nice blouse and a skirt. When she plopped on the couch her skirt rode up just a few inches, showing off those shapely legs. I tried hard to keep my eyes off of her. She looked really good.

"Get comfortable," I said sarcastically. "I might have had a woman in here, you know."

Some time had passed since Julie, so she had no problem going back to the woman jokes.

"Please. You've got as much luck finding a woman as I do a man."

I smiled. Cindy had been single since her senior year in college. She always kept saying it was because she wanted to focus on school. Well, she was done school, and still single. Something else must have been going on. She could get any guy she wanted. I never brought it up.

I grabbed a soda from the fridge and tossed it to her. She caught it neatly.

"Read the paper."

"I will as soon as you pull your skirt down a little."

She looked down at herself. "You okay?"

"Yeah. To be honest, your legs are distracting."

She smiled, and looked pleased. She stood up, her thighs once again hidden. "Better?"

"Yup, thanks. What am I looking at here?"

"The article on the bottom right."

It didn't take me long to read it. It was about Cindy and the accounting firm her father co-owned. Apparently Cindy donated her share of the money we found to charity. Or rather, her firm did.

I looked at her. "You gave away your money?"

"I couldn't keep it," she said. "I just, uh, couldn't keep it. Christ, I had trouble sleeping. So I talked about it with my parents. And they said if I decided to donate it, to give it to the firm first so they could get a write off and a little publicity. But my name wasn't supposed to come up."

I looked through the article again. Her name was mentioned a few times. But Taylor Madison, her father's partner, was mentioned everywhere. Looks like their plan worked.

"How did this even get written?"

I could see her getting angry. "Taylor. He had a reporter come to the firm for a tour and everything. I donated money for autism so he could talk about how wonderful the firm is. They used me. My father didn't know it would go that far. I'm so pissed off."

I put the paper down. I gestured for her to sit while I went back into the kitchen.

"I can't sit now. I'm too mad."

"I can't believe you gave away your share."

"Yeah, well, I didn't have a ghost telling me it was okay."

I couldn't see her face from the kitchen. I couldn't tell if she was being sarcastic or not.

"Well, if you want, I'll split my share with you."

There was silence. After pouring some sauce into a pot I poked my head out of the kitchen.

"Cindy?"

Her eyes were locked on me. "You would do that, wouldn't you?"

"Do what?"

"Give me eight thousand seven hundred fifty dollars."

I smiled. "You better stop with that human calculator crap. But yeah. What's mine is yours. You want half?"

She didn't say anything. Just continued to stare at me. Finally she sat on the couch and reached for the remote. "No, thanks. But I will take some spaghetti."

"Coming right up."

There was a knock at the door, followed by it cracking open a few inches. I recognized a blond head.

"Hey," Alicia said. "Is it safe to come in?"

"Quick, Cindy. Get your clothes on. Hide the blow-up doll. Put the goat away. Mop up the floor. Untie me."

Alicia stepped inside. "Thanks, big brother. You just gave me enough nightmares to last a few months."

"That's what big brothers are for. Have a seat. The chef is at work."

Alicia rolled her eyes and sat next to Cindy. "Spaghetti again?"

Cindy winked at me. "Yeah, but no one boils noodles like Alex."

I pointed at her. "Thank you. You get a bigger plate."

"Lucky me."

I went back to the kitchen to finish up. I listened to Alicia and Cindy talk while they flipped through the channels. It was fun when I didn't get involved and they both went into girl mode.

"So Leese, how are you and Shawn doing?" Shawn was her current boyfriend.

"We're okay. But he says he doesn't want me to get my hair cut."

"Hey. Screw him. It's your hair, you do what you want with it."

"Do you like it like this?"

"Yeah. You kind of look like Reese Witherspoon."

"Except uglier," I called out.

"Hey. I don't care if you gave me a lot of money or not. You'd better shut up and make my food in there."

"Cindy, smack her for me."

"Hell no. Don't get me involved. Then you'll both be hitting me."

There was silence for a second. Then I heard some whispering. Back and forth, hushed tones. Weird. They never whispered around me. We didn't keep anything from each other.

"What are you two whispering about out there?"

I tried to step out to see what was going on. I bumped the handle on the spaghetti pot and knocked it from the stove. I didn't think, just reacted. I reached out and grabbed the pot with both hands before it hit the floor. Boiling water splashed all over the stove, the floor, and me. I set it back on the burner and took a step back.

"Alex? You alright?"

Alicia and Cindy both rushed to me. Alicia gasped and hurried to the hall closet to grab the mop. Cindy grabbed some paper towels to try to soak up some water.

"Damn, Alex. You okay? What happened?"

"Just me being clumsy."

"You're soaked. Does it hurt?"

"Nah. It only got the clothes. Be right back."

I went to the bathroom and pulled my shirt off. I studied every inch of me, turned my hands over a few times. I grabbed a scalding hot pot with my bare hands and got boiling water all over me.

I didn't feel any pain. I didn't even have a mark on me.

I looked in the mirror and shook my head. It was getting to the point that nothing surprised me.

Invisibility.

Walk through solid objects.

And now, burn-proof. It was why my kindergarten nurse didn't find any burn marks on me after a lighter was put to my arm.

"You okay in there, clumsy?"

I'd tell them later. "Yeah, I'm fine."

I went searching for a clean shirt in the bedroom with my back to the door. When I finally found one I turned to see Cindy leaning in the doorway. I had no idea how long she was there, but I realized she was just watching me. She had a smirk on her face.

"Get a shirt on, Alex."

"That's what I'm trying to do."

"Good. Your body is distracting."

She smiled and left. Comments like that from Cindy were enough to make a night.

I was about to find out just how much she meant to me.

CHAPTER 9

It had been a particularly bad day at work. I loaded the wrong freight on the wrong truck. It caused quite a hassle to call the truck to get them back in and straighten everything out. My boss chewed me out, rightfully so. But as I sat there in his office I realized that loading trucks all day wasn't what I wanted to do forever. I wished I had Cindy's motivation to realize a goal and achieve it. Ever since we were little she wanted to follow in her father's footsteps. She just loved numbers and math. I can't see how.

Even Alicia had a goal. She wanted to be a vet. She loved animals, even though Mom never let us have any growing up.

Me, I had no idea.

I didn't have any particular skill. Unless you count talking to ghosts. I could do things no one else could do. But I didn't see how that could turn into a job. I couldn't see what purpose it served.

I was on my way home from work, still angry. I was at a red light when suddenly the intersection in front of me was gone.

I was no longer in my truck. I saw Cindy. She was in front of her work, waving goodbye to her father.

Then I was back at the intersection.

Then it was gone again. Cindy was stretching out on the sidewalk. She was dressed to run.

I was seeing all this in quick flashes that disoriented the hell out of me. I realized that I was seeing Cindy each time from the same angle.

From a car in the parking lot outside her firm.

She was being followed.

Cindy was in danger.

The simple fact hit me as someone behind me started laying on their car horn. This jarred me from the visions I was having and brought me completely back to my own head.

I stomped on the gas.

I tried to keep calm. Everything was working against me. I was about twenty minutes away from Cindy, and that was with good traffic. She had a cell phone, but I didn't. I knew at that moment, she was starting her jog through the city that she sometimes did when she got tired of jogging near home. I also knew someone was following her. Why, I didn't know. But somehow, I knew my best friend was in trouble. It was no different than knowing when an unseen ghost was watching me.

I weaved in and out of the streets near my work till I hit the parkway. Then I sped at ninety miles an hour toward the city. As I drove I was assaulted with more visions. Each one took me out of the truck for just a few seconds. If I didn't crash, it would be a miracle.

I could see Cindy jogging down the city sidewalk. I was in a vehicle following her slowly. It felt higher up, so I guessed it was a van. I wanted to look around, see who was driving. But these visions I was having, they weren't under my control. I couldn't look around or see anything besides Cindy jogging.

My very last vision though, at the bottom of my field of vision, I could see a pair of hands holding a rope.

I had to slam the brakes to keep from hitting the car in front of me. Traffic suddenly stopped. Three lanes of traffic funneled into two, and no one could move. I was just on the edge of the city.

I turned my truck off and climbed out. I got a few looks and shouts from the drivers around me, but I didn't care. I ran to the first car in front of me and leaned into the open window. The driver was a middle-aged man fiddling with his radio.

"Sir, please!" I said. "I need your cell phone!"

I surprised him. He jumped and leaned away from me. "I don't have a cell phone. You have an accident?"

I didn't answer. I ran to the next car. This driver was a woman dressed in a power suit in her mid thirties.

"Miss! Please, I need to borrow your cell phone! I need to call the police!"

She didn't even respond. She leaned away and pushed a button to raise the windows. I put my hands on them to try to hold them down, but that didn't work. I got my fingers out just in time to avoid some pain.

I was actually tempted to smash the glass and steal whatever phone she had, but knew that wouldn't help.

I started running as fast as I could. The city was huge, but I knew exactly where Cindy was. She was running near the Eighth Street Park. I knocked a few people over rounding a few corners, slowing me down even more. I had to leap over a dog that someone was walking.

I took a shortcut down an alley that I knew ran into Eighth Street. When I hit the sidewalk I stopped to study the street. I could see Cindy ahead of me on the other side. She jogged at a steady pace. I kept losing sight of her cause of all the traffic going back and forth.

"Cindy!"

She stopped and turned around. She looked confused at first, then smiled and waved.

A white van pulled up next to her, the brakes squealing. I couldn't see what was going on. I started running one more time. The van sped away five seconds later, and Cindy was gone.

I didn't bother looking out for traffic, and almost paid for it. As I ran across the street I could hear tires screeching and a horn. The Jeep Wrangler actually didn't miss me. I vanished just in time to let it slide right through me. I didn't miss a step. I ran after the van. I could see it making a left at the next light. So I made a left as well. Although I decided the sidewalk wasn't going to work.

I ran directly into the building next to me.

I ran through brick, drywall, desks, a board meeting, anything that was in my way. As I passed through an office with a window I could see the white van on the street. I had the angle to it. I just had to keep running.

Strangely, I wasn't getting tired.

I passed through the last wall and made it onto the street. I was fifteen yards away from the van. I could make out the driver, an older man probably in his fifties, very grizzled.

I took a breath and dove into the side of the van. As soon as I felt my feet clear the side I reappeared. I collapsed inside the van and bumped my head into the other side.

I looked up to see the back of a large man. I could tell what was going on. He was trying to tie Cindy's hands, and she was fighting back.

"This bitch won't sit still," he said. "Ah! She fuckin' bit me!"

He raised his first overhead. I was on top of him before he could bring it down. I wrapped an arm around his neck and squeezed as hard as I could. I heard him gasp for breath and start to fight me. He stood up quickly and threw my head into the roof. I almost lost my grip for a second, but then Cindy was helping. She punched the man right in the balls. He was done after that. He fell into a heap.

Cindy's hands were halfway tied. I saw the driver struggle to drive the van while reaching for a gun at his side.

I seemed to be getting new abilities all the time. But I didn't think any of them involved bullets.

I threw the side door open. I grabbed Cindy's shoulders, and we both jumped.

If the van had been moving any faster, the landing would have been deadly. A stroke of luck there, as we weren't moving too fast. We both fell forward between two parked cars. Luckily I hit the ground first, and Cindy landed on top of me. I got scraped up, but nothing serious.

"Alex!"

She recovered faster than me. She was pulling me to my feet. I helped her undo the rope around her wrists, then held her face in my hands. She grabbed my wrists. She started to shake, but held in whatever emotions she was feeling.

"Are you okay?"

She nodded. "You?"

I smiled and hugged her. If I ever lost her, I don't know what I'd do. I cared about her so much that apparently I could sense when she was in trouble. I needed her in my life, plain and smile.

And those two men tried to take her away.

I watched the van drive down the street. Up till then, I was worried, terrified. Now I was angry.

I looked at Cindy. "Listen, get to the police station, and stay there. Okay? I'll be there soon."

I tried to leave. She held onto my arm. "Where are you going?"

"To follow them."

She shook her head. "No. Alex, don't be stupid."

I gently pulled free from her grasp and grabbed her shoulders. "I'll be fine."

I turned and ran. I vanished once again. Hopefully Cindy wasn't freaking out behind me, as I know she was watching me. She knew what I could do, but never seen me do it out in the open.

As soon as I saw the van making a left, I cut across the street. I ran through a few cars and even a person on the way over. It was a very strange feeling to know that nothing could stop me. I couldn't outrun a van. But I didn't need to follow the road.

And I also didn't seem to get tired when I was vanished.

Running felt weird. I could feel myself breathing, feel the muscles working. But they didn't tire. No pain, no fatigue. I ran full speed, and just didn't need to slow down.

I ran through a McDonald's and a laundromat to get to them. I knew I couldn't jump inside the van again. I couldn't fight two guys with guns. I needed to follow them. But I knew if they headed toward the beltway, I'd lose them completely.

I followed them for twenty minutes as they drove through the city. Sometimes I didn't have a problem keeping up and could run next to the van. But then they'd take a sudden turn and I'd have to run through cars and buildings to keep up.

They finally pulled into the driveway of a beat-up house. Shingles were falling off the side. There was trash all over the yard. The two men didn't speak to each other as they got out of the van and headed toward the front door. They stepped inside with me right behind them. One of them kicked a coffee table out of frustration in the messy living room.

They went right to the basement. I floated down through the living room floor just in time to see one of the men turn on a light and the other sit down in a chair. The one who turned on the light started pacing.

Finally, they spoke to one another.

"Marcus, you fuckin' idiot."

"Me? What did I do?"

"I told you to grab the woman. That's it. That's not so fuckin' hard. You grab her, you pull her in the van. Why'd you pull that guy in?"

"Look. I don't know where that fucker came from. He was just there, Tony."

"Oh yeah. Like a ghost, right?"

I smiled as I stood in the corner.

Like a ghost. Exactly.

"Fuck you. Anyway, we trying again?"

"Eh, the bitch will go to the cops. They'll watch her a while. Nah, not for a few weeks. We'll go to her apartment."

I finally had the chance to study Marcus and Tony. They looked to be around the same age. Early fifties, maybe. They both looked like they'd seen better days. Both white men, didn't look to be in too bad a shape. Both desperately needed a shave. I could tell by the way Tony paced and Marcus sat and stared at his partner that Tony was the leader of their little duo.

"Fuck. Our one solid shot at getting the bitch, and we fuck it up," Tony said.

"Are you sure she's even the right one?"

Tony grabbed a newspaper from the corner and tossed it angrily at Marcus. "Read it yourself."

I was confused. I crossed the basement and looked at the paper over Marcus' shoulder. It was the same newspaper article that Cindy had showed me. The one about Cindy finding money and donating it through her firm.

"You getting it now, asshole? She found that money. And she's got the rest of it."

"It just says she found it near the woods."

"How many people you think bury money around the woods near rich douche-bag's houses? I'm telling you, she found the old man's stash. Or she knows who did."

My jaw dropped. It was all becoming clear.

"Maybe you shouldn't have killed the whole family," Marcus mumbled.

"Hey, enough of that shit, alright? That was twenty years ago. So I got a little trigger happy. So what?"

I reappeared. I was a step behind Marcus.

"You killed George McEllen and his family for a hundred grand?"

Marcus jumped from the chair and stood by Tony. Both their eyes grew wide. Marcus pointed.

"That's him!" he said. "He was in the van!"

Tony fumbled grabbing his gun from the inside of his coat. By the time he had it out and raised, I was already gone.

I shook my head as I circled around them. They didn't even know I was five feet away. They were in their thirties when they killed George and his family. All just for money. Or maybe not. As I looked at Tony, I thought he probably did it for pleasure.

He waved his gun around aimlessly. Marcus stared at each corner with a look of panic on his face, like he'd seen a ghost. I had to be careful. One small mistake by me could end badly.

There was a toilet in the far corner. I took my time getting in good position near Tony. Then I reappeared, grabbed his gun, and tossed it in the toilet. By the time he could react, I was gone again. The whole trick took me two seconds.

They didn't even go for the gun again. I had a huge advantage over them. Fear.

Marcus grabbed a pipe from the corner and tossed a loose two-by-four to Tony. They stood close together in the center of the basement.

"What the fuck are you!?" Tony shouted.

I smiled. Somehow, some way, I hoped George was watching. I would make sure they never hurt anyone again.

I stood in front of Tony and reappeared again.

"Boo!"

Marcus swung as hard as he could, but he was too slow. He swung through me and nailed Tony hard on the side of the head. Tony cried out in pain and fell to one knee.

Marcus had seen enough. He dropped his pipe and ran for the basement door. I let him go. Tony was a few steps behind, but he wasn't fast enough. I kicked the door shut, then vanished again. Tony ran full force into it and fell to the ground. The side of his face and nose were bleeding. Marcus never came back to help him. I heard him leave through the front door upstairs. Guess there's no honor among thieves, or killers.

Tony was pushing himself backwards along the ground. He looked desperate to get away from me. I let him see me now. There wasn't anything he could do to me.

I did see him angle toward the toilet. I grabbed the pipe that Marcus dropped and slowly stalked Tony. When he put his hand in the toilet to go for the gun, I stomped the lid down on his hand. I heard some bones break.

Tony looked up at me, terrified. As I stared down at him I noticed there was a red glow on his face. Weird. Was something on me glowing red?

"Please don't kill me!" he shouted.

Again, odd. Did I look like a killer?

"You're gonna go to the police and tell them what you did."

"What?!"

I nodded. "The police."

"Fuck you!"

I leaned on my knee, putting more pressure on his hand. He winced.

"I know who you are." I noticed my own voice sounded different. "I can go myself. But it'd be easier for us both if *you* did."

Tony gave me one last defiant look. "I can run forever."

"And I can *haunt* you forever." My voice was deep and gravely. It scared even me. "Every time you open your eyes, I'll be there. Go. And when they ask you about Marcus, you turn him in. Understand?"

The glow on his face grew brighter. He closed his eyes. "Yes! I will! Just get the fuck away from me!"

Marcus wasn't anywhere to be seen, but that didn't matter. Tony was scared to death. He almost ran the three miles to the station, with me right behind him.

He ran into the waiting area and started screaming.

"I need to confess!"

He was so wild the police actually tackled him to the ground, handcuffed him, and dragged him away.

After he was gone I reappeared outside the police station and rejoined the normal world of walls and getting tired when running.

Cindy pushed open the double doors to the station and walked outside. She kept looking back in. She was still dressed in her running clothes. When she saw me she stopped.

"That was him, wasn't it? The guy driving the van? Jesus he just ran inside! The cops beat the shit out of him!"

I nodded.

"What happened?"

"I'll tell you later. But they won't bother you again."

She walked forward and hugged me. She was calmer than before, but I could tell she wasn't yet over being pulled into a van and tied up.

"Come on," I said. "Let's go home."

We turned around, and I had to stop one last time. I saw three people standing across the street from the station. I could just barely see through them.

It was George and his family.

He held his daughter Pam's hand. His other arm was wrapped around Sharon, his wife. I saw him whisper something to his daughter. She waved shyly. George and Sharon waved as well.

Then they were gone.

I couldn't get the smile off my face. For the first time in my life, I finally felt like I'd done something really meaningful.

"Alex? You okay?"

"Never better."

*****

It was a long night. We didn't talk much for a while. We walked back to her work to get her car. Then she had to drop me off near the parkway to get my truck. I got there just in time to wave off the tow-truck guy.

We didn't get to the apartment until nearly ten o'clock. We didn't even need to say a word. She followed me inside. I gestured for her to sit down while I poured her some water. I kept my distance and sat on the weight-bench. It was a good five minutes before she spoke.

"Please don't tell anyone about tonight."

I nodded. "Not a problem."

She was quiet again, lost in her own thoughts. I turned the TV on just to break the silence. I flipped through a few channels before I settled on the local news, and was surprised. News sure does travel fast. The hot news anchor looked into the camera.

"A twenty-year-old mystery was solved today, when Tony DeMarco turned himself in to police and confessed that he and his brother Marcus murdered local businessman George McEllen and his family in nineteen-eighty-seven. Marcus was apprehended at the bus station a half hour after Tony gave himself up to authorities. The two will be held without bail."

I looked at Cindy. The news anchor saved me from having to explain everything. Cindy looked back at me with her mouth open.

"They thought I had the money, didn't they?"

I nodded.

"How did you know? How did you know where I was?"

"I, uh, *sensed* it somehow. I saw visions of you in trouble."

I was quiet for a minute.

"Are *you* okay?" she asked.

Amazing. Cindy was nearly kidnapped, and she was worried about *me*. She could tell I was upset. I tried to hide it, but obviously didn't do a good job.

I was afraid. I was afraid of what I was gonna find out about myself next. Tony was absolutely terrified of me. That ate away at the back of my mind.

"I'm fine. Are you okay?"

"I think so. Can I use your shower?"

"Yeah. Bottom shelf in the closet is clean towels."

She nodded. She was halfway down the hall when she turned around again.

"You saved my life."

I nodded. "You'd do the same for me."

She didn't hesitate. "Yeah, I would. Well, except maybe for the turning invisible part."

She went into the bathroom. As I watched her I realized I had a small crush on her.

And the guilt hit me harder than ever.

CHAPTER 10

Neither Cindy or I told Alicia or any of our other friends about what happened that day. Not exactly good memories you want to bring up. I didn't ask Cindy about any details of what happened in the police station. Did she report everything? Would she have to go to court? Did she just wait there?

It took a week, but our somber moods slowly drifted back to us laughing and making fun of each other. Alicia actually thought we were fighting for a while.

My crush on Cindy was just that, a crush. I was smart enough to know it was there, but I knew it would fade eventually. As soon as she got another boyfriend, I would get it through my head that there was no way in the world someone as incredible as her could care about someone like me that way, and the crush would fade.

Then Alicia broke up with Shawn, hey boyfriend.

She called me after work on a Monday. There was no drama, no cheating or anything crazy. Apparently he just wasn't happy, and he broke it off during the school day.

She tried not to show it, but she was devastated, much more than I'd seen with any of her other guys. She came over the apartment nearly every night that week. She actually cried on my shoulder, which she had never done. We were close, but stuff like that always went Cindy's way.

She was starting to seem a little better when I got that strange phone call at work. I was loading a truck when I heard my supervisor calling my name. I looked over to see him with a pinkie to his mouth and thumb to his ear. I went to his office and grabbed the phone.

"Hello?"

"When you gonna get a cell phone?" Alicia asked.

"As soon as I become a movie star. What's happening?"

"When you get out of work stop by the house."

"Everything okay?"

"No."

"What's going on?"

There was silence for a moment. "I don't want to talk about it over the phone. Just get over here after work. I have to show you something."

She hung up.

As I walked back out to the dock I could only think of one thing.

Alicia was pregnant.

I tried to keep calm. I had no clue as to what was going on. But I knew it was bad. I'd never gotten a call like that from Alicia before. Nothing was ever important enough to call me at work.

As soon as I punched out I drove straight to my old home. The house was completely quiet. No TV, no music, nothing. I went into the dining room to see Alicia sitting at the table, staring at the wall. She looked completely out of it.

"Alicia?"

She looked at me and smirked. Then she looked back at the wall.

"What's wrong, sis?"

She took a deep breath. I had to cut her off before she started.

"Wait just a sec. I have to ask. You're not pregnant, are you?"

"What? No! Damn, Alex, I'm not stupid."

"I know, I know." Relief washed over me. "Okay then, I think I can handle anything else."

"Don't be too sure."

Now I was afraid. I sat across from her. "What's going on?"

"I was looking through Mom's clothes. I wanted to borrow a dress for the next time we all went out. You know, gotta impress the guys now."

I nodded.

"Well, I guess I'd better just show you."

I followed her upstairs to Mom's room. She opened the closet and grabbed a folder full of papers in the corner.

"This is right where I found it."

She handed me the folder. I skimmed through it, not quite knowing what I was looking at. A lot of legal documents, it looked like. Not exactly surprising, since Mom's a lawyer.

"Look at the last thing in there."

I flipped to the end. The last document was a little easier to follow. It was a certificate of adoption from the state of Pennsylvania. It had my name on it, along with Gary and Joan Teague, who I thought were my parents.

I was wrong.

I was adopted.

I stood there staring at it for a minute. Alicia was quiet. I looked up, and my eyes fell on a picture of Alicia, Mom, and me, when I graduated high school, sitting on the dresser. It was so obvious that it hit me like a ton of bricks. I didn't look like Mom. I didn't look like Alicia. I always guessed I looked like my father, who I didn't remember.

"Alex, what does all this mean?"

"Well, I guess there's only one way to find out."

I reached for the phone on the dresser and did a very stupid thing.

"Who are you calling?"

I didn't answer. The phone rang seven times.

"Hello?"

"Hey, Mom."

"Alex? Hey honey, how's it going? I can't talk long. I'm having lunch with the team right now."

"Mom, am I adopted?"

There was a long silence that seemed to stretch forever.

"Ah, okay. I guess that's my answer," I said.

"Listen, honey-"

"Nah, Mom. It's cool. I gotta run."

I hung the phone up. A harsh thing to do, and I regret it.

"She said yes," I told Alicia.

We were quiet for a minute.

"This doesn't change anything," Alicia said.

"This changes *everything*, Alicia. I mean, who the hell am I?"

"You're my brother."

I closed my eyes. That suddenly sounded so alien to me.

"I'm gonna go. I'm gonna borrow this folder. I'll call later."

I left the house without saying another word. I drove around for a while before heading back to the apartment. I didn't bother eating. I unplugged my phone and sat on the patio outside my living room.

I had a sister that I was very close to. I had a best friend that looked out for me ever since grade school. I had a mother that had raised me to be the person I was, despite all the obstacles she faced. With all that, I'd never felt so alone.

The sun was nearly gone. I still leafed through the folder from Mom's closet. I couldn't make any sense of the legal jargon. All I knew was the name of the adoption agency, Heavenly Heart, and their address in Blossom, Pennsylvania.

I heard the sliding glass door move behind me. I turned to see Cindy standing there, looking hot in her business clothes.

"Hi."

I smiled, but didn't say anything. I honestly wasn't sure whether I wanted her company or not, but I didn't object when she sat in the chair next to me.

"Alicia's been trying to call you."

"I unplugged the phone. Not really in the mood to talk. I guess you've talked to her?"

"Yeah. She told me what was going on. She wanted me to check on you."

"I'm okay."

"Liar."

I didn't say anything.

"I guess it should have been obvious. You're ugly. Alicia's cute."

Not the best timed joke, but I smiled. "Yeah. I should have known."

"My parents used to joke about it whenever we talked about you at the house. About you probably being adopted. I never thought they would be right."

"What do you and your parents say about me?"

That caught her off guard, and she changed the subject. "Don't worry about it. But tell me what's up."

"I'm freaked out. I can walk through walls, talk to ghosts. Now I find out I'm adopted. I...who am I, really? I think it's just everything happening at once, you know?"

That's all I could say. My thoughts were so jumbled. But I think that about summed it up. There was also the fact that my sister wasn't really my sister. My mother wasn't really my mother.

"Alex, is there anything I can do for you?"

I shook my head. "Nah. I'll be okay, really. I just have to soak all this in."

"Okay. I'll leave you alone. But if you need me, you come get me. I'll do anything for you. You know that, right?"

I smiled. "Yeah, Cindy. I know. Thanks."

She slapped me on the back and left.

I didn't sleep at all that night. I had so many crazy thoughts. What if I was some kind of government experiment that they let loose? What if I was part alien?

I had a past of some kind, before my adoption. According to the paperwork, I was adopted a few days after I was born. Why did my birth parents give me up? What happened to them? Why was I able to do the things I could do?

There had to be answers for me. But I wouldn't find them moping in my apartment.

I had to go to Pennsylvania.

CHAPTER 11

I put in for a week's vacation the next day at work. It was short notice, but my supervisor was okay with it. When I got home I packed up a suitcase of clothes. I printed some directions to the adoption center from the computer. It was a very quick decision to make, but I knew I had to do it. It wasn't like me at all to do something completely spontaneous, like leaving the state. I just needed to know more about who I was.

I drove over to Alicia's to let her know what was going on. I hadn't talked to her since the previous day. I wanted to let her know I was okay, that she was still my sister.

When I opened the front door I heard Alicia talking to someone in the dining room. I walked in and saw another blond head at the table. Totally a surprise.

"Mom."

"Hi, Alex."

I was speechless for a moment. "When did you get home?"

"A few hours ago. Alicia picked me up at the airport."

"But your case in California?"

"They can live without me for one day. I fly back out tomorrow morning. But I had to talk to you." She looked at Alicia. "To you both."

I looked at Alicia. She looked worried for me.

I sat at the table. Mom looked down for a second. I saw her hands were actually shaking. I reached out and grabbed them. That seemed to calm her.

She pulled a picture out from inside her jacket.

"That's my ex-husband, Gary. Alicia's father. A year after we got married, we decided we wanted a child. But the doctors told me that wasn't possible. There was a problem with my eggs, and I couldn't have children."

I looked at the picture. I had never seen who I thought was my father

89

before. That didn't seem odd to me until that moment. Sure enough, I didn't look like him either.

"So, we adopted you. And things were okay. But then it turns out the doctors were wrong. I could have children, and I became pregnant with Alicia. About a month after that, Gary left. He said he didn't want two children. He even thought I went as far as getting the doctors to lie when they said I'd never have any. He really lost it."

"What an asshole," Alicia said.

I knew then for a fact what I always believed. My mother was the strongest woman on the planet. To go through what she did, succeed at her job, and raise two children. She was amazing.

"Why didn't you tell me, Mom?"

I could tell the fact that I continued to call her Mom relaxed her. She would always be Mom.

"Because it doesn't matter," she said. "You're still my son. You're still Alicia's brother. None of that will ever change."

She was right, and I knew it. But there was another thing to consider.

I could do things that people shouldn't be able to do. Maybe my birth parents knew why.

If I couldn't walk through walls, or turn invisible, or talk to ghosts, I don't think I would have cared to find my birth parents. But that wasn't the case. I had to find out why I was different.

I didn't say anything. I got up from the table and circled around to Mom. She stood up and I gave her a strong hug. Alicia joined us for a nice family hug. In fact, I think it was our first one.

Alicia looked at me, and I could tell what she was thinking. She was wondering if we should tell Mom about what I could do. My eyes told her *No*. Sibling communication.

"You two are my family. Simple as that. But I need to know where I came from."

Mom nodded. She was trying to hold back tears. "I understand."

"Is there anything else I should know, Mom?"

She shook her head. "Not really. We adopted you from Heavenly Heart, you never stayed there. It's a shelter for children. They just handled all the paperwork. We took you right from the hospital."

"And you never met my biological parents?"

"No. Nowhere to be seen. And to be honest, we didn't ask any questions. We didn't want to talk to them, and have them end up changing their minds."

I nodded. "I'm going to Blossom. I want to see the place."

"How long?"

"I took a week off. But I won't be that long. I want to find my biological parents. Then I'm coming right back."

Alicia looked at Mom without missing a beat. "Can I go with him, Mom?"

I shook my head before Mom could even answer. "No. Thanks, Alicia, really. But I don't want you missing that much school."

Mom smiled. "Well, the man of the house has spoken."

Alicia looked disappointed, but she smiled. "You'd better at least tell Cindy. She'll be pissed if you don't."

I didn't because she was at work when I got to the apartment. But Alicia was right. It wouldn't be right not to tell Cindy. I could see her whipping my ass when I got back.

I gave Alicia and Mom one more hug goodbye before I left. They both made me promise to call them everyday till I got back. I drove back to the apartment. I saw Cindy's car parked outside, so I knew she was home.

I slowly poked my head into her living room.

"Yo Cindy! You in here?"

"Yeah. Don't come in the bedroom. I'm getting dressed."

"Damn. Just one little peek?"

"Eh, alright. Just one," she joked.

I closed the door behind me. Cindy popped out of the bedroom wearing jeans and a tight tee-shirt. Her hair flowed just a little behind her shoulders. I noticed what she was wearing quite often. She looked good in anything. It was scary.

"Hey. I was gonna make a sandwich. You want one?"

"Nah, thanks. Actually I can't stay long. I'm leaving for a few days."

"Really? Where to?"

"Blossom, Pennsylvania."

She gave me a puzzled look.

"Where I was born, apparently."

She nodded. "Ah. On that famous journey of self-discovery, like in the movies?"

I laughed. "Not quite. I want to find my real parents, ask them how the hell did you make a kid who can walk through walls, and come back here to my dull life."

"It's not that dull. I'm in it."

"This is true."

She brought a hand up to her chin, thinking about something. "How long will you be gone?"

"The plan, seriously? I have a week off. I want to go there, get some answers, and get back as soon as possible. Then I want to lounge around in my underwear for the rest of my time off and have some fun."

"Boxers or briefs?"

"Actually boxer-briefs."

"Nice mental picture. I could call my father right now and get a week off.

Just give me a half hour to pack."

I was stunned. "Huh?"

"We'll take my car, cause I can't drive a stick. That way we can take shifts."

"You're not coming, Cindy."

She looked hurt. "Why not? You don't want me to?"

Just the opposite. I loved Cindy's company.

"That's not it."

"Well, what is it then?"

It took me a moment to find the words. "I feel like I'm leeching."

"Leeching?"

"Yeah. You always look out for me. Makes me feel guilty."

She was quiet for a moment, just looking at me. "Are you joking?"

"No. Why?"

"Alex, you saved my *life*. Did you forget about that? I owe you a lot more than a car ride to Pennsylvania."

"You don't owe me anything."

She went quiet again. There was something in her eyes. I couldn't tell what it was. There was something going on in that head of hers.

"Cindy? You okay?"

She looked away, almost like she was embarrassed. "Yeah, I'm fine. Yes or no question. Do you want me to come with you?"

I hesitated before finally giving in. "Yeah, I do."

"Was that so hard?" she said with a smile. "Give me thirty minutes."

"Thanks, Cindy."

"I watch out for you. You know that. Jesus, it's not like we've known each other eighteen years or something."

I laughed.

We threw our bags in the back of her car. It was a three hour drive to Blossom. I could do a three hour drive easy, but Cindy's company was nice to have. She pulled her shoes off and hung her feet out the window. We didn't say much for about an hour. In fact, she fell asleep. Of course, that was the perfect time to steal looks at her. Since she was reclined back in the passenger's seat, her tee-shirt bunched up a little, and showed off that sexy stomach of hers. Her chest rose and fell as she slept. An absolutely gorgeous woman, and she never talked about it. She never said it out loud, never called someone else ugly. Well, except me, of course. Beautiful, intelligent, kind, and so humble. I wondered sometimes if she really knew how incredible she was.

We were about an hour into the drive. I had the ballgame playing quietly on the radio. Right in the middle of me staring at her, she started talking.

"Alex, can I ask you a question?"

I quickly shifted my gaze back to the road and felt my face growing hot.

Was she awake the whole time? Did she know I was gawking at her?

"Yeah," I said, trying to play it cool. "What's up?"

"What did you see in Julie?"

I looked at her with curiosity. She was looking at me now from her seat, still reclined. A strange question, but I liked it. In the middle of everything that was going on, finding out I was adopted, seeing visions of Cindy in trouble, walking through walls, I needed something normal to focus on. As always, Cindy helped keep me grounded.

I thought about the first night I met Julie. Our normal goofy crew was running around Baltimore Harbor. We saw Julie and a group her friends dancing right by the water. She caught my eye immediately. At first I thought she was interested in Dave, but it was Cindy who pointed out she was "giving me the look". We ended up hanging out as one big group that night, and Julie and I connected.

"She was hot, confident, nice smile, laughed at my stupid jokes. She used to love the way me and you acted."

Cindy sat up. "Ah, confident. So you like confident women? Julie used to always talk about how hot she was. She knew guys looked at her."

I reluctantly nodded. "Yeah, maybe confident isn't the right word."

"So what else do you look for in a woman?"

I laughed at the question. "It'll be a long time before I date anyone now."

"Why do you say that?"

"Well, first, I gotta make sure she doesn't mind that I work at a shipping dock. Then I gotta make sure she doesn't mind me being some kind of freak."

"You're not a freak."

"And then there's you."

"What about me?"

"The woman's gotta be able to put up with you. Remember Marie? She used to always say she didn't want us being friends. Too damn jealous."

Cindy smiled. "Yeah, I've been through that too. My exes were always jealous of the white boy Alex."

"What? You're kidding."

"Nope, no kidding. Promise me something. We'll always be friends, regardless of who you date."

I looked at her. A weird request. She should know we'd always be friends.

"Of course, Cindy. Come on now, who else is gonna look after you?"

She smiled, but then she looked sad.

"What's up?" I asked.

"Nothing. Who's winning?" she said, pointing to the radio.

I decided to let it drop, but there was something going on she wasn't telling me. And I would get to the bottom of it eventually.

"Orioles. Three to one."

"Nice. Maybe we'll finally win one."

I drove the rest of the way to Blossom. Cindy offered to drive, but I didn't give the wheel up. If it was a longer trip I might have, but didn't need to. Blossom was a small town. It wasn't like a suburb where everything blended together and there was plenty to see on the way to the city. This was an isolated town out in the middle of Pennsylvania. It was ten o'clock when we got there, so I knew there was no use in looking for Heavenly Heart.

I pulled into the first hotel I could find, which was a Holiday Inn Express. I was surprised. Given the way the town looked I didn't think they'd made it to Blossom.

I met Cindy at the trunk to get our bags.

"Is this place alright?" I asked her.

"Hey. As long as there's a bed, it's perfect." She looked around at the empty streets. "This place looks dead."

"Hey, this is my hometown you're talking about," I said with a smile.

"Yeah, no wonder you're an oddball."

The lobby was completely empty except for a bored elderly man behind the counter. His name-tag read Marvin. I already liked him because he had a ballgame on under the desk. I could hear it as we walked up. He reached down and lowered the volume.

"Good evening," he said simply.

"Hi. I hope you have rooms open?"

"Nope. We're all booked."

I stared at him. Words escaped me. Then he smiled.

"I'm just funnin' ya. Don't think we've ever been full here. How long ya staying?"

Good question. I didn't have an answer.

"Uh, at least one night. Maybe two?"

"That's no problem. Stay as long as you need to. Just remember to check out before eleven when you want to leave. It's seventy-two a night."

I handed over a credit card and signed a form. He gave me a key.

"Thanks. Hey listen, do you know where Heavenly Heart is?" I looked at my directions. "It's an adoption center on Church Street?"

He eyed up Cindy and me. "You two looking to adopt?"

Cindy reached over and grabbed my arm. "Oh no," she said. "We won't have to adopt, will we, my stallion?"

I barely held in my laughter. I shook my head. "Nah, no adoption here."

Marvin didn't smile. "It's three streets over from this one."

"Thanks a lot. Goodnight."

We laughed all the way up to the room. Cindy could make me laugh so easy. I stopped laughing when I slid the electronic key through the lock and pushed the door open.

"What the hell is this?" I asked.

Cindy walked past me and dropped her bag on the floor. She gave the room a look over. Normal enough. Dresser with a mirror, tiny refrigerator, TV, bathroom in the back.

"What's the problem?"

"There's only one bed."

Cindy shrugged. "So?"

"Don't these places usually come with two?"

She sat on the bed and kicked her shoes off. "Don't know. It's been a while since I shacked up with a guy in a hotel room. What's the big deal? We have little sleepovers all the time."

"Yeah, but that's with a couch and a bed. We're missing one here."

"Would you stop your bitching and get in here."

I stepped inside and shut the door. I was already stressed out. I didn't want to spend my first night in Blossom sleeping on the floor.

I tried to ignore it. I started thinking about the general plan. I sat on the dresser across from Cindy. She leaned back and crossed her legs, looking very sexy.

"Okay. So tomorrow morning we go to the adoption place. They tell me what I need to know. Then I go talk to my parents. I'm hoping we'll be heading home tomorrow night."

"They might not even live here, you know. Maybe they moved to Brazil, for all we know."

I never really thought about that. "Well, if they did, then we're still heading back. I'm not driving to Brazil."

"Sounds good. And I hate to cut this short, but that drive was rough. You mind if I go to bed?"

"Go for it. I'll setup camp on the floor."

"Don't be a dumbass, Alex. You can sleep next to me. I promise I won't try to jump you in the middle of the night."

The sad part was if she did, I probably wouldn't stop her.

My heart skipped a beat at the idea. I knew then this crush wasn't exactly fading away.

But I could control it. Hell, if I could control my ability to walk through walls and turn invisible, I could control a crush on my best friend. It would go away. I would kill it, it would just take time.

"I'll stay on my side of the bed. I promise."

She smiled. "I know, Alex. Man, stop throwing a fit. You can have the bathroom first."

I heard her changing clothes while I brushed my teeth. I knew I'd have a hard time sleeping. I was still wound up from the drive. But I knew I couldn't stay up late. Tomorrow was going to be a crazy day, and I had to get rest.

I left the bathroom to see Cindy wearing flannel pajamas. She disappeared into the bathroom while I went through my bag, and immediately I realized something.

When I packed, I thought I'd be alone. I didn't pack any kind of pajamas. I had sweatpants, but that was it. That would have to do. I quickly put them on. I even kept my shirt on. It would be a hot night.

I crawled into bed and turned the light out on my side. A few minutes later Cindy joined me. It was probably a funny sight. I was *all* the way over on my side. Another inch and I would have fallen out of bed.

"Jesus, Alex, you act like I have the plague or something."

"Just trying to give you space."

"Would you calm down? We're gonna bump into each other tonight, you know. What is your problem? Stop being a baby."

My problem was I was attracted to my best friend. But I quickly shoved that aside. I had to, or it would take over my thoughts.

"No problem here," I said as I gave myself some more of the bed.

"Finally. Goodnight."

She turned her light off, and the room was covered in darkness.

I was right. I couldn't sleep. I laid perfectly still with my hands behind my head and staring at the ceiling. Cindy was curled on her side with her back to me. After about ten minutes she started talking.

"Alex."

"Yeah."

"No matter what happens tomorrow with your parents, just remember I got your back."

I smiled. I could tell by her voice that she was half asleep. She probably wouldn't remember a thing tomorrow.

"Same here, Cindy. You know I'll be the best man at your wedding."

I couldn't hear what she said next. Something about a broom.

"What? Couldn't hear you."

She didn't respond. She was already in dream land. I just laughed quietly.

All of a sudden, without a single warning, Cindy turned over and threw a leg over my waist and an arm on my chest. I froze every muscle. I didn't even breathe. It took about ten seconds to realize she was simply moving in her sleep, and not trying to straddle me. I finally let my breath out and relaxed. Then she actually scooted closer and used my arm for a pillow. Her face was about an inch from mine.

I smiled and wrapped my arm around her. She sighed quietly and squeezed me. I'd had my share of girlfriends, but never been so excited, just to have someone close. I knew I'd be on the floor before long, only because I was so tempted to run a finger along her cheek. And we couldn't have that. Besides, I knew she was probably dreaming about an old boyfriend, and not me.

CHAPTER 12

I'm not sure what time I woke up the next morning. It still felt early, but the sun was up. Cindy and I were in the same positions that we fell asleep in. I was on my back. Cindy was snuggled up close to me. I could feel her breathing, and it relaxed me.

I felt my own heart beating hard in my chest, but for a change it had nothing to do with Cindy. This was the day. I knew it. It was the day that the mystery about me that had been building up would finally get some answers.

Somehow, in the back of my mind, I knew I wouldn't like the answers I got. My biological parents abandoned me. There was no way that could have a good reason behind it.

Cindy's breathing stopped, and I felt her body tighten up.

"Alex?"

"Morning."

"Oh, Christ."

She literally jumped out of bed. I did the same thing, not knowing what the hell was going on. She stared at me from the opposite side of the bed. Her eyes were wide, her hair a mess. Her eyes fell to the bed, then back to me.

"Alex, I'm so sorry," she said. She couldn't find words. "I didn't mean...you know...it was an accident."

I was confused. "Uh, Cindy, *what* was an accident?"

"I didn't mean to get so close. You know, sleeping. I should have stayed on my side of the bed."

I held in my laughter. "Yeah, what the hell is your problem?"

It took her a moment to realize I was joking. Then she smiled. "You ass."

I laughed. "No biggie, Cindy. Hell, I saw you naked. I guess we're even."

"Not really. I call shower first."

"Go for it."

It took about an hour to get ready. During that time I kept peeking out the hotel window, trying to get a small view of daytime Blossom. We were right across the street from a restaurant. A few people walked the streets, but not many. I did notice that everyone stopped and said hi to each other. Interesting. I thought you only saw stuff like that in the movies.

We eventually left the hotel room and climbed in her car. It took us about half an hour to find Heavenly Heart. It was very close to the hotel, but we went the wrong way once, adding to some travel time. We parked across the street and I gave it a hard look.

I'm not sure what I expected to see. I'd never seen an adoption center before. It looked a lot like a school. Lots of rooms, lots of windows. A large gate enclosed the place. I saw a few guys mowing the grass and trimming the bushes. A sign saying Heavenly Heart stood near the front sidewalk.

I took a breath. This is what I came for.

"Are you okay?"

I nodded, then looked at her. "Cindy, if I forget to tell you, thanks for coming with me."

She smiled warmly. She didn't say anything, just put her hand on mine. Which I'm almost embarrassed to say sent little bolts up my arm.

"Okay," I said. "Let's get this done."

We left the car and walked across the street. I saw a middle-aged woman walking her dog. She gave me a long look. I guess they weren't used to visitors in Blossom. She finally gave me a half smile and wished me a good morning. I did the same.

We opened the front door and stepped into a rather large lobby. There was a set of stairs going up to the left. There was a large desk in the center with a bored-looking woman on the phone. Behind her and to the left and right were doors leading further into the center. A boy probably around ten was sweeping the floor, and not looking too happy about it.

The woman ended her call as Cindy and I sat across from her.

"Good morning," she said. "How can I help you?"

I pulled out the certificate from my folder.

"This is me," I explained. "This place handled my adoption. I'd like to know who my parents are."

You couldn't get any more direct than that. She looked over the certificate.

"Alex Teague," she said. "Do you have your driver's license and a second form of ID? A lot of records are in the computer, but I'll have to look. And who is this with you?"

"Cindy Marshall."

"Are you two married?"

I tried not to laugh. Strange question. I can only guess the woman was just nosy.

"Nah," Cindy said. "We're sex buddies."

I turned to make sure the ten-year-old couldn't hear. Apparently Cindy didn't like the nosiness either.

The woman only smiled uncomfortably. I handed over my license and a credit card. The woman started typing quickly at the computer while she talked.

"Back then all records were paper, kept in file folders," she said. "We have been shifting over to computer files though, but I'm not sure if we've hit that year yet. Ah, this might be it."

I actually saw her face turn white before she pushed a few more keys on the keyboard.

"Nope, I was wrong," she said. "Looks like that record isn't in the computer. Which means it's in a box in storage. If you come back tomorrow I can have it pulled for you."

I didn't believe her. She suddenly looked sick.

"Are you okay?" I asked.

She nodded quickly. "Yeah, just not feeling good. In fact, I'm gonna run to the bathroom."

She got up and went through the door behind her, leaving us alone with the ten-year-old.

I looked at Cindy and shrugged. We got up and left through the front door.

"Sex buddies?" was the first thing I said to her.

"Hey, she was sticking her nose where it didn't belong. What the hell does that have to do with adoption? She wanted to jump your bones."

I stood by the driver's door while Cindy circled around. We looked at each other over the roof a moment.

"Do you believe what she said?" I asked.

"Not at all."

I turned back toward the center. Something weird was definitely going on. "Me neither. Stay here a sec. I'll be right back."

With that, I vanished. I stuck my fingers into the driver's side door, just to double check. Before I could cross the street, I heard Cindy.

"Wow. My sex buddy is a freakin' ninja."

I laughed, knowing she couldn't hear me.

I walked through the front door to see the same woman who helped us sitting at the front desk once again. This time the ten-year-old boy was gone. There was an older man standing behind her. They both stared at the computer monitor. I circled around them and listened.

"He was right *here*," the woman said. "Can you believe that?"

"What did you tell him?"

"I told him to come back tomorrow. *I* don't want to get involved. He was so cute, too. But shit, Mister Simmons, I grew up hearing that crazy story."

"That may be, Denise. But we can get in serious trouble for withholding information."

Denise shrugged. "I'll just say I made a mistake. That's all."

Mister Simmons smirked and stared at the monitor again. "The town would talk if they knew he was here."

"Hell, what do you think I'm telling my family as soon as I get home?"

I looked over their shoulders. On the monitor was a wealth of jumbled information that I'm sure they could figure out at first glance. To me, though, it was Greek. I only saw my name once, but I did see something that caught my attention.

Previous Guardian: Elizabeth Fields.

Was that my mother?

I left the center with a few phrases bouncing in my head. Crazy story. The town would talk.

What the hell is going on?

Cindy was reclined back in her seat. I walked right up to her window and reappeared.

"Gotcha!" I shouted, and grabbed her shoulder.

She jumped and gave me a look. "Alex! You asshole!"

I laughed like a little kid as I climbed behind the wheel.

"My previous guardian was Elizabeth Fields," I said.

"Why would that woman lie?"

"I don't know. But apparently I'm some kind of town legend or something."

"At least you're a legend somewhere. No one likes you back in Maryland."

"Aww. *Everyone* loves me."

"Not if you keep scaring people like that."

"What can I do to make it up to you?" I was just kidding. But I realized I sounded very flirty.

"Don't ask me that. I'll have you giving me a full body massage."

Wow. What punishment. I tried to push the picture from my head. "Well, you ready to make one more stop?"

"Sure."

I thought Elizabeth Fields would be hard to find, just because that's my luck. I was wrong. Her name was listed in the phone book, and a guy at a gas station gave me decent directions. Everything was close in Blossom, and it didn't take no more than an hour to pull up outside her house. It was close to two o'clock.

I didn't get out of the car right away. I turned off the engine and sat there, staring at her house. It looked like it had seen better days. The yard was growing out of control. I could barely see the front of the house with all the bushes in the way. The fence looked like it was near collapsing.

Cindy didn't say anything. She knew I was lost in my own little world, just reflecting on everything. I finally talked after a few minutes.

"Three days ago I thought I had everything under control. I'm a freak, I know. But I was a freak that knew where I came from. Now I'm sitting here looking at what might be my real mother's house. I handled all the ghost crap, but this adoption thing is killing me."

"Look, I know it's easy for me to say. But you have to put all this behind you. This will help. You can't let all this get you down. Besides, I'm *glad* your real parents gave you up."

I gave her a look. Strange thing to say.

"I don't know what I'd do without you," she explained. "So yeah, I'm glad. Believe me, Alicia, your mom, my parents, and me, we'll never complain."

I smiled. I knew I'd told her, and I thought it many times, but I was glad Cindy came along with me.

"Okay, let's go."

We crossed the street and I knocked on the front door. Cindy stood a step behind me. I felt my heart hammering as I heard the door open and a woman stood before me.

Slightly graying hair, although it used to be brown. She looked maybe close to fifty. She was probably a little shorter than me, around Cindy's height. Her expression suggested she was having a bad morning. Or perhaps *every* morning was bad. She eyed me up and down, a look of irritation on her face.

"What?" she said. Her tone said it all.

Strangely, all the thinking I'd been doing, I didn't have sentences planned out in my head.

"Uh, hi."

"Yeah, what do you want? You lost?"

"No, I-"

"Look, everyone in the neighborhood knows I don't like anyone knocking on my door. Now get going."

She tried to shut the door in my face. I had to wedge my foot in the doorway to stop her. Her face turned red from anger.

"I'll call the police!" she nearly screamed.

She was forceful, direct. I had no choice but to be the same.

"I'm guessing you're Elizabeth Fields. If you are, you gave me up for adoption twenty-three years ago. I want to know why."

She eased her grip on the door. Her mouth slowly fell open. She looked me up and down, then a look of sadness crossed her face. Obviously I was bringing bad memories with me.

"Come on inside."

We did so. She closed the door behind us. The inside of her house looked nothing like the outside. Very nice, homely. Antiques littered the place. No TV, I noticed. Where I thought a living room would be was a little library. I liked it.

"Thirsty?" she asked. There was still an edge in her voice.

I looked at Cindy. She shook her head. "Nah, we're good. Thank you."

We followed her into a tiny dining room. It looked like we interrupted a light lunch. She sat down in front of a glass of tea, a sandwich, and a book. We sat across from her.

"So, what's your name?"

The question surprised me. Didn't she know?

"Alex. Alex Teague. This is my best friend. Cindy Marshall."

She nodded. "It's good to have friends. I used to have friends. But not anymore. Not since that day."

"That day?"

She waved her hand. "In time. So, I'm guessing you're wondering who I am? Why I was listed as your guardian?"

I nodded. "Miss Elizabeth, believe me, I'm wondering a whole bunch of things."

"Call me Beth. Well, for you, I guess you can call me Aunt Beth."

"Aunt?"

"Yeah. I have some questions for you too."

"I probably don't have any answers."

"You might be surprised. I'm guessing there might be a part of you that you keep from everyone else, even Cindy here. Ghosts, maybe? Spirits? Demons?"

I was excited. Beth knew something. Finally, I would get some answers.

"Yeah," I said. "But Cindy knows. She knows everything about me."

"Tell me. Tell me about yourself. Maybe we can tell each other things."

I told her everything. I told her about getting rid of the demon in Tammy's house in high school, and the encounter at Homecoming with Susan a week later. I told her about George McEllen and his family, and my discovering that I could turn invisible and walk through walls. That *really* caught her attention. I told her of how I could sense when Cindy was in danger, and how I dealt with the two men who tried to hurt her. That's when Beth started actually taking notes. Also, Cindy grabbed my arm when I told that story. I never really gave her the details. I wondered what she'd have to say later.

I must have talked for a half hour. When I was finally done Beth looked over her notes, and started shaking her head.

"This isn't possible," she said.

I laughed a little. "Yeah, which *part?*"

She ignored me. "Seeing into the spirit realm is one thing. But *moving* into it? Not possible."

"What are you talking about?"

She looked up at me with a face full of doubt. "People can't move through walls, my little nephew."

I didn't like her condescending tone. I stood up and moved away from the table. "Now don't blink," I said.

I vanished. Beth gasped and jumped out of her chair. Cindy just laughed. Apparently she was getting used to me.

"He does that whenever I try to take his clothes off. Annoying white man."

"I can see how that would be distracting. Alex? Are you there?"

I backed up a few steps and reappeared, just so Beth could see that I could move when invisible as well. "Believe me now?"

Beth's hands started shaking. "Fuck. I think I'm gonna have a heart attack."

"Are you alright?"

"I guess he pulled it off. Well, kind of. Just the wrong person."

"Who is *he?* Pulled off *what?*"

Her face lit up. "You can help. I'm sure of it."

"Whoa, hey!" I raised my voice a little. Beth was almost out of it, not even looking at me. I waved a hand in front of her face. "You want to include us in your little talk here?"

"I'm sorry I didn't believe you. I have to take you somewhere. To help someone. After that, I'll give you answers."

"Wait a minute. Help someone? What are you talking about?"

"A family on the other side of town. One of the only ones left that will actually look at me if they see me on the street. Their house has spirits."

I raised my hands and sat next to Cindy. "I think I've had enough haunted houses in one lifetime."

"Please. Alex, to put it simple, I won't tell you anything unless you come with me."

I dropped my gaze and shook my head out of frustration. I just wanted answers, then to go home. Looks like I had to jump through hoops to get them. I gave Cindy an amused look.

"And this is supposed to be family here."

Beth started cleaning up her lunch. "You don't know the half of it."

"Are you okay with this?" I asked Cindy. "I can drop you off at the hotel and come back later."

She took a deep breath. I don't blame her for not being enthusiastic. She'd been with me in Tammy's house and George's house. It wasn't exactly fun.

"You know I'm right behind you, fearless leader."

I nodded. I caught Beth giving us both a look, as if she'd never seen such closeness or loyalty before.

We all went together in Beth's station-wagon. I probably should have gotten her to prepare us a little for the next haunted house in my life. But to be honest, I didn't exactly like Beth. I didn't want to talk to her. Besides, I already had a pretty good idea of what to expect. I'd walk inside the house, and get cold. Then I'd see some ghosts.

Blossom must have been bigger than I thought. The "other side of town" was a twenty minute drive. The sun was starting to set when we pulled up next to a quaint little home. It looked about as haunted as my apartment. Neatly cut grass, white picket fence, a mailbox with the last name Baker written on it. It certainly didn't look ominous or haunted.

But then again, Tammy's didn't either.

CHAPTER 13

We followed Beth up the sidewalk to the front door. After a few knocks a woman in her forties answered.

She was attractive, but looked like she was in the middle of a bad day. Probably a bad year. Huge circles under her eyes. Her shoulders were slumped, like the happiness had been drained from her. She managed a smirk when she saw Beth, but it quickly fell into a frown.

"Beth," she said. "What are you doing here?"

"Hi, Nancy. I tried to call before we came over, but the phone was busy. Is it okay if we come in?"

Nancy laughed sarcastically. "Not at all. We could always use more company."

Her statement was lost on me until we stepped into the living room. Then Cindy and I froze.

"Whoa."

There were people everywhere. It looked like a crime scene on TV. There was a guy setting up a camera in the corner. Another was hanging a microphone near the TV. A woman sat on the couch writing in a book of some kind. There was a man wearing a red flannel watching everything from where the dining room started. I could tell just by looking at him he was Mister Baker. He didn't look happy, but he did look exhausted, just like his wife.

Nancy and Beth retreated to near the stairs and started talking. I couldn't hear what was said, but I could see they were talking about me.

And of course, like I expected, the cold chill hit, like the temperature dropped twenty degrees.

"Wow," Cindy said. "Think there's any hot guys here? It's almost like a club."

"Yeah. I'll go get us some alcohol."

"You don't drink."

She was ruining my joke. "You're supposed to say something about us getting drunk together."

"Nice thought."

A man holding some kind of gadget stopped in front of us. He wasn't much older than us, wearing dirty bluejeans and a backwards baseball cap.

"Hi," he said. "We're with the university. I'm just taking some EM readings. What do you guys do?"

Cindy and I looked at each other.

"Uh, I drive a forklift and load trucks."

"I'm an accountant."

He was silent for a moment. "No shit? Really?"

"Yup."

"Well, okay. I'm Dan."

"Alex. This is Cindy."

He went on his way.

"Let's go," I told Cindy. I was getting claustrophobic with so many people in the tiny living room. But I knew we could probably move freely in the house without getting stopped. I just had to get away.

We walked past Mister Baker, who barely looked at us, and went upstairs. There was one person at the end of the hall setting up a camera, but that was it.

"Finally, a bathroom," Cindy said. "Don't leave without me."

Cindy closed the door behind her. I laughed.

"Come on, you have to eat your soup. You're sick."

It was a girl's voice, coming from an open bedroom down the hall. I poked my head in to see a yellow painted bedroom. So yellow it almost hurt my eyes. A little girl in a pink dress was playing next to her bed. She was probably seven or eight. She had a tiny table setup and a few stuffed animals all sitting in chairs. They all had plates in front of them, which I'm guessing had imaginary food.

The girl looked up and saw me. "Hi," she said politely.

"Hello. What's going on in here?"

"Teddy won't eat his soup," she said. "But he has to or else he won't get better."

"Ah. I guess he's not feeling good."

"No. I had to keep him home from school."

I laughed and stepped inside. Cute kid. Looked a lot like Nancy.

"I'm Alex."

"Hi. I'm Rachel. That's Teddy. That's Marvin. That's Bunny. And that's Jerry."

I looked at her little stuffed animal family. I had to laugh at Jerry the

Lizard. Who names a lizard Jerry?

"It's nice meeting you."

I turned to leave.

"Are you gonna make it go away?"

I stopped dead in my tracks. "What's that?"

"The monster."

She had my complete attention. I sat across from her Indian-style.

"Tell me about it."

"It comes out at night. It walks around the house. Sometimes it stands over my bed and screams at me. At first Mommy didn't believe me. But I think she does now."

Given the amount of people downstairs, I'd say Rachel was right.

"The man from our church came over last weekend," she continued. She hung her head. "But he couldn't help us."

"Rachel." She looked up at me. "I'll get rid of the monster."

She smiled. She believed me. The scary part was that I believed myself as well. I'd done it once already.

I left her room. I noticed two more bedrooms. One was at the end of the hall and looked pretty big. Obviously Mister and Mrs. Baker's. I poked my head in the other one to see a teenage girl laying on her bed. Probably a year or two younger than Alicia. She had a pair of headphones on and was reading a magazine. She looked more like Mister Baker. When she saw me she pulled her headphones off angrily.

"I told you guys. No cameras in here! Damn perverts."

I held my hands up. "You see any cameras here?"

"Who are you?"

"Alex."

"What? You like a ghostbuster or something?"

I leaned in the doorway. "Having a bad day?"

"Are there still fifty people downstairs?"

"Yeah."

"Then yes, I'm having a bad day. They can't help anyway."

"What have you been seeing here?"

She looked surprised. "You're asking me?"

"Yeah."

"Wow. No one's asked me anything yet."

"Your sister said she sees a monster."

She shook her head. "No, I haven't seen anything. A lot of noises, things banging around. Footsteps at night. And just...feelings, you know? Like I'm in the shower and it feels like someone's right outside watching."

I nodded. Then Cindy grabbed my arm, scaring the hell out of me. She laughed.

"I knew I'd get you eventually. Finally."

"Funny."

She looked into the bedroom. "Hey, he's my man. Don't try to steal him."

"Good luck in ghostbusting, Alex."

"Nice meeting you, Danielle."

She smirked. "Didn't even tell you my name. I thought you might be the psychic that every group drags along with them."

"Nah. It's on your wall back there."

She turned red from embarrassment.

Cindy and I went back downstairs. There were less people than before. I noticed some guys outside hovering near some vans. They must setup their equipment, then do their watching from the outside.

Mister Baker was in the kitchen making dinner. Nancy was in the living room talking with Beth and the woman I saw earlier with the notebook. There seemed to be some tension there.

When we stepped into the living room everyone got quiet. I could only hear Mister Baker working in the kitchen. The three women stared at me.

"Hello, everyone," I said. I tried to keep my voice polite.

The lady with the notebook stepped forward and extended her hand. She looked to be somewhere in her forties, although nowhere near as attractive as Nancy.

"Hi. I'm Judy Strictland. I'm the clairvoyant on the team."

"Alex Teague. My friend, Cindy Marshall."

"Pleased to meet you. Look, I'll get right to the point. I was talking with Nancy and Beth. I really don't think it's a good idea if we work together."

"Work together?"

"Yeah. Our energies might clash. We might sense different things, influence each other. You understand?"

I looked at Beth, who didn't say a word. She dragged me along, and wasn't going to defend me, I guess. I was tempted to agree, and leave the house. But then I wouldn't get my answers. I also remembered Rachel's face upstairs, talking about the monster.

"I wouldn't worry too much. I really don't kick out a lot of energy. I don't think I'll get in the way."

"This is serious," Nancy said.

"You're right. It is. Rachel upstairs says a monster is here. Are all these cameras and microphones gonna get rid of it?"

"We have to understand what's here. We need time and equipment to do that. Surely you've done this before?"

"Not like this," I admitted. "It's all new to me."

Beth finally spoke up. "Nancy, you've known me forever. We're not trying to compete with anyone here. We're just trying to help. We'll stay out of everyone's way."

Nancy thought for a moment. Then she nodded. Judy let out a little disgusted sigh, but didn't object.

"May I go upstairs?" she asked.

"Sure. I'll go with you."

"Me too," Beth said. "I'd like to see the girls again."

The first floor finally had some breathing room, and less tension. I was still freezing, but I could deal with that. It was only Cindy, Mister Baker, and me.

"I'm gonna go talk to him," I whispered to Cindy.

"Okay. I'll be on the couch. Keep your energy to yourself."

"I'll try."

I walked into the kitchen. Mister Baker had a ton of ground beef cooking on the stove. I wasn't exactly sure what he was making, but it smelled good.

"Mister Baker."

He looked at me. "Call me Doug. Hungry? I'm making plenty for everyone."

I was tempted. Cindy and I had eaten very little. "I might grab something later, Mister Doug. I wanted to talk about what's going on here."

He took a deep breath. "I've told everyone a hundred times. Told the priest last week. Told the first ghost nerd crew who was here. I'm a little tired of talking about it."

I held up a finger. "Just one more time. I don't have a clue of what's happening."

He looked me in the eyes. I guess he believed me, because he started talking while working over the stove.

"It started six months ago. Rachel was the first it all started happening to. She said she started hearing noises in the middle of the night. Footsteps, loud bangs. No one else didn't hear anything, so we didn't believe her." He looked guilty when he said it. "Then Danielle started hearing things, although not as bad as Rachel. It got to the point where Rachel wouldn't sleep in her own room."

"What have you and your wife heard?"

A look of anger crossed his face. "At first it was just noises. Mostly at night. Doors banging, quiet whispers. But then last month," he paused, trying to compose himself. "It tried to *choke* my wife. In her sleep! She said she could feel the hands around her. And sure enough, there were bruises on her neck."

We were both quiet. I could see him fuming.

"How do you fight something you can't see?" he said. "We've had every fuckin' expert out here. We've had the house blessed. Things only got worse after that."

"You can't move?"

He laughed sarcastically. "Easier said than done. We're already so far in debt. And buying another house would mean we'd have to sell this one. Would *you* buy a haunted house?"

I nodded. "Good point."

"So, what's your story?"

"Excuse me?"

"You a holy man? Or another psychic like the other two we've had here that can't tell us shit?"

He was angry. Can't say I blame him. "To be honest, I don't know."

We were done. I sat next to Cindy in the living room. She playfully punched me on the shoulder.

"So what's up? We having fun yet?"

I shook my head. "I can't believe we're here," I complained. "How the hell did this happen?"

"Don't worry. We'll be back in the apartment watching the O's lose soon enough."

I smiled. I suddenly missed that more than anything, watching the Orioles lose with Cindy.

"What do you think of my aunt?"

"Not very friendly. But she doesn't beat around the bush. I like that. You do look like her a little."

"Wonderful."

"So, what's going on here? Do you sense any ghosts or anything?"

"Well, not yet-"

I stopped mid sentence. Funny timing. I could sense its eyes. It was in the dining room watching Doug in the kitchen. I could feel its hate, its anger. It wanted to hurt Doug. I think it wanted to hurt everyone.

What was it? Ghost? Monster? Something else? I wasn't sure yet.

"Alex? You alright?"

I didn't answer. I heard footsteps and voices as Beth, Nancy, and Judy walked down the stairs into the living room. Judy was speaking into a cell phone, I guess to the people outside.

"The upstairs feels empty," she said. "Do you have anything on the cameras?"

She froze at the bottom of the stairs. Beth and Nancy stopped behind her. She stared into the dining room, about where I was looking.

"There's great evil here."

A little dramatic, I thought. Like she was auditioning for a movie. But I agreed with her.

"Yeah. It's in the dining room."

"How long has it been there?"

"Not long. I just picked up on it."

"I don't see anything?" Nancy said.

Doug looked into the living room. "Everything okay in there?"

Judy closed her eyes. "Who are you? What do you want?"

Its eyes shifted to Judy. I stood up from the couch. "Be careful. It's looking at you now."

There was a noise that sounded like a deep, guttural moan. It made my skin crawl. Only Judy and I could hear it.

There was a loud slap. Judy staggered back into the arms of Nancy and Beth. Doug left the kitchen to check on her.

It had struck Judy. She had a hand on her cheek. I could sense it close to her. It reared back to strike again.

"Hey!"

It stopped. I could sense it looking at me now. I couldn't see it. No one could see it. But it didn't matter. I knew everything it was doing. I'm not sure if even Judy could say that.

"That's right. I know you're there."

I put a hand behind me to keep Cindy near the couch. She was loyal to a fault, and always wanted to be next to me. I needed her behind me. The truth was I only barely knew what I was doing. It was focused on me, and that's what I wanted.

"Leave them alone." I smiled at it. "Deal with me."

Judy glared at me. "Don't *taunt* it!"

I realized something that chilled me to the bone.

Whatever it was, it was *afraid* of me.

There was a loud scream. Again only Judy and I heard it. She covered her ears. Then it was gone.

They all helped Judy to her feet. I stood there motionless, almost in shock. I have to give it to Judy, she was calm and collected, unlike me.

"It's afraid," she said. "It's afraid of something."

There was a knock at the front door. Dan poked his head inside. "Judy! We got major shit on the EM and cameras! Come check it out!"

Judy looked at me. Suddenly, we were a team. "Will you stay here?"

I nodded. Judy and Dan left the house. I watched them disappear into a van parked outside. Cindy had a hand on my elbow.

Doug took a deep breath. "What the *hell* just happened here?"

Beth looked at me. I really couldn't offer much information. I knew they were all in danger. But I also knew it feared me.

"It's usually active at night?"

Doug nodded. "That's when it's the worst."

Beth's eyes got big. "It gets worse?"

"Is it okay if I stay the night? I'll stay right here on the couch. You'll never know I'm here."

Cindy looked at me. I could tell she wasn't happy. Can't say I blame her. None of this was part of the plan when we first climbed in the car back in Maryland.

Doug took a deep breath and shared a long look with his wife. "Can you get rid of whatever is here, or what? We don't want to live with it. We don't want to make peace with it. We want it gone."

"I think I can."

"If you're comfortable on the couch, knock yourself out."

I heard Cindy make a noise behind me. She left the house. I excused myself and followed her. She stopped on the front lawn and put her hands on her hips.

"I'll get Beth to drop you off back at the hotel," I told her. "You can pick me up tomorrow morning."

"This is *stupid*, Alex. Shit, are you even thinking? What do you think you're gonna do? Play exorcist? What if you can't help them? What if whatever this thing is *hurts* you? It bitch-slapped that woman in there."

"It can't hurt me, Cindy."

"How do you know?"

I shrugged. "I just do. That thing is afraid of me. I know I can get rid of it. I can help that family. Please trust me."

She paced back and forth for a moment. I could tell she was fired up.

"You know I trust you. That's not the problem. And I know you're an amazing person. You can do things I can't really understand. But I just don't want anything to happen to you. That's all. You're playing with another haunted house. When we were eighteen I left you at Tammy's house all alone. I've never forgiven myself for that."

I didn't know that. I was the one who told her to leave. Had she been beating herself up all these years?

I grabbed her shoulders. "Cindy, it's okay. You didn't leave, I told you to go, remember? And nothing is gonna happen to me tonight. Just come get me tomorrow morning."

She shook her head. "I'm staying. Not getting rid of me this time."

I smiled. "Never gonna have another friend like you, am I?"

"Definitely not as cute as me."

We walked back up the sidewalk together. I felt a small stab of sadness. I definitely wouldn't find another woman like Cindy. I'd have to sit back and watch her date other people forever.

We went back inside. Doug agreed to let Cindy stay with me. I can only imagine how desperate they were if they were willing to let a team of complete strangers wire up their house, and two of them spend the night. We actually ate dinner with the family, and I can say I really liked them. Rachel was a good kid, and so was Danielle. Rachel ate quietly while Danielle told us all about her school life and new boyfriend. Doug took me on a personal tour of the house, and despite the cold chills, I didn't sense anything else going on. It was weird knowing that as we walked and talked, cameras and microphones were watching our every move.

Judy hung around a little while longer. She was constantly taking notes, closing her eyes, and talking on her phone. Like me, she didn't sense anything else going on. I wouldn't say she was exactly warming up to me, but she didn't give me any attitude. Eventually she left in her car. Apparently she and her team took shifts, and she'd come back in the middle of the night to basically spy on the house from their techno-vans out there.

Beth didn't stay. She left with the promise of picking us up the next morning. Strangely, my thoughts weren't anywhere near her. I wanted to help Doug and his family.

At about nine Nancy put Rachel to bed. The little girl gave me a quick hug before she ran upstairs. This both warmed my heart and made me nervous. What if Cindy was right? What if I really couldn't help? What if I let everyone down?

Danielle disappeared to her room not long after, talking on the phone to one of her friends.

It was just Doug, Nancy, Cindy, and myself, watching TV in the living room. It felt awkward at first, but after a while, we started having normal conversations. We covered a little bit of everything. How Doug and Nancy met, what they did for a living, some funny kids' stories. Nothing was out of the ordinary. The house didn't shake. I didn't sense any unusual presences watching us. We watched half a movie until around eleven. Then Doug announced he was going to bed. He hovered near the couch where we were sitting for a moment, and extended his hand.

"Thanks," he said. "Thanks for trying to help us."

I shook it and nodded.

He and Nancy went upstairs. A few minutes later she came back down with a few pillows and blankets.

"I'm not sure how you two want to do this," she said. "We've only got the one couch and the chair in the corner. But this should keep you warm."

I accepted everything, but didn't think I'd be sleeping much.

"Goodnight, you two."

For the first time since that morning, Cindy and I were alone. We heard everyone walking around and settling in upstairs, then it was quiet except for the TV, which I turned off.

Cindy kicked her shoes off. I didn't even have a chance to move before she lounged on the couch and laid back against me. I was shocked for a moment. I had to free my arm from under her and rest it on the back of the couch. Weird position for us. Nothing sexual or anything, but more than usual. We usually only touched if our hands reached inside the popcorn bowl at the same time during a movie. If either of us had a boyfriend or girlfriend, they probably would have been mad. But I wasn't complaining.

"Just get comfortable," I said sarcastically.

She looked at me upside down. "Are you bitching?"

I was braver than usual. "Hot woman leaning against me. I think I'm fine."

She flashed me that bright smile, and squirmed to get comfortable. I felt a little awkward. My attraction to her still hadn't died down, and her touching me was sending my head in all kinds of different directions. She was a little more touchy than usual. She always kept her hands to herself. Weird.

I reached up and turned the living room light off next to us. The room went dark, except for a streetlight just outside the living room window.

We didn't say anything for a minute. I could feel Cindy breathing next to me. She leaned her head back against mine. Again, not very helpful. She smelled wonderful. I wanted to wrap my free arm around her shoulders, but resisted the urge.

"Sitting in the dark. Waiting for a ghost," she said. "Should I be scared?"

"Nope. I'll take care of everything."

"What do you think Leese is doing?"

I smiled. "Probably out guy hunting right now."

Cindy was quiet. I sensed something was wrong.

"Everything cool?"

"Yeah. Just tired."

She was lying. But I didn't press the issue. "Well, I can sit on the floor. You can have the couch."

"Hot guy letting me lean against him. I think I'm fine."

I smiled. I tilted my head toward hers and smelled her hair. It felt great to feel her hair just barely touching my face. I wanted to hold her so bad. A thought flashed through my mind of us kissing. The guilt attacked me, and I forced the thought away. I hoped she didn't feel me getting so close.

She fell asleep first. I peacefully watched her for another hour before passing out myself.

CHAPTER 14

I wasn't sure what time it was when I woke up, but it was late. I don't remember dreaming. There also wasn't any of that sleep lag that hits when you wake up early. I just opened my eyes. I was aware of Cindy sleeping soundly against me. She had a blanket covering her.

I was also aware of something in the dining room watching me.

My eyes slowly slid into focus. I looked in the dining room, but I couldn't actually see anything. But I knew it was there. I looked down at Cindy sleeping. My arm was around her shoulders. She held on to it like it was a pillow. I kept perfectly still.

I looked up. Instead of seeing nothing this time, I saw a shape. It was a silhouette of a large man. I could make out a pair of arms, a head, legs. He was tall. Besides that, I couldn't make out any other details.

I quickly shifted my eyes away, as if I didn't see it. I even stretched out my free arm like I was tired. I didn't know if this game would work, trying to fake out a ghost. But it was worth a shot.

I closed my eyes and leaned my head back against the couch. I heard footsteps, walking right toward me. As it drew closer, I could hear it breathing. Heavy, labored breaths. It was inches away from my face. I held my eyes closed. The hairs on the back of my neck stood up.

"You can't help them," it said in that strange hybrid voice that I hadn't yet gotten used to. It brought back memories from five years ago. "They're all mine now."

Anger mixed in with my fear. I wasn't the same person I was five years ago. I wanted to reach out and grab whatever it was. I wanted to hurt it, like it was trying to hurt the Baker family. I resisted. Judy was right about one thing. We had to know what was happening first.

It leaned away. It crossed the living room and aimed for the stairs. I could still hear its footsteps, slow and steady.

The Bakers were in trouble. It wasn't a ghost they were dealing with.

It was a demon.

I gently squeezed Cindy's shoulder. She slowly woke up and turned to look at me.

"What time is it?" she asked.

"Listen. Stay here, okay? I'm going upstairs."

A look of fear touched her face. "It's here?"

I nodded. "Just stay here. Please."

"Be careful."

I slowly crossed the living room, vanishing as I did so. I'm not sure what good walking through walls or being invisible would do, but it made me feel safer. Walking up the steps, my feet didn't make a single noise. I felt like a ghost myself.

I half-crouched in the middle of the hallway. I couldn't hear a thing. Only a little bit of light came in from the girls' open rooms. And that light was just from the moon outside.

I heard whispering from Danielle's room.

I slowly poked my head through the wall into her room, just enough to get my eyes in.

It was no longer only a silhouette. It looked like a man. Three-piece suit, slicked down jet black hair. The only thing that didn't look human were its eyes. Pure black, like marbles.

I knew it wasn't a ghost.

Danielle tossed and turned, in the middle of a nightmare. The demon leaned over her, whispering just a few inches from her face.

"You should kill them. All of them. They all hate you. Start with your father, so your mother and sister can see. Then cut your mother's throat. Slow. You'll feel so good."

"Hey!" I shouted. I stepped inside the room.

The demon heard me. It stood up and whirled around.

It screeched at me. I almost had to cover my ears. It reached down and grabbed Danielle by the throat. Only then did she wake up. She tried to grab a hand she couldn't see.

"Get away from her!"

I ran forward and grabbed it by the shoulders. It spun and punched me in the chest. I fell to the ground, but didn't feel any pain. The demon, on the other hand, howled in pain. It cradled its hand in agony. We locked eyes, and I could see it all over its odd-looking face.

Fear.

Then it vanished.

Danielle was sitting upright in bed, searching the room. I appeared not too far from her. Probably not the smartest thing. She started screaming. I almost had to shout over her.

"Danielle! It's me, Alex!"

She slowly quieted down while rubbing her throat. "Something just tried to-" She didn't finish her sentence. She broke down crying.

I quickly crossed the room and wrapped her blanket around her. I felt terrible for her, but knew I didn't have time to comfort her.

"Listen. Do not move from this bed. Okay? No matter what you hear."

She nodded. I ran into the hallway. At the end of the hall I could see Doug and Nancy at the door to their bedroom. Rachel was right behind them. Danielle's shouts woke them up.

"What's going on?" Doug asked.

I didn't get a chance to answer. Suddenly Doug bent over, like he'd been punched in the stomach. Then he flew backwards near their bed.

"Doug!" Nancy shouted.

She and Rachel retreated into their room to check on Doug. The bedroom door was slammed shut by an unseen hand, and all I heard were screams.

I ran down the hall. A voice at the bottom of the steps made me pause for a moment.

"Alex!"

It was Cindy. I pointed behind me. I was strangely calm. "Go stay with Danielle."

I heard the front door downstairs open, followed by some familiar voices.

"Nancy! Doug! Are you alright?"

Judy and her crew.

I didn't waste time saying hello. I vanished as I went down the hall and went through their bedroom door.

The entire room was shaking. The bed, dresser, everything, was bouncing up and down. The window opened and closed, finally causing a pane of glass to break. Doug, Nancy, and Rachel were huddled in the corner. The demon stood over them. It leaned inches away from Rachel, who had her eyes closed and ears covered. I didn't know if she could see it, but she could obviously hear it. Nancy cried while Doug held his family.

"Kill them, you bitch!" it shouted at Rachel. "If you don't kill them, I'll kill you! I'll *make* you kill them!"

It grabbed her. Rachel let out a deep breath, but didn't draw another.

It was trying to possess her.

I wasn't afraid anymore. I was just angry.

I walked up behind it and wrapped my arms around its waist. It screamed in pain. I lifted it up and backed away a few steps. The activity in the room, beds bouncing and windows slamming, slowed down a bit. My arms felt like there was a small current flowing through them.

The demon twisted around and grabbed me by the throat. However, as hard as it tried to squeeze, it couldn't. I saw the frustration on its face. For whatever reason, I was immune to whatever it could do.

I punched it hard in the face and grabbed it by the throat. I didn't even squeeze very hard when it fell to its knees. That's when the room grew quiet except for the Bakers crying.

"Please!" The demon started begging. "Please don't send me back!"

I had no clue what it was talking about. But I didn't loosen my grip. It started to fade away until it was finally gone.

Right before it vanished, it changed, just for a second. The skin melted away into red flesh. Its eyes turned bright red.

It looked like a monster, a red demon.

So that's what they really look like.

I fell to one knee, mentally tired more than anything else. The bedroom door burst open behind me.

"Alex! Are you in here?" That was Cindy.

"Nancy? Is everyone alright?" That was Judy.

The Bakers all stood up and ran out, going through me in the process. I was still vanished to the real world. It was only after I heard the Bakers hugging each other in the hallway did I reappear. Cindy was waiting the whole time in the doorway. She ran up and gave me a quick hug, then held me at arm's length to inspect me.

I felt terrible, but that was more emotions than anything else. I just witnessed a demon try to destroy a family. And somehow, once again, I made it go away.

We walked into the hallway. I didn't realize it, but Cindy was actually supporting me. My arm was over her shoulders while I half leaned against the wall. Everyone looked at me. In the living room beneath us I could hear people filing into the house. They were excited. Good for them.

"How the hell did you get in there?" Doug asked.

Rachel ran forward and hugged me. I had a feeling I'd be throwing up before too long. But Rachel's hug told me it was all worth it.

Danielle was behind her parents. Her eyes never left me. I could see a mixture of fear and curiosity. She was the only one who saw me vanish and reappear.

She smiled at me. I knew my secret was safe with her.

*****

The early morning hours were hectic. I mostly sat on the couch with Cindy. But Judy and her crew combed the house. They waved their little microphones and cameras around. After a few hours, Judy came to the same conclusion that I already knew. The house was safe.

They tried to ask me a few questions, but I managed to duck them for the most part. Doug shook my hand. Nancy cried and gave me a hug. I have to admit, it made me feel great. I did something good for someone, and this time they were alive.

If it weren't for Judy and her crew, I might have stayed around longer. But at nine o'clock when I saw Beth pull up outside, I almost leaped from the couch.

"I have to run, everybody."

Doug wanted me to stay longer. Rachel even offered me a plate of her imaginary food. But I politely shook my head. It was time to get moving.

Beth met us on the sidewalk outside. She gave me a nod.

"A demon?" she asked.

My eyes grew wide. If she had said that one simple word yesterday, I might have been better prepared. I guess it was my fault for not asking.

"Yeah. It's gone now."

"Incredible."

We were almost to her car when I heard Judy's voice. She was coming out of one of their vans.

"Alex! Can I talk to you a sec?"

I took a deep breath and looked at Cindy and Beth. "I'll be right back, guys."

Beth nodded. "Okay. I'll see how Nancy's doing."

I walked over to Judy. She waved for me from inside the van. I joined her, and they closed the door behind me. Their van was crowded full of monitors and equipment I couldn't begin to understand.

It was just Judy and Dan, the EM guy I met yesterday.

They both stared at me for about ten seconds. Neither one of them spoke.

"Uh, guys?" I said. "What's up?"

They looked at each other. Dan pulled out what almost looked like an MP3 player. "We had this recording inside last night. It's made to record EVP phenomena. The way it works-"

Judy cut him off. "Let's spare him the lesson. Alex, you saw we had camera and recorders all over the house. We do that so we can hear what people can't. Maybe get a glimpse into the world that spirits come from."

I nodded. "Okay."

Judy nodded to Dan. He pushed something on the player.

Sounds of my little adventure last night started playing. That voice still made my skin crawl. It was full of static, but still audible. "Kill them, you bitch!...make you kill them!..." A pause, then the demon's panicked voice. "Please don't send me back!"

Dave turned on one of the monitors and played with some buttons. I was treated to a view of the Bakers' upstairs hallway, near Danielle's bedroom. The image was all red. Infrared, maybe? There was no audio. What looked to be a moving ball of static came up the stairs. I knew it was me. Then the static moved into Danielle's room. A minute later, I could see the Bakers and

Rachel standing in front of their door. Then I came out of Danielle's room, in the flesh. That's when Dan paused it.

"Static goes in. You come out," Judy said.

Dan pointed at the screen. "You can even see your shadow fall into the hallway, out of nowhere."

Damn cameras. So many people setting up, and I forgot all about them.

"Hold on. It gets better," Judy said.

Dan resumed the video. It was at the part where Doug's bedroom door closed. I walked away from the camera, down the hall, and stopped to talk to Cindy. I faded away slowly, replaced by that ball of static, and went into Doug's room. The video was only a few minutes long, but it felt like forever when it happened.

"Now the only real eyewitness we have is Danielle. She says she didn't see anything strange. She woke up, and you were already there checking on her. But she was tired, and maybe she actually saw something else. What did she see, Alex?"

I didn't like her tone. Not quite accusing, but angry curiosity.

They had everything on camera. There was no use coming up with an elaborate lie. But I didn't need to tell the truth either. I was angry myself. I just wanted to leave. I shrugged. "Does it matter?"

I thought I saw a vein in Judy's neck. "Of *course* it matters."

"Why? There was something in the house trying to hurt that family. I got rid of it. Shouldn't that be the end of the story?"

She sighed. "How many houses do you think we study a year?"

"I have no idea."

"This house will be our sixty-seventh this year. I've been there for every single one of them. We do the same thing, each time. We study, study, study, for weeks. And as much as we've learned, only one time were we able to figure out exactly what kind of spirit we were dealing with. It took three different exorcisms to get rid of it. Now here you come, in less than a night, help the Bakers, and it's obvious you don't know what you're doing."

I wasn't sure if she was insulting or complimenting me.

"Are you asking me something?"

Now she was mad. "*Who* are you?

I looked at Dan. "It was nice meeting you."

"Hell, do you want a job?" Judy asked.

I paused and gave her a look. "I'm still trying to figure out a bunch of things right now. Shit, if you study that tape, and learn something, *you* let *me* know."

"Look me up. University of Virgina, if you're ever in the neighborhood."

I gave them both a smile and left the van. Cindy and Beth were both waiting by the car. Cindy kept an eye on me as I climbed inside.

"Everything cool?" she asked.

"Oh yeah. They just wanted to show me the highlights of the night."

I was quiet on the way back to Beth's house. Still tired, I guess. Cindy however, wasn't, and she did a great job of filling Beth in on the details. Beth seemed impressed, but not surprised, and again I had to wonder what this long lost relative knew about me.

It was finally time to find out.

CHAPTER 15

After returning to her house she poured a glass of tea while Cindy and I sat at her dining room table. She was going painfully slow, like she was trying to make this whole thing longer than it needed to be.

Or maybe she was nervous about something.

"Do you want something to drink?" she asked. Cindy did, I did not.

"So I did what you wanted," I said, trying to push things along. "Now would you mind telling me about my family and who I am?"

She put the iced tea away. "That you did. The Bakers are one of the only families around that will actually treat me nice, ever since, well, forever. So I owe you. You're ready for this?"

I laughed. "After last night, I think I'm ready for anything."

"We'll see."

Her tone scared me.

She leaned against the counter and took a deep breath. She sat across from us and stared at the notes she had taken the day before. It was a while before she spoke.

"Alex, you're not really human," she said. "You can't be. No human can do the things you do."

I gave Cindy a look, not quite believing what I was hearing. "That's it? That's all you can tell me?"

She held up her notes and started reading. "Walking through walls. Disappearing from normal sight. Getting attached to a person or place." She gestured to Cindy. "These are all things a ghost or demon does. Not a person."

"Ghost or demon?"

"Look, this is how it works." She pulled a piece of paper out of her notepad and held it up. "This is the living world, *our* world." She placed it on the table and ripped out another sheet. "Now, this here is the spirit world. Spirits and souls usually find their way here when they die. It lays on top of our world. But the boundaries are different, which is why they walk through walls and we can't see them." She placed the *spirit* piece of paper on top of the *living*. She started dabbing holes into both sheets with a knife. "Now, these pinholes are the places that are like a gateway between the two worlds. These are your haunted houses, your mass murder sites, hospitals, places like that. This is where normal people can sometimes get a glimpse into the spirit world. Psychics can usually peek in when they want, although they don't get the whole picture, like they're wearing sunglasses. You understand so far?"

I looked at Cindy. She shrugged and gave me a half smile.

"Yeah, we're with you."

She ripped out a third piece of paper. "This is the demon world. It's not a good place. Luckily it's a little harder to get to, even from the spirit world." She placed it on top of the other sheets and only punched a few holes, to get her point across. "There's far few gateways, thankfully. Demons aren't pleasant, as you've seen. They feed off of energy and fear. They'll try to possess anything, human or spirit. And once they get a foothold into the spirit or living world, they're nearly impossible to get rid of."

I thought back to Tammy's house and dealing with Richard. He was possessed by a demon while alive, and that possession continued while he was a ghost, till I showed up. What a nightmare.

"I don't think you're just seeing into the spirit and demon worlds," she continued. She tapped her pieces of paper. "You're actually *moving* into them. Out of our world, and into theirs. That's how you can touch ghosts and demons, and move through walls. It's almost like you're half-living, half-"

She didn't finish her sentence, but she didn't need to. I could guess how it ended. Half-ghost. Half-demon. Something along those lines. I didn't like the sound of either one.

I had to fight it, even if it made complete sense.

"I've never seen any demon world," I said.

"Be thankful for that. You don't want to."

I had more questions. "How can I hurt demons? Fuck, how did this even happen in the first place? Does it have anything to do with my parents?"

Beth looked hesitant. "I can answer some of that. I guess I should show you instead of talk. Follow me."

We all went upstairs to a tiny bedroom. Bed neatly made, nice curtains. No pictures, which I thought was a little odd. There was actually a TV in the corner.

"Have a seat."

As we sat on the bed she searched through her closet. After a minute she pulled out what looked like an old shoe box. She blew off a layer of dust and popped the lid. Inside was a video cassette. She took it out very carefully, like it could hurt her.

I did see a pained look in her eye.

"I've watched this a few times, but not in a long time," she said, then looked at me. "I used to wonder whether I'd show it to you one day."

I gave Cindy a glance. A lot of drama over a simple video tape.

I saw her hand actually shaking as she put the tape in the VCR.

The first thing I heard was a woman's scream. It scared me at first, but then I heard some other people, all talking over each other. There was a woman laying on a bed screaming her head off. The camera was shaking all over the place, obviously a homemade video. I started to recognize the scene.

"Is someone giving birth?" Cindy asked.

Beth nodded. Her face was starting to turn white. "Alex's mother, Sarah. My sister."

My jaw dropped and I stared at the TV.

My first glimpse of my biological mother. In excruciating pain, giving birth to me. There were people all around her, lending support. I didn't see any doctors, though. In fact, it didn't look like a hospital.

Cindy looked at me with a smile. I'm not sure why. Maybe she felt like we were finally getting some resolution. I felt kind of weird. I'd never seen a pregnancy video before. Never thought I'd see my own.

There was another voice out of camera view.

"You're doing fine, honey. Be strong."

Some strange chanting started. The camera panned over to a man who looked like an older version of me. There were men standing on each side of him. They were all dressed alike, wearing black robes.

"What the hell is going on?"

Beth paused the video. She was visibly shaking and almost looked sick. She pointed to the man in the middle.

"This is your father," she said. "Mark Fuller."

"What's he dressed weird for?" Cindy asked.

"He was the leader of a cult. Your mother was, too. Those guys you see there, his best friends. You can't see them, but your mother is surrounded by them."

"*What?*"

She resumed the video. To be honest, I wished she hadn't. The camera panned back down to Sarah Fuller. She continued to scream in pain. One of the scary things, as if I needed to think more scary thoughts, was that the sounds of the chanting almost drowned her out. I've heard the voices of demons and ghosts, and the sounds of a haunted house. They don't compare to the sounds of that chanting over my own birth.

The video showed me being born into the world, a disgusting mess. My father cut the umbilical cord. Beth paused it once again.

"Are you sure you want to see the rest?"

Cindy and I looked at each other. She looked as disturbed as I was. "There's more?" she said.

"Where did you get this?"

She hesitated. "I'm the one filming it."

She pressed play. My father cleaned me off with another black robe. Then he carried me over to a table. The camera followed his every move. I heard my mother's voice off camera.

"I love you."

Mark Fuller smiled. "I love you too, Sarah."

The chanting grew louder. I couldn't count them, but a lot of people surrounded the table I was put on. They all wore hoods, unlike my father.

He pulled a huge knife out from under his robe.

"What the fuck?" Cindy said. She grabbed my arm.

He raised the knife over my little baby body. Cindy buried her head in my shoulder.

Before he could thrust it down, there was an inhuman scream. My father was stunned. All the other members of the cult jumped to their feet and looked around. Then the camera started moving as well, searching for the scream.

There was only a single voice, my mother.

"Mark? What's going on?"

A body flew in front of the camera. Following that were some more screams.

The camera went wild, moving all over the place. I heard my father screaming at his followers to find the demon and trap it. I could hear people dying. Beth's screams were the loudest, being right next to the camera. She dropped it to the floor.

"This is where I ran," she told us.

A stream of blood fell down the camera lens. A female body fell just inches away. My mother. Her eyes were wide open, staring right at me.

The carnage lasted maybe three or four minutes. Then all went quiet. The only thing you could hear were my cries in the background. The camera angle barely showed the table I was on.

It looked as if the shadows in the room actually started to crawl toward the table, toward me. I watched in horror as they crawled up the table. My crying turned into something inhuman for a few seconds.

Beth stopped the video.

"There's nothing else. It's just you crying for another ten minutes before I get there with the police. This was in a run-down church on Patt Street."

I didn't speak for a minute. Cindy dug a hand into my shoulder.

"What...*was* that?"

Beth sighed. "Alex, I was in a cult that your father was the leader of. He and Sarah decided to have a child for one reason. To capture a demon, and take its power."

Cindy stood up. "I can't listen to any more of this."

She left the room. Smart woman. But I had to hear the rest of it.

"Go on."

"It was some kind of ritual. You were the sacrifice. Then your father would steal a demon's powers. But something went wrong."

"Gee, you fuckin' think so?"

A tear rolled down her face. "Something that we couldn't see, killed them all. Ripped their throats out. Tossed them around like they were nothing. I'm only alive because I ran away."

"I can't believe this."

"I was your legal guardian after that. And I gave you up for adoption."

I can only imagine the look on my face. "At least you did something right."

She pointed at the TV. "Your father was very convincing. We all followed him, even Sarah. I was a stupid kid. I have to live with that for the rest of my life."

I wanted to throw up. I was having trouble thinking clearly. I sat there like a zombie. Beth kept on talking.

"The town knows I had something to do with it. It's a local legend now. They all hate me. I can't say I blame them."

That image was still stuck in my head, the one of my own father holding a knife over me.

"The church was supposed to be a very rare gateway, one that ran through all three worlds. I really don't know what happened. Your father must have underestimated the power of the demons on the other side. Or the ritual was wrong somehow."

I glared at Beth. "He's *not* my father."

She ignored me. "Either way, I think somehow you absorbed that demon's energy. Who really knows what power you have."

I stood up. I was sweating and didn't even know it. I felt nauseous. I popped the video tape out of the VCR.

"I'm taking this." It wasn't a request.

She nodded. "It's yours."

I went to move by her. I was more than ready to leave. She grabbed me by the arm.

"Alex." She opened her mouth, but didn't say anything. Her face was streaming with tears. "I'm so sorry."

I didn't show any emotion at all. "Goodbye," was all I said.

I would never see her again.

Cindy was waiting for me outside by her car. We didn't say a word as we drove back to the hotel. I played that whole thing over and over again in my mind.

My biological parents were in a cult. They had me, just to kill me for a ritual. And instead of my biological father becoming all powerful, apparently I did instead.

A very short summary of something that fucked with my head a long time.

CHAPTER 16

As soon as Cindy and I got back to the hotel, she started packing. I sat on the bed and put the tape in the VCR. Gotta love hotels that haven't upgraded to DVD players yet. Cindy folded a pair of shorts and shoved them in her traveling bag. She noticed what I was doing.

"Uh, Alex?" she asked. "You ready to go?"

"Not yet. I want to watch this again."

"Why?" There was irritation in her voice.

"I just need to."

"Aren't we done here?"

"Yeah."

"Then why don't we go home?"

"We will. I want to watch this first."

"You should burn that tape and forget you ever watched it."

Yeah, right. Very easy to say.

"I can't, Cindy. I have to know what happened."

"You're starting to obsess over this. You said we were coming here to find your parents. Well, we did that."

I looked at her. "What killed them? Why didn't it kill me?"

"Watching that disgusting tape isn't gonna answer that."

"It might."

I pressed play. Cindy angrily slammed her traveling bag closed and went to the door.

"What is your problem?" I asked. "Where you going?"

"I'm going for a walk."

She left. I shook my head and studied the tape as best I could.

I easily watched it for hours. Cindy never came back. I knew she was really mad at me then. She was right. Watching that massacre over and over

129

again didn't answer any more questions. But I did notice a few things.

When Beth got wild with the camera, I paused it a few times. I could actually see strange shadows on the walls all around. They looked like they were moving. In one shot, I saw one of Mark Fuller's followers missing a hand, with blood shooting out of his arm. They didn't stand a chance to whatever killed them.

I also noticed that Sarah didn't hold me once. I went right from the womb to that sacrificial table. They didn't address me by name. Probably never even thought of one for me. No need to, when you only plan on having your child alive for five minutes.

There was one last thing I noticed. As I watched that video, I thought less of them as my biological parents, and more as Mark and Sarah Fuller.

The sun was starting to set when I finally had enough of watching the tape. Cindy hadn't come back yet. I didn't worry, as this was like her. When she was mad at me, she just stayed away.

I looked around the hotel room for everything I'd have to pack. Before I did so, though, there was one more thing I had to do to put my mind at ease.

I had to see the place. I needed to see it with my own two eyes, and not on a TV. After that, we would leave, and I'd never come back.

I went down to the hotel lobby. The same man who had been working there the night we checked in was back again. He recognized me and gave a nod.

"Hey. Where's that pretty young lady of yours?"

I smiled. Everyone loved Cindy. "Probably out wishing we hadn't come here right about now."

"Ah. Blossom isn't the most exciting place. You take care of her."

"Hey, listen. I hear there's an old church somewhere around here."

He looked at me and shook his head. "Everyone wants to see the old church when they hear about it. Hell, some people come here just to see the damn place. My advice, don't. A lot of bad memories there, son."

"What do you mean?"

"Mark Fuller, everyone liked him. Then the whole town finds out he was a devil worshiper or whatever, using a church of all places for his little meetings. People don't like to talk about it. And they especially don't like seeing tourists walking around the place."

"I'm not a tourist."

"Ah. More personal for you, I take it? Look, if you need to see the place, it's two streets over. You can't miss it really. You can walk there from here. But be quick. Besides getting the stink-eye from the people who live around here, that place has its own share of ghost stories, as you can guess."

Just what I needed. More ghost stories.

I nodded. "Thanks a lot."

"No problem."

I walked the two streets over, noticing that Cindy's car was still in the parking lot. It was a nice night for a walk anyway. When I got to the street, I realized that I didn't know which way to turn. However, the guy was right, it was hard to miss. I could see it a little further down.

I stood in front of it for a moment. It looked exactly like you'd think a twenty-year-old church that no one wanted would. No glass in the windows. No front door. Grass that hadn't been mowed. No visible sidewalk of any kind. But I almost chuckled when I saw there was a gate with a chain and lock wrapped around it.

I searched the street for anyone at all. No one out tonight, except for a dog watching me from a neighbor's yard. Gotta love quiet towns. I did see a few living room lights on, but no one was looking right at me.

I vanished and walked through the gate without a problem. Then I appeared right away. An ominous feeling crept over me as I approached my birthplace, but I pushed it aside.

That familiar cold chill hit when I stepped inside. There was just enough light out to let me see without any problems. It looked like a hurricane had hit the place. There was graffiti everywhere. Many of the old benches were missing, or just plain destroyed. I could actually see old yellow police tape on the ground mixed in with the debris.

This was where I was born. This was where a lot of people died.

As I walked around, I could see familiar settings from Beth's recording. The bed where Sarah gave birth to me was in a heap in the corner. Not too far away, near the front of the church, stood the table where Mark placed me. It was still standing after twenty-three years.

I reached a hand out to it.

"Well, hello."

The voice was right behind me. I spun to see a man standing ten feet away. His feet were missing. He just kind of hovered there. He wore a smile on his face, and right away I knew he, or it, was evil.

There was a blood curdling scream to my left. I turned to see a skeleton pinning a woman down. He was slowly sawing at her neck with a knife. Blood shot everywhere, but she refused to die.

Suddenly, horror surrounded me. The light from the outside took on an eerie red glow. There was a man on his back not too far away from me. He was in half, his legs just a few feet away. He was trying to grab his spilling intestines and shove them back inside. Near the front was someone missing an arm shoving a woman's head into a bucket of water, laughing the whole time. The entire floor of the church was covered in blood. I don't know how many people, and monsters, were there. I honestly couldn't count.

"We've got a new one to play with," the creature in front of me said.

My first small taste of the demon world.

I ran through the church, stepping on someone's guts as I did so. I made it to the front door and stopped in my tracks. The town of Blossom was gone. The only thing beyond the church's walls was a barren landscape. A red moon was high overhead. Things that weren't human ran like wild animals, chasing each other and torturing people as they ran in fear. Screams and cries of pain filled my ears. This was a scene right out of Hell. An arm shot from the ground right in front of me. My heart jumped in my chest and I backed up a step. Some kind of creature pulled itself out of the ground.

"Where do you think you're going, spirit?"

I backed up into the church. Sounds that I would never forget echoed all around me. Blood being spilled, flesh being eaten, organs being ripped out. Yet the victims weren't dying. The demons wouldn't let them move on from the demon world.

I heard a voice behind me that was familiar.

"Please help me."

I turned to see Mark Fuller. Something that looked half-human, half-dog was poking its thumb in and out of Mark's eye socket. Sarah wasn't too far away. She crawled towards Mark with her hand out. A demon walked by and cut it off. She screamed in agony.

I looked around and realized that everyone I saw was in Mark's cult. I saw a few familiar faces from the videotape. This was the price they had to pay for trying to manipulate the demon world.

"We've got a spot picked out for you."

The demon tried to reach out and touch me. It stopped when a new voice echoed around us.

"Alex? Are you in here?"

I turned to see Cindy walking into the church. She was almost completely invisible. It was obvious she wasn't seeing into the demon world, but only the living, as she didn't react in horror. She was just beyond us, and for that I was thankful.

The ghastly voices of the demons spoke around us.

"Another human!"

"She looks delicious."

"I want to taste her!"

"Let me touch her."

One of the demons approached her, its claw stretched out. All of the fear, all of the terror that was inside me disappeared. There was only rage. I don't know where it came from. I ran forward and grabbed the demon by the neck with one hand. It was missing half its face. A maggot fell from its mouth to my arm. I ignored it. It snarled and raked my arm with its claws. I felt nothing. In fact, it seemed to hurt the demon.

"You won't get near her," I said. My voice was different.

It hissed at me.

I tossed the demon like a softball into another that was eating someone's arm. That had everyone's attention, demon and otherwise.

"Listen!" I shouted.

Everyone and everything froze. My voice echoed all across the church. I suddenly felt stronger than ever before. They were afraid of me, and I was feeding off their fear.

Like a demon.

"If you get near that woman," I pointed to Cindy. She continued to study the church, unaware of what was going on in a world over top of our own. "I will punish you."

A demon decided to test me. It ran toward her. I extended my hand and the demon stopped, in pain. I somehow pulled it toward me, with just my mind. It thrashed as I grabbed it in my hands. The demon was about my size, but I lifted it over my head easily and snapped its back over my knee. I didn't kill it. I don't think you can kill a demon. But it cried on the floor in pain.

They dropped their focus on Cindy and all eyes were on me.

"It's *him*!"

"The one with our power!"

The once living people who gave their hearts to a cult stared at me as well. I can only imagine what was going through their minds.

I smiled. Just a minute ago, I was terrified out of my mind. Now the only thing that scared me was the fact that I wasn't afraid, if that makes any sense.

I spoke once again. I was different. I don't exactly know what the demon world is about, but I'm in charge there. I knew it. *They* knew it.

"I'm guessing everything here is surprised to see me."

There were a few hisses and snarls. Another demon ran at me. This one was naked with a gaping whole in its chest. I didn't even have to do anything. It swiped at my face, but it didn't hurt at all or leave a wound of any kind. It fell to the ground, holding its claw.

I was surprised when every demon knelt and lowered its head. The less human looking ones did the same thing.

"Master," one of them said.

"I'm not your fuckin' master."

"But we're inside you." That thought scared me. "What do you want from us?"

I gestured around the room. "These people you're holding on to. Let them go. Let them move on."

"Master-"

"Do it."

There were some groans of protest. Then slowly the mutilated spirits started to vanish. Where they went, I have no idea. I bent down in front of Mark Fuller. He was still missing an eye. Sarah held on to him with her one good arm. They were laying in a pool of blood. I felt nothing for them.

That also scared me.

"That...was...*my* power," he muttered.

I was angry. Even after twenty years of torture in the demon world, he was still the same evil person I only saw glimpses of on that video tape.

"You're welcome. And fuck you."

He and Sarah vanished.

I did more for them than they ever did for me.

The demons still bowed before me.

"You'll be back," a demon said with a smile.

"You won't be able to resist. You're part of us."

I said nothing. I willed myself to vanish from the demon world. It wasn't any different than moving between the living and the spirit. Of course, with the exception of the pleasant scenery.

The red glow of the demon world faded away. I was back in the church with the moonlight pouring in from where windows used to be. No ghosts, no demons. Even the cold chill was gone. I started to process what just happened. My confidence and strength were gone once again. The sight of blood and body parts flashed through my mind. Mark's last words, basically condemning me for stealing his power. Nausea washed over me. I leaned on a broken bench.

Cindy was near the sacrificial table with her back to me. She ran a hand along it. "Jesus, this place is creepy."

"Yeah. Tell me about it."

She jumped and turned around. "Alex?"

"Yeah."

She saw I wasn't doing good. She was at my side in a second. She put a hand on my chest to help me keep balance.

"What's wrong?"

"I'm fine. Just a little dizzy."

"Don't sneak up on people like that."

She backed away to give me some space. The nausea left and I started feeling alright.

I wanted to go home. There were still questions. How did I have the demons' power? What else could I do? But I was done. No more questions. No more digging into my past. I'd already regretted nearly everything I'd learned. I wanted to go home, go out on the weekends with my friends, hang out with my sister and best friend, load a few trucks at work. No more demons. No more spirits.

"Look, I'm sorry I got mad at you earlier," she said. "I just...didn't want to watch that tape again. I wandered around town, got something to eat. I saw this church and thought maybe this was the place, you know?"

"You're right. This is it."

"You want to look around?"

"No. You were right, Cindy. We should have left. There's nothing for me here. I'm done asking questions."

She nodded. "Okay. I'll drive home this time."

I helped her back over the fence and we went straight back to the hotel. We packed and left. I almost left the tape in the VCR, but decided to take it with us. I was quiet the first hour of the drive back, just reflecting on everything.

CHAPTER 17

A human with the powers of a demon, who could cross between three worlds. Nice. What the hell did that mean for the future? How would I tell my future wife that? Of course, that would assume I'd ever date again. Between having a crush on Cindy and feeling like a freak, how would I ever date anyone? How would I live a normal life, ever?

Then there was Mark and Sarah Fuller. I hated them so much, but I made the demons let them go. I started to regret that on the drive home, and I felt guilty for it. I hoped that meant I was still mostly human.

There's a lot of problems twenty-three-year-olds have. Worrying about that old car. Trying to get that new girlfriend. Trying to find a direction for a career. I was worried about my demonic powers.

Still, our little trip put one thing into focus. My *real* family.

We crossed the Maryland state line when I turned to Cindy.

"Hey, where's your phone at?"

"My purse. Behind the seat. Maybe you should get your own cell phone."

"But then I'd have no use for you."

"Funny."

Alicia answered the house phone after a few rings. I felt bad, her being alone at the house without her big brother an apartment away. That feeling went away when I heard music and voices in the background.

"Cindy?" she said, obviously reading the caller ID.

"Try again."

"Shit. Hey Michelle! Turn that music down! How you doing, big brother?"

I smiled. "You wouldn't be having a party, would you?"

"On a school night? Please. Just a few friends over."

"Alright. I won't tell Mom. Cindy and I are heading home now. Just wanted to check in, tell you I love you, all that corny family crap."

"I love you too, Alex."

A voice in the background. "Aw! She loves her brother!"

Then another. "I love him too! Have you *seen* Leese's older brother?"

Alicia was mad. "Hey, would you two shut up?"

I laughed. "Go do your thing. Stop by tomorrow for dinner."

"Cool. Say hi to Cindy for me."

I hung up and dialed another number.

"Hello?" Mom sounded exhausted. It was close to eleven o'clock on the west coast.

"Mom. How you doing?"

"Alex? Hi." She sounded tense, a little afraid.

"Cindy and I are driving back now. We'll be home tonight. Just wanted to call and let you know everything's cool."

"Glad to hear it. Honey, I'm so sorry I didn't tell you everything earlier."

"You got nothing to be sorry about. I love you. I'm so glad you're my Mom."

There was a pause followed by a sniffle. "I wasn't there for you growing up. I was either in school or working. You practically raised Alicia while growing up yourself."

"Mom. I'm who I am because of you. Alicia and I are lucky. Don't ever forget that. I love you."

"I love you too." We were quiet a moment. Afraid to admit I almost felt a tear coming on. I held it in. "Okay dear. I think I'd better go. I'm having dinner with a client, and I don't think it's too smart if I start crying."

I laughed. "No problem, Mom. I'll call tomorrow."

I put Cindy's phone away. She was looking at me.

"What? What's up?"

She smiled. "You're gonna have me calling *my* folks soon."

"Nothing like seeing your biological parents try to kill you to make you realize there's worse things than your sister waking you up in the middle of the night cause of bad dreams."

"Yeah, true."

"I couldn't have done this without you, Cindy. Thanks for coming with me."

She looked surprised, then embarrassed. "You know I'd do anything I can for you, Alex."

"Same here."

"Great. Can we have sex now?"

I laughed. If only. "I probably couldn't handle you."

"Nah. We'd do fine."

I looked at her. Weird thing to say. Obviously she was kidding, but those jokes definitely put pictures in my head.

I was saved from having sexual thoughts of my best friend by a roadside restaurant. We grabbed a quick dinner before heading back home. It was late when we pulled up in front of the apartment building. We grabbed our bags and stood in front of our doors. I was still wide awake, but Cindy looked tired.

"You going to sleep?" I asked.

"Yeah. I'm beat. But I got a few more days off. I'll stop by tomorrow morning when I wake up."

I smiled. Things were already feeling normal again. "Cool. See you tomorrow."

It felt great to stand in my own living room. Just a few hours ago I'd seen things I'm pretty sure no person had ever seen, nor *should*. Blood-filled churches, a world just outside our own, spirits being tormented for decades. But standing in my own quiet apartment, I felt I could at least try to put some of that behind me.

I did feel overwhelmed as I turned on the TV and poured a glass of tea. How was I supposed to deal with something this big? When I finally got over my little crush on Cindy, how would I tell the next person I had feelings for that I had a little bit of demon in me? Would anyone be able to accept me?

I sighed as I crashed on the couch. I tried not to worry about it too much. One thing at a time. Right now my biggest priority was trying to enjoy the rest of my days off.

It was around midnight when I finally passed out on the couch.

I wouldn't get much sleep.

*****

I awoke in the middle the night in a cold sweat. The TV was still on. I sat up quickly, a little *too* quickly. Dizziness took over and I came very close to throwing up all over the carpet. I had a quick mental flash of a bathroom that wasn't my own. I recognized it right away as Cindy's. Then I saw another flash of Cindy on one knee in front of her toilet.

I wasn't sick. She was.

I slowly stood up and took a deep breath. I was fine once again. That definitely wasn't fun.

I left my apartment and knocked quietly on Cindy's door. It was unlocked, like usual. I poked my head in.

"Hey, Cindy!" I whispered. "You in here?"

Her apartment was completely dark except for the open bathroom. The light spilled into the hallway. I heard a sound that I'd heard many times, the sound of someone leaning over a toilet. It lasted a few seconds, followed by Cindy's weak voice.

"Alex? Get out of here, please."

Like a good, stubborn friend, I didn't listen. I softly shut the door behind me and walked down the hall. I peered in the bathroom to see Cindy on all fours, wearing her pajamas. Thankfully I couldn't see any details of what she was putting in the toilet, or I might have joined her. The sound was bad enough.

She got done another round and turned to look at me. She looked terrible. Her face was almost green and dripping with sweat. Her eyes were half closed and puffy from exhaustion.

"Come on, Alex. Leave. This is embarrassing."

Cindy's hair only went a little past her shoulders. But it was still long enough to cause some issues when throwing up in a toilet. I sat on the edge of the bathtub and held her hair back. I was just in time as she gripped the sides and went one more time. I had to look away. Funny thought. I got done seeing blood and guts not too long ago, and came out of that fine. But I could barely handle my friend throwing up.

"Goddamn restaurant food." She collapsed next to the toilet. "Last time I stop at a place I've never been to."

I felt bad for her.

"What the hell are you doing up?" she asked.

"I wasn't. I sensed you were sick."

She managed a smile. "Let me get this straight. I get sick, and you sense it?"

"Yup."

"Damn. You must be in love with me."

Her eyes grew big and she leaned in the toilet once again.

She was right. That's when I first realized it. It wasn't a simple crush I had on Cindy. It wouldn't go away. It wasn't just a matter of Cindy being gorgeous. She was the one I wanted to be with. As I sat there on the tub next to her, holding her hair back while she puked, with her looking the worst she's ever looked, I realized I was in love with her.

Wonderful. As if I didn't have enough to keep me up at night.

"Shit," I complained.

"Huh? What's wrong?"

"Nothing. How you feeling?"

"Like shit."

I tried to grab her under the arms. She forced me away. "I can get up by myself."

I backed up with a smirk on my face. My Cindy, always strong and stubborn. As she stood up, I saw her knees shake a little. I caught her before she could fall.

"I'm dizzy."

"I can see."

I scooped her up in my arms.

"What the hell are you doing?"

"Come on, Wonder Woman. Let's get you in bed before you pass out in the bathroom. Then I'd have to take pictures and put them on the Internet."

She smiled and wrapped her arms around my neck. "I should get sick more often. A free lift is always nice."

I was a step away from her bedroom when she stopped me. "Uh, can't go in there. I, uh, threw up on the bed."

"Nice, Cindy."

I carried her to the couch and gently lowered her down. She threw an arm over her head and closed her eyes. It took me a few minutes to get her settled in. I grabbed a spare blanket and pillow from the closet, and the trashcan from the kitchen, in case she had just a little more in her. I took her blankets off the bed and put them in the washer right next to our apartments. When I finally got done, I thought she had fallen asleep. I carefully took off her slippers and tucked her in. I turned the bathroom light off and was nearly to the front door when she talked to me.

"Alex?"

"Yeah?"

"Stay here. Keep a sick woman company."

I sat in the chair across from the couch. She had the most comfortable chair in the world. I settled in and leaned my head back.

I had no idea how I was gonna deal with my feelings for her.

"Remember Steven? Freshman year of college?" she asked me out of nowhere.

I did. An ex-boyfriend of hers. Asshole. Cindy fell head over heels for him. It wasn't her fault. He hid his nasty personality pretty well in the beginning.

"Yup. You miss him, don't you?"

"Ha. Please. Remember when I got the flu? His idea of taking care of me was trying to have sex."

"Yeah I remember. When Alicia found out I thought she was gonna kill him."

"Yeah. It's sad, isn't it? You take better care of me than any boyfriend I've ever had."

I could hear the sadness in her voice. It wasn't like her to reflect back on old boyfriends. I guess being sick brings out that crap. Despite how I felt about her, I had to make her feel better.

"Don't worry, Cindy. You'll find that guy who drives you crazy."

She was quiet for a second. "I hope you're right."

"I'm always right."

"At least I always have you as my whitest friend. That's depressing," she joked.

Friends. That's what we were. I had to repeat that to myself over and over to get it through my thick head. I was mad at myself for that little stunt I pulled, carrying her to the couch. That wasn't what friends did. That's what guys did when they were looking for any kind of excuse to touch someone they had the hots for.

I had to stop that sort of thing.

"Goodnight, sickie."

"Night, Alex."

CHAPTER 18

I had a few relaxing days off till the weekend. I spent most of it with Alicia and Cindy, and some time alone relaxing in the apartment. I did surprisingly well with Cindy. I was determined not to let my feelings for her rule me. I shoved them deep down. If I could control all the other crazy things I could do, I could control my feelings as well.

The first thing I did when Alicia came over for dinner was give her a hug. Definitely put everything in perspective, and the bottom line was that it didn't matter at all that I was adopted. I was lucky, and I knew it. I would never take Mom and Alicia for granted.

It was Friday afternoon. I had a nice lazy morning watching a few movies, then decided it was time to hit the weights. I had two hundred thirty pounds over my chest when the front door swung open.

"Alex!" she said. "What the hell are you doing?"

I didn't respond until I was done eight reps. I racked the weight and sat up. Cindy stood near the front door with a shopping bag from the mall.

"Well, I'm trying to give all the women something to look at."

She rolled her eyes. I laughed. She knew I was only kidding. I didn't have an ego, which made my ego jokes all the funnier.

I stood up and grabbed the curl bar from the floor. I looked at Cindy, and could have sworn I saw her looking me up and down. Nah. Wishful thinking.

"I talked to Tina while I was at the mall. Her and Dave are heading out tonight. You game?"

The gang. I hadn't seen them in what felt like forever. "Yeah. I'm up for that."

"Cool. If you're nice I'll dance with you. See if we can get you a woman by making them all jealous."

"I'm always nice."

"Then you'll get a dance."

She flashed that bright smile and left. I wished I could let myself think she was flirting with me. But I knew better.

The time passed pretty quickly, which always sucks on a Friday night. Before I knew it the sun had set and I was getting dressed to go out. I walked the three steps to Cindy's and opened the door. The gang was already there. Dave and Tina were wrestling in the middle of the living room. Jenny was in the corner talking on her phone. I could see Alicia talking in Cindy's room. I couldn't see Cindy, but I didn't think Alicia was talking to herself.

"Alex!" Dave called. "What the hell is up?"

That brief greeting let Tina sneak up and put Dave in a headlock. He gave in so he could feel her ass.

"Hi, Alex," Tina said.

I laughed and waved. Jenny nodded at me from the corner. I pointed at her, my way of saying hi. I headed back to Cindy's bedroom and jumped in enthusiastically. Cindy was sitting on her bed, looking serious. Their conversation came to a stop when I popped in.

"How are my two favorite females?"

"Damn. Look who's here," Cindy said.

I rubbed my hands together. "Okay guys. I need your help. There are about one hundred women outside mobbing my truck. I need to get them to go away."

"Just go outside and take your shirt off," Cindy said with a smile. "That should do it."

"If I do that, then one hundred becomes five hundred. I can't risk it. It's too dangerous."

Alicia rolled her eyes. There was an awkward silence. I didn't sense any bad moods, but something was up.

"Guys? Did I cut in to something? What's up?"

Alicia shrugged. "Nope. Nothing going on here. Right, Cindy? Nothing *ever* going on here."

Cindy flashed Alicia a dangerous look. Alicia walked out of the room.

What the hell was that all about?

"Cindy?"

She shook her head and stood up. "Everything's cool. How do I look?"

A black skirt that stopped at the lower thigh. Black sandals. A tee-shirt that showed most of her slender arms.

She looked beautiful. Gorgeous. Sexy.

"You look alright."

"Thanks. Everyone ready to go?"

"Depends on if Tina whipped Dave's ass or not."

We walked in the living room to see Tina on top of Dave. He was on his back with his arms stretched out. Tina's chest was pressed right in his face while she had a hand on his stomach.

"Alex!" he called. "I lost! Whatever will I do!"

"Looks like you won to me."

"Shhh! Don't tell *her* that!"

"Everybody ready?"

"Yes! Let's go get drunk!"

I gave Alicia a look as we all left the apartment. Something was definitely wrong. We locked eyes for a moment, and I could see the frustration there. Not with me, but with Cindy. She gave me a smirk.

Typical Friday night driving into the city. I drove my truck, Alicia her car. We could hear people on the sidewalks, generally acting like idiots. Laughing, screaming, drinking, fighting.

It felt great to hang out with my friends again. Dave had me laughing at least twice a minute. Jenny was her usual quiet self, but we talked for a few minutes about what was going on in our lives. That guy she met at the club the last time we were out didn't pan out, and her job was going okay. Tina, as always, had her hands full putting up with Dave.

I paid my fifteen bucks and walked into the club. People everywhere, of course. Loud music. Women wearing as little clothing as possible. The guys floated around like wolves looking for prey.

"Bar!" Dave shouted. He grabbed Tina's hand and led her away. I laughed.

"Let's get a spot," Jenny suggested.

We stopped near the corner of the club. That way we could talk and the ladies could float out to dance if they wanted.

It wasn't a terrible time, but something was going on between Alicia and Cindy, and it was obvious. I left it alone. I'd get it out of them eventually. They barely said three words to each other. After about an hour there, and some alcohol was flowing through Dave, Tina, and Jenny, the women made their way to the dance floor. Only Alicia stayed behind. Dave and Tina were doing some kind of distance flirting thing. It was like she was dancing only for him. I know he loved it. He blew her kisses while she licked her lips and danced with Jenny. I knew what he'd be doing later.

I was glancing around the club, looking at the sights, when my eyes fell on Cindy as she danced. She was looking back at me, giving me a smile. She was amazing. The way she danced, the way her clothes fit her, wow. I couldn't take my eyes off her. My usual guilt settled in, but I still looked her up and down, giving her a playful thumbs up. She knew I was watching, and she didn't seem to mind. She actually gave me a small wave. Was it my imagination, or was something happening a little past friendship?

My heart stopped for a second. Was it possible?

I felt a set of eyes on me. I turned to see Alicia looking at me. In that one moment, she knew what was going on, and I knew *she* knew. Sibling communication.

"You got the hots for Cindy," she stated.

I opened my mouth, but didn't say anything. My face was turning red, but I think the glow from all the lights hid that.

"Alicia, don't tell her."

"Well, why don't you?"

"Because we're friends."

"How long has this been going on?"

"I don't know. It doesn't really matter."

"Dammit, Alex. Why haven't you told me?"

"I don't know. I thought she was hot in middle school. But what the hell are you supposed to do about that? We've known each other since we were five. It's too weird."

She shook her head, like she was disappointed in me. I was surprised.

"What's on your mind?" I asked.

Before she could speak I noticed something past her on the other side of the club. I saw a woman that I recognized with her hand on a guy's hip. She was leaning into his ear, whispering. Whatever she was saying, he liked it, as he was all smiles.

It was Victoria.

The gorgeous redhead that tried to squeeze the life out of me. The woman who threatened me right in the middle of the club the last time I was there. The woman who asked me what I was.

"Alex? What are you looking at?"

Cindy sneaked up on us. She put a hand on my shoulder and slowly swayed back and forth.

"Hi guys. What's going on?"

I was distracted enough to put a hand on Cindy's hip. I didn't even give it a second thought as her hand was on my shoulder. I realized what I did and quickly pulled it away. I think the red on my face was noticeable that time.

"Sorry."

She smiled. "Accidents happen."

It didn't even dawn on me that she didn't remove it herself. My eyes were still locked on Victoria. I saw her take the stranger's hand and start to walk away.

"I'll be right back," I said.

Cindy followed my gaze and noticed who I was looking at. "Ah! The redhead! So you *do* like her?"

"No. Just need to talk to her." I looked at Alicia. "And you two stop fighting and make up."

"Don't forget. I owe you a dance."

I kept my eyes on Victoria. I had to push my way through some people to keep up with her. I saw her look back at the stranger a few times with a flirty smile on her face. A far cry from the woman who confronted me in the middle of the club all those weeks ago.

My heart sank as I saw them head through a side exit door. I knew that door led to the alley next to the club. I only wanted a minute of her time, to see what her problem with me was. My thought was she was psychic, and knew I was different. But after we had our chat I'd have to reenter the club through the front and push my way through everyone once again.

I threw open the exit door and walked outside. Quite a difference stepping from a club to the night air. I wiped some sweat off my head. I was actually a little creeped out. The alley was dark. I could only see light coming from the mouth of the alley, near the front of the club. Who knew what was lurking in the shadows.

Then I remembered. I had demonic powers. What the hell should I be afraid of?

I heard a noise behind me about twenty feet away. I froze every muscle and held my breath. A quiet noise which slowly got louder. It sounded like a man moaning. I thought it was in pain for a moment. Then I realized it sounded like sex.

I took a few careful steps down the alley. The moaning grew louder, followed by what sounded like sucking noises that chilled me to the bone. It just didn't sound right.

The moaning was coming from behind a large dumpster. The first thing I saw was a pair of legs sticking out from behind the metal bin. Then I saw a shapely ass in a pair of jeans straddling someone. The moaning hit a new level, and I knew it had to be sex. But something was still wrong in the back of my mind. Maybe it was the simple fact that it was in an alley, or the fact that I saw only clothes, and no skin. But I had to keep looking.

I recognized her from the back as Victoria. She had her mouth clamped on the guy's neck she'd taken from the club. I could see his face, and he was in heaven. His eyes were shut and his legs shaking. Victoria didn't make a sound, which was odd to me.

I saw a stream of blood flowing down the stranger's neck.

"Hey!" I shouted. "What are you doing?"

Victoria whirled around. I wasn't prepared for what I saw.

Her eyes were a bright red, throwing light across the alley. Blood dripped down her mouth onto her chin. Two large fangs stuck out of her mouth, about a half inch longer than the rest of her teeth. She licked the blood from her lips with her tongue, a motion that scared the shit out of me.

I didn't have time to react, although I admit I have no idea what I would have done anyway. One second, I was standing there watching her sitting on top of the stranger, who was either unconscious or dead. The next second, I was slammed up against the brick building behind me. She had one hand wrapped around my throat, and I was a few inches off the ground. I had trouble getting air.

"What the fuck are you doing here?" she said. Her long teeth made her speech slurred.

I was a split second away from vanishing when some bright lights hit us from the front of the alley. She dropped me to my knees. We both turned to see an unknown number of silhouettes approaching us. I heard a whoosh through the air and heard it stop right above me where Victoria stood. She fell to her knees next to me, and I could see the arrow sticking out of her chest. My jaw dropped. I had no clue what the hell was going on.

"Hello?" I called, still trying to catch my breath. "What's going-?"

I never finished. I was hit with a tazer, the worst pain I ever felt in my entire life. My body shook uncontrollably for a few seconds while the juice flowed through me. Then I collapsed next to Victoria.

I heard voices before I drifted into unconsciousness.

"...Are we clear?..."

"...Is he human?..."

"...Check his pulse..."

"...Help me lift her...fuckin' bitch..."

"...Too bad we can't fuck her first..."

"...Don't touch that damn arrow!..."

Then I was out.

CHAPTER 19

I have no idea how long I was unconscious. The first feeling I had when I opened my eyes was claustrophobia. I was in total darkness in an uncomfortable position. I tried to sit up and hit my head.

I was in the trunk of a car.

I tried to twist from my side so I could lay on my back, and felt someone next to me. My hand touched a breast, then an arrow.

Victoria.

I drew back quickly, although I had nowhere to go. I couldn't see her, and that scared me even more. I held my breath to see if I could hear her. The only thing I could hear was the sound of the moving car I was in.

Then I heard voices. Very close. Had to be the people in the car, the ones who killed Victoria and tazed me.

"Did you see that bitch fall like Iraq?"

"Yeah. Good shot, Jones."

"Thanks. Look, are you sure she's not gonna go for our throats when we get there?"

Laughter. "This is your first time, right?"

"Yeah."

"She ain't gonna do shit, as long as you don't pull out that arrow. Once their heart is pierced, there ain't nothing they can do except die."

"What about the guy? He had a normal heartbeat, right? That means he's human?"

Silence.

"I feel bad, but he was in the wrong place at the wrong time. Just don't tell Bachner. He hates it when people get in the crossfire. Hell, the guy was probably working for the bitch anyway."

"She *is* hot though, isn't she?"

"They're *all* hot. Doesn't make them any less dangerous."

"Put some music on, man."

"Sure."

Sounds of heavy metal mixed in with their voices. I couldn't hear what they were saying.

I stared at the darkness where Victoria was. I knew nothing about her. The first time I met her she threatened me. Now I knew she had fangs and drank blood. She tried to choke me.

I could easily vanish and leave the trunk, but I felt we were going fast. That didn't sound like a safe plan.

So, Victoria and I were partners.

I simply had to get the arrow out of her.

I took a deep breath and felt around for it. I grabbed it with both hands and pulled up. Instead of moving the arrow, her whole body came up instead. I felt sick to my stomach. I had to pin her down with an arm under her breasts and yank the arrow with my other hand. It moved a few inches. It made a sick, sloppy sound. I pulled a few more times and finally felt the arrow loosen from her skin.

She moaned in pain. I was shocked as hell, but had enough awareness to feel for her mouth with my hand. I felt her bloodstained fangs.

"Shhh," I said.

She took a few deep breaths. She winced and I felt her cover the hole in her chest with her hand. I pulled my hand away.

"Thank you," she said. "What's going on?"

"We're in a trunk. Hell, that's all I know."

"Alex." I somehow wasn't surprised she remembered my name. "When they get to whatever remote place they have in mind and open this trunk, they're gonna try to kill us. Now, I know you're not human. And you probably have a good guess that I'm not either. We can take them. Question is can you mentally handle that?"

"Do...you mean kill?"

"I hope not. I try so hard not to kill. I only kill when my life is in danger, when there isn't any other option. But now might be one of those times."

"I don't think I can."

"Okay, fine. You stay out of the way then."

The ride got rougher. We definitely weren't in the city anymore.

"I'm bleeding bad. Getting weaker. I need blood."

I didn't say anything, just scooted further away from her. I could feel something warm and sticky all over my hands. I knew it was Victoria's blood.

The car slowed to a stop. A series of car doors opened and slammed shut. The ride was over.

"McGee, help me carry the bitch. Jones, drag the guy in the woods. Heins is on his way now with a shovel."

"Why do I gotta dig a fuckin' hole?"

"Cause you're the new guy."

Victoria tensed up. "Heins."

Obviously she knew the guy.

"Alright guys, let's get this party started."

A key hit the trunk lock and turned. The light from the moon and a few flashlights rushed in to replace the darkness.

I didn't even see Victoria move. There were three guys peering in at us. Then she had her fangs buried in someone's neck.

There were a few startled screams as Victoria took her victim to the ground. I was still climbing out of the trunk when she jumped to her feet and swiped at the chest of another guy. Her hand was no longer a hand, but a long talon with dangerous looking claws on the end. Blood sprayed from the man's chest onto Victoria.

I climbed to my feet in time to see a truck pulling up not too far away. Three more guys jumped out, armed with crossbows. One guy had what looked like a damn flamethrower.

"Victoria!" I screamed.

She looked up. Two crossbow bolts whizzed through the air. Victoria was already moving at a speed that I could barely see. She moved a few feet to the right. The bolts struck a tree next to me.

The distraction was enough for the last guy from the first car to stab her in the shoulder with a wooden stake. Victoria yelled in pain and fell to one knee. She slugged the guy in the stomach so hard he flew back and landed right next to me. His head bounced on the bumper of the car.

But she was hurt. She pulled the stake from her arm and dropped it to the ground. There were three men out of the fight, but three more standing fifteen feet in front of her. Two were trying to reload their crossbows, but one pointed a flamethrower right at her.

I finally made my legs move. I ran toward Victoria. I don't know what I thought I was doing. Being the hero? Being the brave guy trying to save the woman? Just being stupid? I could do amazing things. Talk to ghosts and demons. Move into their worlds, which let me turn invisible and move through solid objects. But I wasn't fireproof.

So I thought.

I pushed Victoria out of the way as hard as I could. As she tumbled to the ground, I heard a jet of flame heading right at me. I didn't have time to vanish.

I felt the fire engulf me. I screamed, because that's what you were supposed to do when fire hit you. I felt it dancing up and down my skin. It made me itch, it even tickled in certain spots. I felt the cool night air blow through the holes in my clothes the flames were leaving behind. But there was one odd thing.

I didn't feel any pain.

I looked at my hands. The flames were beautiful, a wild mix of orange and blue that flowed across me. Then the fire vanished into my skin, like it was moisturizer.

I looked at the three men still in front of me. They had forgotten all about Victoria. Their eyes were locked on me.

I glanced down at my clothes. My shirt was almost completely burned away, except for some scraps. My bluejeans were now black.

He squeezed the trigger on his flamethrower once again. The fire embraced me. It felt like a hot shower. I screamed, not in pain, but rage. It didn't sound like a normal scream. It was demonic. It's hard to believe that sound was coming out of me.

They were trying to kill me. They dragged me away from the city, with the intention of burying me in the woods. The cold harshness of that fact settled in, and it infuriated me.

These were not good men.

And they would pay.

I laughed as the flames tickled me. They were terrified, and I sucked in their fear like a baby does milk. I felt myself growing stronger.

I looked through the flames to see two crossbows aimed at me.

I vanished. The bolts passed through me harmlessly.

"What the fuck-"

They didn't have the chance to finish. I reappeared right as my foot was headed into Flamethrower Guy's balls. His eyes bugged out of his head and he fell uselessly to the ground. The guy on the right tried to swing his crossbow at me. I vanished and felt it pass through me. Then I grabbed it out of his hands and vanished again. I couldn't make it vanish with me, but it fell to the ground. I timed a hard headbutt to his nose. He didn't have a chance to stop it, as I reappeared just inches from his face.

Victoria was up again. She was at my side in a second. She grabbed the guy on the left by the neck, lifted him from the ground, and reared back her fangs. She froze, though. I followed her gaze to what she was looking at.

There were two more trucks driving down the dirt road toward us. It was my first chance to get a good look at where we were, and I didn't recognize it at all. We were definitely in the middle of nowhere. It was a large grassy field, with a thicket of trees right behind us.

"That's Heins," she said in that slurred speech.

Three minutes ago I wanted nothing to do with any of this. Now, I was confident. "They don't have a chance."

She dropped the last guy to the ground. He started crawling away. Victoria looked at the damage we'd done. Blood everywhere. People moaning and bleeding on the grass.

"You're probably right. But let's go," she said.

She ran into the woods behind us, with me right behind. It became dark as the moon could no longer reach us. Victoria slowly outran me. She didn't have any trouble seeing in the dark at all. She weaved her way in and out of the trees and bushes without missing a beat.

Then suddenly, I didn't have a problem seeing either.

The darkness faded away. It was replaced be a dull gray, like it was dusk instead of the middle of the night. I could see everything too.

My first experience with night vision.

That still didn't stop Victoria from creating distance between us.

"Hey! Slow down!"

"I already *am* running slow."

I heard a whoosh right by my ear. A crossbow bolt lodged into a tree as I passed it. It missed me only by a few inches.

I risked a look behind us. We were being chased. At least five people. All were carrying a crossbow or a damn bow and arrow.

I vanished. Instead of running around trees and bushes, I started running through them. I didn't get tired.

I could see the trees clearing up ahead. What I didn't see was Victoria standing still where the ground stopped on the edge of a drop that was about five hundred feet to the raging river below.

I saw her at the last second. I panicked and reappeared, hoping she could slow me down. She turned in time to see me on top of her. We collided, and over the edge we went.

I felt a quick, sharp pain in my back.

I was disoriented as hell, but saw her hand flash by my face, and I reached out and grabbed it. I kept her from falling. My arm felt like it pulled from the socket. Somehow, I was still up on the ledge. Victoria grabbed my arm tightly and looked up.

The river slowly started to get larger.

"Do those work?" she asked.

"What?"

She pointed at something to my left and right. I followed her finger, and my jaw dropped.

We weren't on the ledge. We were both falling toward the river. Or rather, *floating*.

Sticking out of the middle of my back, and acting like a parachute to slow our fall, was a set of huge wings.

I could feel them, somehow attached to the muscles in my body. I could *sense* them, just like you can close your eyes and know your arms are there. They shook a little as they glided along the night sky. I was so stunned looking at them I didn't catch what Victoria was saying.

"Alex! Are you listening?"

"Huh? What?"

"Can you move those things? Control them?"

"I...don't know."

She sighed and looked down. She gripped my arm tighter. "Well, I hope you can swim then."

I could hear the water rushing over the rocks as we drew closer. Victoria hit the water first. I was right behind her and was surprised at how cold it was. Luckily we didn't have to swim. The river was only about four feet deep. She made it to the river bank easily, but I was having a tough time. The newly discovered wings sticking out of my back made everything harder than it should.

"Uh, a little help?" I called as I got closer.

Victoria reached out and easily yanked me out of the water with one pull. We both collapsed on the ground. I had no idea what my wings were doing, but I could feel them moving behind me.

"Hey, you want to keep those things to herself?" Victoria said. Apparently I was bothering her.

"Are we safe here?" I stood up and leaned against a tree.

"Unless those fuckers can fly, yeah, we're alright. It'll take a while for them to get down here."

She started checking herself for other injuries. I figured I should do the same. Besides my ruined clothes, I was fine. Victoria had blood all over her, including her arrow wound. But it didn't look like it was bleeding.

"Aw, dammit," she said.

"What? What's wrong?"

She held up something for me to see. My night vision was gone. I had to squint to see what it was.

"The iPhone," she said. "Cost me six hundred bucks. It plays music, email, Internet, phone. I love this little thing. Now it's broke."

She threw it to the ground. I shook my head. We were almost killed, and she was worried about an iPhone.

"I'm, uh, very sorry about your iPhone."

"You should be. This is all your fault."

"*My* fault?"

"Yeah. Why'd you follow me in that alley, anyway? Or you want me to believe you have a damn pair of bat wings, and don't know how to use them?"

I looked at my wings. Very strange thing to say. *My* wings. She was right. There weren't any feathers, like a bird's. They look a lot like a bat's.

"Hey, would you get off my ass? You got shot with an arrow, and I pulled it out of you."

She was quiet, then nodded. "Yeah, you're right. Sorry about that. I'm just a little pissed. Look, let's get moving. We at least gotta get out of here."

"Where exactly are we going? Where the hell are we?"

"Don't really know. Depends on how long we were out, we could be anywhere. But I smell a road, this way."

She started walking into the woods. I followed her.

"You can smell roads?"

"Yup. Got a good nose. It really kicks in when the blood is nearby, which I need really bad right about now."

I didn't ask any questions, at least not yet. I was afraid of the answers.

I kept getting my wings hung up on trees and bushes. It annoyed the hell out of me. I kept having to walk sideways. I couldn't control the huge things at all, and they were sticking straight out, making me at least ten feet wide.

"What's the plan?" I asked. "Go to the police?"

She laughed sarcastically. "Yeah, right. And tell them what?"

"Well, what do we do?"

"*We* don't do anything. This isn't your problem. You were in the wrong place at the wrong time. But they'll leave you alone. I'm the one they want."

"Who are they? And who are you?"

"I know you got a thousand questions right now. And I'll be more than happy to fill in the blanks, *after* I get home, get a nice shower, and a good drink."

I looked her up and down. We were both soaking wet, but I was in far worse shape than she was. At least she *had* clothes. The only thing I was wearing was a half burnt pair of jeans and waterlogged shoes. Still, she had a point. No use playing trivia pursuit while we walked through the woods.

And what a walk it was. We must have walked two miles before we finally got somewhere. She had a hell of a nose. I could see a car break through the trees up ahead, then another.

We were at a highway. I didn't recognize it, so I had no idea where we were. Victoria stopped just before the trees ended and turned to face me.

"You might want to put those things away," she said, pointing at my wings.

"I don't know how."

"Alright, look. Close your eyes." I did. "Now, I want you to picture yourself standing with a giant set of wings hanging out of your back."

"That shouldn't be too hard."

"Okay, now, I want you to picture them disappearing. They go away, and you're back to normal. Or, at least, whatever you call normal."

I tried to do as she said, but I could still feel them. My right one even brushed against a tree, and I could feel it all the way through the wing into my back. Very strange sensation. Then there was that pain in my back again.

"Good job."

I opened my eyes. "It worked?"

"Yeah. Looked pretty weird too."

Nice. A woman who survived an arrow in the chest was calling me weird.

"Okay, let's go."

I followed her up the embankment to the highway. I was only along for the ride. I had no idea what was going on, but Victoria had a natural leadership vibe to her.

I don't know what time it was, but it must have been the wee hours of the morning. There weren't many cars on the road.

"How do I look?" she asked as we stepped over the railing on the shoulder.

"Like a train wreck."

"Well, I know that. But do I still look sexy enough to flag someone down?"

"Are you joking?"

She wasn't. She waved at the few cars that passed by. It only took the third one to pull over and back up to us. Inside was an older man in a suit. Late work night? Crazy party? Who knows. But he rolled down the passenger's side window.

"Well, hello there," he said with a smile.

"Hi," Victoria said. She went through that change that I'd seen before. A minute ago she was forceful and direct. Now her voice oozed with sexiness. "My friend and I had a little accident."

He looked her up and down. Whether he was looking at her ruined clothes covered in blood, or her nice body, again I don't know.

"Yeah, I can see that. You need a lift?"

"Nah. If I could just borrow your cell phone?"

"Certainly."

He handed it over. She dialed a quick number, and looked at me. "You have money to pay for a cab?"

"Yeah, why?"

"My purse is locked in my car back at the club."

The club. Oh man. As far as the gang knew, I just vanished, chasing after Victoria. They were either worried sick, or furious at me. Especially Cindy and Alicia.

I glanced at the phone as Victoria handed it back. It was almost four in the morning. There was no sense in calling. They were already in bed. They'd understand, once I explained everything to them.

The driver offered one more ride to Victoria. She politely refused, and he took off. Victoria sat on the railing.

"We wait for a cab here?"

"Yup. I told him right by the sign on the beltway leading to the interstate."

"Okay. This is definitely new."

"Tell me about it."

I sat next to her. We were both quiet, lost in our own thoughts. I wasn't thinking much actually. I was still absorbing the fact that I was fireproof and could grow a set of wings.

It took twenty minutes for the cab to get there. He insisted on taking us to the hospital, but Victoria refused, and gave him an address on the outer limits of the city. It took another forty-five minutes to drive there. Quite a high cab fare.

CHAPTER 20

I sat in the cab in silence. Victoria did the same thing. Near the end of the ride I noticed she was getting a little jittery, looking out the window and shifting in her seat. We ended up in a nice neighborhood, but I was even more amazed at the house we stopped in front of.

House is the wrong word. More like mansion. A huge wall surrounded the place, with an electronic gate to keep people out. Even the cab driver gave Victoria a doubtful look as we climbed out of the cab.

"You're sure this is your place, lady?"

"Last time I checked."

I paid the man and he drove off. I stood there stunned while Victoria punched a few buttons on a keypad next to the gate, which slowly opened. She turned around to look at me.

"You coming?"

I followed her up the long sidewalk, taking everything in. Huge lawn. It must have taken an army to keep it neat. The mansion was two floors and a lot of windows, and bars over every single one. Next to the sidewalk was a driveway that led to a garage attached to the mansion. The whole place was simply impressive.

She fumbled with her keys a moment before throwing open the front door. I followed her into a huge hallway, and it was a strange contrast from the outside.

There was absolutely nothing. Nothing on the walls. No pictures or decorations. As we passed the huge stairs leading upstairs and a few other rooms, I stole peeks in them. They were bare too. It wasn't dirty or dusty, just empty. Very strange.

We stopped at a large door near the end of the hallway. It had a keypad similar to the one at the front gate. She punched a few numbers and pulled it open. She led me down a set of stairs into the basement.

Again, I was amazed.

The basement was probably the size of most people's houses. I have no idea of the square footage, but it was huge. It was like a studio. There was a kitchen along one wall, a living area in the corner, complete with awesome home theater system. Her bedroom was in plain view for everyone to see, as well as a pool table, and a heavy duty computer system. The only room I could see was in the far corner, and I could only guess that was a bathroom. There wasn't a single window. It was obvious she lived completely out of her basement.

She grabbed a phone from near the couch and dialed a number.

"Hey, Jim. It's me. Listen, I need a favor. It's a long story, but my car, and also a blue Chevy truck, are in the parking lot of Lumbermill's. Could you tow them to my house for me? The code's still the same. Thanks a lot."

She hung up. I noticed that she was familiar with my truck. I didn't ask any questions.

She looked at me and took a deep breath, slumping her shoulders. We were both exhausted.

"What a night, huh?" she said. Then in one quick motion she grabbed her shirt and pulled it off. I saw a glimpse of a white sports bra and a nice chest before I turned away. I heard more clothes coming off. "What's the matter, Alex? Haven't you seen a naked woman before?"

"Every now and then. But I usually have to turn on the charm first."

"Well, when you get to be as old as me, you stop caring about modesty."

As old as me. She only looked a few years older than me. I wouldn't even guess thirty years old.

She passed me, holding her wet clothes. It took a lot of effort to not look at her nude body as she headed toward the bathroom. I was impressed with myself. I knew if it were Cindy, I don't think I would have been able to pull it off.

"I'm gonna take a quick shower," she announced. "Make yourself at home."

She vanished into the bathroom. I heard the shower turn on.

Make myself at home. I was standing in the middle of a stranger's huge well-furnished basement, wearing nothing but wet, burnt clothes, and I was supposed to make myself at home.

I studied her place while she showered. No pictures of anyone. A large DVD collection. Instead of any closets, she had a few dressers and a couple of racks holding her clothes.

The shower turned off. She came out wearing nothing but a towel, which wasn't that long. Her wet red hair hung just behind her shoulders. Very sexy woman. I have no doubt she had no trouble getting men to notice her in the clubs she went to. Or dragging them into the back alleys.

"It's all yours," she said. "Just leave those nasty clothes in the bathroom. I'll dig up something for you."

I said nothing. I was hesitant to take a shower, but I knew I could definitely use one. I didn't exactly trust Victoria, but I didn't think she'd hurt me. It wasn't like she could anyway.

The shower did feel good. I made it quick, just enough to get the drops of blood off me and relax a little. When I got out I saw the bathroom door was open with a pair of shorts and a tank-top folded on the carpet. I grabbed them quickly and put them on.

Victoria was dressed, wearing a pair of jeans and a baggy white shirt. She was lying on the couch with her feet up. I sat in the chair opposite her and leaned on my knees. I wasn't comfortable enough to lean back.

"Sorry, no underwear," she said with a smile. "Don't get a lot of male company." She looked me up and down, not even bothering to hide it. The word *predator* came to mind. "You can fill out a shirt though, can't you."

I could say the same for her. "Thanks for the clothes."

"Sure. So, Alex," she said. She sat up and swung her legs into a sitting position, almost rivaling some of Cindy's sexy moves. "You're probably lost right now, aren't you?"

I nodded. "I don't even know where to begin."

"Well, let's start with you. You're not fully human. I sensed that when I first laid eyes on you. But you got a normal heartbeat. So what gives?"

I took a deep breath. "It's a long story. But somehow, I've got demonic power. And more and more keep coming out all the time."

She nodded. "Ah. Was this on purpose? I mean, did you do this yourself?"

I scoffed. "Yeah, right. My *parents* did this. But it backfired on them."

Victoria laughed. "Wow. I've seen all kinds of crazy shit. This century has been the worst, with all this technology popping up. Some weird experiments going on out there. That's what I thought you were. Some kind of experiment."

"And what exactly are you?"

"Oh come on. I'm sure you figured it out by now. I'm a vampire."

I knew that. The clues were all there. Sucking blood with large fangs in the back of an alley. An arrow through the heart. People using crossbows as weapons. But even though we were saved from a violent fall into the river by a pair of wings that shot out of my back, I convinced myself that there was no way vampires could exist.

"A vampire," I said.

"Yup. If you really have demonic powers, then you know all about the demon world, the spirit world, blah blah. Well, *our own* world has some pretty freaky shit in it too. Vampires, werewolves, witches. It's full of the supernatural."

I was quiet for a moment, just taking it in. "Are they all like you?"

She smiled and struck a pose. "You mean gorgeous?" Wow, just a strange conversation. Who knew a vampire could be so normal and funny. She got serious. "Everyone and everything is different, Alex. No different than humans. All vampires drink blood. We need to to live. Human blood is the filet mignon. You got vampires out there who don't care how they get it, and they'll suck a person dry. Then you got others like me who only take what they need. You don't need to kill a person to get blood."

"Did you kill that guy back at the club?"

"Hell no. He never came so hard in his life."

"What?"

"When we feed, it's like sex to the person we're feeding from. They forget about what happened usually."

"Who were those people trying to kill you?"

Her face turned angry. "Vampire hunters. They don't care who I am, only *what* I am. They watched too many movies and think all vampires are trying to take over the world. Please. But yeah, I've dealt with them before. Heins is a real piece of work. He just lives to kill. He works for a guy named Bachner. They got a little army going on, all out to kill vampires. Real nice."

I shook my head. This was insane.

"You handling this okay?" she asked. "I think if you can handle having a pair of bat wings, you can handle this."

"Yeah, I'm okay. Sometimes, it's just...too much, you know?" I looked down at the fresh clothes I was wearing, remembering what happened to the old ones. "Sometimes I feel like a monster. This isn't helping."

"I can relate a little," she said. "But you're not a monster, Alex. Neither am I. Our actions make us what we are. I don't kill people. Neither do you, right?"

"No, but when we were fighting those guys back there," I trailed off. "I just felt so powerful. I almost got out of control."

She nodded. "I understand. But I think you have a good heart."

"Then why the hell did you try to squeeze me to death when you first met me?"

Her face turned red. I was surprised. "Because I was wrong. It happens. I've been through some craziness myself. Trust is a hard thing to come by. And when you sense something else that isn't human, your guard goes up."

I didn't like how she kept saying I wasn't human.

"Anyway," she continued. "Bachner, Heins, and his little puppet bastards would have torched me and left me to daylight for sure. You'll always have my thanks."

"Stakes in the heart don't do it?"

She shook her head. "Stop watching movies. If something pierces our heart, we go into a coma. Only daylight and fire can kill us."

"Yeah, me and my damn movies."

"There's something else I should apologize for." I waited for her to continue. "I've been keeping track of you for a while, after that night we met. I'm the one that found your adoption papers. I just put them in a spot your sister Alicia would find."

I absorbed that for a moment. "That means you broke into our house."

"Yeah, I did. I had to know what you were. And once I knew you were adopted, I figured you'd do the rest for me."

"Couldn't go to wonderful Blossom yourself?"

She smiled. "Traveling isn't that easy for us. A simple trip can turn fatal if that sun pops up."

I nodded. A part of me was still mad at her, but I didn't think she was some evil creature.

I leaned forward. This was all just so much to take in. I didn't see how it was all possible.

"Shit, it's the twenty-first century," I said. "How the hell have you kept this a secret? You trying to tell me the government doesn't know?"

"Oh, of course they know about vampires. They're just not going to tell the public anything about it. And I don't blame them. Now as for secrets-"

She laughed and stood up. She walked over to the computer in the corner and motioned for me to follow. She sat down and started typing away.

"This is a video on YouTube that popped up a year ago," she told me. "Just watch."

The video showed a woman lying naked on a table. The angle was high and in a corner, like a security camera. The footage was grainy, but wasn't terrible. A man appeared from the side, dressed in a white coat. It looked like an autopsy, like on TV. Sticking out of the woman's chest was a large wooden stake. The man did some prep stuff, washed his hands, put on a pair of gloves. Then he grabbed the stake and pulled it from the woman's chest. She lunged up and grabbed the man by the hair. She clamped her mouth to his neck. Blood shot and sprayed the wall. They both fell to the ground, her still on top of him.

A minute later, she stood up, and he didn't move.

She looked briefly into the camera. Her chest rose up and down as she breathed hard. She almost looked like a wild animal, her head quickly moving to the left and right. Then she ran out of sight, very quickly.

After the video played I just stared at the monitor.

"That was in France, two years ago. That was a newborn vampire, fresh off a vicious attack that turned her. It's all right there, on the Internet for the whole world to see. And you know what? No one believes it. Everyone thinks it was a scene filmed for a movie. We don't even *need* to keep secrets, Alex. No one believes the truth when it's right in front of them."

I was stumped for words. "Wow. Just...wow."

Wild thoughts ran through my head. Victoria was gorgeous. Were all vampires gorgeous? How old was she? Did she know a lot of other vampires? How many of them were there? How did she know the vampire killers, Bachner and Heins?

"You okay?" she asked. "You look a little pale. And believe me, I know all about pale."

"This is all unbelievable."

She laughed. "You know what's unbelievable? You. I've seen a lot of things. But you're one of a kind."

I frowned. Now I was a freak to humans and vampires.

"Okay, it's bedtime for me," she said. She pulled a business card out of a desk drawer. A *business* card. What the hell did a vampire do for a living? "Take this. Stop by or give me a call sometime. I don't like making friends with people. For a vampire, it doesn't make much sense. But you're different, aren't you?"

"I guess so."

"Your truck's outside. I'll open the gate for you when you're ready."

I nodded. I was very ready to go home.

"It's definitely been an interesting night," I said.

Victoria nodded and smiled. Again she quickly took her shirt off, which signaled that it was time for me to leave.

CHAPTER 21

It was about a half hour drive home. I was tired, confused, afraid of what was happening to me. I wanted to go home and sleep. A part of me knew it was a terrible idea for me to entertain the thought of becoming friends with Victoria, a fucking vampire, but another part of me knew it would happen.

As I walked up my apartment steps like a zombie, the door next to mine opened. Cindy stepped out wearing tight shorts and a tank-top. Time for her morning jog.

Morning. I was out all night.

"Jesus. What time is it?"

She looked at her watch. "Almost seven."

I shook my head. I really needed some sleep.

"So, you *do* like her. Looks like you got lucky. You and Red Hot have a good time? Where are your clothes?"

"Who?"

"Red Hot. That's what I call her."

I laughed. She got serious. "Look, Alex. I'm glad you met someone that you're in to. I really am. But next time, let us know before you disappear, okay? I walked around the club for an hour looking for you. And I was worried."

I looked into her eyes. She wasn't joking. "Cindy, I can walk through walls. What do you think would happen to me?"

"It doesn't matter. A woman still worries, you know?"

I thought about telling her right then, on the apartment steps. *Cindy, you are the one I have a thing for. We should try a real date, and see if there could be something there.* Yeah, real easy words to say. Also a very easy way to ruin an eighteen-year-old friendship.

Luckily reality settled back in. Cindy was my best friend, but she had no

165

feelings for me. I had to keep thinking that.

"Last night wasn't what you think," I told her, and left it at that. Cindy didn't need to hear about vampires and vampire hunters. "But I won't do that again. Sorry about that."

She nodded and gave me that smile. I really must have been out of it, because I almost melted.

"So, uh, you didn't get lucky last night?"

"Nope.

She almost looked relieved. Weird. "Okay, well, I got a run to get to. We're having a cookout over Grandma's house in the afternoon. You know she'll beat your ass if you aren't there."

I didn't want to go to a cookout. But I hadn't seen Grandma in months, and I missed her. She had this magic about her that she could always make everyone around her happy. Absolutely amazing woman. Cookouts at her house were always fun.

"I'll be there."

"Good. And I went easy on you. You should have seen how mad I was last night."

She passed me and left the apartment. I watched her sexy figure bounce away as she started her jog. How she could stay out late at night and jog in the morning was beyond me.

Being in my apartment calmed me a little as I lumbered past the living room and collapsed into bed. My bed never felt so good. I was asleep in minutes. Too bad it didn't last long.

*****

I had crazy nightmares. Visions of demons surrounding me. Some looked human, while others didn't. They clawed at me, begging me to let them leave the demon world. That part of the dream was interrupted by a group of vampire killers trying to kill me. Throughout the dream, I lost more and more of my humanity. My skin was on fire, and the wings on my back were out. The demons and vampire hunters fought each other, and I fought both of them, clawing and ripping at their flesh with claws instead of hands.

I woke up in a cold sweat. My pillow was soaked. I looked over at the clock to see it was only ten in the morning. Three hours sleep. Wonderful. I knew I wouldn't be getting any more for a while either.

I took a quick shower and tried to figure out what I should get in to for the next few hours. I should have probably called each of my friends and apologized for getting kidnapped at the club. But then one thing crossed my mind as I climbed out of the shower.

Wings.

I got dressed and went outside. There was a thick area of trees just behind the apartment complex that separated it from the highway. I strolled back there until I was sure I couldn't be seen at all. Then I took my shirt off. If I really did have a pair of wings inside me somehow, there was no need to ruin a shirt.

I tried Victoria's technique from last night. I closed my eyes and pictured myself, standing there normal. Then I pictured a pair of wings growing from my back.

I didn't feel anything.

I felt silly. I was in the woods behind my apartment trying to wings.

"God, you're a dumbass," I told myself.

I turned to leave.

And my left wing clipped a tree.

I gasped as I looked left and right, and there they were. I was aware of them, just like any other body part. I reached my hand straight back to feel them. There were little hairs across the skin. Like any tickled body part, they reacted. My wings folded up close to my back, which scared the hell out of me. I concentrated, and extended them back out fully. I could see the bony fingers, four of them, running through the skin.

I had wings, and I could control them.

I put a hand to my head. This was what I wanted to see if I could do. And now that I knew, I was freaked out.

I couldn't get a good idea in my head of what I looked like. I couldn't see how they were coming out of my back, but they felt about dead center. And I could do more than just extend and fold them. The fingers and skin were very flexible, and I could wrap the wings in front of me almost.

Very cool? Or utterly terrifying?

The question was answered for me after an hour of examining them, moving them around, feeling them. I decided to move them as fast as they could go. Instead of just extending outward, they beat against the air a single time.

I lifted off the ground about four feet.

I lost my breath for a second, and grabbed a tree as I landed. I folded my wings behind my back. It all hit me like a train.

I could fly.

The wings weren't only for show. They didn't just act as a parachute or glider. They worked.

I looked up through the trees to the blue sky. People were so obsessed with flight that they built machines that could do it. Every kid sometimes pretends he can fly. And everyone's had a dream or two about it.

The first time my wings took me off the ground, I knew I could fly.

It was a moment I'd never forget.

I knew as I stood there I'd be spending many nights in the woods behind my apartment, learning how to use my new wings. But not now. Baby steps first. I had a cookout to get to.

I put my shirt back on and headed to the apartment. I gently opened

Cindy's door. The bathroom light was on.

"Hey Cindy! You in here?"

"Yeah. What's up?"

"You want to head up together?"

"Of course, stupid. I told Leese we'd pick her up, but she said she was bringing a guy."

"Really? It's been a while since Alicia had an eye on any guys."

"That's what I said. So don't give her a hard time. I'll be ready to go soon."

"Alright. Come get me when you're ready."

It was thirty minutes later when I heard the door to my apartment open. I was in the kitchen finishing up the dishes. I poked my head out to say hi.

I froze.

Cindy had on a two-piece bathing suit, with a pair of flowery shorts that didn't cover much. She wore one of those white blouses that you could see through. I looked her up and down. Slim legs, tone stomach. She had a pair of sunglasses resting on top of her head. I stood there with my hands dripping water on the carpet.

"Alex? You okay?"

I felt my face turning red, and quickly went back to the kitchen. I was so frustrated. I hated feeling this way, so out of control. Every weird thing I'd found about myself, I was able to control. I had no doubt I would soon learn how to completely control my wings. But I couldn't control how I felt about Cindy, and it was pissing me off.

"Yeah, I'm good. Almost done the dishes, then I'm ready. So, you trying to give everyone a heart attack?"

I heard her laugh in the living room. "You remember Grandma has a pool, right? Take your trunks with you."

I grabbed them and looked her up and down one more time. I didn't make any effort to hide it. Strangely, she didn't seem to mind. When our eyes met I just shook my head. A sudden courage hit me.

"Cindy, how many people tell you a day how hot you are?"

She smiled and shyly looked away. So modest. "Sometimes I hear it," she said. "But it sounds different coming from you."

"Why is that?"

"Because I actually believe it when you say it."

We stood there looking at each other. There must have been a good ten seconds of eye contact before she finally looked away. My heart was beating hard. Probably should have been awkward, but it wasn't.

"You ready to go?"

"Yeah."

Grandma's street was packed full of cars. I knew most of them were probably for the cookout. It took a while to find a spot near the end of the street. We saw Alicia's car. She beat us there with her new guy.

We went straight to the backyard. The cars were a little deceiving. There were only about twenty people there. Cindy's father was leaning over the grill. Her mother and Grandma were laying in lawn chairs by the pool talking to each other. I saw Cindy's aunt and uncle near the back patio. Alicia was in the in-ground pool playing with some younger kids, but I didn't see any guy with her. I only recognized a few other people from Cindy's work.

"Alex! Cindy!" Mister Marshall called. His voice boomed over the other conversations and the music. He gave us a wave.

Grandma heard our names and looked at us. "You two get over here and give me a hug!"

She looked great. She was close to eighty, and got along very well. She was about Cindy's height, and squeezed the hell out of me.

"Man, Grandma," I said. "Go easy on the steroids."

"Steroids? This is all home grown muscle."

I laughed. Everyone got hugs. Mrs. Marshall stood up and gave out the hugs too. Alicia waved at us from the pool. Cindy started talking with her mom and Grandma while I leaned down near my sister.

"What? You didn't bring Red Hot?" she asked.

I rolled my eyes. Now Cindy had everyone using the nickname for Victoria. "Nothing happened, Alicia. And Cindy told me you were bringing a dude? Where is he so I can tell him to get out while he can?"

Alicia hesitated for a second, and that told me all I needed to know. "He had something else to do. Not really too sure." She tried to hide her tone. But I knew better. She was upset. She flashed that smile of hers. "You getting in?"

"I will later, after I eat something."

A new voice behind me. "Oh really?"

Someone grabbed my shirt and nearly threw me into the pool. He held back, though. He only wanted to give me a scare. I turned around to see Mister Marshall laughing.

"Ah I scared you there didn't I? You're lucky I'm a nice guy."

"You wouldn't do that, Mister Marshall. You're afraid of me."

He traded a look with his wife. "Alex, if I have to tell you one more time to call us Larry and Chandra, you *will* take a dive in that pool."

As the ladies talked only a few feet away, out of the corner of my eye I saw Cindy remove her shorts and shirt. Larry was saying something, but to be honest I have no idea what it was. It took the willpower of the gods to keep my eyes locked on his face. I think Cindy hesitated and looked at me before diving in the pool. I relaxed a little now that she was behind me swimming. The last thing I needed was for her father to catch me staring at her.

Grandma cut between us to get to the patio. I should have seen it coming. She *accidentally* threw her body into me, and into the pool I went. As I got my bearings under water and stood up, the first thing I heard was the laughter. Larry, Chandra, Grandma, everyone on the patio and in the pool, all eyes were on me. Grandma had a fake look of surprise on her face.

"I'm so sorry, Alex," she said. "It must have slipped."

I laughed too and pointed at her. "I'll remember that, Grandma."

Larry laughed so hard he leaned on his knees. "She got you good!"

I froze when a familiar pair of arms circled around me. I felt a warm body press against my back. A head leaned on my shoulder next to mine.

"You just got your ass whipped by my Grandma," Cindy said. "I wish I had a camera."

I was so tense. I wanted her to let go and not at the same time.

"You'd better be careful or you'll be after her."

"I'll be waiting," she said, then laughed and swam away.

I watched as she hit the other side of the pool. I kept my eyes on her even as I pulled off my wet shirt.

Then my eyes fell on Alicia.

She mouthed something without talking. I could read her lips.

Tell her.

Yeah. Easy for her to say.

It was a great time. Good food, great company. Larry filled me in on everything that was happening at the firm, including how well Cindy was doing. I filled them in on how my mother was doing. Cindy's cousins all had a good time, playing in the pool. It was the most fun I had in quite a while.

After a few hours people started to leave. I was talking with Larry while he made one last batch of burgers when I saw Alicia sitting on the edge of the pool by herself. She had her feet dipped in the water, staring at the surface. I walked over and sat next to her.

"So when are you gonna tell her how you feel?" was the first thing she said.

"Never."

"Chicken shit."

"Alicia, give me a break. She doesn't feel that way. The last thing I need is for her to find out, then not want to hang out with me anymore."

She shook her head. "You're both so stupid."

"Huh? What do you mean?"

"Nothing. Just forget it."

"Yeah, forget it. Enough about me, anyway. Where's this guy you were supposed to bring? Who is he?"

She lowered her head. "Nobody. Well, I thought he was somebody. But he called right before he was supposed to come get me and let me know how it all is."

Alicia never had a problem with guys. I'd never really seen her get too attached to anyone. And plenty of guys showered her with attention. So I wasn't sure where she was coming from.

"Are you okay? What's on your mind?"

She shrugged, a sure sign she wasn't fine. "I don't know."

I know how to deal with my sister. Just had to gently but firmly press on.

"Come on. I know something's bothering you."

She sighed. "I'm lonely. I'll be graduating this year. And I've never really had a boyfriend."

"You've dated plenty of guys."

"Yeah. Dated. But I don't really stand out. No one in school ever really looks at me for more than a week at a time."

I couldn't believe my ears. Blond hair, blue eyes, very pretty, very sweet, and she didn't stand out? Was she on drugs?

"Are you kidding me? You worry too much, sis. You can have any guy in school you want. Look, don't stress about it. Hell, I'm twenty-three, and can't find a woman."

"You've got one right there," she said, and pointed at Cindy on the patio.

"Don't point at her. Look, all I can tell you is you'll be fine. You'll find your guy. Now it might not be in high school, but you will."

She smirked. "Spoken like a true older brother."

"Hey. What would you do without me?"

"I don't know. I'm glad you're here, though."

I gave her a smile and nod before someone dove head first into the water not too far from us. Cindy stood up and slicked her hair back.

"Hey guys! Come on in! Everyone's heading inside to watch a movie. We've got the pool to ourselves."

She went under the water. Alicia smiled and looked at me. "I'm gonna head home. You know, you're eventually gonna have to tell her."

"Maybe. Not today, though."

She shook her head and stood up. Cindy broke the surface on the other side.

"Cindy, I'm outta here. Getting tired. I'll call you tomorrow."

"Aw. Okay, Leese. See ya."

Alicia disappeared around the side of the house. I made a mental note to call her tomorrow. I'd never seen her down like that before.

"Alex, get in here with me."

I dropped from the side into the water. I still wore my shorts, while my swimming trunks were ten feet away. *No sense in changing now.*

Cindy started swimming toward me. Before I could figure out what she was doing she leaped up and dunked me under. I swallowed a nice mouthful of water. I came up to hear her laughing.

"When was the last time it was just me and you in the pool?"

I had to think. "Man, eighth grade?"

"Remember Rob, my ex-boyfriend? He used to hate it that you and I swam together all the time."

"Can you blame him? I mean, look at this," I said, teasing while flexing my arms.

"I can't argue that."

I gave her a look. That caught me off guard.

I wanted to believe she found me attractive. But I was afraid to. I don't know why.

"So, what's up with you and Red Hot?" she asked. "She's not gonna freak out that we're friends, is she?"

I shook my head. "There's nothing going on, Cindy. It's a long story, but me leaving the club last night had nothing to do with gettin' it on."

"What was it then?"

I lowered my voice. "More demon stuff. I'll tell you later. I've got a question for you."

"What's that?"

"Why have you been single since college?"

She shrugged. "You know why, Alex. I don't keep anything from you."

"Yeah. I know you wanted to focus on school. But that's done now. So what's up?"

"I just can't find my guy."

"And who's that exactly?"

She paused, and gave me a bright smile. "Are you auditioning?"

I tried to search her face. Was she serious? Joking?

"What would I have to do?"

"Stand up straight."

I hesitated, then did so. The water came up to about my chest. She made her way over and looked me up and down. She circled around me, like she was evaluating me. She stood behind me and gently grabbed my shoulders. Then she jumped up and dunked me again.

"Damn. You keep falling for it," she said through fits of laughter.

"Hey! What are you kids doing out there?"

It was Grandma, shouting from the patio. I pointed at Cindy. "She started it!"

"I did not, Grandma!"

"Don't make me separate you two! I can still do it!"

"Don't worry. I'll keep her in line."

"What!"

Cindy tried to dunk me again. This time I managed to turn around and wrap my arms around her waist to stop her, creating an awkward, and nice, moment. I quickly got my revenge by dunking her.

It was nighttime when we decided to leave. Grandma, Larry, and Chandra were inside watching a movie. We gave everyone hugs goodbye.

172

"I love seeing you again," Grandma told me. "Stop by more often. And take care of my granddaughter for me."

"Please," Cindy said. "It's more like me taking care of him."

"Cindy, you're lucky to have Alex here."

She gave me a playful punch in the shoulder. "Oh I know."

"You drive home safe," Chandra said.

"We will. Thanks for having me over."

"You're family. You know that."

It was a quick drive home. As we got near our apartment doors Cindy stopped near hers.

"You want to watch a movie?" she asked.

I actually didn't. I wanted to get to the woods behind the apartment and practice with my wings. "I don't know. You haven't had enough of me for one day?"

"Who can ever get enough of you? What if I look all pretty and say please?"

"Give it a shot."

She leaned her back against the door and stretched an arm over her head, like a model pose. Then she curled a leg and rubbed it against the other.

Damn.

"Please?"

The wings could wait.

"I guess so."

She smiled and straightened up. "Great. Your apartment. I'll make popcorn."

It was a fun end to the night. We put on *Resident Evil* and munched on some snacks. Cindy curled her legs under her on the couch, my kryptonite. So I know I missed half the movie. She still wore her shorts that she had on earlier. I was half tempted to ask her to wear sweatpants, but didn't want to seem too obvious as to how much she distracted me. Not to mention, it was indeed a nice distraction.

She sat on the other end of the couch, towards the TV. So I could look at her without her knowing. As I watched her I kept wondering. What if? I knew what made her sad. I knew what made her happy. I knew when she needed a hug. I knew when I needed to give her space. Hell, with my demonic senses, I knew when she was in trouble.

Could I be a good boyfriend for her?

We both fell asleep somewhere in the middle of the movie. When I woke up, the DVD had already stopped. Cindy was leaning back on the couch. It had to be sometime after midnight.

I smiled. She was beautiful when she slept. She was beautiful all the time.

I got up, stretched, and went to the hall closet. I grabbed her favorite blanket and pillow. I scooped her up easily in my arms. I laid her out on the couch and covered her up. I stayed there for a moment, just staring at her face. I brushed a loose strand of hair from her eyes, and my finger lingered on her cheek.

"Love sucks," I said.

She moaned quietly and spoke from deep within her dream. "Yeah. Tell me about it."

I laughed and turned the lamp off above her. Darkness filled the room, but only for a moment for me, as my night vision took over. Strange, as I hadn't practiced using it. I could already control it easily. I hoped it was like that with my wings.

I fell into bed. I thought I'd sleep soundly, since I was still going off of a few hours sleep. I was wrong this time, too.

A bathroom trip woke me up. I didn't have any hand towels, so I had to use paper towels from the kitchen.

I walked down the hall and was ready to turn by the fridge when I stopped.

Cindy and I weren't alone.

I turned the light on next to the weight-bench to see someone standing over Cindy. I had to rub my eyes for a second, but recognized who it was.

"Grandma?"

She looked up at me. I was confused. She was wearing a pink nightgown, and ran a hand through Cindy's hair. She looked surprised to see me, when I was the one who should have been surprised. I didn't hear her knock on the door or anything. And why did she drive over in a pink nightgown?

"What's going on?" I asked her. "Everything okay?"

"Alex? You can see me?"

Right then, I knew what was going on. I felt a pain in my chest.

"Aww, Grandma. No."

She smiled and nodded her head. "I'm afraid so, dear. You know, I always knew there was something special about you."

I shook my head. "This can't be. I mean, how? Just a few hours ago you were shoving me into a pool."

"It's just my time, I guess. Believe me, it's strange to wake up in the middle of the night, stand up, and look down at yourself."

She died peacefully in her sleep. I know you can't ask for much more than that. But that didn't ease the pain.

I didn't say anything. I gripped the back of the couch and hunched over. I felt a few tears stream down my face.

"Oh, Alex, honey, don't be sad." She walked through the couch and put a hand on my shoulder. She was surprised that she could actually do so. "I'm eighty years old, and I knew this was coming. I'm so glad you and Cindy turned out like you did. Tell her I love her, and you take good care of her. I know she loves you."

"I will, Grandma."

"I have to visit a few more people. So give me a hug."

I hugged her, and she was solid to me. I could feel her breathing. Then my arms went through her, and she was gone.

I was numb. I collapsed in the chair, leaned on my knees, and cried quietly.

"Alex?"

Cindy was looking at me. She rubbed her eyes and sat up. When she saw my face I could see her concern.

"What's wrong?"

I could barely talk. "Grandma."

"What about her?"

That was all I could say. But that's all I needed to. I could see the sadness touch Cindy's face.

"Is she-?"

I nodded.

It hit Cindy much worse than me. She cried hard. I went over to her and we held each other and cried for I don't know how long.

CHAPTER 22

It was a crazy two weeks after Grandma died. I half expected to see her at her own funeral, but she wasn't there. We tried to be happy and talk about the good times, but everyone cried. I admit, when I passed by pictures of her in my apartment, I'd tear up. Cindy took it real hard. I didn't see her much for a while. She worked late, my guess was on purpose. I'd hear her come home, but left her alone. She knew I would be there for her in a second if she needed me.

I spent those two weeks learning how to fly.

As soon as I got home from work I went right to the woods. It didn't take long at all to get used to my wings. I could move them however I wanted. They were amazing. I'm guessing each one was six feet long. They absolutely dwarfed me. Yet when I folded them in, you couldn't tell at all. They let me do some pretty wild things. I could climb a tree in seconds. I gripped the sides with my wings, and climbed up like a squirrel. I could walk across branches, using the wings to help me keep balance. And leaping from tree to tree, using them to either glide or actually flap them to take a short flight, was nothing short of breathtaking.

Extended, actual flight, though, was something I hadn't tried yet.

I'd come home everyday, leap from tree to tree like an ape, but I never went above the treetops. Every day I'd walk in the woods and look up to the sky, telling myself that "Today is the day". But I never tried it. I'd just do my normal thing, then go home and study bats and birds on the Internet. Hell, I studied how birds and bats flew so much I shouldn't have a single problem when I finally took to the sky.

I was simply afraid.

I was afraid that once I flew through the air, I was leaving a part of myself behind on the ground. I know it sounds dumb. But once I soared through the air, I really wouldn't be human anymore. Aunt Beth and Victoria made it quite clear that I wasn't human at all anyway. But still, I *felt* human, even with all the weird things I could do. But that feeling would be gone once my wings truly carried me into the air.

I had ended another tree climbing and hopping session in the woods. I was in the apartment for maybe ten minutes, making some iced tea in the kitchen, when I heard the front door open.

"Alex? You in here?"

Cindy. I hadn't seen her since Grandma's funeral. She was still in her work dress, looking quite nice.

"Hey, Cindy," I said. "Where you been? How's it going?"

She closed the door behind her. "Just working."

That was all she said. I only guessed she was still down about her Grandma.

"Hungry?" I turned to the fridge. "I can throw something together."

"Nah, thanks. Actually, I need your help."

"With what?"

"I got a date tonight."

It's a good thing my back was to her. I can only imagine the look on my face.

"Oh really? Well, that's good, right? What do you need from me?"

"Just some advice. I haven't done this in two years. What should I wear? How should I act? God, I feel so stupid."

The woman I was in love with had a date. I took a deep breath and buried everything deep down. My chest ached, but I shoved that aside. It was time to be her best friend, not the guy secretly wanting more.

I closed the fridge and turned around with the biggest smile on my face.

"Okay, the love doctor is in."

She smirked. "Please. I'm only asking you cause I'm desperate and nervous."

"Not a problem. Where is the date?"

"We're supposed to meet at Applebee's. Then we're hitting a movie."

I frowned. "Dinner and a movie? Probably a little early for that, but whatever. Dinner first?"

"Yeah."

"Bad idea. I know you. Your nerves will get shot and you'll hit the bathroom halfway through the movie. Remember Alicia's sixteenth birthday party?"

She was embarrassed at the memory. About eight of us went to a movie. She was dating a guy at the time. She got so sick she spent most of the movie in the bathroom.

"Okay. Movie first. How should I dress?"

"Hell, dinner and a movie, wear a nightgown for all I care." I looked her up and down. "Cover that chest of yours up for the night. Wear shorts instead. If you catch him looking at your legs, you'll know he thinks you're hot."

She smiled. "I've caught *you* looking at my legs."

I was embarrassed, but nodded. "And I think you're hot. See how the trap works? And if you guys come back here-"

"Hey. We're not coming back here on a first date."

"Yeah, well. If you do, sit on the couch and curl your legs. That is the sexiest thing in the world."

"Are you serious?"

"Yeah."

She was surprised. "Wow. I only do that cause I hate my feet on the floor."

"Well, whatever the reason. Do that."

She laughed. "I'll remember that. I'm gonna take a shower. Wish me luck."

I shook my head. "Don't need luck."

She turned to leave. Then she turned back around and approached me. She surprised me with a hug.

"I've missed you. Thanks. Thanks for being my best friend."

There was that magic word again. Friend.

"Same to you."

She gave me a final wave and left the apartment.

My knees actually felt weak. I leaned against the wall. I never thought I had a chance with Cindy, so you'd think the pain wouldn't be that bad. I was wrong.

I thought of Alicia, constantly telling me to go for it. All I had to do was tell her how I felt. What's the worst that could happen?

I could lose her as a friend forever.

But was the risk worth the reward?

I went to the bathroom to splash my face with water. I leaned on the sink and tried to calm down. My head was spinning with the same basic question. *Should I tell her?*

I hadn't yet made a decision when I looked at my reflection in the mirror.

I almost gasped.

My eyes were blood red, nearly like Victoria's when I saw her snap a few weeks ago. My face was stone white with the exception of my forehead, which was a brownish color. At first I thought I was imagining it. I closed my eyes for a second. I still looked the same when I opened them.

I looked like a monster. Actually, more like a demon, like one I saw in the demon world.

That's what Cindy's old boyfriend saw in high school. That's what those two men who killed George McEllen saw when they looked at me. They saw a monster.

I *am* a monster.

I closed my eyes hard and tried my best to will my demon features to go away. They did, and I was thankful. But the damage had been done. The truth set in. There was no way in hell Cindy could ever go for me. Hell, *no one* could go for me.

I am not human.

I felt the sadness creeping over me. I was a half demon freak that was changing all the time. Cindy deserved much better.

I left the apartment and went right back to the woods. I was an emotional wreck. I did all kinds of crazy things. I jumped from the top of trees and thrust out my wings right before I hit the ground, gliding just inches above the dirt. I weaved my way in and out of trees at high speed, even pushing off them with my feet to go faster. I had all sorts of air tricks mastered. I could fly whenever I wanted to.

After a good while of practicing, and trying to get Cindy out of my mind, I looked to the sky once again.

"This is the night," I said out loud to myself. "What have I got to lose now?"

Before I could convince myself to actually fly, I noticed Cindy's car parking in front of the apartment through the trees. Strange. I knew I was in the woods a while, but not nearly long enough for dinner and a movie.

I went back to the apartment and opened her door just a crack.

"Yo Cindy? You decent in here?"

Through the crack in the door I saw a purse hit the couch. I opened the door all the way to see Cindy taking her sandals off. She didn't look happy. She looked at me as I stepped in.

"Everything okay?"

"Oh, yeah. Everything's perfect."

She stepped out from behind the couch and stormed into the kitchen. She took my advice. She wore a baggy tee-shirt and a pair of shorts that looked great. Very casual, but Cindy is so hot, anything looks good on her. But I got the hint the date didn't go well.

"What happened? Fill me in. You guys hit dinner and a movie?"

"We saw a movie. That's it."

"He was a jerk?"

She came out of the kitchen with a soda. "Nope. He was fine. A nice, good looking guy. And I caught him staring at my legs."

I smiled, just because I was right. "Okay. He was in to you then. So what happened?"

"Look, Alex, I don't want to talk about this right now. I just want to be left alone, alright?"

There was danger in her voice. I hadn't seen her this angry in a while. I realized as she looked at me that *I* was the one she was angry at.

"You pissed at *me*?" I asked.

She didn't answer, which meant yes. "Can we talk about this later? I'm not in the mood right now."

"Cindy, I'm really sorry if I messed up your date somehow."

She finished her soda and turned to toss it in the trashcan. I heard her mumble under her breath. "You ruin *every* fuckin' date."

"What the hell is going on?"

She raised her voice. "I don't want to talk about it! That's the third time! Am I speaking Chinese here?"

Cindy and her temper. I'd experienced it a few times before, and I'd seen her unleash it on others. We had fights before. Sometimes they were my fault, sometimes hers. But honestly, this time, I had no idea why she was mad at me.

I shrugged. "Cool."

I left without looking back. I actually paced in my apartment for a while. I kept trying to think about what I could have done. As much as I wanted Cindy, I wouldn't sabotage a date of hers on purpose. Hell, she said he was nice and my leg trick worked. What the hell was she mad at me for?

I stopped thinking about it after a while. All I had to do was leave Cindy alone and she'd eventually calm down enough to tell me what was bothering her.

But I was restless. I didn't want to sit in my apartment after Cindy gave me a hard time.

I would have called Alicia, but I knew she was out with her friends, which I was thankful for. I wanted her to get her mind off her recent guy problems, or what she thought were guy problems.

I saw Victoria's business card, still sitting on my coffee table.

I got in my truck and drove toward the city. I couldn't believe I was driving to her mansion. I just wanted to do two things. Get out of the apartment and talk to someone.

I didn't think she'd be home. I expected to get to her place, see she wasn't there, then drive back home. So I was surprised when I rang the buzzer at the front gate and heard her voice after a few seconds.

"Alex? Is that you out there?"

"Yeah." Suddenly, I felt foolish. I didn't call or anything. Kind of rude, actually. "I'm sorry. I shouldn't just drop by."

"Hey, no problem. Hell, I'm surprised the buzzer works. Hold on one sec."

She met me at the front door with a smile. Her clothes surprised me. She wore a pair of tight sweatpants and a sweater. Her red hair was pulled in a ponytail. She looked great, but hardly like a seductive vampire.

"This is a surprise. Come on in."

I followed her through the empty first floor.

"How come there's nothing up here?" I asked.

"Too many windows. Can't let the sunlight in. So I'm always downstairs."

I felt a little awkward as we walked down her basement stairs. It dawned on me I didn't really know what to call her.

"Should I call you Vickie? Do you go by Victoria?"

She laughed. "Call me Victoria, please. Vickie just sounds, blah."

I laughed too. "Okay."

The TV was on in the far corner. Again, I thought that was strange. I knew Victoria would say I watched too many movies. I guessed vampires didn't watch TV. They spent all their time seducing people for blood and roaming the night. But here was Victoria, watching TV.

"You want something to drink?"

She went to a tiny fridge and pulled out a bottled water. I looked at it, then at her. She nearly read my mind and rolled her eyes.

"There's no blood in this fridge," she said. "Man, I'm not that weird. Here."

She sat on the couch. I sat in the chair across from her, the same positions when I was first here.

"So what brings you here?" she asked. "I *never* have company, so this is nice."

I looked down for a second, still feeling a little foolish for even coming to Victoria's house. "I just needed a friend to talk to. We *are* friends, right?"

"Sure. I have to say I've never had a man with demon blood for a friend before. What's up?"

"Sadly, woman problems."

She nodded and smiled. "And I thought we were gonna talk about something supernatural. Again, I like this. I guess we're talking about Cindy?"

I frowned. "That obvious?"

"Yup. I saw it about ten seconds after I first saw you two. Little clues. Body language, facial expressions."

"Well, how does she feel about me?"

"I don't know."

I rolled my eyes. I took that as a polite way of saying "not the same as you".

"Well, I'm not really sure, Alex. I spent most of my time studying you. She thinks you're attractive, I can tell you that. Shit, *I* think you're attractive. If you weren't so hung up on her you'd be in that bed right behind us."

I glanced at the king-sized bed in the middle of the basement. "Can vampires have sex?"

"Would you like to find out?"

I turned red. "Uh, no thanks. But don't take that the wrong way. You're gorgeous."

She laughed. "You're definitely a rare one. I wonder if it's the demon in you."

I was starting to hate that word.

"I was around back when black people were only three-fifths of a person," she said. "It's nice to see people like you not caring about race."

"Well, too bad it's only one way. She just sees me as a friend."

"She told you this?"

"Nope. And I'm not gonna ask, either."

"Why not?"

I laughed a little. "Victoria, even if she did have feelings for me, do you think she could really date this?"

I stood up and lifted my shirt. My wings grew from my back. I extended them fully, nearly touching her basement wall, then folded them up behind me. It was amazing how huge they were. But when I folded them, they took up almost no room. After giving her a good look I willed them to disappear, and they shrank once again into my back.

She smirked. "Hey, I'd date a guy with wings. That would make for some fun sex."

I was finally starting to feel at ease around her. "What a thought."

"I'm just saying. I've fallen in love with vampires *and* humans. No reason why it's gotta be different for you. Alex, it took me a *long* time to get used to being a vampire. I'm not trying to belittle what you got going on, but for us, we go from being human to suddenly being very much in danger from the sun. We stop eating and drinking *everything*, and now it's blood only. Having to reverse your sleep, stay inside like a prisoner for twelve hours a day, and watching everyone you care about age while you don't. Hell, I thought I'd lose my mind for sixty years or so. So if you're the product of some supernatural accident, and the only problem you got is woman problems, I'd say you're doing okay."

I absorbed what she said for a moment and smiled. "Thanks, Victoria. You're right. Thanks for listening to me bitch."

"Anytime. Least I can do for pulling an arrow out of my chest. Anyway, the answer to your problem is simple. Just tell her what's up."

"You sound like my sister."

"Alicia. Smart girl."

I laughed. I *did* feel better, although I had no plans of listening to her or Alicia's advice.

We talked and watched a little TV for about a half hour. It was relaxing, and I admit it helped take my mind off Cindy. I never would have thought in a million years I would have a vampire for a friend.

It was around eleven when her cell phone on the end table rang. She picked it up and excused herself. I watched TV alone for about five minutes when she hung up and put a hand on my shoulder.

"You up for a little ride?" she asked me.

"Where to?"

"The city. Just got a call from my cop buddy, William. He needs a little help."

I stood up. "You help the cops?"

She nodded and I followed her across the basement. "Every now and then. I actually own a few businesses across the states. But if William has something going on that looks like it might be supernatural, I'll lend a hand. And of course he pays me."

"I'm almost afraid to ask, but like what?"

"Well, if a vampire or werewolf goes a little crazy and starts killing people."

"We have werewolves in Maryland?"

"Yup."

What a thought.

CHAPTER 23

We rode her car into the city. Looked like a brand new Porsche, with a folded down soft-top. I knew there wouldn't be anything I could contribute to help the police. It didn't take me long to figure out where we were going. Traffic started to back up, and it wasn't because of the normal reasons. We could see a crowd on the sidewalk not too far ahead, with a cop in the middle of the road directing traffic.

Victoria parked her car and I walked next to her.

"William didn't give me much on the phone, but there might be a body up ahead. You okay with that?"

I flashed back to my quick trip to the demon world. I thought I could handle a single body.

We pushed our way through the crowd until we got to a yellow police tape barrier. A cop was also there. He gave Victoria a quick look up and down, then looked back at the crowd. About twenty yards away we could see a black sheet in the middle of the street. Cops were everywhere and seemed to be gathering evidence. Victoria searched the scene until she found what she was looking for. Her eyes locked on a guy probably in his mid thirties talking to a uniformed cop. She waved at him. William Sloane.

"William! Over here!"

He looked over and approached us. He looked like he'd seen a lot of bad things in his life. He walked slowly, as if he couldn't be bothered to walk fast. He was a big guy, but his shoulders were slumped as if he were tired. Slightly graying hair, steel blue eyes. He tried to smirk as he drew closer, but it didn't quite come off right.

"Victoria. Thanks for coming."

"No problem, William."

He winced. "Fuckin' call me Bill. I hate William."

She ignored him. "What do we got here?"

"Come see for yourself."

He held the police tape up for her. I followed, but Bill put a hand on my chest.

"Relax," Victoria said. "He's with me."

"Ah. Is he a-?" He didn't finish the sentence.

"No, he's not."

Bill gave us both some kind of pass, I guess to identify us to other cops. The three of us approached the black sheet. I felt my heart beat a little harder with each step. But that was it. If it had been a year ago I might have thrown up. It's scary that the sight of my first dead body didn't affect me that much.

Bill leaned down and pulled the sheet back. Young guy, in his twenties, lying there dead on his back. He stared up with a blank expression and his eyes wide open. His skin was pale white. He looked normal enough. He wore a tee-shirt and bluejeans.

Although it was hard not to notice the bite marks on his neck.

Victoria saw them too, and made a sound of disgust.

"Shit," she said. She knelt down to study closer. Then she actually put her nose to the man's neck and started sniffing.

"Tell me it's not what I think it is," Bill said.

"Oh, it's what you think."

"Damn," he said. "When the hell does your kind start attacking in the middle of the street? We haven't got a single witness yet. This whole thing just bugs the shit out of me."

"Has the body been touched?"

"Nope. What you see is what you get here."

Victoria started sniffing up and down the body like a bloodhound. It didn't take a genius to see that obviously vampires had strong noses. Her face stopped just above the man's ankle.

She pulled his pants leg up to reveal another set of bite marks.

"What the hell?" she said.

Bill looked at me with confusion. I was worse off than he was. I had no clue of what was going on.

"Two vampires?" Bill said.

"Yeah."

He shrugged. "And that's weird?"

"Very weird. This has all the signs of a newborn. But that doesn't make any sense."

I looked at her. "Newborn?"

"Newborn vampire. I'll explain later."

She was quiet for a moment, continuing to study the area. Another cop came over and pulled Bill to the side, so Victoria and I stood there over the dead body.

I didn't think I had anything to offer Victoria, but as I stood there something ate at me. Something was bothering me, and I couldn't figure out what it was. Some detail that I couldn't quite see, but I knew was there.

"People just don't get bit and turn into vampires," Victoria said, leaning close to my ear. "There's a lot of different factors. Blood type, heredity. So believe it or not, vampires are rare."

I nodded. "So two newborns are *extra* rare?"

"You catch on fast. Exactly. Something isn't right."

"Okay. How do you know newborns did this?"

"Just a feeling. A seasoned vampire, like yours truly, will never be seen, and would never leave a body. This strikes me as a newborn, crazy and out of control for blood. And two sets of bites, well, you can add."

"Did *you* kill anyone when you were first turned?"

She gave me a look. She may have said we were friends, but it was obvious she didn't appreciate the question. "No, I didn't."

I left it at that.

She searched the street. "Okay, so two newborns wake up somewhere around here. They're confused and thirsty. They attack someone in the middle of the street and kill him. Their senses kick in after that, their humanity. They need to run. Their instincts tell them somewhere dark and safe." Her eyes fell on something and she smiled. "Like right there."

She pointed over the crowd to a corner butcher shop on the other side of the street. The place was closed, like all the other small shops nearby.

"A butcher shop?" I said.

"Yup. Shit, I can smell the blood all the way over here." She gestured to Bill. "William! We'll be in touch. I'll call you tomorrow."

"You better, *Vickie*."

She talked to me as we pushed through the crowd and crossed the street.

"William is a good man. I met him when he was a rookie. He's actually saved my life a few times. Typical stupid cop. Married to the job. I've tried to get him over the house a few times just to watch a movie, but he won't."

I shook my head. "I still have trouble seeing you sitting on the couch watching TV."

"I only go out to feed. When I first saw you I thought you were another vampire, moving in on my territory. It was only when I heard your heartbeat that I knew you weren't."

"I still don't know what I am."

"And you probably never will. Get used to that, Alex. Accept that, and live your life. Don't throw years away searching for an answer that might not be there."

I nodded behind her, and realized something. Victoria was suddenly my mentor. Also, there was something personal in her words. I wondered if she had searched for an answer she couldn't find.

Without another word we stopped in front of the butcher shop. Victoria studied it for a moment and stared into the darkened storefront. She walked around the side and circled toward the rear of the place. I was a step behind her. The back door was open.

She gave me a smirk and nodded. "Jackpot." She lifted her head and sniffed around the door.

"Smell anything?" I asked.

"Just a lot of meat and blood. I'm not gonna be able to pinpoint anything in here. So be careful."

"It's a little dark."

"That's okay. I can see in the dark."

I felt foolish. So could I, and I had forgotten.

As soon as we stepped inside the first thing I noticed was the smell. It was horrible. I wasn't sure if a butcher's shop normally smelled like that or not. Victoria didn't seem bothered by it at all, which was amazing considering her nose was stronger than mine. I gagged a few times, and Victoria gave me a strong look and put a finger to her lips.

It was pitch black, but I willed the darkness to vanish, and the light gray swirled in. Over a few seconds objects and shapes came into focus. A table with cleavers hanging from the side. Large freezers. A door that led into an office. A set of double doors that led to the front of the store.

Victoria continued to sniff the air.

"Smell anything yet?" I whispered.

She shook her head.

She stared at the office door for a second, then walked past it to the double doors. She pushed them open slowly and searched the room before moving another inch.

I saw movement in the corner, near the locked front door.

Victoria saw it too, as her head locked in that direction.

I squinted as hard as I could. Even though I could see better, I couldn't see completely. It was just dark enough near the front of the store that I couldn't see anything.

But I could hear it.

It sounded like an animal, low to the ground, tearing and gnawing at something. The fact that I could hear it and not see it sent shivers up my spine.

Apparently Victoria could see it, as she leaned over and started talking to it. She kept her distance, though.

"Hello," she said in that sweet voice of hers. "I'm Victoria. Don't be afraid."

There was a pause, following by more tearing and gnawing.

"Listen, you've been bitten by a vampire. I'm afraid you're a vampire now, too. I know you're confused. But I can help you."

There was a hiss, like a cat. I saw Victoria stiffen. I took a slow step next to her. I could finally see what she saw.

Sitting, curled up in the corner with her legs in front of her, was a woman probably not too much older than me. From the looks of her clothes she was having a night on the town. Torn miniskirt, a spaghetti-strap shirt. Her eyes were blood red, just like my own. She would have been attractive, if it weren't for the blood dripping down the front of her face, and the large fangs. She looked back and forth between Victoria and me while she ripped into a raw piece of steak.

"You need blood. I know that tastes good, but you're gonna get real sick."

No response. Just that same wild look.

"Something's not right here," Victoria said.

I looked at her. From my point of view, that was the understatement of the year.

Something knocked me to the ground from behind. I landed only a foot away from the vampire in the corner. I looked up to see a second vampire, this one a guy, with its arm wrapped around Victoria's neck. He had the same wild look as the other one.

Before I could even think about helping I felt a hand around my throat. The female vampire straddled me. She couldn't have weighed any more than me, but she was strong. She took a quick sniff of my neck, then reared her head back to show off a huge set of fangs. She lunged down toward me, but I was already gone. I vanished, and felt her body sink into mine. Her hand went through my neck and braced on the floor. I quickly stood up, trying to ignore that strange feeling of when I was inside someone else.

I turned around to see the male vampire flying towards me. He went through me and collided with the female. They both tumbled to the ground and scampered back into the corner. Victoria had tossed him like a softball. She was simply straightening her shirt, not a mark on her. She definitely didn't need my help, like I could offer it anyway.

I jumped back to her side, not taking my eyes off of either vampire. She gave me a curious glance.

"Neat trick there."

I ignored her comment. My pulse was racing. Fighting humans was one thing. Fighting vampires, well, I knew I was out of my league.

I looked at the vampire couple. Somehow, I knew they were a *couple*. My guess was they got attacked somehow while having a night out. They crouched in the corner and continued to bare their fangs and snarl at us. They were both covered in blood and smelled terrible.

"It's like they're feral," Victoria said. "This isn't normal."

I tried not to roll my eyes. I had no idea what *normal* was anymore.

Victoria caught a sense of something. She turned around next to me. I did the same.

Two men stood from where we came in, with a third behind them. Vampire hunters. They both had crossbows aimed directly at Victoria. She ducked in time for both bolts to hit the wall behind us. If they were aiming at me, I wouldn't have been able to react in time. I'd be dead.

I heard Victoria snarl next to me. Before she could react the male vampire was on her again. I tried to help her, but the female vampire grabbed me from behind. I vanished, and the vampire again fell to one knee out of confusion, but I was furious. I could vanish all day long, but I couldn't help Victoria if I couldn't touch anything.

Turns out I didn't need to. The vampire hunters already reloaded their crossbows, and fired one more time. Victoria spun around and the bolts pierced the male vampire's back. I saw him go limp and fall to the ground.

The female ran by us and tried to attack the vampire hunters. Right as she drew near, the man in the rear stepped forward and unleashed a stream of flame onto her. The woman let out a scream that would stay with me forever. She flailed about wildly for a moment before falling to the ground.

Before Victoria or I could do anything, the vampire hunter moved the flame toward her. I tackled her to the ground and covered her as best I could. She was crushed beneath me, but it didn't seem to bother her. We were both sprayed with flame, and I could feel my clothes start to burn away. I heard them laughing behind me, which made the anger start to build. I didn't dare move, though. Victoria had her arms pinned between us, and if we rolled an inch either way she'd be exposed to the flame.

"They're done," someone said. "Torch the whole fuckin' place."

"Bachner isn't gonna like that."

"Fuck him. He wanted her dead. Well, she's dead."

"We just killed an innocent guy!"

"Shut up and get moving!"

Victoria's eyes never left mine. I thought I saw a look of panic as we heard the flames spread around us. We heard them pouring kerosene, throwing flame everywhere. After a minute we heard them leave through the back door.

The fire didn't take long to get out of control. The corpses of the two dead vampires were motionless next to us. The smell of burnt flesh made me almost throw up. The legs of a table next to us burned away, and it fell dangerously close. Victoria flinched and shifted uncomfortably.

"Fire will kill me...very quickly." She was afraid, but she hid it well.

I could feel the flames still eating away at my back. If Victoria was gonna make it out of this, it would be up to me. I popped out my wings, knocking things over as I did so. I wrapped them around both of us while trying to pull her into a kneeling position. She kept her arms carefully to herself and leaned close to me. I could see sweat dropping from her hair, while the flames didn't bother me at all. My wings were fireproof, along with the rest of me.

"Good thinking."

I nodded. I pushed her head down a little more while I looked around. I gave a brief thought to crashing through the storefront window, but that didn't feel like a good idea. The way to the back was blocked by fire and smoke. So I looked up.

A skylight.

"Hold on, " I said, and took one last deep breath.

We wrapped our arms around each other, and I beat my wings as hard as I could. Holding a hundred-pound woman, I expected some problems. But Victoria was strong, and my wings were stronger than I thought. The only problem I had was how fast the skylight came at us. I barely managed to get my eyes closed in time before we went through it.

The sound of glass breaking filled my ears. When I felt we were through, and felt the cold night air, I landed on the roof and let Victoria go. I fell to one knee, more from shock than anything else.

"You okay? You hurt?" she asked.

I looked up and shook my head. She gave me a nod.

"Thanks."

"Anytime."

She walked toward the edge of the roof facing the street. I was a second behind her. People were lining up outside to watch the fire. Traffic was already slowed to a crawl, first from the murder crime scene, then a fire. I could hear sirens from a few streets over.

"Look," Victoria said, pointing to the street corner.

While everyone else was focused on the fire beneath us, three men were loading something into a van, only occasionally looking toward the butcher shop. I didn't get a good look at the hunters who tried to kill us, but Victoria and I thought the same thing. That was them.

I heard her make a strange noise, almost like a snarl.

"That's twice now I've let them get me by surprise," she said. "It's not gonna happen again."

Her tone scared me.

One hunter nodded to another. They climbed in the van, and started driving away. Victoria wrapped her arms around my neck, which surprised the hell out of me.

"Follow them." She patted my right wing. That tickled. "I've always wanted to fly."

"Uh, Victoria...I can't really fly. I mean, I've never really done it, except in the woods. And carrying a person? I just don't know-"

She rolled her eyes. Then she let go of me and ran toward the edge of the roof. She jumped, and soared through the air over the street. She landed on another roof and kept running without missing a beat. I watched with my jaw hanging open.

I felt foolish all of a sudden, like I'd let her down. I sounded like an idiot, trying to make excuses.

I could fly, perfectly well. I knew it. My wings could easily handle her weight and mine. But I felt like a freak half the time. I was afraid. Afraid that flying would make me lose my humanity. Afraid of being seen.

I forced it all aside.

I jumped off the roof and beat my wings. I actually flapped too hard at first, as I started to gain more height than I meant to. My wings were so powerful. My first instincts were to go all out, but I didn't need to. A simple flap here and there, and I could glide on the wind.

I could feel my heart beating as I soared across the street. Despite the fact that just minutes ago I was in a burning building, I was excited. No trees outside my apartment, no more hiding. Just pure freedom.

I heard a few shouts below. People were staring and pointing up at me. Feeling a little paranoid, I climbed up a little, to make sure no one saw my face. The city lights were beautiful, a hell of a distraction.

There was a screech of tires below. I saw the van speed up and hang a crazy right turn, almost hitting a few people. Victoria was still running and leaping across the rooftops, looking almost like a little Barbie doll. They must have spotted her, and the chase was on.

I pushed aside the feelings of excitement and focused on what was happening below. Victoria didn't lose pace at all. She jumped down to the street on the hood of a car, crossed the street while dodging traffic, then jumped on top of another roof. It was quite a sight.

The van was easily doing fifty miles an hour on the crowded city streets. Victoria kept up, and surprisingly I did too. In fact, I was starting to pass them. I had to throttle back a bit, glide on the wind a little more.

It looked like it was getting even more dangerous below. Some people crossing the street barely managed to avoid the van in time. It kept weaving in and out of traffic. I didn't sense a good ending to all of this.

Sure enough, I looked up ahead to see an elderly man crossing the street at an intersection. The van was maybe ten seconds to him. There was no way he'd make it across in time. He didn't even know his life was in danger.

I glanced downed below. Victoria was keeping pace with the van, but there was no way for her to save his life. That's assuming she even noticed him ahead of her. It was up to me.

There was only one way to make it to him quickly. I folded my wings behind me, and let gravity do its thing.

A complete free-fall. Nothing I hadn't done a hundred times in the woods behind my apartment. At least that's what I told myself.

The city below rushed up at me. I wasn't thinking clearly, but I did know that if I messed this up, I'd probably kill myself as well as the old man.

I had the angle to him. The question was did I have the second I needed. I was maybe fifteen feet above the street when I tossed my wings straight out. The man saw the van, and was frozen with fear as it barreled up on him. I got low enough, and pretty much slammed into him. I didn't have a choice, there was no way I could slow down. I heard the wind rush out of him as I grabbed him and tilted my wings to gain some height. The van actually smacked my right foot as it went by, almost screwing up my flight. I ran up the side of a building for a second, still holding the man tight. Then I let my wings slowly carry us back to the street.

The man fell to one knee. I went down with him, keeping a grip on him to help hold him steady. He had a hand to his chest and breathed heavily. For a second I thought he was having a heart attack.

"Are you alright?"

It took him a moment. He finally managed a nod. "Shit. I think I have a broken rib."

I felt terrible. It wasn't like in the movies, me saving somebody and being a big hero. But it really was the best I could do.

"I'm sorry. But hey, at least you're alive."

He smiled. "Yeah."

He glanced at my wings. I looked at them myself, and noticed that we had a small audience. Some people stared at the van that sped by. Others were staring right at us. A few people gawked and pointed from their cars, others stopped in the middle of the street and sidewalk. Everyone wanted to get a look at the freak. I felt so exposed.

"Get to a hospital," I told him. I would never know his name, or ever see him again. But I would always remember the smile he gave me right before I hit the night sky once again.

I climbed to just above the buildings. It took me a minute to catch back up. Victoria still kept to the rooftops. The van still tried to steer clear from her. I didn't have a damn clue of what Victoria had in mind, but this had to stop. Someone was gonna get hurt or killed. Hell, maybe either one of us.

Victoria lunged from a corner building. She fell gracefully and landed right on top of the van.

"Victoria! What are you doing!?"

I knew she heard me, but didn't glance my way. She brought her right fist back and pounded on the roof. Then again, and again. She was trying to punch her way inside.

The van took an insane right turn down an alley. I followed. They were hoping to shake her off. It didn't work, as Victoria barely moved an inch. I could see a hole in the roof. Her crazy plan was working.

I saw one of the guys start to climb out the passenger's seat window with a gun. I looked ahead to see there wasn't too much left to the alley. It led to an empty street, and right into an abandoned building, maybe an old factory of some kind.

There was no way the van would be able to stop or turn in time.

I swooped down as fast as I could. Victoria had a hand inside the van, and was trying to pull away at the metal. The guy hanging out the window was trying to hold a steady aim at her.

I landed on the van near her, wrapped my arms around her waist, and flew up once again. The guy fired a shot, but didn't hit anything.

Victoria and I watched from thirty feet in the air as the van nearly flew over the street and into the old factory. It sounded like a bomb going off as they crashed through the wall. Smoke and debris were everywhere. We heard cars from the next street over screeching to a halt.

"Holy shit," I said.

My heart was hammering. Victoria was cool as ice.

"Get us over there."

We floated down to the street and Victoria wiggled free from my arms. She started sprinting to the factory. I was a step behind her. I remembered to retract my wings back to wherever the hell they came from.

The first thing that hit me was the smell. A little bit of alcohol, some shit, and God knows what else. There were a few homeless people running around, scared and confused. The factory must have been a shelter for them.

I was amazed as we drew closer to the van and saw one of the hunters trying to open the back door, going for a weapon. They still weren't done fighting. They were a sturdy bunch of bastards.

"You guys better head out," I called to anyone that could hear. "This ain't gonna be pretty."

Victoria snatched him by the back of the neck and shoved him headfirst into the door. He barely hit the ground by the time Victoria was ripping the passenger's side door off the van. She tossed it behind her and grabbed the man who tried to shoot her. He still had the gun in his hand. She grabbed his hand and squeezed. His face was a mess of pain as I heard bones breaking. Even I winced. I looked at the driver's side to see the third guy leaning on the wheel. He was conscious, but wasn't making an effort to do anything. Shock, maybe.

"You fucking bitch!" he screamed, then spit on her. "I swear to God we'll fucking kill you!"

So much hatred in his voice. It sent a chill up my spine.

She clutched him by the throat and lifted him clear off the ground.

"I want you to tell Bachner and Heins something. Tell them they're gonna start a war they can't win. If you leave me alone, I'll leave me alone. If not, I will kill each and every one of you. Do you get it?"

He managed a nod before she dropped him to the ground. He gasped and rubbed at his throat a moment.

"Get what's left of your friends and get the fuck out of here."

I'd never seen people move so fast. The two that were conscious picked up the third and left through the back of the warehouse through the dark alleys. The homeless people had all fled. The street outside was empty, at least for the moment. We were alone.

She punched the van, leaving a huge dent. She turned and gave me a dangerous look, then an almost sheepish smile.

"Four hundred years old," Victoria said. "You'd think I'd have a better grip on my temper."

I was finally calming down myself, and saw a trail of blood on Victoria's shirt that started from her shoulder. I was wrong. The vampire hunter actually managed to shoot her.

"You're hurt."

She looked down casually. She didn't even notice. "Eh, bullets don't do much to me, at least not in small doses." She started pacing a little. "I just want to live a normal life, you know, Alex? I don't want to go on wild fuckin' rides in the city."

Hell, I could relate to that.

"Anyway, forget about them. There's more important things going on."

"Such as?"

"Those two newborns. Why were they feral? How the hell did they both become vampires? I'm telling you, something's going on here."

"You think those vampire guys have anything to do with it?"

She paused to think. "Anything's possible. But I doubt it. Anyway, it's something we'll have to look in to."

"Uh, *we?*"

"Yeah, we. Alex, I'm gonna need your help on this."

I couldn't believe my ears. "No, you won't. Are you kidding? What am I gonna do?"

"You were *amazing* back there. Who knows what else you can do."

"Victoria, I don't *want* to know what else I can do. What the hell am I even doing here? I should be sleeping."

"Ah, you got something exciting going on this weekend? Gonna pine after Cindy a little more?"

"What do you want from me? I gotta live my life, right? Gotta make money, right? Gotta live normal, like you just said."

"You want to talk money? Five hundred dollars a day. Just to be my eyes. No flying, no crazy heroics. I can't go out in the day. You can. Be my eyes."

Money didn't matter at all to me. Victoria sounded like she really wanted my help, and that's the hook that got me. Victoria sensed it, and put a hand on my shoulder.

"Something important is happening," she said again. "Please help me figure out what it is."

Even as I nodded, I couldn't believe what I was agreeing to.

We left before the cops showed up. Indeed a busy night for them. I barely remember driving with Victoria back to her house, and then back to my apartment.

CHAPTER 24

It was one of those deep sleeps where you don't even remember if you dreamed or not. I woke up, and it actually took me a minute to figure out where I was. I felt my comfortable bed, recognized the morning sun throwing shadows on the closet door. I was home.

I half stumbled to the bathroom and gave myself a look in the mirror. I was surprised at what I saw. I looked terrible. An insane night in the city would do that. A few tiny cuts in my hair from crashing through the butcher shop glass. Huge circles under my eyes.

I was in the middle of making a microwave breakfast when I heard the front door open. I turned to see Cindy. It felt like it had been forever since I last saw her, although we just fought the night before.

I took a quick look down at myself. I couldn't remember what I wore to bed. Luckily I put on a pair of shorts sometime before passing out the night before.

Cindy looked great. Tight pair of jeans, a shirt that showed that slim stomach of hers. She gave me a small half smile, a sign that we weren't fighting anymore.

"Rough night?"

I never lied to Cindy, but wasn't up to talking about the night before. Luckily I didn't have to. Before I could say anything, she lowered her head and looked at the carpet.

"Sorry about last night," she said.

I actually had to think back to our fight. "Hey, no problem. Wasn't our first fight, won't be our last. But what the hell was that about, anyway?"

"We'll talk about that later, okay? I won't leave you hanging, I promise."

I shrugged. Fine. I had other things on my mind anyway. I turned back to the kitchen.

"So when do I get to ride you?"

What a thought. I turned, and actually caught her staring at me.

"Huh? What?"

She smiled. "It's all over the news."

"*What's* all over the news?"

She grabbed the remote and turned on the TV. It only took her a second to find what she was looking for.

I felt my heart sink.

Pictures of me were on the local news. Different angles, different cameras. Some were from cell phone cameras. One was from a traffic camera. No shots of my face, and none of them were very clear. But there I was, flying through the city streets, for everyone to see. They even interviewed a guy while a slide-show of all the different photos played of me.

"Aw man, it was awesome," he said. He stood on a sidewalk while gesturing behind him. "I was right here. The dude actually saved a guy's life. He had these huge wings. It was just nuts. I saw the whole thing. He pulled this guy out of traffic, then started flying away."

Cindy muted the TV. We locked eyes. Part of me thought she was gonna run away. Why not? I'm pretty much a monster. But she didn't. She just gave me that smile.

"So, you can fly," she said. "I thought it was weird you kept going in the woods. Didn't think I noticed, did you?"

"I was gonna tell you, Cindy. Just as soon as I got a grip on everything."

"Oh, I know. Sounds like you had a crazy night. When do I get to try you out?"

I really wasn't hearing what she was asking. Panic started to set in. I did my best to keep it in.

"I can fly." I sat on the couch. "And now the whole world knows."

Cindy knew I was upset, and like the true friend she is, did her best to bring me out of it. She sat next to me and put a hand on my shoulder.

"Hey, it's okay. A lot of the news reports are already saying the whole thing is a fake. It has to be, right? Because no one can fly. You okay?"

I didn't say anything. I kept looking at the TV.

"Look," she said. "Has anyone knocked on your door yet?"

"No."

"Then no one knows. You're safe. Just wear a trash bag on your head next time you take off."

I laughed. That's all I needed, was a laugh and a friend. As always, Cindy made me feel better.

"Thanks, Cindy."

"Anytime." She smiled and rubbed my shoulder, a little more than I would have thought. Or it could have been my wishful thinking. We did hold eyes for a moment, long enough for her to suddenly pull back her hand

and stand up, almost awkwardly. "Well, I gotta head to work."

"On a Saturday?"

"Yeah. We're behind, and my dad's paying double, so off I go. I'll talk to you later. And call Leese. She misses you, and keeps crying about boys. Take her out to lunch or something."

I nodded.

I would call Alicia, but I had a little Saturday work to do myself.

After Cindy left I immediately went for the phone. I had no idea what Victoria's day schedule was like. Did she sleep all day, like in the movies?

"Hello?"

"Victoria. It's me."

"I thought you'd be sleeping. How the hell are you awake?"

"Listen. I'm all over the damn TV. They know about me."

"Who does?"

"*Everyone*. There's *pictures* of me flying through the city."

She was quiet for a moment.

"And?"

"*And?* There is no *and*."

"Please tell me you didn't call just for that. It's not a big deal."

I couldn't believe what I was hearing. "Are you serious?"

"Yeah, Alex. Shit. They've got pictures of Bigfoot and the Lochness Monster. And no one thinks they're real. Well, the funny part is they are, but no one believes it. They won't think you're real either."

"Victoria-"

"Look," she cut me off. "If you're really freaked out about this, I'll take care of it. Alright?"

"What do you mean? Take care of it?"

"Just trust me. You ready to do a little running for me?"

I took a deep breath. To be honest, I wasn't sure I was ready. "I gotta take a quick shower."

"Alright. Head down to the police station in the city. I already talked to William. He's gonna look over the corpse of that guy in the street last night. Bring me a copy of the report."

"You don't have like a fax machine or something?"

"Yes, I do. But I want another set of eyes. And not just a cop's eyes. *Your* eyes."

"Okay. Don't know how much help I can be. But sure."

"Good. Stop by later. And hey?"

"Yeah?"

"How are you and Cindy?"

I was touched she was actually asking. "We're not fighting anymore. She stopped by this morning. Still don't know what her problem was."

"She's a woman. You might never know. But after all this is over, you've got to just throw her down on the couch. Alright?"

I laughed and shook my head. Getting romantic advice from a centuries-old vampire. "Whatever you say, Victoria. I'll see you soon."

Before jumping in the shower I called Alicia. It was short, but not really sweet.

"Hey, Alex."

"What's going on, sis?"

Cindy was right. She was down. "Not much."

"What's wrong?"

"Nothing. I'll be fine. Cindy told me how her date went last night."

"Yeah. She said it went good, then comes home and gets pissy with me."

She laughed, but it was more irritated than happy. "You have no clue, do you?"

"Uh, no. But I guess you do?"

"No. Forget I said anything."

"Alicia."

"Hey, you remember that guy I talked about a few times? Mark from Spanish class? You think I should ask him out?"

I rolled my eyes. Nothing like changing the subject. "Sure, go ahead. But remember what I said. Don't be stressing yourself out."

"Yeah, yeah. I won't. I'm gonna clean the house. Give me a call later, alright?"

I hung up. Obviously she didn't want to talk. My sister and her guy problems. Me and my feelings for Cindy. Oh, and me being a half demon of some kind. Life had its share of problems.

*****

It didn't take long to drive to the city. I parked about a block away from the police station, the same one I forced Tony to turn himself in to, after he and his partner attacked Cindy. That felt like forever ago.

I felt foolish as I stepped inside and walked up to the sliding-glass window separating the front lobby area from the rest of station. I felt like I shouldn't have been there, and I had doubts as to why I was. How exactly was I gonna help Victoria?

"Can I help you?" the lady behind the glass said. She looked bored, and irritated.

"Uh, yeah. I'm looking for William Sloane. He should know I'm coming."

"Name?"

"Alex Teague."

She picked up the phone. "Bill, a guy named Alex here to see you?" She was quiet a second, then hung up. "He'll be right up."

I flashed a small smile and waited. Bill greeted me a minute later. Without the distraction of an insane crime scene, I got a much better look at him.

He didn't look any better than last night. Just looked tired, defeated. It looked like he wore the same clothes from the crime scene, minus the coat. He looked strong, though, tough. He did manage a smirk and nod before shaking my hand.

"Hey, Alex. Put this on."

He gave me a visitor's badge and led me through the maze of cubicle desks and chairs. A lot of noise, a lot of commotion. People were everywhere doing things you'd expect in a police station. Phones were ringing. Desk cops were taking statements from witnesses. Bill didn't say a word, which I liked. All business. He stopped at a desk that I guessed was his and started organizing some folders and punching away at his computer keyboard. He paused long enough to grab a cell phone from his desk drawer and toss it at me.

"This is for you."

"Why do I need a cell phone?"

"Victoria wanted me to give it to you. Said you didn't have one. How the hell can you get by without a cell phone?"

I shrugged. "Just not popular, I guess."

He smirked. "Anyway, her number's in there. I guess you really do work for her now."

"How long have you two known each other?"

He laughed. The laugh seemed to go against his serious look.

"Long enough to wish I hadn't met her sometimes. Vampires, werewolves. I wish I didn't know they were real."

He didn't know the half of it. Demons, ghosts, the list just keeps getting better.

"So, you got a report for her?" I asked.

Before he could answer, a cop led a drunk man in handcuffs by us.

"I'm fuckin' telling you! He flew through the sky! He was like a goddamn giant fucking bat! Or a monster or something!"

Bill shook his head as they walked by. I shifted in my chair, a little uncomfortable.

"What shit are these assholes on now," he muttered, then looked at me. His mind was far away. "What was that?"

"A report? I'm supposed to get a report for Victoria?"

He smiled. "Not yet, but we will in about twenty minutes."

"What?"

"We still have to examine the body."

"We?"

"Victoria didn't tell you? She wants you to get a look at it. I'm not thrilled about it myself, a civvie like you. No offense. But I trust Victoria."

I shook my head, a little angry. I knew it couldn't be as simple as playing mailman for a report.

"Well, what the hell does she think I'm gonna see that you guys aren't?"

"Beats me. She just says you're special, and let you have a look."

I felt a little sick to my stomach. Seeing a dead body in the street is one thing, but *examining* one?

"You ready?"

"I guess."

He got up and led me to the back and down a tight flight of steps. We passed a few sets of doors until we came to a set that required an electronic badge of some kind. He swiped a card and opened the door, but grabbed me by the shoulder before I could walk in.

"You're not gonna faint or puke, are you? I don't feel like mopping shit up on a Saturday."

A quick flash of some of the things I'd seen in my life flashed through my head. A possessed ghost killing his wife over and over again. Visions of demons torturing souls, in my birthplace of all places.

"I'll be fine."

We stepped into the morgue. It was like you'd think it would be. Very cold, very blue. The wall was lined up with small doors, which held tables of who knows how many bodies.

Bill looked at a file folder he had, matching up to which body cabinet he was looking for.

"Our victim, Larry Watling," he started. He wrapped a hand around the body-cabinet handle. "Just a guy in the wrong place at the wrong time. We figure-"

He never finished.

As soon as he opened the body-cabinet door, something lunged out. Caught us both completely off guard. Before I could even blink, Bill was on the ground screaming in pain. The vampire had its weight pressed on Bill's chest, its fangs deep in his shoulder.

I reached down to try to pull it off. It shrugged me off easily, throwing me back a few feet. But it was enough to get its attention.

It lunged at me, but luckily I was a split second faster. I vanished, and it passed through me and crashed into the wall.

I backed up next to Bill, who was starting to climb to his feet. Blood was dripping down his shirt to the floor. We both stared at what used to be Larry Watling.

He half crouched against the wall. He looked to be sizing the both of us up. It looked at us and snarled. Bright red eyes that weren't natural, impossibly pale skin, unkempt hair. It was my first look at a wild vampire in good light, and I'd never forget it.

"This isn't right," Bill said. "This one's acting like an animal."

"Yeah. We found two more like this one."

He lunged again. This time it went for me. My first instinct was to vanish, but I knew if I did, it would smack right into Bill. I took the charge and fell back into the wall. My head smacked off the concrete, knocking me senseless. As I crumpled to the ground, I felt his weight on me. He tried to push my head back and go for my neck. I managed to slip an arm between us, but he was stronger than me. I was a second away from vanishing when he screamed in pain. His hold on me started to slip a little, and he fell next to me, almost in a fetal position. I saw a few inches of a long metal rod sticking through the front of his chest, with the rest sticking out the back. Bill had stabbed him through the heart with some kind of tool used for autopsies.

"You alright?" Bill said, yanking me to my feet.

I nodded, and immediately felt like an idiot. *That* was what was itching in the back of my head last night at the crime scene. As Victoria and I looked over the scene in the street, it just never occurred to me.

Larry Watling wasn't dead. I should have known when I first saw him lying covered in the middle of the street.

I never sensed a ghost at all. I know if it were me, I'd be trying to solve my own murder.

Now here Larry was, lying in a vampire coma on the floor of a morgue, *undead*, of all things.

In all the commotion, Bill didn't see me vanish. That was a good thing, less questions. But he was bleeding bad from the shoulder, and only a single thought hit my mind. He looked at me, and answered before I could ask the question.

"Don't worry. I won't turn into one of them. I've been bit a million times. Even let Victoria suck some blood when she was low."

I sighed. That was a relief.

In fifteen seconds, Bill was calm enough to think. I wish I could say that.

"Fuck. I gotta deal with this," he said, pointing to Larry. "And you gotta get out of here. We'll all talk later."

"What are you gonna do with him?"

"You don't want to know," he said, and gestured to the door.

I nodded, and left the morgue, leaving Bill to do whatever it was he had to do. I didn't give it any more thought. I just wanted to get out. I dropped my guest badge at the front desk and stepped into the afternoon sun.

I sat down at the steps leading to the police station to calm my nerves. The daylight felt good, like it was cleansing me of what the hell just happened. It was good to see people walking the streets, cars stuck in traffic. *Normal* things. Not the strange world I was suddenly thrust in to.

That vampire could have easily snapped my neck, had I let it. It was pure luck and Bill's quickness that saved me. Whatever the hell I was, half demon, human with demon blood, I was starting to feel like I was in way over my head. And the day was only starting.

CHAPTER 25

After unwinding for a few minutes I got up and circled the block to get to my truck. I didn't have any report to give Victoria, so I was just gonna get something to eat and go over to her place.

I never made it.

I didn't even hear them coming up from behind me. Someone hit me on the back of the head with something hard. The pain burst through my skull as I fell to one knee. Then a van screeched to a halt next to me. Two guys jumped out, grabbed me by the arms, and dragged me inside. I didn't have a chance to vanish at all. Abducted right in broad daylight.

By the time the pain in my head started to die a little, I realized I was in the van. I tried to move, but something held my wrist. I was handcuffed to a railing running along the side, my arm over my head.

"Just relax," someone said.

I looked at two guys standing in front of me. My vision was still a little blurry, but they slowly came into focus. I bounced a little as the moving van drove around the city blocks.

"Hi," the man on the left said. "My name's John Bachner. The fellow next to me is Andrew Heins."

The infamous Bachner and Heins. My first look at either one of them.

Bachner was in his forties with light blond hair. Looked normal enough. Medium build. Probably a little taller than me, if we were standing completely straight. He didn't exactly stand out in a crowd, probably a good trait for a vampire killer to have. He looked at me, sizing me up. He had an intelligent look to him, like he studied everything.

Heins, on the other hand, looked to be the complete opposite. No hair at all, an old scar on the side of his face. He looked like he spent all his time in the gym. He had a mean, almost angry expression on his face. When we locked eyes, he spit on the floor of the van in front of me, narrowly missing my shoe.

I pulled my wrist against the handcuffs. I was so close to vanishing from their sight and leaving the van. But something kept me in place. I wasn't worried at all because I knew I wasn't in any real danger, and I have to admit, I acted a little recklessly.

"How you doing? Nice to meet you."

Heins almost snarled.

"You're not a vampire," Bachner said, cutting out any chance of small talk. "Obviously, cause you can get a suntan, like the rest of us. But my men tell me you're not human. I laughed at first, then I see pictures of you flying all over the place. What are you? Some kind of government experiment or something?"

I didn't say anything.

So Heins gave me a nice right fist to the cheek.

My head rocked back. If it wasn't for the handcuffs, I would have fallen.

In my head I saw me doing a quick vanish, then lunging for Heins' throat. Very bad thoughts started to creep in. I hoped it was anger, and not the demon in me. But I kept in control. I kept telling myself I actually had the advantage. They knew nothing about me, and there was no reason to show them what I was capable of.

At least not yet.

"Heins, calm down," Bachner said. He almost looked irritated. He looked at me. "What's your name?"

I almost didn't say anything. But I had a feeling deep down they already knew who I was. They could have also grabbed my wallet if they really wanted to.

"Alex Teague."

"Ah. Okay Alex. I don't know who or what you are. And to be honest, I don't care. You're not a vampire. So I don't want to kill you. I only kill vampires. That's it. But you have made friends with one."

"Are you fuckin' kidding?" Heins roared. "This little punk beat the shit out of our guys. They said they flamed him down and it didn't do shit. Let me put a bullet in his head now."

"Inside the van, Heins? Are you out of your mind?"

They both looked at each other, and I noticed something. Tension. Partners or not, something was definitely going on with them.

"Why do you want to kill her?" I asked, careful not to drop her name. "Just because she's a vampire, doesn't make her evil. She's a good person."

"Tell that to my grandfather," Bachner snapped.

He saw the surprise on my face.

"She didn't tell you, did she? Victoria killed my grandfather, when I was a little kid. And now it's her turn. I've tracked her down so many times, and she's always just gotten away. Well, not this time. I'm only trying to warn you, to save your life. You think she's your friend. Vampires don't have friends. She'll rip your heart out when you don't see it coming."

Heins leaned in close. "So if you don't back the fuck off, and mind your own business, your sister, that hot little black bitch you hang out with, your mommy, they all die. Understand?"

Bachner grabbed his partner's shoulder. "Heins, would you shut the fuck up?"

I didn't look at Bachner at all. My gaze was settled right on Heins. He gave me a hard slap before leaning away.

They knew more about me than I thought. I was stunned at Heins' threats for a second. Then I got angry.

"If you even *think* about my friends and family, I'll-"

"You'll what?" Bachner cut me off. "What will you do? You'll kill us? I'm sorry, Alex, but you don't look like much of a killer to me. More like a forklift driver."

I smiled. I was also afraid. Not of them, but because of the outright evil thoughts going through my head. I didn't feel like myself.

Demon blood influencing me?

"Kill? Nope. That would be too quick. There's worse things. I've seen them. Would *you* like to?"

"What the fuck are you talking about?" Heins asked.

Suddenly, quick flashes of the demon world, all around me. The van was gone, then back again, several times. Each time, more and more demons surrounded me. Some were missing limbs. Others walked around without heads. Some dripped what looked like blood from their mouths and made noises that scared the hell out of me. Snarls and moans.

But they were loyal to me.

"We'll kill them for you, master."

"You're part of us."

Hallucinations. At least, I prayed they were.

"Listen, Alex, nothing is gonna happen to your family and friends," Bachner was saying. He gave Heins an angry look. "All I want you to do is stay away from Victoria. I can't guarantee your safety if you don't."

"Are we done here?" I said. I felt like I was gonna puke.

Bachner shrugged. "Sure. I've said my case."

Heins was furious. "You're a fuckin' idiot."

"Stop the van," he called to the driver. He pulled out a key and undid my handcuffs. "Think about what I said. Be careful who you trust."

"I think I'll trust someone who doesn't burn down butcher shops."

This time, Bachner had a look of surprise, but only for a second. I could read it in his face.

He didn't know.

The van stopped at a light, and I opened the rear door and jumped out. Bachner and I exchanged one last look as he reached out to close the door.

A car honking behind me made me jump and get out of the street. I watched the van drive away and make a right turn.

"I don't think so," I said out loud.

I vanished right in the middle of the sidewalk, not caring if anyone saw me. I started to run. It didn't take me long to catch up, since walls and getting tired weren't a problem.

Me running through the city trying to keep up with a van. It was deja vu all over again. The chase was uneventful. I took a few shortcuts through a few buildings, almost lost them a few times when they picked up speed. But they eventually led me to a warehouse on the edge of town. I slowed up, but still stayed vanished, as I watched the van pull inside a large dock. I ran up and walked inside.

I found their home base.

I looked at everything I could see. There was a makeshift living room in the corner. They had workout equipment that dwarfed anything I had. A large table was against one wall, full of weapons. Guns, crossbows, grenades. They had five vans.

There looked to be about thirty men. Some watched TV. Others were checking the weapons. I saw two guys boxing in the corner.

Victoria was right. It was a small army.

I got inside in time to see Bachner, Heins, and their driver getting out of the van. Bachner and Heins were loud enough to hear anywhere in the warehouse.

"I don't want to hear it, Heins."

"Would you just fuckin' listen to me? I would have had that little punk talking in five minutes. He'd tell us exactly where the bitch is, and we'd be dragging her dead ass into the sun right now."

"You sound like the mafia. Maybe you missed your calling."

"Tell me I'm wrong."

"It's not about that. You don't attack a vampire in their lair. Come on, you should know this shit by now."

"And why not?"

"Because she doesn't live in a goddamn cave. She lives in a house with people around her. We attack her, and innocent people get hurt."

"Oh Jesus Christ," Heins said, rolling his eyes.

Bachner looked over his men.

"Now, I want to know what really happened last night. Did some of you careless bastards destroy a butcher's shop? Did you put someone's livelihood out of business?"

A man stepped forward. I recognized him as one of the guys from the night before. He looked horrible. Bruises and cuts, and a bandage over his right eye.

"I'm telling you, Bachner. That was that bloodsucking bitch. She torched the shit."

Bachner didn't look convinced.

"Everyone listen up. We are in the business of killing vampires. We do not put people in harm's way. We don't destroy people's businesses. We are in control, not those fuckin' bloodsuckers that we hunt. I'm trusting all of you to act smart and be in control. If you can't get with it, there's the door."

"Gonna believe a vampire's bitch instead of your own guys. You're a pussy," Heins said.

Bachner spun around and took a step forward. For a second, I thought fists were gonna fly. They both had a dangerous look in their eyes. Then Bachner calmed down. Heins looked like he would kill him, but something told me Bachner was just as dangerous. He looked over his men.

"There are vampires in this city. You track them, you kill them quietly. Now this is a whole new ball game. They're cooking up something. I want to know what *that* thing is. Get me some answers."

Bachner pointed to something covered in a far corner. Heins followed him, and they argued some more. If it weren't for the fact that Bachner wanted to kill my friend, he would almost seem like an okay guy.

I walked over to where Bachner pointed, to an empty corner where no one was. They had a tarp covering something rectangular. I saw the tarp move a little.

Something was alive in there.

I took a deep breath, then pushed my head through. I felt the tarp, then cold steel. It was a cage.

I was inches away from a male vampire.

He lashed out. Not at me, but at the cage bars. He was wild, like all the other ones I'd seen so far. His hair was a mess. His fangs stuck out just beyond his lower lip. He wore a ruined security uniform that read W.R.S., whatever that meant.

He didn't see me, but that didn't mean I wanted to be near him. I backed out of the cage and took one last look at the warehouse, trying to think about what I was really seeing.

Bachner looked like he barely had control over his own men. He and Heins were at each other's throats. They were on the hunt for more vampires, and they had a feral one in a cage.

Victoria would definitely want to hear about this.

.

CHAPTER 26

It took me almost two hours to make it to her house. I had to run back to my truck, then fight city traffic. I gave her a call on the cell phone to let her know I was on the way. It only took her a second to answer the gate buzzer when I got there.

"Alex?" she said.

"Yeah, it's me."

"Come in. I'll unlock all the doors. Just shut them behind you."

Victoria was pacing near her living area on her cell phone. I had to do a double-take as I got closer. She was only wearing a bra and panties.

I tried to keep my eyes low. Her hair was wet. She must have just showered earlier.

"Okay," she was saying on the phone. "He just got here. I'll give you a call as soon as the sun goes down."

She tossed the phone on the couch and put her hands on her hips. She turned straight at me, not trying to hide anything. Not quite on Cindy's level, but hot nonetheless.

"That was William," she said. "He filled me in on what happened this morning. We're gonna head over to his house when the sun sets. He has some notes he wants to go over."

"Uh, Victoria. Would you mind putting on some clothes?"

"Sorry. Just got out of the shower. Hold on. I keep forgetting you're not comfortable around hot women."

"You're so funny."

She talked while she slipped on a pair of jeans and a tee-shirt.

"What happened to your eye?" she asked. "Make some new friends today?"

I'd forgotten about the love tap Heins gave me. My eye was a little swollen. Luckily it didn't hurt much. "You could say that."

I caught her up on what my day was like while we sat on the couch. I told her about Heins and Bachner, their base, the vampire they had in a cage. She listened to every word.

"So, they found a feral vampire too," she said.

"Yeah. They didn't know what it was."

"That makes two of us. It's good to hear they're just as clueless as we are."

I hesitated with my next question.

"Victoria, is it true you killed Bachner's grandfather?"

She took a breath. "Yeah, it's true."

"What happened?"

I could tell she didn't want to talk about it. But she did. "That was about forty years ago, maybe? I didn't want to, Alex. He was a vampire hunter, just like Bachner. He wouldn't let up, tracked me for a year. I kept sparing his life, and letting him go. I kept telling him, 'I'm not a bad person'. But he wouldn't listen. I kept thinking if I let him live, he'd leave me alone. Then one day he and five other hunters get me in a corner. It was either them or me. I chose me."

"He said vampires don't make friends."

She almost laughed. "He might not be too far off there. It's hard to have friendships with humans when you know you'll outlive them. But you and me, we're friends, Alex. I hope you believe that."

I nodded.

"You look pretty bad."

"Well, thank you."

"I mean tired. Get some rest. We have a few hours before the sun sets. I promise I'll keep my hands to myself. Unless you say otherwise."

I laughed, and stretched out on her loveseat. She was right. I was exhausted. The past few days were starting to get to me.

"No, thanks."

"Damn. I can go to any club and have my teeth in someone's neck in twenty minutes. What does Cindy got that I don't?"

"I wish I knew, so I could maybe get it out of my head."

I was asleep in five minutes.

Too bad it wasn't restful.

*****

I woke up on the couch, but Victoria's basement was long gone. I was in the middle of a red desert with a hot sun overhead. I heard a thunderstorm coming. The sky had a reddish glow. Before I could even wonder what was going on, I saw them all around me.

Demons.

They were feasting on corpses. At least I thought they were corpses.

212

They started to move and moan in pain.

Just like at the church in Blossom.

All I could hear was them eating. Chewing, munching noises. Flesh being ripped from bone. Blood spilling onto the sand. They noticed me, but didn't make a move. I could sense fear. Whether the corpses were afraid of the demons, or the demons afraid of me, I couldn't tell.

A quiet whisper echoed in my ear.

"Let us out."

"No!" I said, anger in my voice.

"You're a part of us. Forever."

Suddenly, the demon world was gone. Victoria was shaking my shoulder. Her pale, pretty face was a few inches from mine.

"You okay?" she asked. "You're having a nightmare."

I swung my legs over the couch and rested my head in my hands.

"That's one way of putting it."

"The sun's almost down. You ready for a ride?"

I was still drowsy, but knew I didn't have much of a choice. "I guess so."

It was dusk outside. The sun had set, but there was still a little light coming over the horizon. I knew she'd say I watched too many movies, but I guessed vampires couldn't come out unless it was pitch black. I was wrong.

We drove for a while in silence. I thought back to the past two days. I wish I could figure out what was going on. But if Victoria was in the dark, there was no way I'd be of any help. I still didn't know why she wanted me along. Probably just for company. She kept tossing out her little comments like she was interested in me, but I knew that was part of how she acted. She was my mentor, and she genuinely wanted to see me with Cindy.

That made two of us.

"What do you think is going on?" I asked.

"I don't know. Some bad blood going around, maybe? Turning vampires feral?"

"Well, it must be pretty strong stuff. Between yesterday and today, three crazy mindless vampires. Good thing Bill is immune."

"Why?"

"He didn't tell you? The one in the morgue took a bite out of him this morning."

She gave me a worried look, then grabbed her cell phone.

"He said he'd been bit before," I said. "That you even drank from him."

She didn't say anything. She spoke in her cell phone.

"William. It's me, Victoria. If you're there, pick up."

Silence.

"Dammit. Okay, we're on our way over now."

She hung up.

"Everything alright?"

"I hope so. Let's just get there."

We parked on the side of a street full of town-houses, way on the other end of the city. His was the last house on the end before one of those huge separating walls stood between the street and the beltway. She knocked on the door.

"William! It's us."

Nothing.

"Fuck," she said.

She looked around for anyone else on the street. There was a group of kids near the other end playing, but they were far away. Victoria took a step back. I stopped her before she could kick the door in.

"Hold on," I said. "We can do this quiet."

I vanished. She'd seen me do it before, but not without any other chaos going on.

"That amazes me every time you do it," she whispered.

I slowly put my head through the front door. The TV was on, but there was no one in the living room. Everything looked normal enough. I couldn't hear anything. I stepped all the way through and unlocked the front door.

"You're just full of cool tricks," Victoria said. "William? Are you in here?"

The only thing I could hear was the news on TV. But Victoria had better senses than I did. She put her nose to the air and sniffed a few times, like a bloodhound.

"Oh no," she said.

"What? What's wrong?"

"Stay behind me."

She slowly moved through the living room. As I took a step behind her, my right wing clipped the couch. I popped my wings out without even knowing. Didn't even feel my shirt rip. I was so mad at myself. It was like premature ejaculation.

I followed Victoria through the living room into the long hallway that went through the whole house. The kitchen was near the back. I got a sniff of what Victoria smelled as we got closer. And it wasn't good.

The scene set itself as more of the kitchen came into view. An open freezer door. Raw meat spread over the floor. A man in plain clothes on his hands and knees licking the blood and juices from the meat. When he heard us he looked up like a wild animal. Long fangs, bright red eyes.

Detective Bill Sloane.

"Oh, William ," Victoria said quietly.

Bill snarled, then dove right at us. I vanished, but it turned out I didn't need to. Victoria moved almost faster than I could see. She stepped in front of me and easily knocked Bill to the ground. She jumped on top of him and pinned his face to the floor.

"William, come on," she said. "Tell me you're in there somewhere."

He responded with another snarl. He reached up and raked a claw across her face. She cried in pain, and it was enough of a distraction for William to throw her off. She crashed onto the kitchen table, which shattered under her.

Bill turned his attention to me.

He took a step forward. I lashed out with one of my wings. I actually caught William off guard. He staggered against the back door.

But that was all. As many tricks as I had, I wasn't any match for a vampire. Luckily, I didn't have to be.

Victoria was already at my side. The gashes on her face had already healed. She had two splintered table legs from the kitchen table.

"William. *Bill*. Please, talk to me."

She sounded almost desperate. In the back of my head, I knew Bill was gone. Victoria knew far more about vampires than I ever would. But this was our fourth feral in just a few days. Bill wasn't coming back.

He took a split second to size us both up. Maybe my wings threw him off, but he decided Victoria was the weaker target. He charged her. She easily drove one of the table legs into his shoulder. She kept a grip on it and drove him to the floor.

"William, listen, you're a vampire now. But we can get through this, okay? Just tell me a part of you is in there."

He tried to reach for her throat. She leaned up a little, still keeping her weight on the table leg. Blood spilled from his shoulder. I was careful in walking up to the two of them. I retracted my wings and pulled them inside my back.

I touched Victoria on the shoulder. "I don't think that's William anymore."

She gave me a quick glance. I'd never seen her so upset. She studied Bill's face.

"You're right."

Before I could say anything else, she reared the other table leg back and drove it into his chest. Bill opened his mouth to scream, but nothing quite came out. He closed his eyes and slumped lifeless. Not dead, but in a coma.

I'm not sure how much time passed before we went into the living room. It felt like forever. Some deep part of me still kept thinking. *We should be leaving, getting out. It's dangerous to stay here. If a neighbor heard, trouble will come.* But Victoria sat on the couch, and I sat next to her.

She was quiet, sitting there staring straight ahead. I would have never thought it possible, but I think I was more together than she was. I risked putting a hand on her shoulder.

"Victoria? Are you alright?"

"I thought William and I would work together for decades," she said. "I, uh, I actually thought I'd go over his house. Have dinner. Hang out. Maybe even give him advice on getting a wife."

I didn't know what to say. "I'm so sorry."

"You always think there will be enough time. Maybe being a vampire can spoil you. But there's never enough time."

That got me thinking about Cindy. I had to tell her how I felt.

"Listen," I said. "I know you're hurting. I'm freaked out myself. But what are we gonna do? We have to leave."

She nodded. "Yeah. He's always taking work home with him. Let me look around first."

"Okay. What do you want me-"

I didn't finish. Bill's living room was gone. I was somewhere else. Another living room full of people. Loud music, people bumping into each other.

I stood up. "What the fuck?"

Victoria grabbed me. I came back to Bill's home for a moment, then I was once again in that unfamiliar living room. "Alex? What's wrong?"

I saw Alicia. She was on the other side of the living room talking to some other girls. They were laughing, having a good time.

Then a voice. Two guys were talking to each other. I couldn't see them.

"That one, right over there. The hot blond."

"Yeah. She's smokin'."

"Did you bring the shit?"

"Yeah. Go upstairs and get in a room. I'll bring her up in a minute."

I was back at Bill's. Victoria had both hands on my shoulders, holding me steady. She was worried.

Then I was right in Alicia's face.

"Hey. What's your name?"

"Alicia. But my friends all call me Leese."

"Well, Leese, you want something to drink?"

A hand reached out and handed her a beer.

I was seeing through someone else's eyes.

Someone who had eyes on my sister, with bad intentions.

"Alex? What's going on? Talk to me."

I gripped Victoria's arms to keep myself from falling. I wasn't sure if it was the suddenness of those quick flashes, or what I saw, but I felt sick. It didn't last long, though. My demon senses always keep me close to the ones I love, and they were telling me my sister was in trouble.

"Alicia," I managed to say.

Victoria simply nodded. "Go. I'll take care of things here."

"Go? Go where? I don't know where she is. I just saw-"

I was panicking. Luckily, Victoria wasn't.

"Relax. Call Cindy. Maybe she knows where she is."

I nodded and started hitting numbers on the cell phone.

"Hello?" She sounded like she was in her car.

"Cindy?"

"Hey, Alex. Where you at? I'm gonna pick up Dave and Tina and Jenny. You coming out with us?"

I hadn't seen my other friends in forever. But that was the furthest thing from my mind.

"Where's Alicia?"

"She won't be coming out. She had a party to go to." She picked up on the tension in my voice. "Everything okay?"

"No. Do you know where?"

"Uh, her friend Stephanie's house. I think she lives a street over."

I did know Stephanie. And I knew where she lived. Cindy was right, she wasn't far from my old home.

But I was so far away.

"Alex, what's going on?"

"I can't talk now, Cindy. But I'll catch up with you later."

I hung up and looked at Victoria. She nodded and gave me a small smile. "Get moving."

I gave her a quick hug and ran through the front door. As soon as I was clear, I popped my wings. I didn't even care who might be watching. I took off.

I made serious time. For the first few minutes I followed roads, as that was all I was used to. Then I started taking a shorter flight, cutting through the night sky.

Flying was amazing, but I couldn't let myself enjoy it. I beat my wings in a steady rhythm. My first flight through the city wasn't very long. This one was a lot longer, and I was afraid I wasn't gonna make it. I really didn't have any idea of what I was capable of.

I made it without breaking a sweat.

I passed over my old house and over Stephanie's street. It wasn't very hard to find the party. A million cars parked along the street, with groups of teens heading in and out of one house.

I flew low through the trees that were in pretty much every backyard. I heard a few dogs barking at me as I passed over. I landed in Stephanie's backyard and pulled my wings in. I walked around the side of the house and walked through the open front door.

Typical house party. Teens everywhere. Loud music blaring. Beer being passed around, and who knows what else. I scanned the living room.

I saw the stairs going to the second floor. I fought panic as the scariest thoughts imaginable filled my head.

I pushed my way through a few groups and hit the stairs. It was quieter on the second floor, with only people coming in and out of the bathroom. There was only one closed door at the end of the hall.

It was locked.

I pulled my hand back and knocked a few hard times.

"Is anyone in there?" I called.

A voice from the other side "Yo! Get your own fuckin' room!"

I recognized the voice from my quick flashes.

I vanished and stepped inside.

Two guys, probably twenty years old, were on a bed with Alicia. She wasn't unconscious, but moaned like she was having a bad dream. One of the guys was holding her hands above her head. The other was pulling her jeans off.

I reappeared, and as I did, threw shadows across the room. They turned around to see me.

"What the fuck, man?"

"How did you get in here?"

I didn't answer. I lunged forward and pushed the one fumbling with her jeans to the floor. I shoved the other against the back of the bed. I went right to Alicia and put a hand on her shoulder.

"Alicia?"

She looked at me with glazed eyes. "Alex? Where are we?"

I got hit hard with something on the back of my head. I fell on top of my sister. Then, before I knew it, I was lifted to my feet and in a full nelson. The dude was strong.

The other guy started punching. One good shot in the stomach almost forced the air out of me. My body wanted to fall, but the guy behind me held me up easily.

"Leave him alone," Alicia said from the bed. She tried to move, but she could barely pull her jeans up.

I got punched two more times. One hit me straight in the jaw. The other connected right where Heins hit me earlier in the day, on the side of the cheek.

That's when I snapped.

I didn't need any demon tricks. Didn't need to throw people around with my wings. Pure rage carried the day on this one.

I felt for one of the guy's fingers on the back of my neck. I grabbed one, and twisted. I heard a snapping sound as he screamed in pain.

I rushed forward and had my hands around the other guy's throat. I forced him against the wall. He tried to break my grip, but I squeezed tighter. I felt the fight start to leave him.

An arm wrapped around my neck. I was dragged backwards. Thank God for that, as I might have killed someone.

The other guy had recovered, and was trying to help his friend. My hand happened to fall on an alarm clock on a nightstand as I was pulled back. I ripped it from the wall. I gripped it with both hands and swung it wildly behind my head. I hit him square in the forehead. He collapsed to one knee. I turned around and hit him two more times. The last time sent him to the floor in a ball.

There was a strange growling. I realized it was me. Or something inside me, trying to get out.

I wrapped the alarm clock cord around his neck and started to pull for all I was worth. I was totally out of control.

Out of the corner out my eye I saw his buddy struggling to get to his feet. His face was still red from when I choked the hell out of him. Right as he took a step toward me I saw a leg come up and kick him right in the balls. His eyes nearly shot out of his head before he crumpled against the wall.

Alicia was on top of him, clawing and punching away. Whatever they'd given her, it must have started to wear off. Or, like me, anger was pushing her.

"You mother fuckers!" she shouted. "Touch my brother? I'll fucking kill you!"

That was Alicia. She was nearly raped, and she was worried about me.

Ironically, seeing her lose control made me start to calm down. I started thinking clearly again. I needed to get my sister away. These assholes didn't matter.

I loosened my grip on the alarm clock and hooked Alicia under the arms. It was tough pulling her away.

"Alicia, relax. It's okay. They're done. Let's go."

"You're damn right, they're fucking done."

She started to let me pull her away. But not before getting one last kick in to the other guy's balls.

She started to fall when we made it to the bedroom door. She wasn't quite ready for a marathon yet. Tears rolled down her face. She managed to pull her jeans up, but didn't have any shoes. I'd buy her another pair later. I just wanted to get her away.

I wrapped her arm around my neck to help support her. We walked through the house, getting quite a few looks. When we made it outside I stopped.

The gang was just pulling up in a minivan that Jenny was driving. It was her, as well as Dave, Tina, and Cindy. They had come to rescue us. I hadn't seen the crew in so long.

Alicia and I were quite a mess. Thankfully, I was in worse shape than she was, at least physically. Her clothes were messed up, and her face stained with tears. My face was starting to swell a little from the few beatings I'd gotten in one day. And now that I was calm, I was starting to feel the pain.

Jenny, Tina, and Cindy took over for me with Alicia. They helped her into the back of the minivan. Dave put a hand on my shoulder. He was all business.

"Do we need to go in there and fuck people up?"

Despite everything, I smiled. I couldn't ask for better friends. They had no idea of what was going on, but they put the pieces together. My crazy call to Cindy, seeing the shape we were both in.

"It's all taken care of. Some guys tried to mess with Alicia. But we beat the shit out of them."

Cindy walked up to us. She looked concerned. She put a hand to my face. I winced a little. "Damn, Alex. Are you okay?"

"Yeah, I'm fine. I'm in better shape than those two assholes in there."

"Assholes? As in more than one?"

"Yeah."

She was mad. "Dammit. Next time wait for us. You can't be doing crazy shit like that by yourself."

"I couldn't really wait. But thanks for worrying, sweetie pie."

I didn't expect the hug. She leaned forward and wrapped her arms around my neck. I hugged her back, a little nervous at the sudden touching. Dave was looking at us with a smirk. I could tell by his look that he knew I had a thing for her. Hell, it probably wasn't much of a secret anymore. But as long as Cindy didn't know, I was golden.

"Come on, guys, let's get out of here," he said.

CHAPTER 27

We agreed Alicia would stay with me at the apartment. The drive was quiet. Alicia didn't say much. Shock, maybe. She cried quietly. She sat in between me and Cindy. Cindy had an arm wrapped around her and stroked her hair. Dave and Tina tried to keep the mood light, just joking and carrying on.

The rest of us watched TV in my living room while Cindy and Alicia were alone in the bedroom. I had to change shirts once again. My damn wings were gonna cost me a fortune in shirts. I caught everyone up on what happened.

"Should she go to the police?"

I shrugged. I didn't know what the hell to do. I could barely talk from the soreness and numbness in my face.

"I really don't know. We all probably should, but I'll leave that up to Alicia. I did kind of fuck up two guys and a bedroom."

Jenny shook her head. "Man, I wish I saw that."

Everyone was surprised. I was always the calm one. Always in control. I was afraid that I'd lost it so bad. I really could have killed those two guys. And with the things I can do, I couldn't let myself ever get that out of hand again.

"Cindy came and picked us up to go out. She told us you two needed help," Tina said.

"I'm sorry I messed up your night, guys."

Dave waved me off. "Man, don't say stupid shit like that."

The bedroom door opened. Cindy walked out with a finger to her lips.

"Sleeping?" I asked.

"Yeah. She cried for a while. She's just shaken up. But she fell asleep."

"The police?"

"She said no."

I shook my head. I didn't know if that was a smart thing or not.

Cindy went into the kitchen and messed with something in the freezer.

"What do you guys think?" Dave asked. "Pizza? Movie?"

I laughed. Everyone was dressed for a night out, and it ended up with pizza and a movie. I was so sore, and the day was so packed, I wouldn't have minded a night to myself. I definitely could have used some time away from vampires. But I also couldn't think of a better way to end it than spending it with my friends.

And Cindy was gonna make it even better.

She came out of the kitchen with the phone and a little ice-bag she made. She tossed the phone to Dave.

"Get some pizza."

"Yes, ma'am."

I was alone on the couch. Dave and Tina were sitting on the loveseat, while Jenny sat on the floor and leaned against Tina's legs. Cindy crossed the living room and sat next me on the end. Then she tossed one leg against the back of the couch and stretched out. She patted the spot in front of her.

"Come here."

I looked at her. "Uh, dear? Shouldn't we save our crazy sex stuff for when no one's here?"

She rolled her eyes. "In your dreams."

I couldn't argue that. It would be a dream come true. She grabbed me by the shoulders and gently dragged me closer. Next thing I knew, I'm leaning back against her. She held the ice-bag against my bruised cheek while rubbing my shoulders with her free hand.

I can only imagine how tense I was.

"Alex, would you relax?"

"Oh, I'm relaxed."

She wrapped an arm around my chest and pulled me against her. She handed the ice-bag to me and squeezed my shoulders with both hands. Her face was right next to mine, watching TV while Jenny flipped through the channels. It felt great.

Dave looked at Tina. "I give you sex, and I never get a shoulder rub."

"Yeah, but you never give me *good* sex."

Jenny laughed.

"I've known this dumbass since we were sperm," Cindy said. "So we can get away with stuff like this. He knows I don't want him."

"How about a kiss? No tongue?"

"Don't push your luck."

I smiled. Dave gave me a fake look of sadness.

Then she leaned close to my ear so no one could hear.

"Maybe later."

I laughed. If only she weren't joking.

We watched a movie while waiting for the pizza. It was actually fun. I didn't know where to put my hands, so I rested one on Cindy's leg next to me. She was in the same situation, so she wrapped her arms around me and rested her head on my shoulder. Wow. She was being a little too touchy. It felt great, but made me want her more. That feeling I could do without. If we were alone, I'd probably spill my guts to her.

About halfway through the movie the door to my bedroom opened. Alicia gave us all a quick look before ducking into the bathroom. We all looked at each other, then I got up from the couch.

I gave the bathroom door a quick knock.

"What the hell? Can't a girl use the bathroom?"

I knew she wasn't using the bathroom. And she knew who was at the door. Sibling communication.

I cracked the door open.

"Alicia?"

She was splashing her face with water. She saw me in the mirror and turned around. Her hair was a mess, and her eyes were still red from crying. She gave me a small smile.

"I probably look terrible."

"You always do."

"Shut up."

I closed the door and leaned against the wall.

"You okay?"

She nodded. "Yeah, I think so."

"You sure you don't want to go to the police?"

"No. What would I tell them? Two guys, I have no idea who or where they are, tried to drug and fuck me?"

I winced. The anger almost built up all over again.

"Besides, I don't think they'll be touching anyone for a while."

We were quiet a second. She looked down at the floor.

"You disappointed in me?"

"Huh? What the hell are you talking about?"

"I keep messing up. The guy, he said his name was Tom, probably a fake name. Anyway, he said he just wanted to talk, away from everyone and the music. And I believed him. I'm so stupid. What is wrong with me?"

I grabbed her by the shoulders. "Hey. You don't keep messing up. And I'm never disappointed in you."

She nodded, and looked relieved. I love my sister. Scary to think our opinions matter to each other. We gave each other a quick hug.

"How did you know what was going on, anyway?"

"My little ghost powers. I'll *always* have your back. Now clean up, and come out and eat some pizza."

We had a good time for the next few hours before everyone started heading home. Cindy went back to her apartment, while Alicia slept on the couch. It was an insane day, but it made me realize how much my friends and family meant to me.

I definitely needed some rest.

*****

I finally got some overdue sleep. It was past noon when I woke up. Alicia was gone. She'd left a note on the table saying she and Cindy had gone shopping. That was good. I wanted to see Alicia relax as much as possible.

I took a shower and was half dressed when the cell phone rang. I took a deep breath before answering. I doubted Victoria was calling just to say hi.

"Hello?"

"Alex. It's Victoria."

"I figured that."

"Is everything alright?"

"Yeah. It was a crazy night. But it's all fine. Everything okay on your end?"

She was quiet a moment. "Yeah. I, uh, took care of William. Left him out for the sun."

"Are you okay?"

"I will be. I grabbed his files and spent most of the night looking them over."

"Find anything?"

"I think so. They weren't officially missing, as it hadn't been a day yet, but William was smart. He's got a report that two people, Shannon Smith and Tom Zimmerman, went missing a few blocks from where the butcher shop is."

"Hmm. Shannon and Tom. Do you think-"

"Yes. I already looked into it. They were the vampires we fought that night."

"Okay. Do you think we can dig into their lives? Try to figure out where they got bit?"

"We can try. They both worked at the same place. Some place called Waylon Research. We should probably start there."

Waylon Research. The two words immediately brought to mind the vampire in a cage at Bachner's hideout. He had a security uniform with the initials W.R.S. on it.

Waylon Research Security.

"Oh shit," I said.

"What's up?"

"The vampire. The one I told you Bachner had. He worked there too, as a security guard."

"Okay. Finally, we got something," she said. "Can you meet me there tonight? Say like midnight or one o'clock?"

"You mean, like, break into the place?

"Exactly. I'll get the address, figure out what I can about the building."

"Do you really still need my help?"

"Yes, I do. Don't worry, after all this is over, you'll get a big fat check."

"I'm not worried about that, Victoria."

"I know."

I frowned. I just wanted life to go back to normal. Hell, it was Sunday, and I didn't make a habit of being up late before a work day. But I knew I wouldn't say no to her.

"Alright. I'll be there."

"Thank you, Alex. See you tonight."

CHAPTER 28

I didn't see Cindy or Alicia for the rest of the day. I guess they had a female day, which was fine by me, as my mind was far away.

It was a restful day. But as the sun set and I made myself dinner, I started growing more anxious. I hoped tonight would be a simple night. I hoped we would go to Waylon Research, Victoria would find what she was looking for, and we'd head home. But what were the chances of that?

Waylon Research was out in the middle of nowhere. A series of turns off the beltway led through a wooded area and a gravel road. Through the trees up ahead I could see a building surrounded by a fence and light posts.

The cell phone rang.

"Alex," Victoria said. "I can hear your truck."

"Where are you?"

"Right by the fence. Far corner, by the light pole. Why didn't you fly?"

I didn't expect the question. "Uh, cause my truck still works?"

"You're making too much noise. Stop right now, back up, and park in the woods somewhere."

"Alright. Don't go nowhere."

I did as she said. Once I killed the engine, I realized there was no light at all.

It took me almost falling in the dark to remember I had night vision.

I closed my eyes, and willed the darkness away. Gray replaced black, while trees and bushes took shape once again. I headed to the far corner of the fence, and saw Victoria leaning against a tree in the shadows. She shook her head as I got closer.

"You can fly and you're fireproof, but you can't be quiet at all," she whispered.

"Hey, give me a break. If I go ghost and start walking through shit, I lose my night vision."

"Poor you."

I stood next to her and stared at the building. Nothing really jumped out at me about it. Looked like a typical office building. Plenty of windows, with a few office lights on. An empty parking lot. Nice little sidewalk leading to the front door.

"You notice anything weird?" I asked.

She nodded. "The security."

I squinted. There was a lone security guard walking around. One time I saw him talk into his radio. Looked normal to me.

"What about him?"

"Just gives me a weird feeling. Security guards don't usually walk around anymore. Most of them sit in nice cozy rooms and watch monitors all night long. Hell, there probably shouldn't be any security at all, at least not people."

"Well, what exactly is this place?"

"Medical consulting. They basically improve hospitals and medicine."

"Okay then. What's the plan?"

She pointed to an open office window on the fifth floor.

"We get in through there."

"Uh, you can fly?"

"No. Don't worry about me. I'll meet you in there."

I shrugged, then vanished and walked through the fence. I walked calmly across the parking lot, invisible to everything. I passed the security guard and walked through the front door.

There were plenty of offices, plenty of what looked to be exam rooms. I didn't pass by a single person.

I walked through the door leading to the stairs and started climbing. It was strange not hearing my own footsteps. I felt a little guilty. Not just at the fact that I was sneaking around, but that I was sneaking around so easily.

I got a little lost on the fifth floor. I had to peek into office doors, as I had no idea of which office Victoria was pointing to from outside. I got lucky, though. I turned a corner and saw a light come on at the end of the hall. I took a peek in, and sure enough, Victoria was sitting at a computer.

I closed the door behind me, and noticed the window was still open.

"How the hell did you get up here?"

"I'm a vampire, Alex."

I waited for her to continue. She didn't. I leaned over her shoulder as she typed away at the keyboard.

"What are you looking for?"

"To be honest, I have no idea. But we have three feral vampires, all with ties to this place."

"What do you want me to do?"

"Just sit there and look cute for a minute. Keep an eye out, make sure security doesn't make their way up here."

I shook my head. Something felt wrong with Victoria paying me five hundred dollars a day to stick my head out an office door.

"So, you talk to Cindy yet?"

The question caught me off guard. Seemed like a weird time to be talking about my personal life.

"Uh, no. The chance hasn't really come up yet. I will, though."

"What are you afraid of?"

"Well, getting slapped in the face and losing my best friend, for starters."

She shook her head. "You don't give yourself enough credit. I keep telling you, if you weren't hung up on her, I'd be all over you. It's a shame we're a few centuries apart."

I laughed. "Yeah. A real shame."

"Seriously, Alex. I just lost a good friend. You always think there's enough time. There *never* is. You know, when I was your age, I-" she cut herself off.

"What? What's up?"

She almost looked amused. "You gotta love computers. Fifty years ago, I'd be tearing apart file cabinets and offices. Not anymore. Check this out."

I looked at the monitor, but didn't really know what I was looking at.

"What is it?"

"I'm just poking around in their file server, seeing what they got. Look at this."

She pointed at a file folder on the screen.

Hominus Nocturna.

"Hominus Nocturna? What the hell is that?"

"Fancy name for vampire."

"Are you kidding? That's sitting right there on their file server?"

"Not exactly. I've picked up a few tricks along the way."

"Well, what's in there?"

"Let's find out."

The file folder was full of videos, probably a hundred or so. I wasn't prepared for any of them at all.

Victoria picked one at random. It showed an examination room. A man was restrained on a table. It only took a moment to realize he was a vampire. He thrashed and struggled, looking a lot like the feral vampires we'd already found. A man in a white coat took some notes, then faced the camera.

"The mixture looks like it has the complete opposite effect of what was intended. Instead of killing the mutant strain, it seems it only makes it stronger. We're gonna keep trying."

Victoria cut him off to load another video. This one showed the same room, except with two vampires restrained instead of one. The same doctor looked into the camera. He paced a little, obviously unnerved.

"We've been unsuccessful in killing the original mutant strain. Although, by sheer dumb luck, we've discovered that this new mutant strain can be passed to ordinary humans." He gestured to the tables. He didn't look comfortable at all. "The, uh, subject on the left is...*was*...a janitor who strayed too close to Section B. We're still working to reverse his condition."

I looked at Victoria. She was cool. I admit, I was freaked out.

She loaded one more, the last one. The same doctor, even though this time he wore plain street clothes. He looked visibly shaken. The two vampires behind him on the tables were motionless. I could see wooden stakes jutting from their chests.

"This will be my last report before I resign my position. The new mutant strain isn't reversible. It should be destroyed. But it seems my supervisors don't agree. I'm worried that it could be made even stronger."

Victoria closed the video. She clasped her hands and stared at the monitor. She said nothing. I was the first one to talk.

"Victoria, what did we just see?"

"They were trying to cure vampirism. Looks like it backfired, and turned into what we're dealing with. He called it a strain? More like a damn plague. And it just doesn't affect some humans, but all of them, and makes them like animals."

"You and me alone, we've already seen four vampires in the city. Who knows how many Bachner and his crew have seen."

"Yeah. This is scary. This is why I hate the twenty-first century sometimes. Our kind and science don't mix."

"What's the next move?"

"He said something about Section B. Gotta be here somewhere. Let's make a stop there."

A new voice, right behind me.

"You can't. There's no time."

I spun around. Victoria noticed my surprise, and spun in her chair. But she didn't see what I saw. My mouth hung open.

"You've got about fifteen seconds before this place explodes."

"Huh? What are you-"

"Get moving. Now!"

I grabbed Victoria. "Come on. We have to go."

I pulled her to the open window. I popped my wings, and ruined yet another shirt.

"Hold on tight."

She didn't ask any questions. She gave me a tight hug.

We flew about ten feet from the window. Then the explosion rocked my ears. I felt the heat at my back. We flew forward, but I didn't have any control. We were heading to the ground.

It was Victoria's turn to save me. She held on tight and wouldn't let go.

She hit the ground first, and cushioned our fall. The air rushed out of my lungs. I rolled on my back, in time to see some flaming debris heading right for us. Victoria was already on her feet and pulling me out of the way.

I only remember my legs moving. Victoria had me by the shirt and led me away from the burning building. A few more tiny explosions went off. I gasped for breath.

When we got near the fence she stopped. I fell to one knee and tried to breathe. She was next to me, holding the back of her head. Vampire or not, she was in pain.

"You okay?" she asked.

I managed a nod. We both turned and looked at the fire. Just like that, the five-story building was up in flames. How in the hell was that possible? Explosives on each floor?

"Shit. I hope no one was in there."

I saw some shapes moving near the front of the building. They started wandering away from the fire, looking lost and confused. I could make out arms and legs. Finally I could see their clothes. But they weren't on fire.

My heart sank.

"There *were* people in there," I told Victoria. My voice cracked a little. "Looks like at least two security guards, and a few late night office workers."

"You...can see their ghosts?"

"Yeah." It was the first time I'd ever seen ghosts of people who had died just minutes before. It was surreal. I'd never seen anything more sad. Just like that, so many lives and families destroyed. "Should I say something to them?"

The voice came from right next to me. "There's nothing you can say."

I turned to look at him. The ghost who had minutes earlier saved our lives. Detective Bill Sloane.

He gave me a quick nod, then gestured to the other spirits, who wandered aimlessly. They looked at each other, then at the burning chaos behind them.

"In about a half hour or so, they'll realize they're dead. They'll probably lose it for a while. Just yell and scream. Then their families will come for them."

"Is that what happened to you?"

"Alex?" Victoria said. "Who you talking to?"

"Yeah," Bill said. "My parents, and my sister who I lost when I was younger to cancer. It was great to see them again. But I told them I had some things to do first."

"Like what?"

"Like put away one more case."

"Are you kidding?"

Victoria tossed her hands in the air. "Alex, please fill me in on what the hell is going on."

I took a frustrated breath and grabbed Victoria by the hand. It was almost by instinct. I had no idea of what I thought would happen.

But my hand started tingling, like it was asleep. Then she took a quick breath. She looked right at Bill, and could see him.

"William?"

Bill was as surprised as Victoria and me. He almost managed a smile.

"I see why everyone on the other side is talking about you. How are you doing that?"

I shrugged. "I really don't know. I don't ask questions anymore."

"William," Victoria said. She took a step forward to touch his face. Her hand went through his skin. She pulled it back quickly. "I'm so sorry. I'm sorry for what I did."

"You drove a stake through my heart and left me for the sunlight," he said. "You did exactly what I would have done. We're cool, Victoria. I don't blame you at all. I blame whoever cooked up that vampire virus."

"Do you know what's going on?"

He nodded. "I think so, at least a little. I'm still a cop, you know. But we can't talk here."

"Yeah," she agreed. "There's a park-and-ride train station just up the highway. Let's meet up there."

I let go of her hand. The tingling vanished, and Victoria could no longer see William.

With a touch, I could let others see into the spirit world.

My mind was going in crazy directions as I followed Victoria up the highway. I thought about the exploding medical center, poor Bill, the insane vampire mess we were in. But my mind kept drifting back to those lost ghosts walking out of the burning wreckage of their workplace. One second, they were working a normal night shift. The next, their ghosts were wandering the parking lot. Everything gone, in less than a second.

It made me think of Cindy. I needed to talk to her, tell her how I felt. Victoria was right, there was never enough time.

The park-and-ride was almost completely empty. Only a few cars sprinkled the lot. I saw Victoria leaning against her car. William stood next to her. It made me wonder how he got there. I guess ghosts teleport somehow.

I took a deep breath as I parked next to her. I wasn't looking forward to the conversation we were getting ready to have. A vampire, ghost, and some kind of demon thing getting ready to talk about feral vampires.

"Alex," she said as I got closer. She looked all around her. "Is William here?"

I nodded and pointed. "Yeah, right next to you."

Victoria held out a hand. I took it. She almost jumped when she saw William.

"Okay," Victoria said. She wasted no time. "What's going on, William?"

He nodded. "I was a step ahead of you in finding that medical center. I was checking it out, and saw some mercenary lookin' bastard with no hair wiring explosives all over the place. He really knew what he was doing."

Victoria snarled. "Heins."

"You know him?"

"Yeah, I know him. Works for an old vampire hunter buddy of mine named Bachner. Why the hell would they want to blow up the medical center?"

I shook my head. Something didn't make sense here.

"Victoria, when I found Bachner, they had a feral locked in a cage. It didn't seem like they had any idea of what it was. I don't think they know where they came from."

"Well, maybe they *just* found out, and decided to kill the labs where the virus was cooked up."

Yeah, maybe. Seemed like a stretch though. The day before, they didn't have a clue. To go from not having a clue, to wiring a building to explode, seemed like a large leap. But something else ate at me.

"Bachner, he wouldn't kill anyone."

"Oh, really? You're a shrink now?"

She was irritated at my defending him. "No. I'm just saying. I know, he hates *you*. He hates vampires. But he wouldn't have killed those people in that building."

"But Heins would."

"Well, Heins works for Bachner."

We were all quiet for a moment, unsure of what to think. It didn't feel like we were getting anywhere. Victoria looked at Bill.

"Did you get a look at Section B?"

"I got a look at the whole place. They had a huge lab in the basement. No humans were there. But they did have about ten vampires locked in cages, strapped to tables. Looked like they were studying them. I'm guessing that's your Section B."

"Okay, so the lab is destroyed, the ferals dead. They kill innocent people doing it, but they wipe out that virus. Now *we* have to make one hundred percent sure the virus is dead and gone."

"How do we do that?"

"Tomorrow, we go to their little hideout, ask Bachner what he knows."

Bill looked at me. "Give me the address. I'll go scope out the place. Then I'll come get you when the sun starts going down."

"I'll have some friends check it out too," Victoria said.

"Okay. Until tomorrow night, then? What do you want me to do?"

"Well, it's early Monday morning already. Go to work."

Easy for her to say.

CHAPTER 29

The day at work went like any other. It was actually refreshing. As much as loading trucks sucked sometimes, I could put behind me all the crap I'd been dealing with over the past few days. Vampires, ghosts, exploding buildings, my sister. It felt good to settle back into an eight hour routine and drive a forklift all day, even if I was exhausted.

An hour after I got home, I was listening to the ballgame, making a simple dinner, when the cell phone rang. I was surprised the call didn't come much sooner. I took a breath, knowing it was time to run out soon.

"Hello?"

"Alex. It's Victoria. You heard from Bill?"

"Nah, not at all."

She was quiet. "That's weird. I had a friend check out that address you gave me. Completely empty."

I sat on the couch, ignoring dinner. So much for another night out with Victoria and Bill. Not if we didn't know where Bachner was. "Are you kidding? I'm telling you, they had a huge thing going on there. Guns, plans, maps, and that damn vampire."

"I believe you. I'm just saying, there's nothing there now. They know we're on to them, and they packed up and left."

"They gotta be somewhere else. Probably still in the city."

"I know. But where? And what the hell are they up to? Bad things are gonna happen if that vampire they have gets out."

"I wouldn't worry about that too much. They must have blown up the research center to cover up the virus. They're vampire killers. They don't want that to spread. Believe it or not, whatever the hell it is they cooked up in that place, I think Bachner and us are on the same side."

"Maybe. But I'll feel much better when we find Bachner and he says 'Yes, we killed the last feral and the virus is dead.'"

"Then he'll go after you."

"Well, he can certainly try."

The front door opened. I turned to make sure it was Cindy. She gave me a smile and wave. She just got off work herself, wearing a gray skirt with a white shirt and gray jacket. Looking hot and professional. She stopped for a second, seeing I was on the phone. I motioned for her to come inside. Despite all the crazy things going on, I missed her.

"What's the next move?" I asked.

"We find them. It's that simple. I got some friends out snooping around. And I have no idea what Bill is doing, but hopefully he'll get with you."

"So we wait?"

She didn't sound happy. "Afraid so. The sun's down, so I'm gonna get to work, hit the streets. You get a night off, rest and relax. I've been pushing you harder than I thought I would."

"I've been handling it so far."

"Yes, you have. Don't worry, I'll call if I need you."

"Okay. You take it easy."

I hung the phone up.

I leaned on my knees. I knew in a perfect world, Bachner had discovered the vampire virus, and killed that vampire they had in a cage. The virus would be dead and gone. Then we could get back to something that was almost normal.

Cindy was getting a soda out of the fridge. I almost forgot she was there. My mind was going in so many directions.

"Was that Red Hot?" she asked.

I smiled. I almost forgot about that nickname. "Yeah."

"Sure you're not interested in her? I can give you some good advice."

"Ha, yeah. Like I gave you? No, we're just working together right now."

"More demon stuff?"

"Yeah, you could say that. Don't worry, I'll tell you all about it later."

"Cool. You know if you need someone to talk to, I'm here."

"I know. But I'm okay. Getting things under control."

She nodded. "I talked to Leese today. She's doing alright. Still a little down, though."

"I'll bet."

"She's lucky she's got a big brother looking out for her."

"That's my job. I'm gonna give her a day or so, then check up on her. She knows she can stop by whenever she needs to."

"Yeah, she'll be fine. She's actually at the game tonight with her friends," she said, pointing at the TV.

I was jealous for a second. We hadn't been to a game in a while. Cindy leaned in the kitchen doorway. I remember when I thought to myself that the next time I got the chance, I'd tell Cindy exactly how I felt. I couldn't the other night when the gang was over. But I was home, and she was with me, relaxing like we always did. There was so much going on, and there might have been no such thing as a perfect time. But it was now or never.

"Uh, Cindy," I said from the couch. I could already feel my stomach knotting up. "We gotta talk about some stuff."

She finished a drink of soda and took a deep breath. "Me first."

I was surprised. "Everything okay?"

"No."

I kept quiet. She tossed her soda away and actually started pacing. She was making me nervous. I had to get up and move too. I got a soda from the fridge, just to keep my hands busy and stand with her. I don't know why, but I was terrified of what she had to say.

"Cindy. You can tell me anything, you know."

She finally stood still long enough to give me a sad smile. "Maybe not this time."

"You want to sit down?"

"No."

I leaned against the wall and waited patiently. It took her about a minute to say something.

"Shit. This has been on my mind forever. And I don't know where to start."

"How about the beginning?"

"That would be high school."

I didn't say anything, just gave her a puzzled look.

"Every guy I've ever dated, they always end up saying the same thing. 'You spend too much time with that friend Alex of yours. Either you stop hanging out with him, or we're through.'"

I smiled. "I had a few of those talks too."

"Yeah. And every time, I picked you. Didn't do much for my dating."

I was tense. I didn't like where this seemed to be going.

She started pacing again. Her hands were actually shaking.

I tried to brace myself for the friendship-only talk.

"I can't believe I'm doing this."

"Cindy, what's going on?"

I took a step toward her and put my hands on her shoulders. She backed away, almost like I was a snake. I put my hands up and stepped back.

"Sorry."

She looked frustrated. "No, Alex. I didn't mean-"

She made a disgusted sigh and rested her hands on the back on the couch.

"When college started, I kept comparing every boyfriend to you. I wanted them all to be like you. 'Why can't they all be like Alex?' Then it finally clicked one day. I wanted *you*, and couldn't have you. How the hell do you tell your best friend you got eyes for him? All I've been trying to do is find excuses to get close to you. I even moved right next door."

My jaw hung open a little. She wasn't done.

"So I watched you date all these other women, who I knew weren't right for you. Every day, trying to hide being jealous. I was getting sick of it. So last week, I finally decide to try to move on, and go on a date. And it's the same shit all over again. I just wanted him to be you. He was a nice guy, but it wasn't fair to him."

So *that's* why she was mad at me. It was making a little more sense.

"Sorry, I'm rambling. I've been whining to Leese about this for a year now. I know she's getting tired of hearing it. So here goes." She took another deep breath. "Alex, we should try going out a few times. You know, like *real* dates. We both know each other better than anyone else, and I think there could be something between us. What do you think?"

I'd never seen her so nervous. It was actually funny. For so long, I struggled with my feelings whenever I was around her. She did the same, even longer than me, and I never even realized it.

I stood there staring at her. So much went through me. The first girl I'd ever known. We both stood up to the kindergarten asshole together. She knew most everything about me, even the fact that I had wings inside me. Here she was, in my apartment, stuttering over her words to ask me out on a date.

"Uh, Alex? Say something? Did I mess that up? Want me to leave you alone?"

I wanted to kiss her so bad.

So that's what I did.

I caught her off guard. I kissed her harder than I meant to. She didn't respond for a second, and I heard her make a startled sound. I thought I went too far. I was getting ready to pull away when I felt her hands slip around my neck. And off we went.

There was definitely something between us.

We wrapped our arms around each other and just kissed. Real light, getting used to each other's lips. I lost track of time, but she eventually pulled away. She had the brightest smile I'd ever seen. She was still shaking a little.

"Did you want to say something?" she asked.

I shook my head. Our lips were only inches apart. "Nope. You pretty much covered it."

"Leese kept telling me. I didn't believe her."

She laughed, and we kissed some more. After a while, it was my turn to pull away.

"Cindy, listen," I said. "You really don't care? You know, about me-"

I didn't even get a chance to finish the question about me not being completely human. She shut me up with a kiss. She pushed my lips apart with her tongue and pressed up against me. Her body felt great. Our breathing started picking up. It wasn't just a kiss anymore.

I was making out with my best friend. Our hands started going all over the place. The gentleness faded away, and passion took over. We'd known each other since we were five. We used to play in the dirt together in her parents' backyard. We used to babysit Alicia when we were in middle school. Maybe it should have felt strange, but it didn't at all.

She was the first one to go for the clothes.

I felt her hands grabbing at my shirt. I didn't fight her trying to take it off. I helped her shrug out of her coat and took her shirt off. Just an amazing body. With a smile on her face, she shoved me backwards. I fell over the arm of the couch and landed on my back. I looked up to see Cindy in her skirt and bra. I can't remember if my mouth hung open or not, but whatever I did, got a laugh out of her. She climbed on top of me, very slow, very sexy, and pressed her chest against me as she kissed me again.

"I guess you don't mind me being a freak. I mean, I do have wings," I managed to say, this time with a smile, instead of a frown.

She returned the grin and looked at me. She had a glow about her. I'd never seen her happier, and I was the one she was happy about. Wow. Not even flying through the sky compared to how I felt as she looked me in the eyes. She played with my hair. I had a hand resting on her lower back. Just the fact that our bodies were touching, flesh to flesh, drove me nuts.

"A freak? I thought you were gonna ask if I cared that you were a white boy."

We laughed, and kissed again.

The longer we made out, the more our barriers dropped. It wasn't long before I had her skirt pulled up to her hips and was rubbing her legs and firm ass. She had a hand on the front of my pants and grinded against me. Between nibbles on my ear I heard her quite clearly.

"You don't know how long I've wanted this," she whispered.

"What took us so long?"

She undid the top of my jeans. My heart started hammering. Cindy was gonna take it as far as we could go. And I wasn't gonna stop her. As she fumbled with the snap, I leaned up and kissed the top of her breasts. She moaned and wrapped her fingers in my hair. I wanted her so bad. And she wanted me. I felt goosebumps on my skin as she went for my pants again.

Unfortunately, the goosebumps were only half from Cindy.

"Alex," the voice said.

I turned my head to see Detective Bill Sloane's face staring at me.

"What the hell!" I called out.

Cindy jumped from the couch. I scared the hell out of her. I stood next to her and looked at Bill, who stood behind the couch. His eyes weren't on me, though. He looked Cindy up and down. Can't say I blame him. Only a bra, her skirt pulled up to her hips, showing off a pair of thin black panties. Cindy was looking at me, more confused than afraid. I jumped in front of her with my back to her. She wrapped her arms around my waist and pressed against me. It was strange to cover up someone from the prying eyes of a ghost.

"You got good taste, Alex. Look, we got *major* problems."

"Bill, that's just not cool," was all I could say.

"I would have knocked, if I could. *Listen* to me. We've gotta go."

Cindy was quick. "Who's Bill? Alex, are you talking to a ghost?"

"Yeah."

She gripped me a little tighter. She had some fright in her voice. "Well, uh, is it a good ghost?"

I gave Bill a look. "At least I *thought* so." I held Cindy's hand and stayed in front of her. I felt the same tingling that I had the last time I tried my latest trick with Victoria. I heard Cindy take in a breath behind me, and I knew she could see him.

"Cindy. This is Detective William Sloane."

"Call me Bill. Listen, the warehouse address you gave us, it's empty."

Cindy squeezed my hand. "Holy shit," she said. "Alex, how are you doing this?"

It was tough talking to two people at once. "I got a magic touch. I know, Bill. Victoria called and told me. She's looking for them."

"Well, I *found* them."

As soon as he said it, the ballgame actually went off TV. All there was was a tone and a *technical difficulties* message. Hadn't seen one of those in quite a while.

"The stadium," Bill said. "Those bastards sneaked their little pet bloodsucker to the stadium and let it loose near one of the back doors. Took me forever just to figure out how to get here to tell you."

"What? Camden Yards? The game we're watching *right now*? They're trying to *spread* the virus? Was Bachner there?"

"I don't even know who Bachner is. I don't know their names."

"Bachner? Virus? What the hell is going on?" Cindy asked.

We should have been a little more aware of the fact that we were half naked with a ghost in the room. A minute before, Cindy and I were in our own world on the couch. She was still pressed against my back, but my mind wasn't on her gorgeous body.

I picked up Cindy's shirt off the floor and handed it to her. Then I grabbed the cell phone from the coffee table. It seemed like it took her forever to answer.

"Hello?"

"Victoria, it's me." I heard a lot of noise in the background. She wasn't at her house, but out on the streets. "Listen, Bachner took the feral to Camden

Yards. They somehow got it in. The game actually just went off the air." My heart sank as I remembered. "Leese is *there*. My sister's at the game."

"Calm down, Alex. I'll call back in one minute."

That one minute felt like an eternity. Bill stood there behind the couch, watching us. Cindy grabbed me by the shoulders to stop me from pacing.

"What is going on?" she asked gently.

"They're trying to make more vampires," I said. "Why the fuck would they do that?"

"Vampires? Like people even more white than you, but with longer teeth?"

I told Cindy everything about me, but nothing about vampires. There was so much she didn't know.

"Is Leese okay?" she asked.

"Yeah. I'd sense it if she wasn't. But I gotta get over there."

"Get over there? You're not doing anything stupid."

The phone rang.

"Hello?"

"Alex, it's me. Containment's gonna start real quick."

"Containment? What-"

"*Listen.* This virus will spread through that stadium *fast*. One vampire will turn into two, two into four, you get the idea. We've gotta go and help however we can. Are you with me?"

"Yeah."

"Good. I'll meet you there."

"How am I gonna find you?"

"I'll be the one killing vampires."

She hung up.

I took a deep breath. I wasn't ready for this. But I had to get moving. I grabbed Cindy's hand so she could see Bill once again.

"Bill, can you get to the stadium?"

He looked embarrassed. "Well, yeah, but it took me a while to get here. I'm not an expert on *ghost moving* yet."

"Okay. Get there however you can. Look for me or Victoria."

"Well, how are *you* gonna get there-"

My wings shot out of my back before he could finish. Cindy gasped. She knew I had them, but it was her first glimpse of them.

"Holy shit."

I looked at her. She squeezed my hand a little. A part of me was still afraid she was gonna take off and run. Instead, she gave me a soft smile.

"You okay?" I asked her.

She nodded. "What do you want me to do?"

"Stay here."

"The hell I am."

She was serious. I grabbed her shoulders. "Cindy, we really are dealing with *vampires* here. We have to stop them before they bust out of Camden Yards. *Please*, stay here. Lock the door and all the windows and just lay low."

She didn't look away. Slowly, she nodded her head.

I let her go and clipped the cell phone to my belt. I gave Bill a look.

"Okay, Detective. I'll see you there."

I opened the sliding glass door to my balcony. Before I could step out I felt a hand on my wing. Cindy spun me around and surprised me with a deep kiss. She rested her forehead against mine.

"*Don't* get hurt."

"Don't worry. I won't."

She smiled, and actually stroked my wing. I hate to say it, but it felt good.

"I still want a ride."

I smiled back and turned around toward the balcony. I climbed on the railing and jumped off. I sank for only a second, until my wings started to lift me up.

CHAPTER 30

I flew as fast as I could. I tried to take shortcuts and avoid following the roads. But I had to keep the highway in sight some of the time, as I didn't know how to get to the city otherwise. I made good time. I can fly pretty damn fast.

As I got closer, the shit started to hit the fan.

Traffic started to bottleneck maybe a mile or so outside the city limits. That wasn't anything surprising. What was surprising was the military that was suddenly everywhere. It looked like a war zone. Jeeps, hummers, soldiers standing tall at intersections. As I got closer to Camden Yards, I could finally see what Victoria was talking about. Maybe it wasn't obvious down on the ground. But from the sky it was clear.

The military was setting up a quarantine around the stadium.

Camden Yards has a large fence surrounding the whole thing. At every gate, every single turnstile, I could see soldiers keeping people inside. They also kept people from getting in. The very sight scared the hell out of me. How far would the military go? Was Victoria responsible for all of this?

I hovered far above the stadium, so no one could see me. I could see people running around, though, and even heard what sounded like gunshots.

I heard a helicopter, and had to spin to see where it was. It was heading right for me. I can only imagine how many bullets they'd put in me if they got close enough. A half naked guy flying in midair was certainly going to attract attention.

I dived downward. As Camden Yards grew closer, I could really see what was happening. Just pure chaos. I saw bodies now, in the stands with pools of blood forming under them. People running and screaming, trampling each other. Feral vampires were leaping and attacking. I saw one pin a woman to the ground from behind and sink its fangs into her neck. A group of four attacked a group of teens.

We were too late. It was spreading.

I also saw vampire hunters.

It was a group of three of them, moving through a crowd away from the playing field. They were laughing as they gunned down a few vampires, then drove a stake though their hearts.

I landed on top of the lights high above home plate. I really didn't know what was going on. I didn't know why Bachner spread the virus, yet now had his men killing vampires. I didn't know what the military was planning.

I had a flash in my head. I almost lost balance for a second. I had to grab the light structure to keep from falling.

It was Alicia. I was inside her head, seeing what she saw.

She was in danger.

Hell, *everyone* was in danger.

She was running down the corridor with a group of people. Arms were flailing around and there were screams. I couldn't tell where she was at all. A vampire that used to be a hotdog vendor dove at her feet. He barely missed her and bit the man running next to her. I caught a quick glimpse of Donna, her friend from school, pulling her by the hand.

"We have to get out of here!" she shouted.

I shook the vision off as best I could. I needed to be in my own head. I yanked the cell phone out and called Alicia. I didn't know if she'd answer or not. But I had to try. If she saw it was me calling, she would answer.

I was right.

"Alex, please help," she said. I could hear the panic in her voice. "There's something fucking crazy going on at the stadium!"

"I'm here now. Where are you?"

"I don't know! Shit. We just passed section two-thirty."

"Alright, listen. You can't get out, we're all locked in. Find someplace and barricade yourself. Just hide. You hear me? Then text me when you're safe and let me know where you are."

"Okay."

I hung up. Time to find section two-thirty.

I heard a scream beneath me. There was a man running across the field. Two vampires were chasing him. He only had maybe a few seconds before they were on him.

I folded my wings and jumped off the light rack. I wouldn't be able to fly to him in time, so I let myself fall straight down. Ten feet before I hit the ground I threw my wings out and beat them a single time as hard as I could, then landed on one knee near home plate. Still hurt a little.

The two vampires tackled the man just past second base near the outfield.

"Hey!" I shouted at the top of my lungs.

They both looked up right at me. The two vampires used to be ushers.

Blood ran down their orange and white uniforms and from their new fangs. I could see the red glow in their eyes.

They ran at me. Behind them I could see the man they attacked get up and run away. He certainly wasn't going to help me.

I took a few steps back as the vampires quickly closed the gap. I was afraid, but shoved it aside. I could easily vanish and let them pass right through me. But I had to fight them. I had to stop them from hurting anyone else, or worse, *biting* anyone else.

I lashed out with my wing as the closest one got near. It actually knocked him to the ground, surprising the hell out of me. But then the other was on me.

He tackled me hard. I fell back and my head bounced off the ground. Pain shot through me and I started seeing stars. I had enough sense to throw my arms out, and I caught him under the chin, barely holding him back from taking a bite out of my face.

He snarled and pushed against my face with his hand. Out of the corner of my eye I could see the other one rising to his feet.

There was nothing I could do. I vanished. The vampire fell through me and jumped to his feet. He looked at the other one before they both ran off together.

I stood up slowly, still breathing hard. I was all by myself, invisible to the world. I was so angry. I had all these amazing powers. But there was really nothing I could do against a creature so much stronger than me.

As I once again faded back into the world of the living, my cell phone beeped. It was a text message from Alicia.

Ruby Tuesday near section 240. Come fast.

I flew straight up, then soared over the stadium seats. Most of the outside was empty. I could see dead bodies, and newborn vampires rising up. Most of the people were in the corridors, trying to escape. I looked at the section markers and finally found section two-forty.

I vanished before I even hit the ground. I ran through everything in my way. I tried not to look too hard at the massacre around me. Men and women being devoured. Blood everywhere. I saw a group of maybe eight or so vampires at the front door to the Ruby Tuesday's. I could see people inside frantically blocking the door and every window. I ran through the mob of vampires to get inside.

There were four people. Alicia was there with her friend Donna. A Ruby Tuesday waiter with a name tag of Chris, probably around Alicia's age. An older guy who looked like a business executive. White shirt, dress pants, black tie. They all worked together to put as much crap as they could in front of the place. Tables, chairs, carts.

"I knew it. All along I knew it," Chris said as he pushed another table near the front door. "It's right on the web. Vampires have always been real."

"Chris, would you shut the hell up?" Donna said. "They're trying to get in here!"

"Okay, okay. After this, we're gonna have to start a fire."

"Mister Johnson! Slide that cart over here!" Alicia said.

He did so. "Please, call me Sam."

I appeared behind everyone.

"Is everyone okay?" I said.

They all turned. I didn't think about how I looked. A shirtless guy, appearing out of thin air, with a huge pair of wings sticking out of his back. Sam and Donna took a step back. Chris surprised me. He grabbed a broken table leg and jumped in front of Alicia.

I gave him a look. Thin looking guy. Kind of nerdy looking with short black hair and thick glasses. But he was facing down a demon with a table leg. I was impressed. It was obvious he liked my sister.

"What the hell are you?" Chris asked.

"Relax," Alicia put a hand on his shoulder. "He's my brother."

"Your brother is a vampire?"

She walked around him and gave me a quick hug. She stared at my wings. I just gave a sheepish shrug.

"We'll talk later," I said.

A noise came from the front. The vampires were slowly pushing the doors open, even with everything in the way.

"Come on! Get more up there!"

I started helping. We tossed everything we could get our hands on in the pile. I pushed with all my strength. The group of vampires was slowed, but it wouldn't last forever. I could hear them scratching and tearing at the tables. The windows were already broken. I saw a hand reach through and almost grab Sam by the hair.

We all leaned against the mess we'd made. Donna was crying now. Alicia looked at me, fear in her eyes. I grabbed my cell phone.

It took forever for Victoria to answer.

"Alex, I'm a little busy here."

"We're trapped. Ruby Tuesday's near section two-forty."

"Trapped? How the hell can *you* be trapped?"

"Come on, hurry up. I'm with my sister and some others. They're breaking their way in."

She hung up.

"Help is coming."

The table I pushed against split apart. A vampire had simply kicked it. They were slowly pushing their way in. One barely missed raking his hand across my face.

"Okay, everybody back up," I said. "Get a weapon, anything you can use. We need fire."

"The kitchen's in the back," Chris said.

I looked to the rear of the place. None of us could run back there and make a fire of some kind before the vampires were on us. I didn't see it happening.

"Donna, Alicia, get to the back and hide."

"No," Alicia said while grabbing a broken cart leg.

Chris smiled. "I like her."

She smiled back at him.

We all backed up in a line, just waiting. They thrashed like wild animals as they punched through the tables and carts we put in their way.

"Go for the heart, okay? Like in the movies."

The first one broke through. I lashed out with a wing and gouged out one of his eyes. He howled in pain and fell. Two others tripped over him. Chris and Alicia jumped on the two that had fallen, clubbing them with table legs and trying to jab their broken weapons in their hearts. But moving targets weren't easy to hit.

"Help!" Sam called.

One had pinned him to the ground. The only thing saving Sam was he had managed to push his table leg against the vampire's throat. I grabbed a spoke from a broken chair and thrust down into the vampire's back. Blood fell all over Sam. The vampire went limp and collapsed on him.

It was the first vampire I'd ever staked. I didn't have much time to reflect on it. I pulled Sam to his feet, then heard Alicia scream behind me.

I spun around. She and Chris had somehow managed to drives stakes into the two vampires that had tripped, but three more were pushing their way inside. Donna stood behind us, too afraid to move.

All the things I could do. Talk to ghosts, move through walls, fly, none of that mattered. There was nothing I could do against vampires.

I saw a quick flash of red hair, just behind the vampires. Then one fell to the ground. Then another. By the time the last vampire had a clue that something was happening, Victoria had the end of a railing in its chest.

Everyone was stunned, including me. She knocked a few tables out of the way as she pushed her way inside.

She was covered in blood. Her clothes were ruined. She looked completely in control, which was odd to me. I know I was scared out of my mind.

Bill Sloane was right behind her. He didn't even bother ducking through the door and what was left of the barricade. He simply walked through it. He gave me a nod, knowing I was the only one who could see him. He must have found Victoria and followed her, not able to do anything else.

I looked her up and down. I can guess what she had been doing. I'm sure she would have quite a story for me later.

"Damn, Victoria."

She looked at her arms, which were covered in blood from elbow to fingertip.

"Not exactly clean, I know," she said. "What's going on here?"

"We tried to hold up in here. I think the army is blocking people from leaving. I saw them from up in the air."

"I know. I called them."

"You?"

"Yeah. I still have some friends in high places. We contain this *now*, not let it spread outside these walls. You and Bill, you did good." She looked at her arms. "It might not look like it, but you saved *a lot* of lives."

I gave Bill a look. He took a deep breath and smiled a bit.

"Thanks. And thanks for the help."

She looked at the vampires, all staked on the floor. Then she looked at our little crew.

"I'm impressed. Vampires aren't easy for humans to bring down." She looked right at me. "But you shouldn't have needed my help."

"What?"

She pointed to my wings. "Have you forgotten what you are? These vampires, they're newborn and wild. Humans will have trouble with them. But *you*, you should be able to tear them apart."

Alicia took a step beside me. Chris was right next to her. She put a hand on my wing, then my shoulder.

"Lay off my brother," she said. "He saved us."

"Yeah," Sam said. His tie was loose, his shirt unbuttoned. "I have no idea what he is. But this young lady said her brother wouldn't let her down. And sure enough, he popped in like five seconds later, like a ghost."

Victoria gave me a stern look.

"You keep holding back. I don't know why. But you'd better start letting loose, or we won't make it through the night."

"Hey, I'm not stronger than these vampires."

"True. But you're a damn *demon*, Alex. I know you've got more in you than a fancy pair of wings. Just stop holding back."

Deep down, I knew Victoria was right. Some of my problem was not knowing what I could do. But I knew I had more powers in me. They always seemed to come out when I didn't think, when I ran off instinct.

But I was afraid. I stepped closer so only she could hear.

"If I let whatever's in me out, I might not be able to reel it back in. I have nightmares about demons, and they scare the hell out of me."

She gave a nod. "You'll do fine. You're stronger than you think."

I said nothing, chewing on her words.

"Okay," Victoria said to us all. "The army won't let anyone out till daybreak. It doesn't matter whether you're infected or not. Alex and I have to go help out whoever we can. Put this barricade back up, then barricade yourselves in the kitchen. Don't make a sound, and you'll be okay. We'll come back for you when we can."

"I'm afraid no one's going anywhere."

The new voice came from just outside.

CHAPTER 31

Bachner stepped inside the restaurant. Right behind him was Heins, along with three of their flunkies. Behind them, I saw two of their men fire their flamethrowers, followed by some vampire screams. Alicia and Donna covered their ears. The same two vampire killers stayed outside to keep watch.

"Damn, I'm sorry, Alex," Bill said. He'd been quiet this whole time. "I fucked up. I should have stayed outside to keep an eye out."

I nodded to Bill that it was okay.

Victoria threw her hands up in the air, like she was more frustrated than afraid.

"Come on, Bachner. Don't you have better things to do than be obsessed with your little revenge fantasy?"

He didn't say anything for a moment. He stared at the woman whom he'd been chasing nearly his whole life. He and Heins both had crossbows trained on Victoria. He looked at the humans in the room.

"You four, step away. Move over to the other side of the room." He looked at me. "I wish you could go with them, but you picked your side."

"Fuck you. I'm not moving a step," Alicia said.

I patted her shoulder. She looked me in the eye. I could see she was scared. She could see I was serious, and confident. Everything would be okay. Sibling communication.

She moved away along with everyone else. Chris stood in front of her and held her hand. Brave guy.

"Uh, if I could say something," he said. "I'm still trying to catch up, but the hot lady and Batman did save our lives."

"Shut the fuck up!" Heins said. His first words, and he pointed his

251

crossbow at Chris.

"Would you calm down?" Bachner shouted. He lowered Hein's crossbow with his hand.

I could see Victoria react, just slightly. She noticed the tension between them, like I did when I first met them.

Bachner looked at Victoria.

"I've waited so long to kill you, for my grandfather. So I have to admit, the revenge part is nice. But I wish I could have killed you before spread your filth."

"Me?"

"Yes, you."

She rolled her eyes. "Are you that clueless? Bachner, yes, I killed your grandfather. We both know this. I gave him every single chance I could, tried to pound it through that thick head of his, before he backed me in a corner. I am *not* a fucking monster. Now here you are, following in his footsteps. If you want to kill me, fine, but this feral vampire bullshit that's going on right now, *you* did this, with your little cooked up stolen cure-gone-wrong."

He chuckled angrily. "I've spent my life killing vampires. I don't *make* them. You helped create it in that research center, then blew it up."

I could see Victoria was angry, but also confused. We both could see Bachner actually believed what he was saying.

"Bachner. *Jake.* Listen, and *think.* I know you hate me, and to be honest, I don't like you either. But I'm the one who called the army. I'm trying to *contain* this. I've got sources that told me *you* did this."

"I've never seen him," Bill said, pointing at Bachner. Then he looked at Heins. "He's the guy that was running the show, at the research center, and at the service tunnel here."

Of course.

Bachner was getting ready to say something, then closed his mouth. He was thinking, keeping his eyes locked on Victoria the whole time. A smile flashed across Heins' face, and Victoria, Bachner, and I all realized it at the same time.

Heins.

Bachner turned his head in time for Heins to hit him with the butt of his crossbow. Bachner's nose shattered and blood poured down his chest. He dropped his crossbow and stumbled back into Victoria and me. Of all people, Victoria kept him from falling. As she caught him under the arms, Heins fired his crossbow. The bolt went through Bachner's shoulder, and pierced Victoria's heart. She fell instantly to the ground. Bachner, screaming in pain, went down with her. They were stuck together, Bachner's back pressed against Victoria's chest. I knelt down next to them and grabbed the bolt. Alicia, along with everyone else, was screaming.

"Hey!" Heins said. The two goons behind him aimed their crossbows at me. "Hands off." I let go of the bolt. Bachner was in pain, but lucid. We locked eyes before I stood up.

One of Heins' goons leaned in his ear.

"I'm telling you, boss. That's the freak. Fire don't work on him."

Heins looked me up and down. He shook his head.

"I knew I should have killed you when I first saw you. But Uncle Sweetheart on the floor there wouldn't have it. Just what are you? Some kind of vampire experiment? Like our wonder-cure that ended up making more of you bastards?"

I didn't say anything.

"Alex?" Alicia said from across the room. She looked at Victoria. "Is she okay?"

"I told you to shut the fuck up," Heins said. He gestured for a goon behind him. The goon pointed the crossbow at Alicia.

I felt rage inside me. Just seeing someone threaten Alicia.

"Hey," I said to the goon. My voice sounded different. A quick flash of demons in my head, slobbering and howling. He looked at me. "I'm the most dangerous thing in this room. You'd better point that thing back at me."

He actually did so.

But the rage wasn't going away.

It was like I said to Victoria. I hoped I could reel it in.

"I always knew you were a piece of shit, Heins," Bachner said on the floor next to me.

He laughed. "I've waited a long time to see you on your back where you belong. You're a pitiful excuse for a vampire killer."

"Listen," I said. "Whatever it is you had in mind, it's over. The army's here, getting shit under control."

"How can you say that when you don't even know what I've been up to? Ask that cream puff on the ground there. You know what the hardest part to killing vampires is? Getting help from other people. Convincing them vampires even exist. Well now, I've done that."

I shook my head. It sounded insane.

"You're okay with destroying an entire city, just to prove to the world that vampires are real? That's what this is all about?"

He didn't even hesitate. He smiled and nodded.

"Yes. Sacrifice a few to save the world. The sunlight will kill most of them, me and my men will round up the stragglers. That's the difference between me and you, Jake. I will do what needs to be done. You'll lose sleep if someone's little butcher shop falls to the ground."

"You've fucking lost it. This isn't what killing vampires is all about," Bachner said.

I saw a stream of flame outside. There was a scream, followed by someone poking their head in.

"Boss. We've got a group forming up out here."

"Alright. Time to go, boys."

I looked at Bill. He nodded, knowing exactly what I wanted him to do. It was all he could do, really, to follow them.

"What should we do with them?"

Heins looked at all of us. "They'll be dead by morning anyway. Kill him." He pointed at me. "And we might need some hostages. Bring the two girls."

One of the goons smiled, and looked at Alicia and Donna. "Now we're talking."

And that was it. I snapped.

I vanished and ran toward them. They barely had time to look surprised. I vanished in and out, landing punch after punch, but disappearing before they could get their bearings. I swung at the guy who leered at my sister and her friend. I caught him twice on the nose. I knocked the other goon to the ground with my wings.

I didn't see Heins slip through the front door.

Alicia called my name. I turned to see the goon whose nose I broke aiming his crossbow at me. I vanished, feeling the bolt pass through me. The bolt hit the wall behind me.

One of the goons who was keeping watch outside stuck his flamethrower inside the door. Alicia and the rest had gathered around Bachner and Victoria now, making sure they were okay. I stood in front of them and spread my wings.

At first I thought I was hit in the face with a bucket of warm water. Then I realized it was the flame. It felt great.

"Alex!" Alicia called.

They were all safe behind me.

"I told you!" someone shouted. "Fire doesn't do shit!"

I ran forward, not quite seeing where I was going. I reached out where I thought the fire was coming from and grabbed the nozzle. I pulled hard and knocked the guy off his feet. He was alone, Heins and his men had left him. I punched him hard a few times in the face. He looked up at me, terrified.

I was close to the front of the store, and could see the vampires running. Three of them stopped and looked at me. I looked at the man who had tried to burn me and my friends.

"Mind slowing them down for us?"

It wasn't a question. I grabbed the gas tank off his back before pushing him out of the restaurant. The three vampires tore into him quickly. He screamed in agony as they pinned him to the ground.

I didn't even flinch.

I turned back to the others.

"Sam! Take this."

He stood up and looked at the flamethrower I was handing him. It would have been funny any other time. A well-dressed businessman holding a flamethrower.

"How the fuck do I use this?"

"I don't know. Just stand at the door and pull the trigger."

Alicia and Donna were kneeling next to Bachner. Alicia was crying.

"Get ready for some pain," I told him.

"Felt nothing but pain my whole life."

I grabbed the bolt and broke it off as close as I could to his shoulder. Then I grabbed him and pulled him up. He yelled and let out a deep breath when the bolt was clear.

Bachner moved fast. He grabbed some kind of mini-crossbow strapped to his ankle. A regular boy scout. He fired a single shot that barely missed Sam's head, who was staring at us. He hit the heart of a vampire trying to make his way in. Sam wasn't paying attention to the front door, and if it weren't for Bachner's quick reflexes, who knows how that would have ended.

"Focus!" Bachner shouted. "Come on, man. Be careful with the flame, though. Or you'll burn us alive in here."

Sam nodded, and gave a light spraying to the next vampire that tried to climb in. He didn't kill the thing, but it did run away.

"A fuckin' mutiny right under my nose," Bachner said as he put a hand to his shoulder. "Unbelievable."

"Well, just goes to show yo. Some humans are assholes. And some vampires are actually okay."

He looked at me. I saw what might have been a little remorse in his face.

Alicia grabbed me and gestured to Victoria. "Is she dead?"

I was gonna grab the bolt sticking from her chest, but Bachner bent down next to her.

I could almost see the emotions he was dealing with.

He'd chased Victoria his whole life. She was the reason he hunted vampires. She was motionless in front of him with wood in her heart. She was finally vulnerable. Revenge was his for the taking.

He grabbed the bolt and gave it a few pulls.

Victoria's eyes grew wide and she took a huge breath when the bolt was out. She winced in pain, but still kept quiet. I could see her nose twitching, like she was sniffing the air.

Then she pounced on Bachner.

"What the fuck!" he yelled.

She locked her mouth onto his shoulder wound.

"It's okay!" I said. "She's just getting some blood."

"Get the fuck off me. Get off me!"

I pulled gently on Victoria's shoulders. She let go and fell backwards on her ass. Bachner scooted away, and they made eye contact. Blood dribbled down Victoria's chin. Her fangs were out now, a sure sign she was weak, slightly out of control. She looked up at me.

"Heins?"

"Gone. But he couldn't have gone far. The army's not letting anybody out of here."

Bachner shook his head. "That won't matter. I'm sure he's got an escape plan."

"Yeah. You trained him well, right?" Victoria asked, ice in her voice.

"Guys?" Sam said near the front. "I'm hearing a lot of noise out there."

Victoria stood up. I was surprised she extended a hand to Bachner. And he took it.

"What is he doing?" she asked.

"He wants this thing to spread," Bachner said. "Probably stumbled on the virus, and figured he'd make use of it. I didn't know anything about it, cause I'm an idiot."

"No arguments here. He needs to be stopped."

Bachner didn't hesitate. "Yeah, I know."

"Where's he staying? You have a hideout of some kind?"

A new voice, right by Sam. It was Bill.

"A helicopter came and picked them up. Don't know how they got out with the army flying around. But they did. I heard them talking about an old office building on Russell Street, right behind where Buster's used to be."

Bachner was confused. He thought I was staring at nothing. "Kid? You lost your mind?"

"An old office building on Russell Street. Make sense, Bachner?"

He nodded. "We got a few places. Gotta keep moving, you know? That's one of our best."

Victoria looked at Bachner and me. I didn't even notice that Alicia, Donna, and her new friend Chris were right with us. Just one big happy group.

"Okay. I'll take care of Heins. Alex, you and Bachner stay here and help clean up this mess. Now steer clear of the army. They won't kill you on purpose, but they do have to contain this." She looked at the humans. "You all stay here. When we leave, you block off this door. Then you go back in the kitchen and block off there too."

"No," I said.

She glared at me. "What?"

"Bachner, if you're as good as I think you are, this base of yours, I'm guessing it's vampire-proof?"

"As close as we could get it. UV bulbs in the ceilings. Backup generators. A vampire even walks through the front door, it's toast. And it makes sense for him to hide there until daylight, then kill whatever's left over."

"You won't be able to do it," I told Victoria. "But I can."

She gave me a little smile. I think she might have been proud of me, finally taking control.

"You just gonna walk in there and kill them, Alex? Can your conscience handle that? Because mine can."

I smirked. I knew what needed to be done. No more holding back.

"They won't have a chance."

"Wait, wait," Alicia said. "You're talking about sending my brother in against those guys?"

"I'll be fine, Alicia. Trust me." The last two words sounded weird. My voice mixed with demons.

"You be careful, kid. Heins, he won't be playing."

"Neither will I." I looked at Victoria and Bachner. It looked strange to me, the two of them standing side by side. "You two play nice now."

I looked at Bill. He nodded. "I'll meet you over there."

Bachner reloaded his mini-crossbow.

"Okay, let's go."

I gave Alicia a quick hug, but I knew it wasn't goodbye. I was confident. I just had to make sure it didn't turn to arrogance.

"Oh, I kissed Cindy tonight," I whispered to her.

She smiled. "About time."

The three of us left through the front door. Sam and Chris started rebuilding the barricade once again.

Some vampires were chasing someone near the stairs not too far from us. I saw someone standing over a corpse. Just standing there, looking confused and lost. I realized it was a ghost, mourning over his own body. It made me sad, and angry.

I shook my head. I had to stop Heins.

"Good luck," I said.

"Same," Bachner said. "Do me a favor. Give Heins one good shot for me."

Victoria gave me a smile. "See you soon. Don't worry. I'll take care of your sister."

"Thank you."

I vanished and ran away from the stadium. As soon as I cleared the outside walls, I reappeared and flew off.

CHAPTER 32

I got a better view of what was happening from up in the sky. It looked like the army was getting things under control. They were slowly making their way inside, hopefully to save more lives. That surprised me. If they truly knew what was happening, they'd wait till daylight.

Russell Street wasn't too far away. The army presence didn't stop at the stadium. I saw what looked like checkpoints every few blocks. The city was deadlocked. No one in or out. People were standing around in mobs everywhere. It was a scary sight to see. I hoped no riots would happen.

I had to fly into the wind, a bit of a rough ride. I stayed high. I'm sure there was enough panic and camera phones below me as it was. I didn't need to add to anything.

I saw where the old Buster's nightclub use to be, and the abandoned office building behind it. I couldn't see inside too well. There wasn't anyone near the place.

I landed in the empty parking lot. I could have vanished and walked right inside. But I didn't. I wanted them to see me, if they were watching. Give them a chance to run.

Give them a chance to escape from the Hell that was coming.

I tried to prepare myself for what I was about to do.

I still didn't know exactly what I was capable of. But I have the power of demons. I had taken it from them, or they had given it to me. And they talked to me in my head, in my dreams. I was gonna do what they wanted.

Before I could take a step, Bill appeared next to me. He was obviously getting better at moving around.

"They're in there," he said. "Maybe twenty, thirty of them. Some are trying to catch the news on the radio. Others are just goofing off. But they're all armed. Heins is on the top floor, like the company president. He's all alone. It's weird, though, the radio doesn't seem to be covering this at all. Looks like maybe his plan didn't work."

I'm guessing Bill's early visit to me did a lot more good than we thought.

"Victoria called the army *very* fast. I'm sure the coverup is already started."

He nodded. "Okay. So what's the plan? I can go in and do more recon if you need."

I put a hand on his shoulder. "No. Stay *far* away. I'm not sure if what I'm gonna do will affect you or not."

He was surprised. "Alex, I'm a ghost. What the hell can anyone do to me?"

I smiled and walked toward the office building.

I could see my reflection in the glass door as I got closer. I didn't expect what I saw.

My jeans were a little charred from the earlier flame bath. My hair was a mess, and my chest was speckled with blood. But that's not what surprised me.

My face was totally different.

I barely recognized myself. My face was almost swollen. My forehead was a light shade of brown with ridges in it. My cheeks were a bright red, to match my new red eyes.

I looked like a monster. Like a demon.

And that's what I am. I'm part demon. It was time to really embrace that.

I pushed open the front door. An alarm went off. The lobby area was rundown, like I imagine the rest of the place was. The ultraviolet light gave the trash on the floor a purple hue.

I heard people running. Two of Heins' men popped up in a doorway not too far to the right. Looks like they were packing guns this time. Before they could aim, I faced them and beat my wings a few times. The wind knocked them to the ground.

Two more showed up at the hallway to the left. There was a large old desk that a secretary must have sat at a long time ago. I ran for it and dove headfirst across the floor. I vanished right before they opened blind fire. I felt the bullets pass through as I slid through the desk and got into a sitting position. They kept peppering the desk with bullets. I heard the first two guys climb to their feet. There were four armed men, all pointing guns at the desk.

I heard someone talking into a radio.

"The winged freak is here. He disappeared. Get down to the lobby now."

I didn't want to reappear. But I had to give them a chance. I had to at least say I tried to save them.

"Listen, don't shoot," I said. My voice still sounded like a demon. That wouldn't help me get my message across. "You have to leave. Please. Call your friends back and get everyone out of here. If you leave now, you won't get hurt."

There was a short laugh, followed by another click of a radio.

"Okay, we've got him trapped. He's begging for his life. Hurry up."

I shook my head.

One of them jumped behind the desk, his shotgun ready. I was already gone, vanished into the ghost world.

Just one more world to go.

The empty office building slowly faded away around me. The sounds and smells of the city all vanished. I could only smell something horrible that I can't even describe.

I was in the demon world.

It was the same reddish looking desert that I was in before. The demon world was always bleak and barren, except for those rare gateways that reached all three worlds. But this wasn't one of them.

That's because *I* was the gateway.

I was in the middle of hundreds, maybe thousands of demons. None of them spoke a word. They were eating people, ghosts, I guess. Was this Hell? Is this where bad people went when they died? Or were they just lost souls, like my biological parents and their cult?

One demon casually ripped off a woman's arm and licked the end of the stump. Another ripped the dick off a man and shoved it in his mouth. Some looked human, with arms and legs. While others looked like twisted mutant animals of some sort, with four legs. Some even had two heads.

They saw I was there.

They stopped what they were doing and looked at me. Some were drooling with anticipation. One of the ones that looked like a twisted dog tried to lick my leg, but it drew back, like I'd hurt it. For whatever reason, I can hurt demons with a touch.

A few of them bowed before me.

The demons had once said I'd be back, that I was a part of them.

They were right.

"You want to come out and play?" I asked. I still sounded like them.

There was some commotion. They looked excited. One of the dog-like demons looked up at me and wagged its two tails. It drooled blood.

I thought it was cute.

Then I felt guilty and horrible for thinking that.

"It's play time. But no killing."

They looked dejected, but only for a second.

It was time to go back to the real world.

The red desert vanished. I was back in the lobby of the office building, near the front door. It looked like eight men all surrounded the front desk, trying to figure out where I went. I recognized a few of them from the stadium.

I was angry.

"I tried to warn you." They spun to face me. I stretched my wings out, like a cobra extending its hood, then folded them neatly behind me. "But you wouldn't listen. Remember, you brought this on yourselves."

They raised their weapons.

The UV lights blinked once, then went out completely.

It wasn't me that did it. At least, I don't think.

My night vision let me see everything. They fired everything they had, but their shots passed through me. They only succeeded in destroying the door and glass windows behind me.

"Did we get him?"

"What the fuck?"

"Where's the lights?"

Someone grabbed their radio. "Roy, fire up the backup generator."

There was a pause, then a voice on the other end. "Both generators are fried."

"What? What are you talking about?"

I saw the shadows in the room start to move. I think they even grew larger. The men saw it too. They all bunched up near the center.

"What is that? What the hell is that moving?"

There was one inhuman moan. Then another. I could almost feel the air leaving the room, even in the ghost world.

I saw claws reach out from the shadows. A claw raked down the back of one of the men. He fell to the ground screaming.

"Remember!" I called, like I was talking to a bunch of kids. "No killing!"

But Heins and all his men would wish they were dead.

It was a scene straight out of my old visits to the demon world. It reminded me of when I first saw my biological father. My little minions attacked with rage. They came out of the shadows, the corners, the floor. They were everywhere. The men in the lobby all shot blindly. I think they may have even wounded each other.

I followed a stairs sign down the hallway. I didn't even bother running. I saw a demon with its jaws wrapped around some guy's arm. He screamed as he beat the demon on the head with his free hand. The demon looked like it was having a little too much fun. As it chewed on the man's arm, it put a claw to his throat.

"Hey! I said no killing!"

It looked sad, like a puppy. I winced as the demon ripped the man's arm off from the elbow down. It didn't speak, but I could hear a deep voice in my head.

"He's alive, master."

I walked up the stairs. As I passed the second floor, I could still hear screams and demons wailing. It did creep me out.

But I didn't feel sorry for them.

They had their chance to run. They didn't take it. My demons wouldn't kill them, but I doubt they would be able to hunt a vampire ever again.

I opened the door to the third floor. Old offices and cubicles were everywhere. The lights flickered on and off. I heard another scream that sounded like it came from outside.

I ran to the window. Down in the parking lot I saw some of Heins' men trying to escape. Some of them crawled away as fast as they could, demons on their backs. Then I saw the demons vanish. The men who could still run did so without looking back.

I realized the demons couldn't go too far away from me. They were linked to me, just like I was linked to them.

I heard a noise far across the floor in the corner. I could see a rifle sticking out from behind an old desk. Looked like someone was reloading.

Sure enough, Heins jumped up and started shooting at a few shadows. My demons maybe were messing with him, as I didn't see any. He looked terrified.

"You like my little friends?" I asked.

He pointed the rifle at me and fired. I was already vanished. He emptied every round he had into the wall behind me. When he was out he tossed his gun and pulled out a knife. I tried not to laugh.

I saw my demons. They crawled out of the shadows, surrounding him.

"Wait," I reappeared.

"They're all alive, master." It was many voices now. They seemed to come from everywhere. I thought only I could hear them. But the way Heins flinched told me he heard them too.

He pulled a grenade out of his vest.

"Stay the fuck back!" Heins shouted. "Or we *all* die!"

I laughed this time. My demons laughed with me.

"You think that will hurt us?" I asked.

Heins was really afraid. Every time I'd seen the man, it was all tough-man bravado type crap. Now here he was, sweating bullets.

"It doesn't matter," he said. "I've won. The world will know now. No more secrets."

I snarled. I wanted so bad to take him back to the stadium. I wanted him to see the ghosts of the people whose deaths he was responsible for.

"And we both know you're not gonna kill me," he said. "You don't have it in you, kid, or whatever the fuck you are. Deep down, you're a pussy, just like that vampire bitch of yours, and just like Bachner. You won't do what has to be done."

I looked at my demons. They were anxious to tear into him.

But they would do whatever I said. I had total control over them.

"You know what I'm gonna do?" Heins was suddenly getting brave. "I'm gonna find that sister of yours. Then I'm gonna find your girlfriend. And we're all gonna have some fun."

I looked around at my demons. "Play time's over."

They looked dejected. "But master."

"It's *over*."

Slowly my demons faded back into the shadows. The lights came on steady. The thickness in the air seemed to go away. With my demons gone, I could hear the men on the second floor screaming in pain, and calling for help outside.

"Oh, just me and you, now?" Heins asked. He actually put the grenade away and dropped his knife to the ground. "Okay, let's go, freak."

I walked toward him. He could have been trained in one hundred forms of martial arts for all I know. But that wouldn't matter, not for what I had planned for him.

Despite everything he'd done, and how he tried to provoke me, he was right. I couldn't kill him.

But he needed to be dealt with. He was still very dangerous.

He tried to take a swing at me. I wrapped my wings around myself. I heard his knuckles crack against the tough skin. He yelled in pain and held his fist.

I reached out and grabbed his arm.

"You ready to go for a ride?"

The office building faded around us. The air got humid as the dark red landscape took over. The demons were more spread out this time, chasing ghosts around.

Sadly, I was getting used to seeing them eating and devouring what used to be people.

They paused when they saw me.

"Master. Can we play again?"

I looked at the guest I'd brought along with me, Heins. His mouth hung open as he looked at the Hell around him. I still had a lock on his arm.

I didn't know I could bring demons into my world, or bring others into theirs. I was running off of instinct now.

And it felt good.

"No. But I brought you a toy."

"What-what the fuck?" he said. "What you are gonna do?"

"You're right. I'm not kill gonna you." I gave him a smile. "I'm gonna leave you here."

"Are you joking? No, please."

"So long, Heins."

I let go of his arm. He fell to his knees. The demons started circling him. "No!"

I disappeared from the spirit world before they tore into him. Did they kill him? Or let him live as long as possible for more torture? Is it even possible for anything to die in the demon world? I don't know.

I walked slowly back through the office building. I had to walk through pools of blood on my way out. Heins' men still littered the place. True to their word, my demons killed no one. They were in bad shape, though. I saw a guy missing his eyes. Another had a leg missing. They begged me for help. I called 911 on my out the door, but that was it. Compared to Heins, they were the lucky ones.

I didn't think any of them were in any shape to hunt again.

I took a deep breath as I stretched my wings against the night air. I didn't know how much sleep I'd lose. I didn't know how much guilt would eat away at me. Did I do the wrong thing? Was I just as bad as Heins and his men? Maybe. But I thought back to the people in the stadium. I thought back to the people killed at Waylon Research. At least their ghosts could maybe have some peace.

I heard ambulances coming. I flew off into the night sky.

I am part demon. I think for the first time, as I flew away from Heins' hideout, I was okay with that.

EPILOGUE

Two weeks went by. Despite what Heins thought would happen, the vampires of the world didn't just stand up and declare "We exist". And the military and government, well, they kicked off probably one of the greatest coverups of all time.

The whole incident was all over the international news. But according to the government, the military responded to a domestic terror threat at the stadium. They even had mug shots and criminal backgrounds to go along with it. I could only wonder who the poor guys they were showing all over the news were. But the threat had been neutralized, they'd claimed, so the citizens of the country could just relax.

That didn't stop the grainy internet videos. Some of the videos and even some eyewitnesses showed up on the news. But still, it didn't alter how everyone lived their lives. There weren't waves of vampire hunters rising up to fill the ranks. Heins had failed.

Victoria and I said goodbye to Bill.

He had solved his one last case, and was ready to move on. There was no funeral for him, as he was only declared missing. There wasn't a body to bury. But we met at the cemetery anyway. Just a touch from me let Victoria say goodbye to her dear friend. A lot of things had to fall in the right place. But if it weren't for Bill, I could only imagine how many people would have lost their lives, including Victoria and me.

The two talked for a bit. I wish I could have left them alone, but that wasn't possible. We watched Bill walk over a hill. Then he vanished somewhere even I couldn't see. I thought I saw a tear in Victoria's eye.

Things slowly got back to normal. It was a Saturday morning. The phone ringing pulled me out of a deep sleep.

Cindy stirred next to me.

"Who calls this early?" she asked.

She threw a leg over me. We were both still naked from the night before. We were up most of the night, so there was a good chance it wasn't as early as she thought.

"I'd better go see who it is."

She gave me a quick kiss and rubbed my chest.

"Hurry up. I got plans for you."

Cindy and I are together now. I've never been happier. She was still my best friend. We still spent time together, watched TV, had dinner, hung out with all our friends. The biggest different now was we had a lot of sex. She accepted me for who I was, wings and all. There was no way I'd ever be able to tell her in words how much that meant to me.

I answered the phone in the kitchen.

"Alex, it's me."

Victoria. I tensed up. We'd spoken a lot the past two weeks. Every time she called, I expected bad news. Like the military is on the way to your house. Or everyone knows about you and wants you dead. But that wasn't the case. There were videos of me flying around the stadium on the Internet. But you couldn't see my face. And like Victoria said. People don't believe the truth even when it's right in front of them. I was safe.

"What's up?"

"Nothing. Just checking in. Seeing how you're doing."

"I'm good. Me and Cindy, getting ready to have some breakfast."

"Is that what they call it now?"

I smiled.

"I'm happy for you two," she said.

"Thanks. So you just called to talk? No bad news or anything?"

I could almost see her rolling her eyes. "No. No bad news. Everything is okay. Even if it wasn't, I know the right people."

"Okay, cool."

"Listen. I have an early dinner planned with Bachner. But what do you have planned tonight?"

A dinner with Bachner. That was a name I hadn't heard much in the past two weeks. And those two eating dinner was something I couldn't see in my head.

"Dinner? You two are friends now?"

"I don't know if you'd call us friends. But I don't think we're enemies anymore. We got a lot to talk about still."

"That's good to hear. We're going out with our friends tonight. You've seen us all before, at the club."

"You mind if I tag along with you?"

Our little group was getting bigger. Alicia was dating that boy she'd met at the stadium, Chris. After the military, Victoria, and Bachner cleaned up the stadium, Chris was all my sister could talk about. He was almost the complete opposite of her, but she was crazy about him. He hung out with us all the time.

"Sure. You're always welcome. You know that."

"Thanks. I'm gonna go, time for bed for me. Tell Cindy I said hi."

"I will."

I hung up. When I turned around Cindy was leaning against the dining room wall. She still hadn't put any clothes on. Wow, she is gorgeous.

"You awake?" she asked with a smile.

"I am now."

I gave her a hard kiss against the wall. Our breathing started picking up. I was ready to pick her up and carry her back to bed when I felt the goosebumps.

I turned to see someone standing in my living room.

I ducked behind the couch, pulling Cindy with me. I was startled for a second, then annoyed.

Cindy thought behind the couch was where we were going to make our magic, and laid down on the carpet. She tried to pull me on top of her. Funny, looking back now.

"Hold on a sec. Uh, who exactly are you?" I called.

Cindy was confused, then she pieced together what was going on. She rolled her eyes, but smiled. She wasn't afraid of ghosts anymore.

"I'm so sorry," a female voice said. "I didn't mean to interrupt, well, your private time."

I was holding Cindy's hand, so she heard her too.

"Oh, no problem," she said. "Just trying to have sex with my boyfriend."

"So it's true what they say. You can see us. And let others see us too."

I poked my head over the couch. Cindy did the same. No reason for a ghost to see us both naked.

Very pretty lady. Slightly older, wearing a long white dress. Her hair was done up in a bun. She had an old-fashioned look to her. I wondered when she died.

"Uh, is there something I can do for you?" I asked.

"I think maybe there is. My name is Elizabeth Margot. I was murdered sixty years ago. I'd like to hire you to find out who killed me."

I shook my head and squeezed Cindy's hand. I'm so glad I have her. Life was about to go on another wild ride.

ABOUT THE AUTHOR

I live in Maryland with my wonderful wife and four cats. I love gaming, computer technology, movies, and of course, reading and writing. I love science fiction and especially horror. Ghosts, vampires, werewolves, zombies, anything supernatural, all beautiful subjects.

I've been writing since I was twelve years old. There's just something about creating a story that I like. It's always fun to try to come up with something that hasn't been done, or is unique in some way. It's fun to build a character, give him a personality and background.

Visit my website at http://www.glennbullion.com

Made in the USA
Coppell, TX
13 December 2019